I0586160

THWARTED QUEEN

*The Entire Saga about the Yorks,
Lancasters & Nevilles, whose family feud
inspired Season One of "Game of Thrones."*

CYNTHIA SALLY HAGGARD

Copyright © Cynthia Sally Haggard 2022
This book is licensed for your personal enjoyment only. No part of this
book may be reproduced in any form or by any electronic or mechanical
means, including information storage and retrieval systems, without
written permission from the author, except for the use of brief quotations
in a book review.
This book may not be sold, copied, or plagiarized. Thank you for respecting
the hard work of this author.
The moral rights of the author have been asserted.
All rights reserved
ISBN: 978-0984816989
Enquiries: greetings@cynthiasallyhaggard.com
Published by Cynthia Sally Haggard, Washington DC, USA
www.cynthiasallyhaggard.com
LCCN: TX 7-473-955
Edited by Catherine Adams, Inkslinger Editing
Cover Design by Tim Barber, Dissect Designs
Cover images: AdobeStock & Alamy.

Praise for *Thwarted Queen*

"Extremely interesting and cleverly written-I was completely enthralled!—*Lucy Bertoldi, Historical Novel Society.*

"A gripping, well-researched historical novel, revealing a violent age. Cecylee and the other characters are well-drawn, with great subtlety and depth."—*Lindsay Townsend, author of "To Touch the Knight."*

"The author immerses the reader in a complex and vivid world that is depicted with persuasive confidence."—*Curtis Sittenfeld, author of "American Wife."*

"A wonderful novel to introduce Cecily Neville and historical biographical fiction to young female readers."—*Mirella Patzer, author of "The Pendant."*

"Haggard delivers a swift epic that is both entertaining and informing. The writing is crisp and clear, the characters well-defined, and the emotion overflowing. This book has something for everyone—romance, intrigue, and plenty of action."—*US Review of Books.*

AWARDS FOR THWARTED QUEEN

IPPY Gold Medal for Audiobook Fiction, May 2021

Global e-book Awards Finalist, August 2012

Next Generation Indie Book Finalist for Historical Fiction, May 2012

Eric Hoffer Commercial Fiction Honorable Mention, April 2012

Dedication

For my dear friend
Beth Gessert Franks
for all her endurance of

CECYLEE

THE YORKS

CECYLEE NEVILLE, DUCHESS OF YORK, QUEEN BY RIGHT, ABBESS OF THE BENEDICTINE ORDER OF ASHRIDGE (1415-1495).

RICHARD PLANTAGENET, 3RD DUKE OF YORK, (1411-1460). Cecylee's husband.

JOAN PLANTAGENET (born circa 1438, died circa 1441).

ANNE PLANTAGENET, "NAN", DUCHESS OF EXETER (1439-1476).

HENRY PLANTAGENET (born 1441, died as a child), first son of Cecylee and Richard.

EDWARD, EARL OF MARCH (1442-1483), EDWARD IV from 1461. Cecylee's illegitimate son by her lover Blaybourne.

EDMUND PLANTAGENET, EARL OF RUTLAND (1443-1460).

ELIZABETH PLANTAGENET,, "BETH", DUCHESS OF SUFFOLK (born 1444-died circa 1504).

MARGARET PLANTAGENET, DUCHESS OF BURGUNDY (1446-1503).

WILLIAM PLANTAGENET (born 1447, died as a child).

JOHN PLANTAGENET (born 1448, died as a child).

GEORGE PLANTAGENET (1449-1478), DUKE OF CLARENCE from 1461.

THOMAS PLANTAGENET (born 1450, died as a child).

RICHARD PLANTAGENET (1452-1485), DUKE OF GLOUCESTER from 1461, RICHARD III from 1483.

URSULA PLANTAGENET (born 1455, died as a baby).

THE LANCASTERS

JOHN PLANTAGENET DUKE OF LANCASTER, "JOHN OF GAUNT" (1340-1399). Cecylee's grandfather.

JOHN PLANTAGENET, DUKE OF BEDFORD (1389-1435). Negotiated marriage between Richard of York and Lady Cecylee Neville.

HUMPHREY PLANTAGENET, DUKE OF GLOUCESTER (1390-1447), younger brother to John of Bedford.

HENRY VI "HENRY OF LANCASTER" (1421-1471), reigned as KING HENRY VI from 1422 to 1461, when he fled England. In July, 1465, he was captured, and brought to live in the Tower of London. In May 1471, after the Battle of Tewkesbury, he was murdered.

MARGUERITE D'ANJOU "BITCH OF ANJOU" (1429-1482), Queen of England from 1445 to 1461, when she fled England. In 1471, she was captured by the Yorkists, and in 1475, returned to France. She died in poverty in 1482.

ÉDOUARD, PRINCE OF WALES (1453-1471). Son to Marguerite d'Anjou, and possibly Henry VI of England or Edmund Beaufort, 1st Duke of Somerset. He was killed at the Battle of Tewkesbury in May, 1471.

EDMUND TUDOR, EARL OF RICHMOND (1430-1456), son of Owen Tudor and Catrine de Valois, he was married to Lady Margaret Beaufort and became the father of Henry, Earl of

Richmond, later Henry VII, King of England. He died of the plague in 1456.

JASPER TUDOR, EARL OF PEMBROKE (born circa 1431, died 1495), younger brother of Edmund Tudor.

HENRY TUDOR, EARL OF RICHMOND, (1457-1509), HENRY VII from 1485, he was the son of Edmund Tudor, Earl of Richmond and Lady Margaret Beaufort. He won the Battle of Bosworth in 1485, in which Richard III was killed. He married Edward IV's heiress, Elizabeth of York in 1486, and founded the Tudor dynasty. He is the father of Henry VIII.

THE NEVILLES

RALPH DE NEVILLE, 1st EARL OF WESTMORLAND (born circa 1363, died 1425). Cecylee's father.

JOAN DE BEAUFORT, COUNTESS OF WESTMORLAND (born circa 1377, died 1440). Cecylee's mother, she was the daughter of John of Gaunt and his third wife Catrine de Roet.

CATRINE DE NEVILLE "CATH" DUCHESS OF NORFOLK (born circa 1397). Cecylee's eldest sister.

RICHARD NEVILLE, BARON MONTACUTE "SALISBURY" (1400-1460) 5th EARL OF SALISBURY from 1428 . Cecylee's eldest brother.

ANNE NEVILLE, DUCHESS OF BUCKINGHAM (born circa 1411, died 1480). Cecylee's sister.

CECYLEE NEVILLE, DUCHESS OF YORK, QUEEN BY RIGHT, ABBESS OF THE BENEDICTINE ORDER OF ASHRIDGE (1415-1495).

RICHARD NEVILLE, 16TH EARL OF WARWICK "WARWICK THE KINGMAKER", (1428-1471), one of Cecylee's nephews.

ISABEL NEVILLE,"BELLA" DUCHESS OF CLARENCE, COUNTESS OF WARWICK and COUNTESS OF SALISBURY "BELLA" (1451-1476), elder daughter and heiress of Warwick the Kingmaker.

ANNE NEVILLE "NANETTE" PRINCESS OF WALES and
DUCHESS OF GLOUCESTER "NANETTE" (1456-1485),
younger daughter and co-heiress of Warwick the Kingmaker.

THE PLANTAGENETS

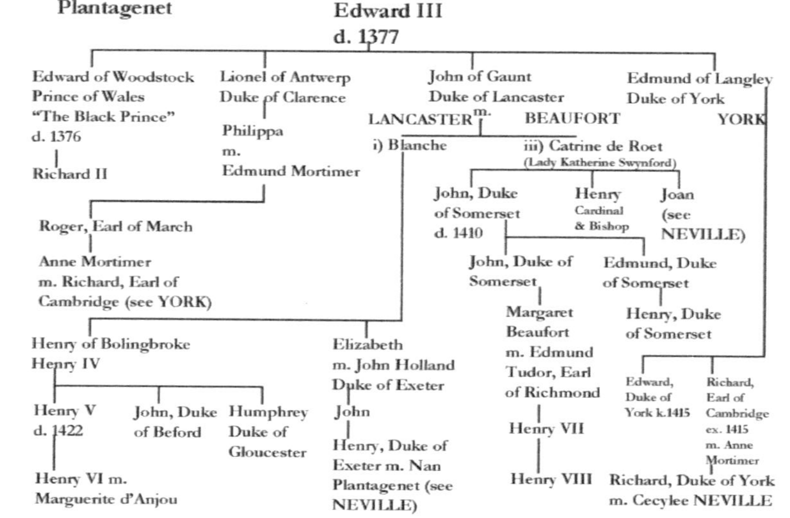

THE NEVILLES

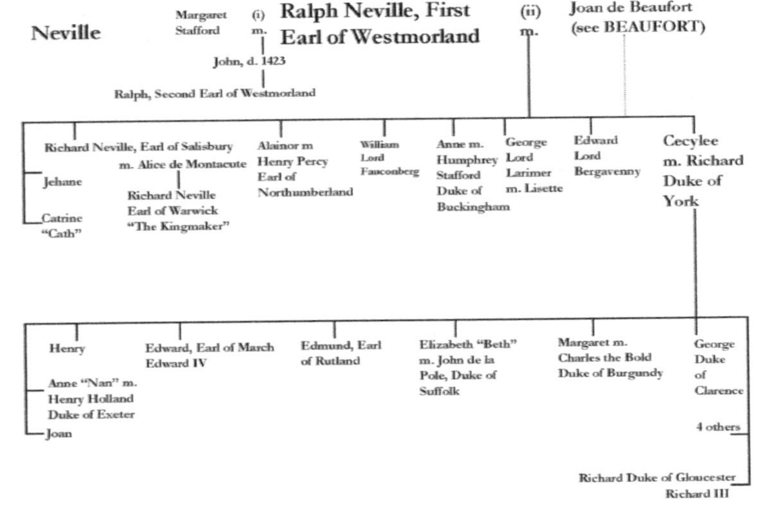

Map of England & France in 1422

MAP OF FRANCE IN 1453

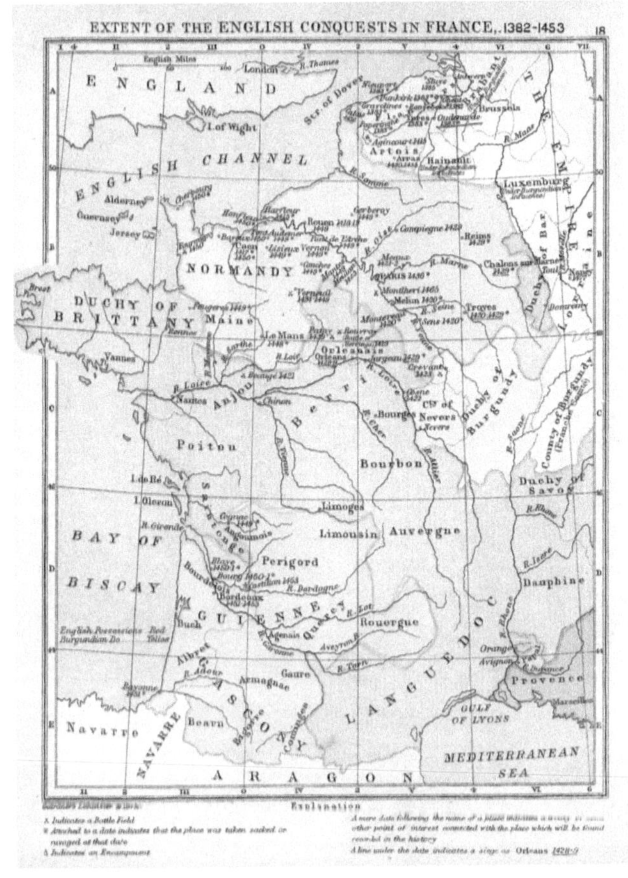

PROLOGUE

She useth to arise at seven of the clocke,
and hath readye her chapleyne to saye with her
mattins of the daye,
and mattins of our lady;

FROM ORDERS AND RULES OF THE
PRINCESS CECILL
QUOTED BY JOHN WOLSTENHOLME
COBB (1883)
HISTORY & ANTIQUITIES OF
BERKHAMSTED

Berkhamsted Castle, Hertfordshire, Feast of Saint Joseph
March 19, 1495

Now I am ready to speak, for death will be with me by year's end.

The House of Tudor shall declare this tale a lie. They will say I'm an impostor. Let there be no mistake about my identity. As proof, I lay forth my name in its true construction:

CECYLEE

Queen by Right
Duchess of York
Abbess

I am Cecylee—not Cecily or Cicely. My name has been corrupted by those who claim to have the ear of the present King of England, one Harry Tudor, Earl of Richmond, a self-styled King Henry VII. Let those who seek to dismiss my testament compare this sign with the many documents signed as Duchess of York and Queen by Right.

I have had other names. I was born Lady Cecylee de Neville in May 1415. In the year 1424, I became Duchess of York. Admirers called me the Rose of Raby. Enemies called me Proud Cis. I am the mother of Kings Edward IV and Richard III. I have seen my sons kill their opponents and even their kin.

Folk think me saintly, for I hear Mass several times a day. I hear religious texts while I dine; I spend hours on my knees in prayer. This causes them to disbelieve some of the unflattering stories whispered about me. Folk are too kind if they imagine that a pious old woman couldn't have sinned. It grieves me greatly to say this, but late in life, while I was living in the countryside as Abbess of a Benedictine Order, I was responsible for the murder of two of my grandsons.

In these pages, I make confession, using my voice and the voices of others important to its weaving.

Book I: Rose of Raby

*"A gracious lady!
What is her name, I thee pray tell me?"
"Dame Cecille, sir."
"Whose daughter was she?"
"Of the Earl of Westmorland, I trowe the youngest,
And yet grace fortuned her to be the highest."*

*FROM A FIFTEENTH-CENTURY BALLAD,
ANONYMOUS*

CHAPTER 1

Castle Raby, Scottish Marches
The Feast of Saint John
June 24, 1424

Today they tell me I must behave.

I'm not allowed to laugh loudly, stare, or make remarks.

I must put on my best gown, the pink silk damascene with the long train, balance my heavy headdress on my head, and play my psaltery. The king's uncles are coming to visit.

Today, they decide if I'm suitable enough to be made Duchess of York and maybe queen. Richard Plantagenet, Duke of York, the boy I'm supposed to marry, is only thirteen, but they say he will be the richest peer in the kingdom when he reaches the age of twenty-one.

"But that's not for years," I point out. "I'm only nine years old. Why do I have to do this now?"

"Richard is the king's cousin," Audrey, my mother's maid, tells me. "If the king were to die, Richard would be king. Your father wants to secure your future now."

I sigh. Sitting in stuffy rooms listening to Mama and Papa and all those important people they know wearies me. If you are the Earl of

Westmorland, like Papa, and the king has given you the task of guarding the English border against the heathenish Scots, then you must want to know many such people. But I prefer to frolic under one of the huge trees that surround the castle.

I turn my head slightly, and Audrey mutters as she stuffs my thick blond hair into the netting under the headdress. Sliding my eyes to the right, I can just make out the shapes of the trees through the newly glazed windows of our rooms in Bulmer's Tower.

Bulmer's Tower is a five-sided tower shaped like an arrowhead that stands apart from the rest of the towers comprising Castle Raby. It can be easily defended from a sudden raid on the castle, so Papa decreed that all of us should live here. The trees seem small and very faraway.

Mama enters my chamber, carrying my psaltery. Her eyes look pink. Silently, she scrutinizes me, her lips pinched, as Audrey curtsies and steps aside. Then she takes my hand and leads me up the steep spiral stairs to the solar.

"How much are you willing to pay for her?" says a deep voice.

Mama clenches my fingers so tightly I yelp.

"That is John Plantagenet, Duke of Bedford, the senior uncle to the king." Mama, Joan de Beaufort, Countess of Westmorland, turns me around so that I have to look into her eyes. "He's just been made regent of France and rarely comes to England. It is a high honor for him to visit us, Cecylee."

"But you don't seem happy," I remark as we peek through the arras.

Mama shakes her head and puts her fingers to her lips.

"Two thousand marks," replies Papa.

Through an opening in the richly woven tapestry, I find Richard
standing in one corner, his hand running through his hair. For the
past six months, he's been living at Castle Raby. When I asked why,
Papa pinched my cheek and said it would be well if we got
acquainted. I try hard to be pleasant, but he is so serious. He's
dressed in black. Couldn't he think of some other color?

Duke John looks around the solar, his sharp eyes taking in Papa's
glazed windows, the newly installed hooded fireplace on the north
wall, and the rich hangings. He reminds me of a merchant at a fair.

"Four thousand?" he says.

Papa stares at his lap as if he's just discovered something
fascinating, perhaps a pulled thread, on his silver and blue robe.
Ralph de Neville, Earl of Westmorland, must never be too quick to
compromise.

A cough erupts as a gentleman enters from the door opposite and
bows. I turn to Mama.

"That is Duke John's younger brother, Humphrey Plantagenet,
Duke of Gloucester. He lives in England and acts as regent for the
king."

"How old is the king?"

"Three years old."

"He's ten years younger than Richard then."

Mama quietly shushes me.

Duke Humphrey smiles at Richard. Perhaps they are friends. I
did hear someone say that Richard always stays with him when he
visits London.

Duke Humphrey shakes his head.

Richard smiles faintly.

Duke John sighs. "Three thousand?"

"'Tis a goodly sum," says Duke Humphrey. "Three is the sign of
the Trinity. 'Tis the perfect number."

Papa strokes his white beard. The corner of his mouth quirks.
Then he roars with laughter. "Done. Let us drink to it."

Mama gives me a look, which means to stay here behind the
arras and be quiet. She goes to Papa. "You know I am not happy with
this."

"Cecylee needs to marry," replies Papa. "This betrothal will make her Duchess of York, and you know where that might lead."

A duchess! I wiggle with excitement. That would make me more important than Mama! She says softly, "I care little for that kind of future. I want my Cecylee happy in her life."

"Don't be ridiculous," snaps Papa.

Duke John looks surprised. He holds his wine cup high in the air and stares at Mama. To my surprise, she kneels.

"She is my youngest daughter and only nine years old. Do you have to do this now?"

Papa bangs his cup on the arm of his chair, ruby-red liquid sloshing to the floor. "Mind yourself, my lady," he hisses, wagging his finger, as Jenkin rushes to clean it up. "Never contradict your lord in public."

Drawing a handkerchief from her long triangular sleeve, she dabs her eyes.

Papa helps her up, leads her to her seat, and signals for wine.

Mama looks straight at me and nods.

I run into the room. Suddenly all eyes are upon me. I dip a deep curtsey, rising smoothly and without wobbling, the way Mama taught.

Richard bows and smiles, then frowns. I smile back, trying to coax that frown away, and when his features smooth out, I turn to Mama. "What shall I play for the company? Shall I do *I Cannot Help It If I Rarely Sing?*"

Papa slaps his thigh and bellows with laughter.

Mama smiles: "Why not sing *This Lovely Star of The Sea?*"

Settling onto the window seat beside Richard, I nestle the psaltery into the crook of my elbow, pluck it, and began to sing. I love to sing; it's so good for the spirits.

"This Rose of Raby has spirit as well as beauty," says Duke Humphrey after listening for a few minutes.

"She's not shy," replies Papa, smiling.

Duke John winks at Richard. "I know you must be eager to wed."

Richard colors a fiery red, making the gentlemen laugh heartily. I sigh.

"When is the ceremony to take place?" asks Duke Humphrey.

"I wonder if it could be this year," says Papa, "in October, on the Feast of Saint Luke."

I strum my psaltery with a flourish and finish the song.

"What are you going to sing now?" whispers Richard.

"Wait and see." I glance at the adults, who are busy talking, and play softly *I Cannot Help It If I Rarely Sing*.

"Cis!" exclaims Richard, laughing softly. "Your lady mother—"

"It's too late now, isn't it? Shush! How can I talk to you if I have to sing?"

Richard smiles and sinks back onto the cushions next to me. He looks less serious.

"Where will they live?" asks Duke John.

"Where would you like to live?" whispers Richard.

I think for a minute. I don't want to be far away from Mama. "Do you have a castle close by?"

"I have many castles, Cis. But not here."

"Oh." I turn away. "I don't wish to move."

"I know that you, my lords, have much on your minds," says Papa, bowing. "So, I wondered if they could be betrothed rather than married. That way, both Richard and Cecylee could continue to live here."

Richard nudges me. "Did you hear what they said?"

I nod and smile. I pluck my psaltery and take a deep breath:

A gardyn saw I ful of blosmy bowes
Upon a ryver, in a grene mede,
There as swetnesse evermore inow is,
With floures white, blew, yelwe, and rede—

"What is that song, Cis?"

"It was written by Granduncle Chaucer. I made up the tune myself. Shall I teach you?"

Richard puts a hand on my arm, for Duke Humphrey speaks. "Is it not true that you have a large number of soldiers garrisoned here at Castle Raby?"

"Indeed," says Papa, "I am warden of the western march, and I have to patrol the land from here to Scotland."

"I like not the idea of rough soldiers being so close to this pretty rose."

Duke John stares at me. "Why not have little Cecylee and young Richard live at court with their cousin King Henry?"

"But Cecylee will be safe here with me," says Mama, hands tensing on her chair.

"This is a serious issue," says Papa slowly. "It is true that I have a large garrison of soldiers here because of the Scots raids and because of the lawless nature of this country."

"We would not want our wild rose plucked before her time," says Duke Humphrey. "Young Richard here is close to the throne. It would not be seemly if his wife-to-be were caught in a rough soldier's embrace."

Confused, I turn to Richard. "What are they talking about?"

"Your virtue," he replies, reddening.

"But there is no blemish on my virtue." I frown.

Richard pats my hand. "You would not be able to defend yourself against any man determined to take you. You have not the strength."

"I have a good kick. And I know where to aim."

"Cis!" Richard pulls down the corners of his mouth. He looks strange, but then I see he is trying not to laugh. "How do you know that?"

"Audrey." My mother's maid has been with her for hundreds of years and knows everything. I ease the psaltery into a comfortable position, strum for a minute or two, and then sing a song I composed to please Mama:

I once was in a summery dale,
In one such little hidey-hole,
When I heard a great debate

'Tis my favorite song, and it always makes Mama laugh. She says it is very old, perhaps one hundred and fifty years old, written by someone unnamed, but I make it my own by strumming loudly on the heavy accents of the poem, particularly the words "stiff and stark and strong." I look up, expecting her grin, but Mama looks pinched around the lips. She signals for me to stop.

"How would you guarantee her safety?" asks Duke John.

"I could give her apartments in the keep for her very own use," says Papa. "They are accessible only through a flight of steep and narrow stairs. There is a guardhouse underneath those rooms, which could be garrisoned by my most trusted men."

Duke John comes closer. "You want this marriage so much; you are prepared to lock your daughter up?"

My mouth opens, I look at Mama.

She stares at the floor, her fingers tensed around the bunched fabric of her silken skirts. Suddenly she looks up and glares.

She glares at Richard.

CHAPTER 2

Michaelmas
September 29, 1424

I fly upright in bed; something wet has touched my ear. A hound regards me mournfully with his large brown eyes. Laughing out loud, I snuggle up to him in the pile of furs. An Irish Wolfhound with wiry hair, long legs, and floppy ears, Clavis is a birthday present from Papa. He said, now that I'm growing up, I should have a hound. It would attack whenever I'm in danger, just like the saying, they are gentle when stroked, fierce when provoked. I retorted, who would dare to accost me, the youngest daughter of the greatest lord of the land. Papa said only, better to be safe than sorry.

I lie in my new apartments in the keep, the bed in the main chamber, a large room made of flat white stone. The windows are so high up I have to angle my head to see the castle courtyards below. I miss looking out at my trees, and I'm tired of the faint stench of latrines that makes its presence felt, even on cold days.

To the right of the window opposite my bed, a door leads to a small room where Jenet sleeps. Next to my bed, another door leads down a steep spiral staircase to the guardroom. When Jenet enters this morning, I hear the scrape of metal and the sound of male voices. She curtseys, pours a jug of angelica water into the bowl and waits. I turn away, burrow under my furs, and cuddle up to Clavis, who growls appreciatively. I giggle as I count under my breath. How long will it take for Jenet to speak? Once, I counted all the way up to three thousand before my new maid timidly asked if I wouldn't like to wash my hands.

This morning, however, is different. The door bangs as Audrey surges into the room.

"Get up, my lady!" she shouts. "Your sisters, Ladies Catrine and Anne, have arrived!" When she tugs the bedclothes off the bed, Clavis jumps up and barks. I shiver in the damp chill of the large stone room as Audrey calls for hot water to be brought up from the kitchens for a bath.

"My lady's uncle writes beautifully, and in English too, so we can all understand it. Even a humble shepherd can understand what Master Chaucer says, not like those priests forever muttering in Latin." Audrey is small and brown like a sparrow and never stops talking.

I yawn. "How I long to leave." Audrey attaches the wide triangular sleeves to my gown over the pink silk chemise. "I haven't been allowed out since midsummer."

"You know that's not true, my lady." Audrey ties the laces into a bow. "Duke Richard often takes you out."

I make a face. I want to go out with someone who laughs loud and gallops as swiftly as a greyhound. Richard is always worried about something. He thinks I will fall off my pony if I'm not careful. But I don't want to be careful; I want to soar up into the sky like an osprey.

16

At least today, I'll be allowed out for a few short hours. I wriggle in blissful anticipation, and Audrey mutters under her breath.

"Where is Papa?"

Audrey kneels to adjust the long train of my silver and dark green dress.

"He's ridden out, hasn't he?"

"Never you mind," says Audrey.

"I wish he would ride out more often, so I could visit Mama in Bulmer's Tower."

"Mind your tongue, my lady," says Audrey, motioning for Jenet to drape the fur mantle over my shoulders. "You should not speak ill of your lord father. He rode out at dawn to head off another Percy raid."

"Are they going to attack us?" I ask.

"Mayhap," says Audrey.

"But why?" says Jenet, going pale.

"The Percies and the Nevilles," says Audrey. "They have these huge private armies to stop the heathenish Scots from their border raids. The Percies are supposed to be patrolling the eastern marches and the Nevilles, the western. That would be all well and good if the Percies and the Nevilles saw eye-to-eye. Naturally, they do not."

"What mean you?" says Jenet faintly.

"They fight each other," I say. "Sometimes they don't notice that the Scots have launched another border raid."

Audrey sits to put her clogs on. "If you've got loads of men roaming the countryside armed to the teeth, you get all kinds of banditry. You get raids, skirmishes, ambushes."

"But in Picardy, it wasn't like that," murmurs Jenet.

"We are not in Picardy, ma petite," replies Audrey. "Here, in the far north of England, it is wild, dangerous, unruly. Ungodly, you might call it."

Jenet crosses herself. "If we're going to be attacked, shouldn't we be making ready?"

"Never you mind," replies Audrey. "My lady is in Bulmer's Tower. That can be defended in any raid."

"What about the king?" asks Jenet, drawing close her red woolen mantle. It is her most prized possession, all she had of value when she left Picardy in northern France after the death of her mother to come to serve me under the guidance of Audrey, her mother's sister. Audrey tells me that she has around fourteen years.

"The king's writ does not run here," I say.

"And that is why your lord father gave you these fine apartments in the keep, in the middle of the castle, to keep you safe," says Audrey. "Truly, he knows what is best for you." She picks up my train.

"But I hate being mewed up." I pick my way onto one of the wooden walkways that criss-cross Castle Raby. "I want to be free." My voice is taken away by a gust of wind.

"My lady and I speak French, of course," says Audrey to Jenet as they follow. The gusting wind makes the wooden walkway sway. I sway in time to it. These walkways allow the soldiers to patrol our defenses and get from one tower to another easily, but the wind makes the journey somewhat perilous. "But we don't do as some jumped-up persons do, which is to speak loudly in French to show off in front of their servants."

Another gust knocks my cone-shaped headdress to the side of my head. I giggle, for I must look very peculiar. I stop so that Jenet can replace it on my head.

"I would never tell my lady this to her face," continues Audrey as we walk sixty feet above the ground, "but do you really want to understand what Master Chaucer says? It's such rubbish! There he is, as bold as brass, criticizing the church. And then there is that vulgar tale told by a miller about the young woman who cuckolds her husband by pretending the flood is upon us."

She pauses to let the material of my train flow down the wooden staircase taking us into the top of Bulmer's Tower.

"Take the *Wife of Bath*," says Audrey as we enter Bulmer's Tower, "that dreadful woman with her four hundred pounds of linen on her head, her five husbands, and all her talk against chastity. 'Tis proper scandalous, I tell you, and no fit subject for a young lady."

I bite my lips to prevent myself from laughing; if I want to hear gossip, I best look stupid. I take the fur mantle off, give it to Jenet, and enter the solar.

Mama is reading aloud:

> *You have two choices; which one will you try?*
> *To have me old and ugly till I die,*
> *But still a loyal, true and humble wife*
> *That never will displease you all her life,*
> *Or would you rather I were young and pretty*
> *And chance your arm what happens in a city*
> *Where friends will visit you because of me,*
> *Yes, and in other places too, maybe.*

"It's the *Wife of Bath* today," mutters Audrey to Jenet.

I curtsey to Mama and sit on the window seat, picking up the tunic left for me to embroider. Truly, it is a glorious day. The sun throws beams of light across the floor where my betrothal gown is laid out in a pool of blue velvet. The betrothal is less than a month away. Yesterday my half-sister Mary, a daughter from Mama's first marriage, finished stem-stitching the hem, which reads *Cecylee, Duchesse of Yorke* in a scrolled pattern. 'Tis very fine.

Audrey takes off her clogs and kneels on the carpet to draw a design for the skirts with her wand of chalk. It looks like a flowery mead with animals. As I am fond of sheep, she sketches in a couple for Jenet to embroider. Meanwhile, Mary wears her usual thin-lipped expression as she laboriously sews the diagonal bands of the Neville crest onto the bodice of my gown. At thirty years, she is already old, married to Papa's son by his first marriage, Sir Ralph Neville.

> *Which would you have? The choice is all your own.'*
> *The knight thought long, and with a piteous groan*
> *At last, he said, with all the care in life,*
> *'My lady and my love, my dearest wife,*
> *I leave the matter to your wise decision.*

Anne puts her sewing down and frowns. Four years older than me at thirteen, she's expecting her first child, being married to the Earl of Stafford. "You mean," she says, "his wife rules him? But how can that be, Mother?"

"What kind of woman was the knight's wife?" asks Mama, turning to Anne.

I cannot contain myself. "She was the one who told him the answer to that riddle, Mama. She told him that what a woman most desires is sovereignty. She wants to rule her own life, her husband, and her lover."

Mary looks up and frowns. I toss my head and smile. Mary is always sour, always quick to find fault, always hard to please.

But Mama's lips quirk at the corners as she shakes her head at me and says, "Let Anne respond, my love." She turns to Anne. "How would you describe her?"

"She was very well-read," says Anne, slowly. "She quoted Dante, Catullus, and Juvenal. So she could read Italian and Latin. Perhaps the knight, her husband, let her make the decisions because she was so wise."

"But is education the same as wisdom?" asks Mama.

Anne is silent while I look around. The late September afternoon sunlight is bright on the round carpet of Mama's solar. It is peaceful here, away from the swirling winds outside. A bee hums. Silken threads whisper as Mary and Jenet pull their needles through the velvet. A spoon tinkles against glass as my eldest sister Cath, visiting from the estates of her husband, the Duke of Norfolk, stirs a distillation of rose petals. I yawn and quickly bend over the tunic I am embroidering, a betrothal present for Richard. I've selected purple velvet to betoken his royal blood while embroidering the hem in a pattern of songbirds. The yellow thread makes their song bright and cheerful.

"No," says Anne at last. "But it helps to develop your mind, to give you discernment, to learn to discriminate."

"Indeed, it does, my love," says Mama, patting her hand.

I cover another yawn. I'll fall asleep soon if nothing interesting happens. I put my sewing down, got up, and poured a cup of wine for Cath. It might make her talkative. Though past twenty-seven, she seems young because she is so merry.

"Cath," I say. "Did Queen Alainor of Aquitaine have great learning?"

Catrine, named after our mother's mother, Catrine de Roet, sips her wine quickly, loving to talk about the past. "That's not what makes her so famous. When she was married to King Louis, they went off on crusade together, and Queen Alainor and all her ladies dressed as Amazons. They wore breastplates, carried swords, and rode like men."

"And what about King Louis? Was he dashing?"

"He was dressed as a monk and walked a great deal of the way."

I am crushed that my heroine should have to put up with someone like that. He sounds worse than Richard. "They seem rather ill-sorted," I say. Cath bursts out laughing.

"That marriage didn't last long," she remarks. "Once Alainor got her divorce from Louis, she married Henry of Anjou, who was thirteen years younger—"

"Thirteen years younger?" I gape at her. "A younger husband? I didn't think that was allowed."

"Cath!" says Mary. "That's enough. You shouldn't fill Cis's head with such ideas." She turns to me. "Pick up your embroidery, child; you have much to do, so it is suitable for Richard to wear."

I absently finger the tunic before me. A much younger husband would not even be born yet, for I am only nine—

"Mary," says Mama. "Cecylee knows her duty."

"Not as well as Anne," says Mary, her lips thinning.

This is true. Anne sits there, quietly sewing. I don't know how she does it. How can you concentrate on something as dull as embroidery when all these tales are inviting you to imagine all sorts of things? I eye Richard's tunic and turn to Mama. "Is it true that a woman may marry only once?"

"That depends on canon law," replies Mama.

"Bishops and the church determine that?" asks Anne.

"Men! Men always do!" I exclaim.

Mama takes some time to explain what canon law is. I pick up Richard's tunic. Perhaps it would be well to finish it soon, so I can make something pretty for myself.

"It's ridiculous, all this talk about canon law," says Audrey under her breath. She sits down beside me and threads her needle with silver thread. "I ask you, most women are lucky if they manage to survive one husband, with all those pregnancies, let alone several. Men always want the same thing." She bites off the silver thread with the one tooth that is left in the side of her mouth. "They don't always stop to think if their favorite sport is good for their young brides. Look at Lady Anne. She was only twelve when she married the Duke of Buckingham last year, and now she's expecting her first child at thirteen."

I look up to see Mama's reaction. But she talks as if nothing has happened: "Most people don't worry about remarrying nowadays. You can marry as often as you please—provided that your husbands are dead first." She smiles at me, then turns to Anne. "Which women have power?"

"Abbesses," says Anne. "They may ride out of their convents and conduct business with important men."

"Widows with rank and money," I put in quickly. "Once your husband is dead, you may do as you please. You can manage your land, plead lawsuits, spend your own money." I throw back my head and peal with laughter, contemplating the luxury of so much freedom.

"Makes you wonder why more husbands are not bumped off," says Audrey, "when wealthy widows have much more power than rich wives."

A hush descends. Anne and Jenet stare, their needles suspended in mid-air. Mama bites her lip. Catrine looks amused. Mary stands. "My lady mother, how can you countenance this? If you do not curb her, Cecylee will imagine she can do as she pleases."

"You're too hard on her, Mary," says Catrine.

"Life is going to be hard on Cecylee," replies Mary. "You know she has no choice in the matter of her husband."

"I am well aware of that," says Mama, flushing. "But I see no reason why Cecylee may not enjoy the girlhood that is left to her."

"My lady mother, your judgment is usually faultless, but you are blind about Cecylee," continues Mary.

Mama rises. "You know the sacrifices I have been forced to make."

"How can you expect her to be a dutiful wife?"

"I never see Bess, my eldest, because she lives on the other side of the mountains."

"Filling her head with the Wife of Bath only makes things worse."

"I never see Jehane because she is a nun."

"You never say no to her."

"Alainor is lost to me because she is married to the heir of our worst enemy, Henry Percy, Earl of Northumberland."

"Cecylee is acquiring a temper to go along with her haughty ways."

"Anne and Catrine must live with their husbands and can make only rare visits."

"And you do not see this because she winds you around her finger as if she were reeling in a day's catch."

"And the only reason why I see you, Mary, is because you are married to a Neville and live at Castle Raby."

"You're so jealous—" says Catrine and then stops.

The unmistakable sound of mail-shod feet climbs the spiral staircase. It sends prickles up the spine. Quick as a flash of steel, Cath bundles Master Chaucer's manuscripts into a chest and shuts the lid.

"Mama—" says Anne. But Mama takes my hand and says, "If it's the last thing I do, I'll not be parted from my Cecylee."

Papa enters the solar.

Mama grips my hand tight.

Papa narrows his eyes. "Well, my lady?"

Mama draws herself up. "You agreed that Cecylee could visit me in Bulmer's Tower—"

"What's this I hear about never being parted from Cecylee?"

I flick my gaze from Papa to Mama. "Mama means that she would like me to visit more often."

Papa fingers his beard as he glances at me. He gives a harsh bark of laughter. "So be it!" he exclaims. "Provided you include young Richard in your visits." He strides to the door and turns. "It would do the lad good to spend more time with the ladies, do you not agree, madam?" And laughing, he pounds down the stairs, his mailed foot striking each stone step.

Mama's fingers clutch mine as we both sweep him a low curtsey.

CHAPTER 3

Feast of Saint Luke
October 18, 1424

My eyes snap open.

The day of my betrothal, my stomach spasms into knots.

Why be betrothed now? At nine, I'm expected to enter a woman's estate, with a woman's cares and responsibilities. Where is my girlhood? I don't want it to end. I'm comfortable with Mama and enjoy my studies. I don't see why all of this can't continue.

Maybe I can delay things.

The door opens. Jenet pours warmed water into a bowl and hands over a linen napkin to dry my hands and face. She stokes the fire into a blaze before helping me into a fur-lined robe. I put my feet into fur-lined slippers, Jenet wraps her red woolen mantle tight, and then we file onto the wooden walkway for our cold and invigorating walk around the kitchen tower to the chapel.

A crisp cold morning, the sunlight cuts through the golden leaves of the trees. Smoke curls lazily from the castle kitchens where servants labor to prepare the betrothal feast. As we emerge from the staircase into the chapel, the deep bell tolls, calling people to early morning Mass.

Today, a large crowd gathers, my kinfolk having ridden into Castle Raby to take part in the celebrations. As I enter the chapel, I catch a glimpse of my eldest brother Richard Neville, Baron Montacute, who has twenty-four years. He stands at the front of the chapel with Alice Montacute, his sixteen-year-old wife. They've spent the last month traveling 300 miles from their estates in the south of England, bringing with them their baby Cecily, named in honor of me.

I look around. My two half-sisters, four sisters, and several brothers are all in attendance. My betrothal to Richard is part of a double ceremony, for my seven-year-old baby brother Edward will marry a wealthy heiress and bear the title Lord Bergavenny in right of his wife. His wife-to-be, Lady Lisbet de Beauchamp, stands next to him. She has a pale face, pale pink lips, pale hair, and pale blue eyes. She stands very still. You would not think to look at her that she is my age. Edward is two years younger, so she is lucky enough to get a young husband she can boss around.

After Mass, I go back to my apartment in the keep, accompanied by Jenet, who has to wash and dress me and do my hair. I am so busy concocting my plan I don't notice the ladies gathering to greet me. A well-known voice makes me jump.

"Cecylee, sweeting, guess what I have for you."

"Cath!" I exclaim. "I'm busy—"

"Listen to her Impatience, the next Duchess of York."

I blush.

"Don't you want to know?" she cajoles, hiding something behind her back.

26

I sigh and resist stamping my foot. Bother Cath for getting in the way.

"What is it?"

"You have to guess."

I close my eyes as I rack my brains. Why does Cath have to be so irritating? "A mirror," say I, guessing wildly.

"My baby sister is as cunning as a fox!" exclaims Cath as she brandishes the object in front of me. I focus my eyes on something very bright that reflects the light. It is a mirror, a beautiful silver mirror with a matching silver comb. Both have sinuous decorations on the handles and edges; my name carved discreetly within. I am struck dumb.

"Really, Catrine!" exclaims Mama, a twinkle in her eye. "You encourage Cecylee to be vain."

I look up. My sisters, half-sisters, sisters-by-marriage, their maids, and other female relatives fill the apartments. As the laughter dies away, the sound of a soft footfall comes, and Anne appears with Humphrey, her new baby boy, the future Earl of Stafford. Even though it's now three weeks since the birth of her son, Anne looks pale and has violet shadows under her eyes.

"I'm fine, Mother, truly," she says in response to Mama's unspoken question. "I just tire easily."

"Sit by me and rest," says Mama. She takes the baby from Anne while Cath goes to the kitchens to oversee the refreshments.

Anne sits down, and from her sleeve, she produces a small package wrapped up in linen. She smiles at me.

Another present! I unwrap it to find a purse made out of sky-blue silk and lined with dark blue damask. My name is embroidered in seed pearls on the front.

"Did you make this?"

Anne nods.

I hold it up. The embroidery is finely wrought with small, neat stitches and no knots or threads hanging loose—so different from my own travails, so perfect.

I give it to Mama; she examines it with gentle fingers.

"You can take that to the fair," says Anne, "with money in it from Richard to buy yourself some luxuries."

My cheeks warm. Even my quiet sister Anne has noticed Richard's attentions, how he always presents me with tokens of his affection like sewing scissors, thimbles, and needles—things I need for the everlasting embroidery I am supposed to do. When the fair comes, he buys me headbands, snoods, veils, hairpins, earrings, and necklaces. I delight in these presents, but should I really accept them?

"It is beautiful," says Mama, kissing Anne's cheek. "How you found the time to do it when you had to ready yourself for your first child, I do not know. Cecylee, my love, thank your sister."

I hug my sister tight as Mama wipes tears away with her fingers.

More company arrives in the shape of Richard's fifteen-year-old sister Isabel, married to Sir Thomas Grey. Mama greets her, trying to prompt a smile from her sad face, and settles down to gossip with the ladies who now preen themselves in front of their mirrors.

I tiptoe away.

When I reappear sometime later, I am just in time to see the women from the kitchen struggling up the stairs with buckets of warm water. Jenet tests the temperature of the water with her elbow, then helps me out of my clothing, and I step into the tub. She washes my hair in rosemary soap, then tenderly smoothes an oily paste made of finely ground almonds onto my skin to cleanse it, washing it off with angelica water. After that, she helps me out of the tub and dries me off.

With her help, I put on silk stockings and tied the garters just above the knee. When I stand, I hold my arms so that Jenet can pull the ivory silk chemise over my head. Then Jenet braids my hair into plaits. She coils the plaits around my head, pins them, and then carefully covers her handiwork with a hair net.

As I relax under Jenet's gentle ministrations, the door bangs, and Audrey appears.

"My lady," she says to Mama, "I cannot find Lady Cecylee's gown. I swear I had it with me this last hour, and now it's disappeared." She turns to Thomasina, Cath's maid, and Gunilda, Anne's maid. "Don't just stand there. Help me find it. Search your ladies' things."

A hubbub ensues. I smile as I calculate how long this will keep everyone busy. I find a quiet corner, fold my hands, and keep my eyes downcast. I count things; trees, sheep, ospreys. I am just getting started on castles when I sense someone standing in front of me. I glance up and see Anne.

"Cis," she whispers, "where is it?"

"Where is what?" I ask.

"You know what I mean," whispers Anne. "Where have you hidden your gown?"

"I haven't," I say.

Anne opens her mouth to say something when the door opens. Cath reappears, followed by servants bearing food on trays and cups of wine. There are pies made out of game, several different kinds of cheese, round flat rolls of manchet bread, mead and hippocras, a spicy wine.

The servants put the food down and withdraw while Cath takes in the crowd of women surrounding Mama, gesticulating and wailing over the disappearance of my gown. Her eyes flick over to me. She beckons.

I make my way slowly over, clenching my hands as she fixes me with a firm look. "Stop playing games," she hisses. "You cannot hurt Mama in this way—"

"In what way?" I say.

"I know you've hidden it, you little prankster," Cath continues, her voice rising. "Where is it?"

She says it in such a loud voice, it reaches to the ends of the earth. Everyone has heard everything, and the room grows quiet. The weight of many eyes fall on me, their expressions a mixture of exasperation, pity, amusement, and disappointment. I flush to the roots of my hair.

The silence holds. Then the door opens, and Mary appears.

"I found this in my bedchamber, concealed in my garderobe," she says, shaking out the bundle in her arms to reveal the missing gown. She glares at me. "Someone must have put it there by mistake."

I twist my hands, hang my head. Mary's the dressmaker of the family, and I thought I could conveniently hide my gown amongst everyone else's finery.

"*Cecylee!*" says Mama. Just that one word, but it makes me cringe with shame.

The room rustles as remarks fly. "Such wild manners," whispers the Countess of Warwick to her neighbor. "I would never let my daughter behave in that way."

Mama reddens and bites her lip.

"Let me," says Anne, taking the dress from Mary and smoothing it out. "I'm already dressed, so I can help Cecylee." With Anne helping, Jenet slowly brings the heavy velvet, midnight-blue betrothal gown over my head. They lace it up at the sides and attach the triangular sleeves over my long-sleeved chemise. Jenet places the blue velvet head-roll on my head and pins on the translucent silken veil. Anne helps me into the shoes, pointed poulaines made of matching dark blue velvet with the Neville crest on top.

The dress is ablaze in silver embroidery. There is the Neville crest at my bodice, and the bullion knots on the skirts give way to a silver, flowery mead with horned sheep. At the bottom around the hem is embroidered *Cecylee, Duchesse of Yorke*. I am ready.

The gentlemen rise and bow as Mama, and I enter the great hall, followed by the ladies. On that never-to-be-forgotten morning, the great hall looks magnificent, decorated with apples, autumn roses, and sheaves of corn. The lighted wax tapers make the stone walls and silverware glow, and new rushes of meadowsweet give off a sweet scent of newly cut hay and flowers.

Cardinal Beaufort, Mama's younger brother, clears his throat. "We are met here today to witness the betrothal of Richard Plantagenet, Duke of York, to Lady Cecylee de Neville."

Richard smiles at me. I ignore him, staring instead at the finely embroidered handkerchief placed into my hands by Mama.

Cardinal Beaufort raises his voice. "If there be any among you who know why Richard, Duke of York, and Lady Cecylee de Neville may not be betrothed, say you so now, or forever hold your peace."

I look around. Surely someone will say something.

They do not.

Cardinal Beaufort turns to me. "My child," he says, "do you consent to this betrothal?"

I tense. I look at Papa, and he nods. I look at Mama. She nods also.

"Yes," I murmur, looking down.

Cardinal Beaufort turns to Richard. "Duke Richard, take you Lady Cecylee's hands."

Richard's warm and moist hands take mine. I make a supreme effort not to snatch them away. While Cardinal Beaufort speaks the words that bind us to marry at some future date, I stare at my blue velvet slippers. I don't look at Richard until Cardinal Beaufort is in the middle of marrying little Edward to Lady Lisbet.

"Does this mean I don't have to be locked up anymore?"

Richard stares at me. He draws himself up. "You must stay in your apartments."

I set my lips into a line.

"I may be King of England one day."

"I hate being locked up because of you."

Richard flinches. "Cecylee," he says, "calm yourself. I am here to protect you."

"I don't want your protection," I mutter, looking away.

"One day, you will be my wife."

"But I don't want to be your wife if I have to be locked up like a caged animal."

"I am the heir to the throne."

"I hate these chains!"

"You must do what your lord father tells you."

"I want to be free!"

"Cis!" A deep bellow casts a pall.

I freeze.

Papa strides up, putting his hands on his hips and glaring at me. "Well?" he says. "What do you have to say?"

I do not know what to say. Truly, my lord father, and I do not see eye-to-eye on this matter.

"My lord, it is nothing," stammers Richard.

Papa shakes his head. "Lord Richard, you are too kind. Mark my words, you will be ill recompensed for being so. Cecylee must learn to bear the consequences of her actions."

I lift my head. "I told him I did not want to be locked up."

"And why are you locked up?" asks Papa softly.

"I don't know," I murmur.

"Speak up, my lady."

"I don't know."

Papa grasps me by the arm. "Don't you? Then I shall have to teach you, my fine lady. Until then, you will show the company that you know how to behave. Is that understood?"

I look at the floor, moisten my lips.

"Is that understood?" thunders Papa.

I flinch. "Yes, my lord father."

He glares at me.

I sweep him a low curtsey.

He stalks off.

Richard lets out a long breath. "Are you affrighted, Cis?"

"No."

"Isn't he going to punish you?"

I am silent.

"You have greatly angered him—"

With a flourish of trumpets, the food arrives in a procession of platters set down first on the high table, then on the lower tables. Silently, Richard takes my hand and leads me to the place of honor in the middle of the high table.

The feast begins with thick turnip soup, flat manchet bread, and goat cheese; platters of green beans, sweet peas, and carrots follow. There is pike stuffed with a mixture of breadcrumbs and herbs. While the dishes are being cleared away, the first sugar sculpture is presented, created by Audrey's son. On one platter is Castle Raby with a rose in front of it, to honor me, the Rose of Raby. On the other platter is a white lion to symbolize Richard, who has taken the White Lion of March as his personal badge in honor of his late mother, Lady Anne de Mortimer.

At another flourish from the trumpets, the meat course arrives. There is a Swan and a Boar's Head with an orange in its mouth, followed by a large piece of beef dressed in rosemary and sage. At the end of the procession, servants carry silver sauce boats, salt cellars, and pipes of wine.

The feast ends with another subtlety of the Lady and the Unicorn. The Unicorn bears an unmistakable resemblance to Richard, showing him sitting docilely at my feet. Richard reddens upon recognizing himself. But roars of laughter from Papa and the applause of the guests mask his embarrassment; everyone rises and drinks our health. The minstrels strike up a lively air, and Richard leads me into the hall for the first dance. How I love to dance! I even manage a smile for Richard.

At last, afternoon melts into evening, and Mama takes me by the hand. We bid our guests a "God go with you" and leave.

I don't have to wait long. I'm sitting by the fire with Audrey in attendance, dressed only in my chemise, when Papa strides up to my room, birch twigs in hand. He makes me bend over and lifts my skirts. The twigs cut into my bare skin. I try not to cry out, but soon give up.

I am furious.

Why shouldn't I be free?

Why should I be forced to marry someone I don't want?

I hate Richard.

I hate my lord father.

I hate men.

I will never forgive them.

Never. Never. Never. Never.

Never. Never. Never.

Never.

Never.

CHAPTER 4

Feast of Saint Ursula & The Blessed Virgins
October 21, 1425

I bring the pony to a stop. Before me, sprawled on the ground, lies my lord father, Ralph de Neville, the Earl of Westmorland. His right leg sticks out at a funny angle. Next to him kneels Richard. He is weeping.

"Help me off," I say.

We've been riding from Sheriff Hutton to Middleham to transact business and collect revenues. I have been allowed to come along, accompanied, naturally, by Richard. We ride in the middle of the party, surrounded by knights, when we hear a sudden shout. I dig my heels into Doucette to make her go faster, but the docile little pony merely snorts and continues at her customary pace while Richard's gelding surges to the front of the line.

I disengage myself from Richard and stand over my father. Is he dead? I stare at him hard, but he doesn't move.

A thunder of hooves reverberates, and my brother Salisbury vaults off his horse. Instantly, everyone doffs their hats and kneels.

Father is dead.

Salisbury motions everyone up and stands beside Richard. "Did you see him go down?"

Richard shakes his head.

"He clutched his chest, grimaced, and tumbled off," says Sir Ralph Neville the Older, riding up. Sir Ralph is one of father's numerous younger sons by his first marriage, thus my half-brother.

Salisbury bends over and places a stubby finger on father's forehead. "He's as cold as marble," he mutters. He fishes two golden sovereigns out of his leather pouch and places them over the lids to close them. Then he straightens up and gives orders for father to be borne to Castle Raby.

I stand still, looking at father. He doesn't move. I stare at the fallen leaves on the ground, then lift my eyes to the huge oak tree that stands in my path. It has been blasted by a summer storm and is dead. Underneath it is the green shoots of new trees. Papa is like that oak, sheltering us from storms. What will become of us now? What of Mama? Will she have anything, or will she be forced to beg like those old women I see by the edge of the road when I ride my pony into Staindrop?

"He's already acting as heir!" exclaims Sir Ralph.

I look up.

Sir Ralph clutches the reins, causing his stallion to prance.

"I thought he was," says Richard.

"Well, you thought wrong," snaps Sir Ralph, swinging his stallion around. "My nephew and namesake is heir. I must ride to Brancepeth and tell him so before that upstart takes more than is his right." He digs his knees in, and the stallion bounds off across the desolate moorland.

I stare after the rapidly fading figure of Sir Ralph Neville the Older, the cold wind snapping my veil. I am ten years old. It has been just over a year since I was forced into that betrothal with Richard. The seasons have rolled around, bringing in the bright, chill days of October.

What does this mean? I know, of course, that Sir Ralph is my father's second son by his first marriage. Sir Ralph's elder brother, Sir

John Neville, died some five years ago, and so Sir John's eldest son, Sir Ralph Neville the Younger, stands to inherit.

Or does he?

What about brother Salisbury? He is the eldest son of my father's second marriage to Mama, Joan de Beaufort, and father has always treated him as the heir. Salisbury has royal blood flowing in his veins like me, for our mother's father, John of Gaunt, was son to King Edward III. Has father actually gone against English law and custom and disinherited the children of his first marriage?

"Where's he gone?" I turn to see Salisbury standing there.

"Brancepeth," says Richard.

"Aye, he would," mutters Salisbury, flicking mud off his blue velvet tunic. "We have not a moment to lose." He claps his hands. "We ride to Raby."

"To Raby!" shouted the men in response.

I follow Richard as he strides beside Salisbury into the great hall of Castle Raby. They bow before the high table, where Mama presides in state. Before her, stands a tall young man I do not recognize.

"He's already here," mutters Salisbury.

The stranger turns, and I draw breath, for Sir Ralph Neville the Younger is the veritable image of my lord father. Salisbury smiles and takes the new Earl of Westmorland by the elbow. "Congratulations, my lord, on your new title." He looks meaningfully at the servants. The entire household rises to its feet, and the steward proposes a toast.

"Wass-hail," they roar. "May you have good health." A great noise fills the hall as they clank cups and goblets, precious metal, clay, and pewter, to drink to the new earl.

The second Earl of Westmorland flushes with pleasure and rubs his hands as he looks around the handsome old hall. His gaze lights on me. "Is this little Cis?"

I make my curtsey.

"Yes, my lord," says Mama. She makes a small gesture in the direction of Richard. "Are you acquainted with my lord of York, her betrothed?"

Richard inclines his head. Sir Ralph makes a perfunctory bow in return and continues to stare at me. I lift my chin, a flush mounting into my cheeks.

The new earl chuckles. He turns to Salisbury. "When do you and your lady mother leave for Bisham Manor?"

The great hall grows silent as Salisbury narrows his eyes. At last, he says: "I thought you knew—"

"Knew what?" snaps Westmorland.

"I thought you knew that your grandfather left most of his lands to my lady mother."

I glance at Mama.

"No!" roars Westmorland. "I am the heir of the late earl's eldest son. These lands are mine by the laws of England."

Salisbury beckons to his scribe. "Show my lord of Westmorland a copy of his late grandfather's will."

Westmorland glances at it, then balls the document between his fists. "God's teeth!" he explodes. "I am to be Earl in name only!"

"You get Brancepeth," says Salisbury.

"Aye, but Castle Raby, Sheriff Hutton, and Middleham with all their vast holdings go to that—" he breaks off abruptly and flushes.

"They go to my lady mother," says Salisbury.

"Which you get when she dies."

"I do not think we should be talking of the death of my lady mother."

"As if you don't have enough land, with all those rich holdings in the south your wife brought you when you married."

"My lord father did not want my lady mother to be destitute."

"And what do I get? Nothing, except for Brancepeth and a few paltry manors in the north of this country on poor land."

"You are the Earl of Westmorland."

The new earl glares, his blue eyes looking as icy as his grandfather's. He stalks out of the hall.

There is silence for a few moments, then conversations rumble.

Richard turns to Salisbury. "What do you suppose he'll do?"

Salisbury sighs. "I know not. But we haven't seen the end of this."

"He'll go to the Percies to seek their aid in taking our land," says Mama. "I heard he plans to marry Lady Elizabeth Percy."

"But she's old enough to be his mother!" says Salisbury.

Mama purses her lips and shrugs.

"I must see to our defenses." Salisbury bows and leaves.

Richard glances at me, but I take my place beside Mama. Richard looks around the room as if seeking someone, then bows to Mama and leaves.

Mama puts down her knife and draws a handkerchief from her sleeve. I see that she is weeping.

"Mama," I say softly.

She takes my hand and attempts a weak smile.

"Papa?"

She nods. "Your brother tells me he didn't suffer." She gulps. "But I miss him so. I can't believe he's no longer here."

"But—" I don't quite know how to put this. "You didn't always agree."

She brushes her tears away and takes me gently by the shoulders: "Understand this, my love, your father and I were the best of friends."

"But—"

"Of course, we didn't always agree. You'll understand when you're a married lady yourself."

I frown.

She leans forward and whispers. "Look what he did for me. He left me everything of value in his will."

I look at her, and it is as if everything becomes lighter. I smile.

Mama smiles back.

"My lady!" The steward appears, bowing. He engages Mama in a long discussion.

I pick at my food but can't eat. Suddenly, the hall seems unbearably hot and stuffy. I long to get outside. I want to think about everything Mama has told me. When the steward has gone, I lean forward. "Mama," I say. "It's such a glorious day. May I ride out on Doucette?"

Mama nods absently.

I rise, filled with sudden energy. After a year of being mewed up in the castle keep, I will be alone.

I run.

I run with a speed I didn't know I had, my heart pounding in my chest.

I don't know where I get the energy, for I haven't run in such a long time.

I head for Bulmer's Tower and fly up the stairs towards Mama's bedchamber. I fling myself onto her bed, gasping and sobbing.

Audrey appears. "My lady Cecylee. Whatever has happened?" She takes me by the shoulders. "Why, child, you are a sight to behold, your headdress gone, your hair wild, your clothes torn—" She pales. "Did someone try—?"

I nod, unable to speak.

"Who?"

"The new earl," I manage to gasp out.

It is nearing dusk by the time brother Salisbury returns, followed by Richard and a large party of men—mostly untrained recruits carrying pitchforks, shovels, and other farm implements.

I doze in Mama's bed, dressed in a clean silk chemise. I've been given a bath, my bruises and scrapes treated with a salve. Mama strokes my hair and tells me I've been very brave, that I did right to run away. She promises she'll take care of matters, that I should worry no more.

I gaze at her, unable to speak, tears sliding down my cheeks. I can feel his slimy hands cup my breasts, and smell his foul breath on my cheek. Every time I think of it, I shiver violently and retch into a bucket.

Mail-shod feet pound up the stairs. Audrey opens the door a crack and drops a deep curtsey. Mama rises from her place on the window seat, taking Salisbury into an adjoining room.

Eventually, Salisbury leaves. I hear him speaking to someone outside: "My lady mother wishes to see you." Then I hear the bang, bang, bang of feet going downstairs.

There is silence for a while, then Richard's voice fills the room. "I am more sorry than I can say about the death of your lord husband."

"I dare say you are."

Silence. I hear the rustle of parchment as if someone is searching for something.

"We came back as soon as we could, madam."

Silence. More rustling. A chair scrapes. "I hold you responsible for Lady Cecylee's safety. It is your duty to protect her."

"But Cis does not welcome my visits."

"Why did you leave?"

"To help Salisbury raise his men."

"Did you not notice the way Westmorland stared at her?"

Dead silence.

"I thought you hadn't noticed."

"Did he not ride to Alnwick?"

"I had no men to spare to see that my daughter was safe."

"I thought it made sense to help Salisbury with his levies."

"If her hound had not bitten Westmorland, Lady Cecylee would have been ruined."

"Ruined?"

"I am saying she would have been forced to marry him."

"Marry him? But I thought he was going to marry Lady Elizabeth."

"Are you so doltish you could not see what his game was?"

Silence.

"He could have demanded Castle Raby and the other manors as her dowry. And we would have been unable to refuse."

I am a pawn in the greedy and unscrupulous hands of men. I lean over the bucket and retch up the rest of my dinner.

"If you want Lady Cecylee, impress me. Show me you are truly worthy."

"I am a Plantagenet, the Duke of York."

"An empty title. Where are your lands? Held by the Crown. Because your father was executed as a traitor."

"But I have been promised my lands back once I reach my majority."

"You're only fourteen now. That's seven years away."

I hear a crackle, someone opening a document.

"I will continue to hold your wardship, but I think you should reside with your brother-in-law."

"I will go to Sir Thomas Grey directly," says Richard. "But in the matter of my wardship, I beg you not to break my betrothal to Cecylee. I consider the promise I made that day a sacred vow."

"You are not married to Cecylee. I made sure of that."

"I would like to see Lady Cecylee, to bid her farewell."

My heart drops into my stomach. I'm so ill; I'll humiliate myself in front of him.

"You are not yet worthy." Mama's voice shines into the darkened room: "No."

CHAPTER 5

Bisham Manor, Berkshire
April to May 1437

On the death of my lord father, the marriage negotiations fell into the hands of Salisbury. Fortunately for me, brother Salisbury is more at home commanding his soldiers than persuading Mama to discuss my marriage, so he doesn't try too hard to press Richard's case. Enjoying a girlhood my sisters never had, every May for the next eleven years, I set off with Mama and Salisbury into the north of the country to manage our vast estates in Yorkshire and Westmorland. We go with a heavily armed escort, for the new Earl of Westmorland continues to feud over the Middleham estates, and the Percies make occasional raids. Every October, we return south to Bisham Manor to spend Christmas with Salisbury's wife, Alice, and their growing family.

Alice and other ladies of my age and status grow old and ill as they birth one child after another. Still, I have no husband. Yet while this makes me sigh with relief, thanks to father, I'm styled Duchess of York and am always announced as such. I haven't seen Richard in eleven years, and with leisure, I ponder: What should I do with my life?

The answer comes from an unexpected quarter. Now that Mama spends half of the year at Bisham Manor in the south of England, the abbess of Barking Abbey makes it her business to call frequently upon her half-sister. Abbess Margaret de Swynford travels with several nuns in her train and is kind enough to bring her cousin Elizabeth Chaucer and her half-niece Lady Jehane de Neville with her. And so Mama is able to see a niece, as well as a daughter she believed to be lost.

Lady Jehane, my long-lost sister, has cultivated an air of quietude that draws others to her. She listens attentively as I tell her about my dilemma.

"Richard is not a bad person," I say. "I think he's fond of me or was. But I don't love him, and I don't think he could make me happy. Indeed, my whole being revolts at the idea of being tied down in marriage."

"There's no reason why you couldn't take the veil."

"But I couldn't leave Mama."

"Of course not. She has set much store by you, her youngest daughter." Lady Jehane gives me a smile, untinged with bitterness. "But one day, Our Blessed Lady will gather our lady mother into her arms. If you're not married by then, you could take the veil. I would help you."

My soul soars. I would be spared the rigors of childbearing. I would have opportunities few other women dream of. I could cultivate my mind and improve my handwriting and my grasp of languages. I could learn to make medicines. I could lead a life of quiet contemplation.

I would have a measure of freedom.

But Richard achieved his majority in 1432, obtaining his vast estates back from the Crown. He became the wealthiest peer in the land. Then, in 1436, the king's council decided that Richard of York should replace the king's uncle as governor of Normandy and regent of France, the Duke of Bedford dying unexpectedly at the age of forty-six.

Becoming governor of Normandy was quite a coup for a young man of twenty-four, but it was not a coup for me as Richard now pressed his suit with more vigor and persistence. In April 1437, he even returned to England from Normandy.

Now, he demands to see me.

I recoil.

I remember well how my lord father gave me a beating after I'd dared to question his right to lock me up. I have the scars to prove it. The last time any man touched me was when Sir Ralph Neville lifted my skirts in the stables at Castle Raby. Even now, that humiliation makes me shudder.

The world of men is filled with violence, and I want none of it.

I am seated on a low stool, singing softly, surrounded by brother Salisbury's children, when the crunch of gravel reaches my ears. Looking up, I find a young man.

He is well dressed in rich hues of velvet, as befits a noble. He fingers his heavy gold collar, decorated with white roses done in enamel. From this showy bijou drops a huge spear-pointed diamond.

A prickle wends its way up my spine. There is a silence as he stares at me.

"Need you something, my lord?" I enquire.

Absently fingering the diamond, the young man stutters out a reply. "My lady Cecylee—forgive this intrusion—I see you know not who I am." He takes a deep breath. "Remember you a boy named Richard?"

God have mercy upon my soul. I look down at my lap. I had better get this over with and quickly. I look up and lock eyes.

He reads my face hungrily as if concerned about my feelings. Then he smiles. His smile transforms his face, lighting up his blue-grey eyes and imbuing his expression with warmth and delight.

I cannot help it. I smile back. "Richard, it is you!" I exclaim. "Only you look different. I had not expected to see you look like—"

"Like what, sweetheart? You mean old and ugly?"

I tilt my head as I take him in. "There is a different feel about you." I frown, trying to reconcile the serious, rather pompous boy I'd known with this attractive young man who kneels before me. Then I blush. What am I thinking? I do not wish to marry.

"I see my intrusion has discomforted you, my sweeting, for the which I am sorry. I should not have come upon you this way."

I graze him with a glance. Is he making fun of me?

"We promised once to marry, my lady, but I'd not force you to it against your will." He leans forward. "Is it still your wish to become my wife?"

I thin my lips and veil my eyes with my lashes. So, this is why brother Salisbury has been closeted inside all morning. They must have been signing the marriage papers. Naturally, no one bothered to inform me.

I rise. "You know me not, my lord," I say. Then I sweep out of the garden.

I go to Mama. I do not have to say anything, for she takes one look at my face and nods.

I am gone within the hour.

A message reaches me at vespers the next day: my lord of York arrived to pay a visit but was turned away. He will return in a week.

I smile and toss the note into the flames.

A week later, at the appointed time, Richard, Duke of York, claims admittance to Barking Abbey, where I enjoy the hospitality of Abbess Margaret de Swynford. Lady Jehane has kept me company during this time, and I have attended every Holy Office. I find the quiet darkness of the church where the nuns murmur their prayers soothing to my spirits.

I will tell Richard no, then stay here and take the veil.

I sit in my chamber when he appears. The windows face out onto Abbess Margaret's herb garden. The scent of rosemary and sage fills the room. Audrey and Jenet sit in a corner, engaged in sewing. I read a book in Latin, making notes about it in French.

Richard stares at this scene while I turn to my book.

"How did you learn Latin?" he asks, sitting down beside me without invitation.

"While I waited for you to return, I decided to educate myself," I reply. "My brother Edward was learning Latin, so I begged my lady mother to let me sit in on his classes. Eventually, his tutor Doctor Eusebius agreed to take me on as his pupil."

"I see," says Richard. His eyes strain to look at the title of the book on the table. I give it to him to examine. It is Boethius's Consolation of Philosophy. He stares at me. "Do you like philosophy?"

"It makes you think hard about things," I say. "It is very consoling in times of crisis."

I put that book down and opened another. Again, Richard cranes his neck. I hold it up for him to see. The City of Ladies by Christine de Pizan.

Richard's eyebrows lift as if he's never allowed that a woman could write a book.

"Christine de Pizan was a learned lady, highly regarded by the Queen of France," I say. "This book is a retelling of history from a woman's point of view." I pause and turn to be sure I have his attention. "Have you noticed that history is always told from a man's point of view?" I smile. There.

He stares back but does not recoil. "Cecylee, you are full of surprises," he finally says. "I never would have guessed that the pert, contrary young lady I used to know has turned into a scholar and an ascetic."

I lower my eyes. "You don't have to marry me if you think it unseemly to have such a well-educated wife—"

I stop because Richard is kissing me. On the lips. I shudder. No one has ever done this before. I close my eyes; I'm grasped firmly yet gently; the warmth of his body penetrates my fine woolen gown. At the softness of his lips, I feel myself begin to swoon. "Cis. Don't tease. You know more than anything I want to marry you. But you treat me so badly."

"Don't," I say. "Don't—"

But he kisses me again. I can't help it. His kisses are gentle and respectful, and he holds me softly in his arms. To my surprise, I find myself melting into him.

"You see me for a few hours, then you take fright and rush off in that reckless way you have, forcing me to cool my heels for a week while I'm panting with impatience to see you—"

He sounds like a lover. Does he love me? Is there anything for me in this marriage, apart from an exchange of money and land? "Am I really so difficult?"

"Difficult. You've never been easy. If I weren't madly in love, I'd be tempted to give you a good shaking."

I gaze at him.

He gazes back; his eyes fixed on mine. He looks as if he might care how I feel.

"I'm sorry, Richard," I find myself saying, now calculating. "But I did have to think. It was too much for me after so many years of not seeing you, of not expecting us to marry, of not expecting you to love me or even be very interested."

He should be horrified by this speech. Instead, he looks hurt and —baffled. "How could you think that? I've always been intensely interested in you."

I put my hand on his arm. "Now, Dickon, don't be angry. When my lady mother gave me the girlhood which my sisters never had, and I educated myself, many people told me that no gentleman would want to marry me, and I'd have to spend my days in a convent."

"But, Cis! You don't understand! I love you! I want your company!"

I give him another hard stare. But he meets it without flinching. He takes my hand and brushes his lips over it. I shiver with pleasure. "Have I now proved to your ladyship's satisfaction that I will be a good and loving husband?"

I come to. He hasn't proved anything. I rise and search through my books. "There is just one more thing."

"One more thing?" His voice mounts higher. "Cis, how much longer do you plan to torture me?" He moves closer and puts an arm around my waist. Again, I feel a pleasurable sensation radiating from his touch. I don't understand it. Surely, after the mistreatment I've met with at the hands of men, I should be dead to amorous advances.

I ignore my feelings, find my book, and say, "Only until you've read this." I hand him The Wife of Bath's Tale. "It has some things to say about women, which I would like to discuss with you."

Richard groans but does not lose his temper. Instead, he takes me in his arms and kisses me. "And that will be all? You promise?"

"Promise," I say. If he can swallow that, maybe I should marry him. But I am nearly sure it will enrage him. In which case, I shall refuse him.

Richard sighs. "I don't know why I allow this, but I will read this … tale and return tomorrow morning." He strokes my cheek with his finger. I close my eyes at the unexpected intimacy of his touch.

The next day Richard reappears. "That's a rather subversive story, Cis."

I look straight at him. "Do you agree with it?"

"You mean that women want to have mastery over their lives in the same way as men? That is what you want me to remember?"

"Yes."

Normally marriage negotiations are handled by my liege lord, my father or brother, without taking my views into account. Yet here I am, twenty-one years old, old enough and well educated enough to act as my own advocate. At this moment, I know I have the makings of a ruler, just as Mama said.

I draw myself up. "Remember, Richard. I have a soul to keep. That is why the church allows women to give or refuse their consent to marriage. It is important to me that my soul be well matched to that of my husband. Women are not things. We do not want to be viewed as good only for making babies. It is insulting to our intelligence and to our feelings to be treated thus."

Richard's mouth opens, horrified.

I experience a moment of disappointment. But after all, he is a man. What did I expect?

"Cis!" he stutters.

I stare into the abbess's garden as I brace myself for the tirade. I smile.

But Richard does not say anything for a long time. I had forgotten about these silences. I take a deep breath.

"We could make beautiful children," he finally says.

I whirl around and glare at him.

He takes a step backward.

I fold my arms tight across my body. "I do not wish for a lord and vassal relationship. I want you to love me as your equal."

"But haven't I given you every reason to believe that?"

"I have to give up all my legal rights to be your wife."

"You would be Duchess of York."

"And what would you do if I displeased you?"

"A marriage vow is a sacred obligation."

"Women have the dice loaded against them."

"Cis!"

"Every time a woman has a child, she goes to the gates of death."

"What are you saying?"

"To please her husband, she is usually required to have one child after another, which is bad for her health."

"Do you take me for a brute?"

"If she displeases him, he can take away her children and lock her up."

"Do you expect me to ride roughshod over your feelings?"

I stare at him. Yes, I do expect him to ride roughshod over my feelings. But something about the way he looks at me prevents me from saying so. Instead, I merely remark, "I don't know you."

"We have known one another since childhood!"

"We have not seen one another in twelve years."

"That was not my wish. I always wanted to see you."

I twist my hands together. I can hear the longing in his voice.

"My love, I think you worry too much. No one could love you as much as I. You must know I don't want a caged animal for a wife, but someone to love me."

I finger my crucifix.

He kneels. "Don't you want to experience the joy of having a husband who loves you?" He takes my hand. "Don't you want to have children to adore?" He kisses my hand and puts it over his heart. "Are you telling me, Cis, that you would prefer to live out your life in your brother's household when I am offering you my hand, my heart, everything I have?"

Unexpected tears come to my eyes. I realize I am wilting through a lack of love. A life ruled by prayer now seems colorless and lifeless.

All my life, I have spent in my head. The tips of my fingers resonate with each beat of his heart. He kisses each finger of my hand, front and back. The gentle pressure of his touch makes me tingle. I glance at him. He is attractive, lean, muscular, and well-dressed. "Come to me, my love," he murmurs, "I adore you. You would be safe with me."

I look away. He sounds hungry for me. What would our wedding night be like? I shiver and close my eyes.

Richard gently kisses each finger. "Would two months give you long enough to get ready?"

Two months? That is not much time. On the other hand, I feel powerful sensations of longing I did not know I possessed.

"Yes—" I sigh out that word on the thread of a whisper, without looking at him, to hide my blushes.

"When?"

I pull myself together and stare at him. "The feast day of Mary Magdalene."

But Richard laughs, his face warming with merriment. "Cis, you really are—"

"Mary Magdalene is much misunderstood," I inform him stiffly.

"My love, of course, if you wish it," he says instantly. He rises and takes my face between his hands. "But have I your promise that we will marry then, in two months' time, on the twenty-second day of July, in the Year of Our Lord 1437?"

"On one condition," I say. "I wish to stay here another week. I need to prepare myself."

Richard treats me to another one of his long silences. Finally, he says, "I have a request also. Of course, you may stay here for another week, but I would ask that you allow me to visit you every day and then escort you back to Bisham." He folds my hand into his. "It would be cruel to deny me the pleasure of your company."

What am I supposed to say to that?

Book II: One Seed Sown

As long as I am alive, in truth,
no one will have the joy and pleasure of my love
except for this flower

FROM PLUS BELE QUE FLOR
MONTPELLIER CODEX, 13TH CENTURY

CHAPTER 6

Rouen Castle, Rouen, English France
Feast of Saint Anne, Mother of Our Lady
July 26, 1441

On a day when hot winds carried the sharp scent of herbs, I was riding back from a visit to the merchants of Rouen—one of several—when I heard the thunderous sound of hooves galloping towards me.

I stopped my palfrey on the slope that led up to the castle.

Was it Richard? He'd ridden out with his army to relieve Pontoise only two weeks ago, and I did not expect him so soon. I clutched at the reins, causing my gentle palfrey to snort and arch her neck.

Life as Richard's duchess was not as bad as I'd feared. I acquired a taste for gorgeous satin and thick velvet gowns of every hue, for fur robes, supple gloves, elegant boots, and jewelry. I grew to love the wink of precious gems, emeralds, rubies, and sapphires, and in the summer months, I loved the subtle luster of pearls with lighter silks. Richard proved to be a considerate husband, sparing no expense to fit up his various residences for my pleasure. The only thing he would not tolerate was refusal when he wanted to bed me. He was gentle but persistent.

And so, I bore him three children in four years.

I hated the discomfort of pregnancy and the messiness and pain of birthing, but my children were lovely. My eldest, three-year-old Joan, whom I named after Mama, was the apple of my eye. She was a charming child, already showing great beauty and saying the funniest things. Her sister, two-year-old Nan, was a much quieter soul who glowed with contentment when playing with animals. Baby Henry, born in February, was only five months old and had yet to make his mark on the world. But Richard had been thrilled to have an heir.

Through the thin, semi-transparent fabric of my veil, I dimly saw a gentleman bring his white gelding to a stop with a flourish and vault off.

I pushed the material aside with my gloved hand.

Much younger than Richard, I guessed his age to be no more than twenty. He wore a tunic of dark green velvet over stockings that were half green, half gold, with the seam straight up the middle of the front of each leg. The tunic was shorter than usual, and the eye-catching stockings drew attention to those legs, long and very shapely.

"Your Grace," he gasped in elegant French as he dropped to one knee in the dust. "You forgot this."

He handed up a package that contained my new dress, stiff with jewels.

I looked into a pair of laughing hazel eyes.

"Have I seen you before?"

"I was riding through Rouen when I saw your entourage. I'd heard much of your beauty, so I reined in to see if I could get a glimpse of such rare loveliness."

I turned my head to hide a faint blush. "How did you notice my package?"

"I saw it as soon as you left."

"How fortuitous that you should happen to be there at that precise moment."

His boots were coated in dust.

"Have you come from Pontoise?"

He nodded.

"Have you news of my lord?"

"Indeed, I do, my lady. He is in good health and spirits, and his campaign against the French is going well."

Richard and I arrived in Rouen a month ago so that he could take up his post as governor of Normandy. The city of Rouen was the English capital of France, but the French had been trying for the past several years to wrest control of English France. Pontoise was an English town near Paris that controlled a strategic crossing over the River Oise. Whenever the French wanted to use this crossing, they were forced to pay English tolls, and this they did not like.

In early June, three weeks before our arrival, the French laid siege to Pontoise. But Richard appeared at the head of a large army, bringing his best generals. He was determined to teach the French a lesson. While the men fought the French, their wives and children kept me company.

At my asking, the young man went into detail about marches and counter-marches, night-crossings, and chases back and forth across the River Oise. His brown hair bounced as he gestured the army's movements with his hands, his lips equally mobile and expressive. He smelled of almonds, of nutmeg, and of some exotic spice I could not place. This was such a contrast to other men I knew, who smelled of dogs, horses, mud, and—other unmentionable things.

Who was he? Where did he live?

"Why don't you stay awhile and refresh yourself?"

I led the way into the great hall of Rouen Castle, summoned the servants, and saw that he was well furnished with refreshments. When I was assured that he had what he wanted, I left.

Around an hour or so later, I reappeared.

He was singing a chanson, accompanying himself on his lute. As soon as he saw me, he rose.

He devoured me with his eyes.

My new dress was of blue-grey silk with yards of material that floated around me as I walked. Pearls adorned the bodice. Pearls swirled in patterns down the sleeves. Pearls inscribed my name around the hem. I wore a matching heart-shaped headdress with a fine gauze veil.

It had been hard to decide which jewels to wear, for I had chests filled with them. It had taken Jenet a whole hour to find them all.

Eventually, I chose a sapphire and pearl necklace with matching earrings.

The silence lengthened as he gazed at me.

I lifted my chin and stared back. What would happen now? But our silent reverie was interrupted by the appearance of the other ladies. Word must have got around that an attractive stranger had arrived, for they wore their best dresses, coloring their cheeks and lips with rouge. After two weeks of nun-like seclusion, while our men battled the French, we were dying for male company.

The young man got up and bowed, kissing each hand with a flourish.

I took in their finery and glanced down at my gown.

"You look ravishing, duchess," murmured the young man. "You need no addition to your attire."

Richard's sister, now Isabel de Bourchier, married to Baron Henry Bourchier, bit her lip.

Lady Bess de Vere, married to John de Vere, twelfth Earl of Oxford, interrupted. "Do you know Plus Bele Que Flor, The One To Whom I Submit Is More Beautiful Than A Flower?"

"Now, how does that go, my lady?" said the young man as he sat and strummed some chords on his lute. "The One To Whom I Prostrate Myself Is More Lovely Than A Flower?"

Lady Margaret Beauchamp, Countess of Shrewsbury smiled. *"The One Who Lets Me Play For Her Is More Lovely Than A Flower."*

"No," replied my sister-in-law Lady Lisette Beauchamp, married to George. *"The One Who Lies Beneath Me Is More Lovely Than A Flower."*

I laughed. *"No indeed. It is The One Who Commands My Obedience Is More Lovely Than A Flower."*

"You are looking very well, Cis," remarked Isabel in her distinctive voice. She lisped her rs exactly as Richard did. "That is quite a magnificent dress; I have never seen so many pearls. Who is that?"

Silence fell as I faced Isabel.

Lady Isabel de Bourchier was an unusually thin lady of thirty-two years. Of course, it would be Isabel asking the awkward questions, with her habit of watchful silence. "This young man, Isabel, has come from Pontoise."

Isabel turned towards him. "And you are?"

"My name is of no consequence, my lady." The young man rose and bowed gracefully.

Isabel's elegantly thin eyebrows rose. "Are you saying that you are of no consequence?"

There was silence.

"Where are you from?"

"A country far from here."

Isabel thinned her lips.

"Isabel," I said, touching her arm. "He has come from Pontoise. He has news of the campaign."

Immediately the ladies clamored for news about their husbands, all of them among Richard's generals: Isabel's husband, Baron Henry Bourchier, Bess's husband, the Earl of Oxford, and Lisette's husband, my brother George, Lord Latimer.

I held up my hand. "It's such a fine evening, with many more hours to run. Why don't we sit outside? We can discuss Pontoise."

I signaled to the servants to follow.

The young man put down his lute and offered me his arm.

I led everyone to an area out in the garden screened by yew, which made for a private kind of outside room. Inside this space were tubs of roses, rosemary, thyme, and small orange trees. A turf seat stood in the middle, looking as if three benches had been put into an oddly shaped triangle with a side left open. Sitting on the seat gave us a view out of this small garden through a doorway cut into the hedge. This view led the eye into the larger pleasure ground, where a fountain fed the bathing pool.

I sat in the middle of the seat, with the young man on my right and Isabel on my left.

The others took the remaining places.

I turned to the young man, and he began his tale while the servants set up a table at the open side of the three-sided seat and brought cold beet soup, cheese, and manchet bread, followed by a salad and hare stew. This was followed by Hippocras and angel wafers.

"The French are playing a clever game," I remarked as I set my wine down. "By not coming out into the open to fight us fairly, they conserve their forces while we wear ours out as we chase after them. Could we not employ a similar strategy to the French?"

The young man raised his brows. "You are quite right, my lady," he said. "What a strategist you are. I would not like to command an army that opposed yours."

I was about to reply when Bess said, "I'm thankful our men managed to cross the bridge of boats at Royaumont without breaking their necks. Our Blessed Lady be thanked for that." She dipped her head like a horse, chestnut curls bobbing.

"Men can be so reckless," agreed Margaret, wiping her fingers with a napkin. Her husband, the Earl of Shrewsbury, had been holding Pontoise for the English along with my brother William, Lord Fauconberg, before Richard's army arrived. Now they joined in his campaign against the French.

"We ladies have to be so strong," declared Lisette, stuffing another wafer in her mouth and licking the honey off her fingers. "Gentlemen have no idea how hard it is to wait and wait with no news." She batted her lashes at the young man. "Would you treat your wife like that?"

"I have no wife."

Lisette opened her small, raisin-like eyes wide. Small and plump, twenty-year-old Lisette was like a pigeon that constantly pecked at its feed. "You don't? A fine young man like yourself?"

"It's not so easy for someone with my kind of life."

"What kind of life? I've never met such a well-favored gentleman who hadn't been snatched—"

"Lisette means only that she is used to married couples," interrupted Margaret, flushing. "In our society, we are married at such a young age." Her voice trailed off.

"Before we know who we are," I said. "Before we even have the capacity to choose—so that we can't."

The young man shot me a sharp look. I twisted my napkin while Isabel picked up her horn-handled knife and peeled an orange.

"Have you heard the story of Black Fulk of Anjou?" she enquired, staring at the young man. She looked around. "Some of us here are descended from him. One day, he discovered his wife in the arms of her lover. Do you know what he did?"

The young man stared at her, unflinching.

"I will tell you," said Isabel, returning his stare. "He made his wife get into her wedding finery. Then he burned her alive in the town square at Angers."

There was silence for several moments, almost as if everyone were holding their breath. Then a sound made everyone turn.

It was Lisette. She slumped, white-faced, into her seat.

Margaret got up. "She is not well," she said, frowning at Isabel, who daintily placed a piece of orange into her mouth. "I must take her back to her chamber."

I signaled to the steward, who bowed and put his hand under Lisette's elbow while Margaret stood on her other side. Between them, they propelled the limp figure back to the castle.

"She makes much out of nothing," said Isabel. "She creates these dramas."

"Your story was not pleasant," said Bess. She turned to me. "Is she easily upset?"

I hesitated. It was a delicate matter for Lisette, married to someone like my brother George, who had an unpredictable temper. Eventually, I murmured, "She is not happy."

Isabel snorted. "Who is?"

I rose. "I fear I must bid you goodnight," I said to the young man. "Margaret might need my help."

The young man bowed. "Of course," he murmured, gazing at me as he kissed my hand.

I stepped into the shadows to hide my blushes while the others bade farewell to him.

"What a charming young man," declared Bess as we went back to the castle. "So well-favored. Do you suppose we'll be seeing him again?"

"You can be sure of that," said Isabel. "He clearly enjoys gleaning information and gossip from wherever he can find it."

I didn't respond.

"I'll see you in the morning," said Bess, curtseying first to me, then to Isabel. She smiled at me as she stifled a yawn and disappeared up the stone staircase.

"You are quiet tonight, Cecylee," said Isabel, giving me a peck on the cheek.

"I am greatly fatigued, madam," I replied, sweeping her a low curtsey.

I spent that night waiting for dawn to break.

CHAPTER 7

Lammastide
August 1, 1441

By Lammastide, the roses had reached their peak and clustered thickly up and over the arbor, providing not only shade but also a wonderful scent that intensified upon the evening.

It was my custom to sit in the arbor, by the bathing pool, with Margaret while we did our needlework. At thirty-seven years, Margaret was the eldest lady of my acquaintance, and during that long, hot summer, she became my dearest friend and confidante. Perhaps this was because Mama had so recently passed away.

How I missed Mama. Though we'd not seen much of each other these four years since my marriage to Richard, our messages brought me great comfort. Now she'd been gathered up to heaven, leaving a great hole in my life. Something Richard didn't understand.

I sighed. Why did he interest me so? I'd scarcely been able to keep him out of mind for the past week. "What do you want?" I murmured. Then, recollecting myself, I said to Margaret, "I wish I could give my lord another son. Little Henry is not strong. I fear he will not make old bones."

"Has he been coughing again?"

"Yes. He seems always to be sick with something, and it is high summer. What will happen when winter comes?"

Margaret leaned forward and patted my hand. "It is not in your hands but in God's. Only God can tell whether your son will be spared."

"Is that so, Mama?" asked six-year-old Eleanor Talbot. Margaret's youngest was the most striking of her three daughters, with fair hair the color of silver and unusually colored eyes. Now, she tilted those violet eyes up to her mother's face.

"What about Our Blessed Lady?"

"Of course, she'd know as well," replied Margaret, smoothing back the child's silky hair.

"But wouldn't she know more than God?" asked Eleanor.

Margaret frowned. "I don't know, my sweet. Why do you think she would?"

Eleanor smiled, revealing even white teeth. "Because she's a lady, and ladies always know more than gentlemen."

"Why do you think that?" I asked. Where had the child got such ideas?

"Gentlemen do not always think with their heads," remarked Eleanor, executing a stem stitch.

"What do you mean, child?" said Margaret. "Of course, they do."

"Not always," replied Eleanor. "Sometimes they think with their pricks."

I flinched, the pleasant summer afternoon gone.

"Eleanor!" said Margaret, flushing. "Where did you hear that?"

Eleanor hung her head and fiddled with her work. "I was repeating only what Chantal said," she murmured. Chantal was a local girl who worked in the kitchens.

Margaret put a ringed finger under the child's chin, tilting it so that she could look directly into her daughter's eyes.

"That is not the sort of thing ladies say," she admonished gently. "You know your lord father wouldn't be pleased. And one day, you'll be a married lady. You'll never be happy unless you learn to curb your tongue."

"Yes, Mama," murmured Eleanor, dimpling. "But suppose I wish to take the veil?"

Margaret was saved from replying by the appearance of a diminutive figure rushing over.

"Mama! Mama!"

Three-year-old Joan threw her arms around my neck. I smiled, taking her in. Joan's dark brown, almost black hair had come free from her headdress and was coiling down her back. She was dressed in a silken dress of dark blue that was stained and badly creased. Yet she looked carefree and happy.

Annette de Caux, both governess to the older children and nursemaid to baby Henry, followed Joan at a more sedate pace. She held Joan's discarded headdress in one hand. "Lady Joan," she exclaimed. "It is not seemly for you to wander with your hair so wild —" She broke off as she caught my eye and sank into a deep curtsey.

I smoothed Joan's loose hair and gathered her into my arms. I covered her soft cheeks with kisses.

Annette sighed and thinned her lips.

Joan tilted her head and smiled. "Mama," she said, clutching at my sleeve with sticky fingers. "Where've you been? I want to play ninepins."

"It's too hot to play now, my sweet," I murmured, brushing strands of hair out of Joan's face with the tips of my fingers. "And I'm busy. I must finish this sewing."

"But you're always busy nowadays," replied Joan, her lips quivering. "I only wanted to play for a little while." She pouted for a moment, then smiled.

I sighed. Joan was breathtakingly lovely, her eyes a deep blue, her face shaped like a heart. Pink roses bloomed in her cheeks. I held her more closely and inhaled her sweet scent.

"Why don't you let Annette take you to the kitchens?"

At this, Joan's face lit up. Annette folded her arms and shook her head.

"Are we going to be allowed to have sweetmeats?" Joan asked, running the tip of her tongue around her rosy lips.

Margaret laughed. "Yes indeed, you sweet child."

"Are you coming too, Margaret?" asked Joan as she scrambled off my lap.

"Lady Margaret," said Annette softly.

Margaret laughed again. "Your mother and I will come soon enough. We can play ninepins outside when it is cooler."

I bent and gave Joan one last kiss. "Go now," I said, giving her a gentle push.

"Come on, Eleanor," called Joan, holding out her hand to her friend. "We can go to the kitchens and eat as much as we like. Mama said."

Eleanor glanced at her mother, who nodded. She made her curtsey and waited for Joan.

Joan blew me a kiss and ran off with Eleanor.

Annette followed, chastising, "You should always remember to make your curtsey to your lady mother. You should always wear your headdress. Your lord father would be gravely displeased to see his eldest daughter behaving like a kitchen wench—" Her voice faded away as she continued to instruct three-year-old Joan on the proper way to behave.

Margaret and I looked at each other and burst into laughter. A sudden cloudburst prevented us from saying any more as we made for the castle swiftly.

An hour passed, the sun came out, and I was smoothing a tuck with my right ring finger on a dress I was making for Joan when I glanced up. My heart pulsed in my throat. Bess was with the young man in the gardens below. Their heads were close together as they strolled along.

"Look at that," declared Lisette. "She's got him all to herself. She never thinks about the rest of us."

"Lisette!" exclaimed Margaret, turning towards her youngest sister.

I pricked my finger. A spot of blood landed in the middle of the flower I'd been embroidering.

Margaret rose, took a basin of water, added salt, and with a linen cloth set about getting the bloodstain out of Joan's new dress.

The door opened, and Bess danced in.

"Such a charming young man," she declared.

"No need to ask whom you've been with," remarked Isabel, snapping her ivory needlecase shut.

Bess turned to me. "The young man's name is Monsieur Pierre Blaybourne, and he's just joined the garrison here at Rouen as an archer."

"Now, why would he do that?" asked Isabel.

Margaret looked at me closely as she continued to rub salt and cold water onto the bloodstain.

"He says he's doing it to protect Cecylee," replied Bess, laughing.

The room went very quiet as three pairs of eyes fell on me. Margaret's grey eyes grew thoughtful, Lisette's currant brown eyes flashed angrily, and Isabel's pale ones bore right through me.

I felt a shiver of a whiplash pass up my spine. I rose from my seat.

"I know nothing of this. I have not seen this…Blaybournea since the day we met a week ago."

Bess laughed and pulled at my sleeve. "There's no need to be so serious. He's invited all of us to the archery butts to see him practice with the other men. They are having a contest now and want us to judge who is the best archer."

Immediately, the solar hummed like a hive. Lisette jumped up and called for her maid to bring her new red dress. Margaret, Isabel, and I put our sewing away and summoned our women for rosewater and lavender water and for pastes made of angelica flowers and ground almonds to cleanse the skin.

Jenet helped take off my everyday blue linen, and I slipped into a dusky rose silk worn over a pale green chemise. I studied my jewel case, deciding on pearls to go with the pink silk while Jenet tidied my hair and rearranged my headdress. By the time Jenet had finished dressing me, the other ladies were ready. Lisette was vivid in red, Bess's dress of the deepest green set off her green eyes and chestnut hair, Margaret wore heavy purple damask, and Isabel wore sky-blue silk.

The shower had cooled off the thundery weather. Outside, a light breeze lifted our veils, and we walked a well-trodden path amongst oak and hornbeam, beech, hazel and hawthorn, followed by servants bearing refreshments.

Just outside the city walls were the archery butts, small mounds of earth and stone used as platforms for practice targets. The targets themselves were limited only by the imagination. Sometimes the archers used scarecrows, sometimes a rough plank with crudely painted symbols. Today, they'd set up a well-dressed French soldier stuffed with straw. His tunic bore the royal arms of France.

A knot of perhaps twenty archers gathered a little distance away. They checked the horn knocks on their bows to be sure they held the string properly, waxed the bowstrings to ensure the arrows flew easily, and wound silk thread through the flights of each arrow to hold the goose feather quills firmly to the arrow shaft. As we approached, Blaybourne separated from the crowd, smiling and bowing. He was attired in a brown linen tunic and hose, topped with a leather jerkin, an outfit that blended in perfectly with the other men on the Rouen garrison.

"I am charmed that such lovely ladies should grace our archery contest—."

"Who wins?" Bess asked, fixing her green eyes on him. "Is it the person who shoots the fastest?"

"Or perhaps the one who is most accurate?" asked Margaret.

"Or perhaps the tallest and most well-favored gentleman?" put in Lisette, smiling up at him.

"And what think you, my lady?" asked Blaybourne, turning towards me.

"Shooting accurately and quietly are important, of course," I replied, "but perhaps we should also look at how well kept each archer's kit is because that gives some indication of his character."

He bowed.

"Or perhaps," I put in laughing, as a sudden thought struck me, "it should be how untidy it is."

He raised an eyebrow.

"Yes," I said. "How untidy it is, on the grounds that an archer who can shoot both fast and accurately and yet has the most untidy tackle must have a very quick and agile mind in order to be able to find what he needs in the midst of such shambles."

He clapped his hands and laughed. "An unusual contest. So let me see, the other ladies will judge speed and accuracy."

I smiled.

"And you, my lady, will judge for yourself how untidy he is."

Everyone murmured assent, and we arranged ourselves on the benches under the oak tree like brightly colored birds. The marshal held up his hand, then let it fall. The archers nocked and drew. They aimed, then let fly with hand following string almost as swiftly as the arrows flew. Bow strings twanged, arrows whistled, as the archers reached for the next arrow in belt or quiver, to nock and draw, aim and let fly, in a lethal, unrelenting hail of arrows.

Two archers lined up at a time to shoot, standing sideways in the direction of the target and drawing to ear or jaw. By this method of doublets—which I had suggested—we eventually narrowed the contestants down to Blaybourne and his rival, also tall and barrel-chested, but dark, scowling, and rough in his manners.

Both stood there: the scowling churl frowning as he nocked and drew with his right hand, while Blaybourne faced him, wearing gloves of soft tanned leather, using his left hand to knock and draw. Both arrows flew, but the one from Blaybourne pierced the heart of the stuffed French soldier, who toppled over into a heap of straw and old clothes. There was a cheer, followed by laughter as Blaybourne came back to receive our congratulations.

Even Isabel was quite warm in her praise.

"I've not seen a left-handed archer before," she remarked. "Can you shoot with your right hand too?"

"I'm sure he can," put in Lisette, her usually pasty complexion tinged with pink. She drained her cup of wine. "He could pierce anybody's heart with either hand," she giggled.

Isabel looked at her, but Lisette drained another cup of wine.

"My lady Cecylee, would you like to inspect the archers?" inquired Blaybourne with a bow.

Smiling, I took his arm. "It has to be suitably untidy," I remarked, tilting my head. "Somewhat untidy will not be good enough."

"And what does my lady consider to be suitably untidy?" he asked, laughing.

I felt a flutter in my chest, so I frowned.

"You take this very seriously."

"Indeed, I do. I do not give my favors away lightly."

Blaybourne raised his eyebrows but did not reply.

Each archer laid out his things on a piece of rough cloth. There was the bow, which was about five and a half feet long. There was the bow case, made of canvas. There was the leather quiver to hold the arrows, the arrows with their goose-feather quills, leather belts to tie the quiver around the waist, arm guards or bracers, and finger tabs to protect the fingers from the bowstring. There was also wax, silken thread, horn nocks, and various tools for repair.

At length, I came upon one that was very untidy. As I straightened up, my eyes met Blaybourne's.

"Yours?" I queried.

He smiled.

"You knew—"

"I did not. I left it here just as you see."

I shook my head.

"It is true," he said, "I am naturally untidy. I am always losing things."

Another archer standing nearby agreed. "Yes, my lady. Untidy, that's what he is."

Soon there was a chorus of nodding men.

"How unfortunate," I murmured, "for that means you win."

"How can that be unfortunate?"

"It will make you unpopular," I remarked, looking at the other archers who were staring at me expectantly.

I raised my voice. "I am awarding two prizes. The first is the duke's prize for the fastest and most accurate archer, who has the tidiest kit."

I beckoned to the scowling man who came forward, his face now wreathed in smiles, as I gave him a badge made in the likeness of Richard's white lion. He pinned it onto his tunic with a flourish.

"Next, I present the duchess's prize for the fastest and most accurate archer who has the untidiest kit."

I pinned another emblem onto Blaybourne's tunic. It showed a rose tree with a castle in the background. "It signifies the Rose of Raby, which is what folk called me when I was a girl," I murmured.

"I will treasure this with my life." He took my hand and kissed each finger separately.

My cheeks burned, for it reminded me of a gesture Richard had made when he'd come courting. Why was I being so foolish? My embarrassment was sure to set tongues wagging.

Blaybourne nodded to the marshal, who came beside him and whispered something. The marshal signaled to the men from the garrison, and they departed in the direction of the castle. Then Blaybourne turned to the others watching. "Which of you ladies would like to try your hand at archery?"

Isabel went first, but she needed no instruction.

"How deft she is," remarked Margaret. "I'd no idea she was so talented."

Then he bowed and asked Margaret to try.

"I don't know if I should at my age."

"My lady, you are not old," he said, "and it will do you good."

He handed her his gloves and tied a leather arm guard on each arm.

Margaret drew. The arrow hit the ground in front of her with a thud.

"Try to look up, my lady. And pull to your ear."

This time the arrow whistled off and landed several yards away.

The ladies clapped, but Margaret, breathing heavily, handed the bow and gloves back to the archer.

"I do not wish to tempt fate," she said smiling. "Let the others try."

Lisette went next. Turning her head sideways, she gazed up at him through her lashes while he gave instructions.

"Lisette," murmured Margaret.

The arrow flew but landed only a yard or so away.

"Oh dear," remarked Lisette. "I don't feel very stable. Perhaps if you were to steady my arm?"

She gazed at him and crumpled to the ground.

I took a linen napkin from a servant to wipe her face, which was now beaded in sweat.

Margaret knelt beside her and gently unlaced her red gown.

Bess laid a hand on her cheek. "She seems feverish. We should take her inside."

Lisette opened her eyes. "I don't wish to go."

"You're not well," said Margaret.

"I shall take her back to the castle," said Isabel.

She signaled to the servants, who helped Lisette to her feet and divested her of the gloves, arm-guards, and bow he had given her. They placed her in a litter and took her back to the castle.

Margaret and Isabel followed.

I remained with Bess and Blaybourne, looking at the retreating figures, when Bess said, "I have always wanted to try my hand at archery. May I?"

"Of course, my lady," he said. He tied the leather arm-guards on, handed her his gloves, and gave her his bow.

I felt suddenly weary, so I sat down under the oak tree and closed my eyes.

I must have gone out for a moment, for I came to with a start when he called out, "Perfect, my lady. You will be a fine archeress one day."

"With such an excellent teacher, how could I help that?" Bess replied, laughing.

He was silent.

I rose and signaled to the servants to offer them some refreshments.

"I wondered where you were, my lady; I thought perhaps you'd gone," he said.

"I was seeing about the refreshments. Would you like something? Bess? It is a hot afternoon, and shooting arrows must be tiring work."

"No, thank you," said Bess as she gave the gloves, arm-guards, and bow back to him. "I will go and see if Margaret needs my help."

She disappeared in the direction of the castle.

"Do we need the servants here, my lady?"

I looked at him for a long moment. I knew I shouldn't be alone with him, but—

"Perhaps not," I murmured and beckoned to the steward.

Soon the servants were disappearing down the path to the castle. A breeze stirred, and a bird trilled an arpeggio. We were completely alone.

He touched my arm. "And now it is your turn, Cecylee."

My head jerked up.

Our gaze held. Then he handed me the bow and the finger-tabs and tied the arm-guards on.

I lifted the bow, drew the string back, and aimed. But my first shot fell in front of my feet.

He came closer and, standing just behind me, put his hands on mine. His hands burned into my skin yet gave me strength.

"It's like this," he murmured softly. "You look up, not down, you draw back as far as you can, and then—"

"You take the consequences?"

"Exactly," he said as I fired off a shot that landed several yards away, right in the middle of the painted board that had been chosen as the target.

"That was excellent, Cecylee."

He was so close that I could inhale the spicy scent and feel his body just touching my back. Now, I felt his breath on my cheek. One step more, and he cradled me in his arms. Ignoring my pounding heart, I fired off another shot.

It landed in the ground several yards away.

"Should we continue?" he murmured, brushing my cheek with a butterfly kiss.

I gave him the bow.

"I must stop now."

He kissed my cheek again and squeezed me gently.

"You're not angry with me?"

"No. But this is unwise."

"Indeed, it is. But I've longed for this moment ever since I first saw you."

His eyes were like a clear pool that refreshed my soul. "I feel so drawn to you," he said. "I tried to keep away, but I could not."

"You make me feel as if I've come home," I replied.

Our lips met in a kiss.

I melted. Then I pulled back.

"I must go." I took off the finger tabs and arm-guards, handed them to him, and turned.

He put a hand on my arm.

I gazed into his eyes, my cheeks warming.

"I must go."

I turned on my heel and forced myself to walk away, feeling his gaze scorching into my back with every step that I took.

CHAPTER 8

Feast of Saint Clare
August 12, 1441

Lisette's illness continued, and after ten days, we needed more medicine.

I could have sent a servant to the Abbey of Saint-Ouen, but I was longing for fresh air. I should have gone with an escort, for Richard had enjoined me never to ride abroad without protection. But I was tired of being surrounded by various people. Bess agreed to accompany me, and so, leaving Lisette in the care of Margaret and Isabel, we set off early one morning just after dawn while it was cool.

As we came into the courtyard where our horses waited, a tall figure detached itself from the shadows and came forward. Bess gasped and clutched at my arm, but as soon as the light fell on the figure, she relaxed into a smile.

"Ladies," Blaybourne called, bowing low. "What brings you out so early?"

"Lisette is not well," replied Bess going up to him. "She continues feverish, and we are riding off to the Abbey of Saint-Ouen to get fresh medicines."

"Allow me to escort you," said Blaybourne. He looked at me.

I opened my mouth to decline, but Bess assented.

Blaybourne helped us onto our horses, vaulted onto his white gelding, and we set off.

It was a glorious morning. The air was fresh and cool; the meadows a riot of flowers, with blue cornflowers, pink heather, and yellow meadow-rue. The trees were thickly leaved, and their leaves rustled as we rode past. I held back so that I rode behind Blaybourne and Bess. They spent the entire journey riding side by side, chattering amiably.

I remained silent. I spent ten days devoting myself to Lisette, amusing the children, and playing the gracious hostess to the merchants and aristocrats passing through Rouen, wanting to visit with the governor of Normandy's wife. I expended an enormous effort on keeping my mind off the one thing that kept powerfully drawing me towards it, like a lodestone: my feelings for Blaybourne.

Blaybourne meant many things to me. For one, he was a pleasure to look at. Now he sat gracefully on his gelding, using subtle motions of his long fingers to guide it. Everything he did had a kind of ease and charm, so different from Richard. Richard rarely vaulted onto his horse, for he was becoming stout and often needed his groom to help him up.

Then he was so well-tuned to me; he seemed able to read my thoughts before I was aware of having them. I remembered his kindness and sensitivity at the archery tournament when my fiery blushes had given me away. Every time we talked, our interactions were like a duet, alternating effortlessly with perfect timing, without one having to wait for the other to catch up. With Richard, I always had to remember to be patient, for he ran at a slower speed.

Most alarming of all, I felt the stirrings of something I didn't even know I could feel. It made my affection for Richard seem pallid by comparison. I didn't understand it. How could I feel so passionate about someone I scarcely knew?

And there he was, riding a few feet in front of me, being courteously gallant to Bess. Yet Bess did not seem to be making much progress. She was trying hard enough, telling amusing stories and little morsels of gossip, but Blaybourne seemed distracted, sometimes asking her to repeat things, sometimes not getting her jests.

I sighed. How was I going to make him go away? And what had he been doing in the courtyard at that hour? Had he been waiting for someone? Had he been waiting for me? At that thought, my heart leaped in my throat and started thudding. What was wrong? I never felt this disquieted. I was noted for being serene, yet every time I thought about Blaybourne, my heart interrupted.

I was in such a brown study I didn't notice how far we'd come until Bess pulled on my bridle.

"Cecylee!" she exclaimed. "We're here. Do you not see that?"

I pulled myself out of my thoughts with an effort and attempted to smile, although I felt more like weeping.

Blaybourne walked up to me, frowning. "You look pale, my lady. Perhaps you should sit under this horse chestnut. It provides a goodly shade, and I will get you some refreshment."

This was the last thing I wanted, but conflicting thoughts and feelings left me dumbstruck. I looked at Bess in silent appeal, sure that she wouldn't want to leave me alone with the attractive young man she'd been cultivating for the last half-hour.

But Bess jumped down and said, "I'll get the medicines then." And blowing me a kiss, she disappeared.

I set my mouth grimly as Blaybourne helped me down, willing myself not to notice how it felt to be in his arms. I wandered over to the bench and sat down, examining the patch of dusty ground beneath my feet, each blade of grass, the marks on my boots, the white dust dredging the hem of my gown. At length, Blaybourne returned bearing a tray of cider with pastries warm from the oven. The aroma of those pastries was so seductive I could not help looking up.

It was a mistake.

Blaybourne's eyes were warm, soft, and deep. His mouth curved into a tender smile.

My heart resumed its hammering.

"I don't know what's wrong with me. I don't feel well. I should've let Bess come by herself."

"But then I would have missed seeing you," he remarked as he set the tray down and handed me a cup of cider. "Or is that what you are trying to say?"

"Just what were you doing in the castle courtyard at that hour?"

"Waiting for you. What else could I possibly have been doing?"

"You could have been doing any of a number of things." I lowered my lashes and sipped my cider. Finally, I looked into his face.

His eyes were warm, and his mouth curved into its gentle smile. I smiled back.

He leaned over and kissed me on the lips, a long, luxurious, and increasingly passionate kiss. "My sweet," he murmured. "You know very well I can't keep away from you. I've been waiting for more than a week for you to appear."

"What about Bess?"

He caressed my cheek with a long finger. The sensation made me tingle all over. "No, the question is, do I mean anything to you?"

"You mean the whole world to me. I've been miserable without you."

He held me close, brushing my hair and cheeks with his lips. "Would you meet me in the garden this evening, around compline? It'll be quieter then, and we can spend some precious moments together."

"I'll be there," I promised as he kissed every finger of my hand, front and back.

"I'm the happiest man in the world," he murmured, and then Bess appeared.

Blaybourne rose to help her with her packages. As before, I hung back, so Blaybourne and Bess again rode side-by-side, chatting. I had a strange feeling in the pit of my stomach as if a large piece of lead had lodged itself there. I could hardly believe I was taking such a risk. And what of Blaybourne and the risk he was taking? He was a good archer, but could he fight with a sword? Richard was an excellent swordsman—

My mind veered off into these depths as I attempted to keep my horse from wandering off the track.

Eventually, we reached the castle, and Blaybourne helped Bess down and summoned a servant to look after her packages.

Then he came for me.

He slowly led my horse into a secluded nook between the stables and the gardens, and gently he carried me in his arms as he lifted me down off my horse. We lingered.

Reluctantly, I pulled away. "I must go." I gave him one final kiss.

"I'll be in the garden, my love, at compline."

"By the fountain?"

"By the fountain." And clasping his hand one last time, I flew across the courtyard and up the stairs, tearing myself away from him.

As I entered my chamber, Jenet rose and curtseyed. She was now around thirty but looked as slender as she had at fourteen. Her black eyes grazed me, intense and direct.

"My lady, whatever has happened?"

I blushed.

"An attractive young man?"

"Really, Jenet! What has happened to you? You used to be as quiet as a mouse."

Jenet busied herself in unpinning my veil and removing my headdress.

"I beg your pardon, my lady. I didn't mean to be rude. It's just that I've never seen you look so radiant."

"You never used to be so lively and so free with your opinions when Audrey was around."

"If you remember, my lady, Audrey, loved to talk. It was difficult to get a word in edgewise." She brushed my hair. "I miss my aunt and your lady mother. It is hard to believe they are no longer here."

After Mama died nine months ago at her manor of Howden-le-Wear, near Castle Raby, Audrey was soon dead herself.

"Audrey was devoted to Mama," I said slowly, stumbling through thoughts as Jenet's fingers worked at my hair. "She was her best friend and confidante. She nursed her through all her pregnancies and comforted her when Alainor was snatched away as a child-bride. I remember Mama saying once that she didn't know what she would've done without Audrey."

"And your lady mother was so kind to my aunt," said Jenet. "She allowed her to stay on, even though she had a child out of wedlock. She saw to it that he was trained as a cook so that he could work in the castle kitchens."

An image of Perrequin's elaborate sugar sculptures filled my head. He'd made two of them the day of my betrothal.

There was a pause while Jenet braided my hair into plaits and fashioned them into an elaborate hairdo.

"What did the young gentleman say?"

"It has nothing to do with you."

"Indeed, it does, my lady." She paused to look into my face.

I lowered my lashes and set my mouth into a line.

Jenet sighed. "He didn't make any suggestions—"

My lashes flew up as my cheeks warmed.

Jenet's mouth opened.

I turned away and studied my jewels.

"My lady, I know I am bold for saying this, but you plunge headlong into things—"

"Have you ever been in love?"

"My lady—"

"I am powerless—"

"But you're not, my lady. Don't go to him. He doesn't have anything to lose. You do."

I glared.

"I heard a story this very morning," said Jenet. "I was breaking my fast in the kitchens when a traveler told me a story about an Italian count who murdered his lady wife after he found her in bed with a lover. Chopped off her head, he did—"

80

"My lord would never do something like that!"

"Of course not, my lady," said Jenet, gently turning my head so that she could continue making the hairdo. "I never meant to suggest so. But—"

"We will talk no more of this," I said.

And I kept silent while Jenet finished dressing my hair, washed my face and hands in rosewater, and arrayed me in a richly embroidered green silk dress.

During the rest of that long, hot day, I kept to my seat in the solar next to Isabel as I sewed the children's clothes. My needle flew with eerie energy as I embroidered flowers, made buttonholes, and ran up hems and seams.

The time for compline came and went.

I heard laughter coming from the garden below, and, looking down, saw Lisette with Blaybourne. I blinked. I hadn't known Lisette was well enough to get up. When Margaret flew to her side, trying to convince her to return to her room, I understood.

Lisette put her hand on Blaybourne's sleeve. "It's such a lovely evening. Will you not walk?"

I did not hear his reply, but Lisette threw her head back, laughter bubbling up from her throat. Blowing him a kiss, she was escorted back into the castle by Margaret.

Without thinking, I got up and craned my head through the window.

Blaybourne raised his hand and beckoned.

I clutched at the heavy draperies.

"Is something wrong, Cecylee?" said Isabel. "You mustn't let silly little Lisette get on your nerves. She's not worth your time."

I resumed my seat. "You are quite right," I murmured when the door flew open, and Lisette came in, supported by Margaret.

"He's taking me to the abbey tomorrow. He said it would do me good to ride out and get fresh air."

Isabel turned to stare at her. "Your husband is fighting in Pontoise. Who could you possibly be talking of?"

Lisette flung herself down.

"I feel much better. I agree with our charming friend. Fresh air will make me feel well again, especially as he'll have to help me on and off my horse. How it will feel to be in his arms—" She closed her eyes and smiled dreamily.

I dropped any pretense of sewing and looked at Margaret. "Is she well?"

"Obviously not," snapped Isabel. She rose. "I will not have it said that we ladies are so uncontrollable we fly towards the first pot of honey we see while our husbands risk their lives in battle."

Lisette rose, hectic spots of red flaring on her cheeks. "I'm going out with him tomorrow."

Isabel turned to Margaret. "I strongly suggest we give her a draught of poppy juice to calm her down."

"I'm not a child!" Lisette stamped her foot, then swooned.

Isabel nodded to Margaret, and between them, they bundled up the limp figure and carried her off to bed.

I sat there, stunned. Were they going to drug Lisette? What had Blaybourne said to her? I closed my eyes and imagined Lisette in Blaybourne's arms. I could feel his breath, hear her giggles, imagine what might happen.

But why should I care? What was he against Richard and four years of marriage? I knew scarcely anything about him—not of his family, where he came from, what his station in life was, or what he was doing in Rouen.

What was he doing in Rouen?

There was a soft footfall, and someone entered the room. My eyes flew open. And there he was.

I rose slowly; the room swirled.

With catlike grace, Blaybourne caught me in his arms.

82

"You shouldn't be here."

"Come, my love."

"I shouldn't."

"I adore you," he said, kissing my cheek.

At that moment, the door to Lisette's chamber opened a crack. But no one came out.

He grabbed my hand, and we ran down the stairs into the courtyard, through the garden, until we came to the private screened-in area.

I turned away to compose myself, for I was short of breath, and the pins in my hair were coming loose.

"My love, do you remember you promised to meet me at compline?"

I put the last tendrils of hair back into place. "I am the governor of Normandy's wife."

"Has someone upset you?"

"Another story of a jealous husband. This time he beheaded his lady wife."

"Who told you that?"

"Does it matter?"

He was silent.

"What about you? Can you fight with a sword? My husband is extremely skilled with his."

"I have ways of protecting myself."

"Do you?"

He flushed. "I am sorry to have troubled you, madam."

He turned and walked slowly away.

I stood there, watching him go, wrapping my arms around me. My fingers were cold. My hands were cold. My arms were cold. I moved towards him. "Don't go!"

Blaybourne turned and raised an eyebrow.

I went to him.

He folded his arms around me. "You are sure?"

I nestled against him and nodded.

He covered my mouth with kisses and stroked me with long, nimble fingers, sweeping me away in a wave that was so fierce, I could no longer fight.

I unwound myself, kissed him on the forehead, and sighed.

Alert in an instant, Blaybourne dressed with deft motions, then helped me into my chemise.

I leaned against him, my hair hanging loose to my waist. "I've broken my marriage vows."

Our eyes locked. "Did you choose your husband?"

"You know there is no choice."

"And if there were?" he asked, stroking my hair. "Would you have me?"

I wrapped my fingers around his. "If I were free. But I'm trapped inside my marriage."

"I could protect you."

"But you're just an archer."

"Do you think so?"

I sneezed.

He put my gown on over my chemise and tied the laces. He was in the middle of helping me with my hair when we heard footsteps. We gave each other a quick glance, then Blaybourne melted into the shadows.

I rose to my feet, fumbling for my shoes.

"Cecylee!"

The cold voice cut through the warm air like a knife.

I drew myself up but couldn't think of anything to say. Isabel's cold blue eyes raked me from head to toe and from toe to head.

My cheeks burned.

"Have you thought of what it would do to Richard if he found out?" she asked, biting off each word in cold fury. I stared at the ground, a whiplash of fear prickling up my spine. "I'm surprised at you, Cecylee. I thought you had more sense."

I twisted my hands.

"I have been so stupid. Here I have been protecting your brother George's honor, trying to get his flighty Lisette to behave when I should have been protecting Richard's honor."

I hung my head.

"Do you not care about Richard?"

"Richard is not Black Fulk—"

"You don't need to tell me that!" snapped Isabel. "He isn't going to burn his wife in her wedding finery, however badly she behaves."

"But—"

Isabel jerked my chin up. "Look at me. Remember your heroine Queen Alainor? Do you know what her husband did to her when she betrayed him? He locked her up for sixteen years."

"Queen Alainor outlived her husband."

"Is that all you can think of, outliving Richard?"

I squirmed. "Queen Alainor lived for another fifteen years and helped her sons rule England."

"You snake in the grass," hissed Isabel, sounding like a snake herself. "You care nothing for the House of York."

"Enough," said Blaybourne, quietly but firmly, materializing out of the shadows.

"How dare you," said Isabel. She turned towards me. "How could you lower yourself with an archer on the Rouen garrison?"

"You don't know anything about me."

As Isabel stared at him, my mind sluggishly went to work, like a millwheel churning up muddy water.

"You have grievously injured my brother."

He was silent.

Isabel leaned forward. "Do you deny it?"

"Did Cecylee choose her husband?"

"What does that have to do with anything?"

"Did you choose your husband?"

Isabel stared at him.

"I understand you had two husbands. Your first marriage to Sir Thomas Grey was annulled, was it not?"

Isabel tightened her jaw.

I scrutinized his face. How did he know that? That happened over fifteen years ago.

"I believe on the grounds of cruelty?"

She was silent.

"Your husband beat you, didn't he?"

I recoiled. An image sprang to mind of Isabel as a young woman visiting Castle Raby on the occasion of my betrothal to Richard. She was pale and thin and complained of pains in the stomach. When I asked Mama about it, she told me it was women's troubles. Now, I wondered. It explained a lot: the watchfulness, the sourness, the pleasure she took in unpleasant tales.

"How dare you cross-question me like this," said Isabel, her voice rasping. "I am a great lady. I am above such things. Yet here you are, digging for dirt—" She went into a spasm of coughing.

He ignored her. "That marriage was not of your choosing, was it? You were only four years old when you were married to him."

I winced. That was bad as anything that had happened to Alainor.

"I do not choose to discuss this with a stranger!"

"As you wish. But remember that you had a terrifying experience with a husband foisted on you when you were a small child. Why can't you be more compassionate to Cecylee?"

"Because my brother is no monster!"

"Isabel," I put in. "I do not expect you to understand—"

"Understand? I do not understand why Richard loves you."

"That marriage was not of my choice."

"Choice! What makes you think you would choose well for a husband?"

"I have a right to choose."

"You should be thinking of the family honor."

"My happiness is at stake."

"Is he well-chosen?"

I folded my hand into Blaybourne's.

"Your behavior has been disgraceful."

"I want to be happy in my life."

"You have grievously injured the House of York, and if I had any say over the matter, you would be severely punished!"

Isabel glared at me. Then she swept off in the direction of the castle.

CHAPTER 9

I did not leave the castle until one evening a week later. The day had been especially warm, Lisette had just recovered, and to celebrate, we went out to the bathing pool to cool ourselves with a bathe in the evening air. We lingered, gossiping and playing with the children, but at length, everyone went in, leaving me gazing at the brightening stars. The night was peaceful, and I ached for some of its quietude before I had to go back into that hot, noisy, and smelly castle.

I lay back in the pool, half closing my eyes to let the sounds of the evening wash over me. I was unaware of anything other than the turmoil of my thoughts, unleashed against the quiet backdrop of the night.

"My sweetest flower, how sad you look."

I started. "What are you doing here?"

"I must talk to you," he said in a low tone.

I stared. Where had he come from?

"You could be carrying my child."

"No."

"I will wait while you dress yourself." He disappeared into the shadows.

I clambered out of the pool, grabbed my chemise, and threw it over my head, followed by my silk gown, which had become water-stained and ruined by my splashes. Sighing, I sat on the bench, finger-combing my hair and making a half-hearted attempt to braid it, when he returned.

"Who are you?"

"Truly, I don't want to talk about myself." He pulled me gently to him and kissed me slowly and luxuriously on the lips.

"You are not answering the question."

"Could it not wait?"

"I have been thinking since last we met. I realize I have agreed to marry someone whom I know not. Isabel is right to chastise me. How can I make such a choice about one whom I know nothing?"

There was a pause.

"Let us start with your name. Is it really Blaybourne?"

He turned away from me and gazed into the bathing pool for a long moment. A breeze stirred faint ripples. I put my hand on his shoulder.

"You may not like what I have to say, for my family is humble. My father was a blacksmith in the village of Blay, near Bayeux in Normandy."

The color drained from my cheeks. I was silent for several long moments. "But you do not have the manners of a blacksmith," I stuttered.

"I was sent to the Abbaye-aux-Hommes in Caen as soon as I turned seven, for my parents were dead, my elder brother had a family to support, and there was no money for my keep."

I stood silent for a long time, trying to imagine this. "Is it usual for poor children to be sent away to the monastery?"

"If they are lucky. Otherwise, they have to beg at the side of the road."

I shuddered. I had seen such children, of course, many times but had never given thought as to what their lives were like.

"I did well at the abbey, so when I turned twelve, they sent me to study languages at the Abbaye de Saint-Maurice on Lake Geneva. I studied Italian and German as well as French, Latin, and Greek."

There he stood, now gazing into the pool. The son of a blacksmith. I had allowed myself to be touched by a peasant. My cheeks burned with shame. But his manners were excellent, highly polished, and courtly. His voice was musical and cultivated. He dressed well. He was clean.

"I know you feel betrayed," he said, flushing and twisting the ring on his finger. It was a sapphire set in silver. His fingers were long, thin, and aristocratic-looking. They did not bear the marks of hard labor.

"You have not led the life of a peasant."

"No. But I started out that way."

"But you have made something of yourself. You were not born with riches as I was. You had to work to make your way in the world."

He gazed at me. "That is a rather unusual thing for a great lady to say."

I put my hands into his. "I've never felt this way about anyone before."

His lips met mine, and we lingered together for a long moment. "Beloved," he whispered, "I hardly dared hope—"

I stopped his mouth with my fingers. "I want to know more."

"I spent a couple of years at the Abbaye de Saint-Maurice. Then I was sent to university, in Italy."

"Where?"

He smiled and shook his head slightly.

"Are you a bachelor?"

"I'm a doctor."

I stared. I'd never met anyone so well educated. The aristocratic men I knew lived and died in the saddle. A vision of myself with this gentleman filled my head. We would study together and have soaring conversations.

"How did you become an archer?"

"I learned various trades."

"Is your name Blaybourne?"

"My name is Pierre de Blay, from the village in Normandy where I was born."

"Where does 'bourne' come from?"

He was silent.

I frowned. "Bourne" was an old English name for stream, like the north-country "burn." Many villages had "bourne" in their name, like Pangbourne, Fishbourne, Nutbourne. "Are you going to tell me anything else?"

"Not now."

"But—"

"All in good time, my sweet. You need to think about what I've said, and if you remember, I wanted to speak with you."

I nestled against him like a bird that had found her home. Suddenly I didn't care where he'd come from, only what he meant to me now.

He held me close. "Would he lock you up?"

"Is that why you wanted to see me?"

He nodded. "Would he harm you?"

I froze. Richard loved me, and yet—

"I would have to hide you somewhere."

"But I am the Duchess of York."

"Today is the twentieth day of August. I will return on the morning of the twenty-third to await your answer. I will meet you in the great hall of the castle where you hold your public audiences."

"But that's too dangerous."

"It will not be dangerous, I assure you."

"But how?"

"You will see, my sweet. Be sure to wear your pearl dress that day." He kissed my hand, bowed, and vanished.

Next day, I took to my bed. "Whatever shall I do when Richard returns?" I asked Margaret when she came to visit me with Bess.

"Perhaps he'll not know."

Bess kissed my cheek.

"Are you not angry?" I asked.

"Why?"

"You liked him well."

"Indeed, I did," replied Bess.

"Why did you leave me alone with him at the abbey?"

She patted my hand and smiled. "I have never seen two people so in love as the two of you. I knew you could not have long with your husband returning. I thought such lovers deserved to have some precious moments together."

Annette entering my chamber woke me. She carried Joan, who sobbed hard.

I cuddled her on my lap. "Whatever is the matter?"

"Madam, I know not," replied Annette. "Lady Joan seemed in good spirits this forenoon. I put her down for a nap, as I usually do. But she awoke screaming. I can do nothing with her."

I turned to the limp figure in my lap, gently cupping my hands around her little face. "What is it, sweetheart?"

"Mama, Mama," sobbed Joan, her tears making a wet patch on my silken chemise.

I stroked her hair and rubbed her back. "Come now, my dearest child. Tell me what troubles you so. Mama is here. You are safe. Whatever is wrong?"

Joan lifted a tear-stained face. "Don't leave!" She buried her face in my gown and sobbed.

I stiffened. "What is this?"

"I know not, madam," said Annette, growing pale.

"Has she talked of this before?"

"No, madam, I don't think so."

"Who has been talking?"

"I would not like to say—"

"Come now," said Margaret, getting up from her place on the window seat. "Remember, your loyalty is to Duchess Cecylee. If someone has upset Lady Joan, she needs to know who."

Annette blanched. "Lady Lisette," she whispered. "She said she would curse me if I told anyone. She told me she would put a spell on me so that I would wither away before my time."

"That's nonsense," exclaimed Margaret. "Lisette should not be saying such wicked things. I'll find her at once and bring her here."

Margaret returned not only with Lisette but with all the women. Jenet was there, and Margaret's woman, Bess's woman, Lisette's woman, and even Isabel's woman. Keeping Joan on my lap, I faced them all. "For the sake of the children and for peace in my family, I ask you not to gossip."

Lisette smiled.

I handed Joan, now quiet, to Annette and rose. "Was it you?"

Lisette remained silent.

"I find my daughter sobbing her heart out. My maid frightened out of her life—"

"That's nothing to what you did. You broke your marriage vows. You sinned against your husband."

I slapped her across the cheek. "You will say no more. Do you understand?"

Lisette faced me, holding her hand to her cheek. Her eyes flashed. "Why should I help you? You always get what you want."

Margaret interrupted. "If you don't promise," she replied, her gentle grey eyes turned to steel, "I could go to George and hint that his wife's behavior was not what he would have wished."

Lisette jutted out her chin.

"You threw yourself at him every opportunity you got," said Bess.

"He didn't want you," said Lisette, rounding on her.

The room fell silent.

Lisette looked from one to the other, her face flushed, her under lip jutting out. At last, she turned to me and made the sign of the Horned King.

"I curse you, Cecylee! May you have a long and unhappy life!"

I fell into a chair. "You couldn't mean that."

But Lisette had gone.

CHAPTER 10

It was a bright hot morning. I sat on the dais in the great hall of the castle of Rouen, struggling to listen carefully to a stream of petitioners. The steward from Fotheringhay Castle in Northamptonshire wanted to pursue a land dispute. There were several merchants from Rouen wanting to show off their wares. There were people from Normandy seeking redress from the governor's wife over land, marriage settlements have gone awry, and taxes.

I shifted in my seat. I should have sent a message to Blaybourne, telling him not to come. But somehow, I had forgotten to do so. I drew a handkerchief from my sleeve and dried my moist palms.

A fanfare of trumpets sounded, and a page appeared, a boy of around nine or so, attired in a white satin tunic and hose. He wore white shoes and had a white hat on his head. He approached the dais bearing a ring on a white velvet cushion.

"My master wishes, madam, to present you with this ring."

As he knelt, I moved forward to accept the present. The ring was magnificent. It was a deep blue sapphire, cut into a strange shape, set into silver. It radiated a deep color in the warm sunshine, matching my pearl dress perfectly.

"Shall I ask my lord to approach?"

"Indeed. I should like to thank him for his gift."

I had entertained many diplomats and visitors from other countries arriving with costly gifts. Vague questions entered my head about this particular diplomat, but they left just as quickly. Another fanfare sounded, and this time a procession appeared. They looked like soldiers, men-at-arms, menservants, and pages—the sort of people an aristocrat would have traveled with him.

The unknown personage was the last to appear. Like his entourage, he was attired in white. But his tunic came down to his ankles, the long sleeves adorned with fashionable jagged edges. He wore a stylish hat with a piece of material hanging down from it, protecting him from the dust of his journey. Altogether, he looked exotic and foreign, perhaps Italian. Perhaps from a place further to the east. I could not place him as he came closer. He exuded a scent of nutmeg and almonds, with a hint of exotic spices.

As I inhaled deeply, I remembered where I had encountered it before.

But now, the herald was announcing the aristocrat's name:

Philippe de Savoy, Count of Geneva.

He bowed and smiled as he held out his hand to take mine.

Then our eyes met.

Of course. His ruse was perfect, for no one would dare challenge a lord of such obvious means.

I swallowed.

The sounds in that bustling hall faded away as he straightened, and we faced each other.

"Madam, I have a long journey to make, and I wondered if you would be good enough to give me some advice. I understand that stormy weather may blow in from Pontoise, and I wanted to know whether Rouen would provide a goodly place of shelter."

"No," I replied.

His eyebrows shot up. Silently he proffered his arm so that I had to leave the dais and walk into the hall with him.

His timing was perfect, for the servants were setting up the tables for the midday meal, and we stole some private moments together amidst the hubbub. He led me to an unoccupied window seat: "My sweet, are you sure?"

I was silent.

He took my hand. "My flower, I know how hard this is for you. But I have everything ready. My groom is outside waiting with an Arabian mare. I have spare clothes. You need only throw this cloak over your gown, and we can leave."

I jerked away.

"I should have told you before," he murmured.

I clasped my shaking hands together.

"I have more people stationed outside Rouen waiting for us to arrive. You would be safe from your husband. There are many places where I could hide you."

"No," I interposed, looking down.

He waited, taking my hand in his.

After a long moment, I lifted my head. "I cannot go with you."

Abruptly, he let go of me. "Is it because I'm the son of a blacksmith?"

I put a hand on his sleeve. "You could not take me and three children."

"You promised to marry me."

"I cannot leave my children."

"We would have our own children."

I shook my head as I took his hand and kissed it. "If I had no children, I would go with you in a heartbeat."

A sound drowned out our conversation. A rumble of hooves. A fanfare sounded, and a shout went up. The men of the garrison, dicing and lounging in the shade of the trees outside, now scrambled to their feet, straightened their tunics, grabbed their weapons, and lined up in formation along the castle walls.

"They're back!" someone shouted. A roar answered.

His face turned as white as his tunic. "You will not come with me?"

"I cannot."

"You have my ring?" He dug into his tunic and produced another sapphire ring, quickly showing me how his ring fit around mine.

"If you change your mind, send your most trusty messenger to me with this ring. If it fits mine, I will know it comes from you."

"Where should I send the ring?"

"The Medici bank of Florence. They will get a message to me. There is a branch in every big city, including Paris and London."

He bowed low, took my hand, and kissed it. "Always at your service and ever devotedly yours." Then he abruptly pulled away, ran outside, vaulted onto his gelding, and rode off before I had time to breathe.

I ran to the window. In the distance, I could make out Richard's pennant bearing his white lion.

Blaybourne rode straight for Richard; my heart slammed against my ribs. He drew his white horse level with Richard's black one, bowed low, and commenced a conversation. Moments later, Richard raised his gauntlet in salutation as the Count of Geneva and his entourage set off south towards Paris.

I watched and watched until I could see him no more, my mind reeling.

But scarcely had I time to think. I sent orders to the cooks to prepare a more elaborate feast and for the steward to bring up pipes of the best wine from the cellars. Everyone flooded back to the castle to greet the governor of Normandy and to hear news of the Pontoise campaign.

I slipped upstairs to the solar where Jenet bathed my tear-stained face with rosewater, re-did my hair, and rearranged my headdress. On impulse, I went to the prie-dieu in the corner of my chamber, closed my eyes, and knelt to pray.

Half an hour later, I made my way down to the great hall into a noisy din of hundreds of guests drinking the health of the governor of Normandy. As I arrived, there was a sudden hush. The men rose and bowed.

My eyes met Richard's. He looked thinner than before, the hard exercise of the previous five weeks showing off a new muscular leanness. I'd never found him so attractive and was overcome with sorrow at what I'd done.

Richard came forward and, taking my hand, courteously led me to the seat beside him.

"Cis," he murmured as he eyed my pearl-encrusted, blue-grey gown with its yards of billowing silk. "You look ravishing." He kissed me lightly on the cheek and whispered into my ear, "I can hardly wait until tonight."

And then he turned and resumed his conversation with a gentleman sitting near him.

My hands shook as I sipped my wine.

At length, Richard turned towards me.

"Tell me about the campaign," I said. And so Richard spent the rest of the meal discussing tactics while I asked many questions.

A fanfare of trumpets sounded, heralding a toast. Richard rose, and I rose, forcing a smile onto my face. The whole hall shook as everyone lifted their cups and toasted the newly arrived Duke and his Duchess.

Afterward, Richard and I, followed by the ladies and their husbands, the army, and the townspeople, rode down into the town of Rouen to celebrate a solemn Mass of thanksgiving in the cathedral. Then we went back to the castle, where the feasting and the merrymaking went on for hours.

I collapsed into an exhausted sleep late that night. Afterward, I was ill for a week. Every morning brought with it the painful knowledge that I would never see Blaybourne again and that I'd hurt a good man who loved and trusted me.

I sat on a seat beside the bathing pool, near to where we'd had our tryst, unable to prevent the tears from trickling down my cheeks. I could see him, hear his voice, smell his scent.

Richard frowned and shot several glances at me as he paced up and down. "You have loyal friends here at Rouen. I have asked everyone what is wrong with you, and I get the same response: They avert their eyes, say you will get better in God's good time, and then change the subject."

I wiped away my tears with the tips of my fingers.

"As your husband, I have a right to know what is going on."

I studied my slippers. "I can't explain."

Richard gently tilted my face so that my eyes met his. His eyes gazed back darkly. "What can't you explain?"

My head drooped as I drew a line in the dust with the toe of my slipper.

"You had an affair with another man."

My head jerked up. As my eyes met Richard's, he flushed.

"It's true! Christ on the Cross!"

He drew his sword, went to a nearby tree, and whacked it.

I recoiled.

The spear-pointed diamond that hung from his gold collar jumped and glared at me in the harsh sunlight.

Richard turned round, his face taut, his mouth snarling. "How could you?"

I squeezed my folded arms against my chest.

He thrust his sword back into the scabbard, grabbed me, and jerked my head back. "Don't I mean anything to you? What about our marriage vows? What about our children?"

I stared back, trying not to see his pain when suddenly he let go.

I clutched at the wooden bench to prevent myself from falling, then got to my feet.

"If you knew how many times I tried. How many times I walked away. How many times I tried to forget about him."

"So, you blame him? By God Almighty and all his saints, if I ever catch him, I'll flay him alive."

"You won't."

"Won't what?"

"Catch him," I murmured, looking down.

I looked up to find Richard glaring at me. A vein in his forehead was throbbing. "And how do you know that?" he said in an icy tone I'd never heard before.

I folded my arms. "I don't even know his name."

"You don't know his name? How could you lie with someone you don't know? Are you so fickle, so shallow, that you pick up anyone who happens along?"

I lifted my chin. "If I 'd been free if I'd not been married and had you and three children to think of—"

"You were thinking of running off with him." He folded his arms and gazed at me keenly.

I turned away.

He drew his sword and walked up and down for several minutes, whacking trees, hedges, anything that he came into contact with. Leaves, twigs, and branches strewed the path. Then he sheathed his sword. "I would banish you now. I would lock you up. But I need your family."

I shivered. I had never heard such cold calculations from Richard before.

"You are a Neville," he spat. "There are political considerations. Salisbury is a loyal supporter. I am constantly in the position of struggling to make my voice heard on the king's council. I would be nowhere were it not for your brother's support. A scandal would make me the laughing-stock of the whole court."

The color drained from my face.

"You didn't think of that, did you?" he snapped, thrusting his face into mine so that I felt the drops of his spittle as he bit each word off.

I stepped backward.

"If your family were not so valuable to my political career, I would punish you as you deserve."

Blaybourne's voice filled my ears: Would he lock you up?

"Are you with child?"

I lowered my head.

"You spend days, nay, weeks in that misbegotten knave's arms. And you expect me to accept his bastard!" He looked around. "It happened here, didn't it?" His eye caught the door in the yew hedge through which the private garden with the turf seat could be seen. He reached out and held my arm in a vice-like grip. "It was on that turf seat, wasn't it? It was in this garden where you spent your time."

"One night," I murmured.

He twisted me around. "Look at me, damn you. What did you say?"

"It was only one night."

"Ha! So, you wish it had been more."

He grabbed me around the waist with one hand, while with the other hand, he gripped my chin so that I was forced to look at him. We gazed at each other in dead silence for several minutes.

"Damn you, Cis," he said between his teeth, letting go of me so suddenly I crumpled into a heap.

"I am cursed!" he shouted over and over again.

I crossed myself. Was Lisette's curse coming true? I wiped the dust from my clothes and hair and rose. "I am here, Richard. I have not gone."

"Aye, but you lie to me. What is his name?"

An image of Blaybourne filled my mind. I couldn't give him away. I resented Richard for assuming he had a right to know my private thoughts and feelings. Was I to have no space to call my own in this marriage? Blaybourne would be my space.

"I think you know, but for some reason, you won't tell me. Come, my love, out with it."

"No."

"No, you don't know? Or, no, you're not telling?"

I stared at the ground.

Richard sprang forward and lifted me up in his arms, holding me in a vise. "You know I could lock you up. I could forbid you to see the children. I could starve you to death."

I shook, then looked him full in the face. "But you cannot make me talk."

He slapped me hard across the cheek. He grabbed me by the arm as I crumpled to my knees, holding my throbbing face.

"Woman. You will speak. I asked you a question. What is the knave's name?"

"I will never tell you."

"You love him as much as that? You would risk all?"

"Yes." I moved to the other side of the seat. "I have never loved anyone before. When you met me after all those years, you were experienced, but I was not. I married you because I had to. I had no notion of what love was like, until now. Here I am. You can do with me as you please. My heart is broken. I don't much care what happens to me now."

Richard moved swiftly to prevent me from escaping and imprisoned me against a tree by putting his arms on either side of me. I closed my eyes but could not get away from him. I could smell the leathery scent of his sweat and hear his heavy breathing.

"Are you with child?"

I was silent.

He tore himself away. "I cannot believe you would do this!" He slumped onto the bench and put his face into his hands.

I stared at him, still backed up against the tree. I did not dare move.

CHAPTER 11

September 1441 to April 1442

When Richard found out that I was indeed carrying another's child, he was not best pleased. He did not shout or carry on but compressed his lips into a thin line. Thereafter, although scrupulously courteous, he was cold.

It didn't help when the quarterly bills came due at Michaelmas, for they were unusually high. During Richard's absence, I'd been unable to resist all the lovely luxuries the merchants of Rouen kept bringing to the castle. Richard did not bother with a confrontation. Instead, he sent a note saying that he'd hired a Master Elbeuf to be comptroller of the household, and if I needed money, I was to consult him. This was a clever way for Richard to keep watch on me, for if he knew exactly how I spent my allowance, he'd know how I was spending my time. I couldn't argue with his logic.

Things continued in this uneasy state through October; then, little Henry sickened as the first frosts appeared. He died on All Hallows Eve, aged eight months. Truth to tell, I'd never paid much attention to the child, being so occupied with getting the entire household to Rouen shortly after his birth and then being caught up in my affair of the heart. Now he was dead, and Richard lost his heir.

As I sat there with my hand on Henry's cold cheek, there was a stir, a glint from the diamond, and Richard arrived. He cleared the room with a look and went up to me.

"Well?" he demanded coldly.

"I do not know what happened."

"You don't know. Why not?"

"He was never strong."

"No, he was not. And whose fault was that?"

He came over and gripped my chin with his fingers so that I was forced to look into his eyes, hard and steely.

"I'm sorry," I whispered.

"You should be. You have been extremely careless, madam, in the care of my son. Riding off to Lincoln in your condition when you were six months gone with him."

"I had to go to Mama's funeral."

"You should have waited until he was born to pay your respects to your lady mother. If you had done as I'd asked and stayed at Fotheringhay, he would have been stronger. And now we would not be dealing with the death of my heir."

Henry was buried in the Abbey of Saint-Ouen.

After that, I did not see Richard for several weeks. As winter intensified its grip, I spent my days sitting in front of the often-smoking fire, cuddling Joan on my lap. One day Joan could not stop coughing. I thought she had a bad cold, but she started wheezing and making gurgling noises. I doused the fire, but it made no difference. I tried to force syrup down her convulsing throat, but most of it spilled onto her clothes. After a long struggle, she turned blue and expired. She was three and a half.

I clutched Joan to my breast while tears rolled down my cheeks. When the priest came, they forced me to drink a draught of poppy juice because I would not hand her over for the last rites.

When I came to, I ran to the window. Someone—it was Richard —was quick enough to grab me. I twisted my head to look at him.

"Let me die."

"What of your immortal soul? That sin would land you in the fires of damnation."

Everything went black.

When I came to, I was lying in bed, and someone was holding my hand. As I gradually surfaced, something glinted through my closed eyelids. Richard sat on a stool by my bed. His face looked grey, new lines carving the flesh around his eyes and mouth.

"You've come back."

I raised myself up and looked around. "Why am I not dead? I should be."

Richard turned his head; the room filled with the sounds of people leaving. He sat on the bed and took me in his arms. "I thought we'd lost you," he murmured, holding me close.

I felt the diamond hard against my bosom. I gently pulled back and looked at him. "But why do you want me? I've wronged you."

"Cis!" he exclaimed, putting his hands on my shoulders and giving me a shake. He stopped abruptly as my eyes filled with tears. There was silence for many moments. "Don't you see how much I love you? I want you, not someone else." He kissed me gently on the lips.

"But I hurt you."

"You've been punished enough." And rising, he dashed a hand across his eyes, turned on his heel, and left.

I didn't see him again for many weeks. We buried Joan in the chapel of Saint Romain, in the castle, so that I could visit her every day.

I made a slow recovery. By some miracle, I didn't lose my child. Every day, I went with Margaret to visit Joan to pray for her soul. Every evening, I went to confession and confessed my sins to Père André, the castle chaplain. It took much time, but in the end, I told him the whole story.

Père André was a wise man and a good priest. He did not fob me off with a few Aves here, a few Paternosters there. He systematically went over my sins, discussing them at great length. Then he recommended books that I should read, starting with The Confessions of Saint Augustine. But the most important thing he taught me was how to pray. I spent many hours on my knees praying during the winter and spring of 1442. That was how I gradually recovered my sanity.

"My lady, do you want to see your son?" Annette de Caux's voice disturbed my reverie. Annette had stayed on after Henry's death, suckling her own child and acting as a governess for little Nan. Now, I engaged her as wet nurse for the new baby.

"Not until I've seen my lord husband."

And there he was, standing in the doorway. I'd scarcely seen him since the day he'd pulled me back from the gates of hell.

Annette, Jenet, and the other women hurriedly bobbed their curtsies and left while Richard came over and stood by the side of the bed.

"A son," he said. "You gave him a son."

I was silent.

"Are you going to send word to him?"

"Do you want me to?"

Richard sighed and sat down on the bed. "At least you chose a nobleman. The master sergeant of the garrison told me that one of the archers was a nobleman of the House of Savoy. He disappeared the day I arrived."

I fixed my eyes on Richard's face. Did he know anything else? Did he know he'd spoken with my lover? How would he feel if he knew Blaybourne was a peasant?

"I'll leave with the baby if you wish."

Richard stared.

"Or, I could stay with you," I murmured hastily, trying to soften his stony look.

"Of course, you're staying with me!" he shouted, seizing me by the shoulders. "I would never let you go. You know that."

"Perhaps you'd like another wife."

"Do you want to leave me?"

I looked at my long-suffering husband as though I were seeing him for the first time. He wasn't tall, but he wasn't fat either. He wasn't exceeding graceful, but he wasn't uncouth. The recent lines around his eyes and mouth made his face more interesting, less bland.

His eyes were his best feature, a clear blue-grey that reflected his every mood.

I hung my head. How stupid I'd been. Kind husbands who stood by you in a crisis were a rarity. And what of Nan? She needed me. It was my duty to hold my family together. I lifted my eyes and put my hand into his.

Richard wrapped his fingers around mine and held on tightly.

I lowered my lashes. Blaybourne seemed so dim and far away. Would I have been welcome if I'd gone to him? Who was he anyway? I wasn't sure if I believed him to be a powerful nobleman, a scholar, or a humble archer. I opened my eyes. "I would rather stay."

Richard drew me close. "The greatest wish I have is for my wife to love me. Could you?" His eyes bored into mine, going darker as they gazed at me.

I touched his cheek lightly with my finger, all hesitations gone. "Yes," I breathed, and he kissed me with more abandon than he ever had before.

"I could never let you go," he murmured over and over.

I leaned my head against his chest and frowned. "But what of the baby?" I asked hesitantly.

Richard stiffened. "Where is it?" he demanded, pulling away and rising.

"I don't know."

"You don't know?" Richard's eyebrows drew together.

"I didn't want to see him until I'd talked with you first."

"I see." Richard went to the door and signaled to Annette to bring the child.

"Would you like to hold him, my lady?" asked Annette.

I looked at Richard. Richard went over to look at the child. "He's big and perfectly formed. He seems robust and healthy. He'd be a good fighter." He fingered his beard. "You know what this means, of course."

I shook my head.

"If I say nothing, he becomes my heir."

I clasped my hands. "Is that what you want?"

BOOK III: THWARTED QUEEN

When she is fully readye she hath a lowe masse in her chamber, and after masse she taketh something to recreate nature; and soe goeth to the chappell hearinge the devine service, and two lowe masses; from thence to dynner, during the tyme whereof she hath a lecture of holy matter…
After dinner she giveth audyence to all such as hath any matter to shewe unto her by the space of one hower;

FROM ORDERS AND RULES OF THE PRINCESS CECILL QUOTED BY JOHN WOLSTENHOLME COBB (1883) HISTORY & ANTIQUITIES OF BERKHAMSTED

Chapter 12

Abbey of Beaumont-lès-Tours, Tours, France
Spring 1444

Enchanted," murmured William de la Pole, fourth Earl of Suffolk, as he stooped to kiss the outstretched hand of Marguerite d'Anjou. A vibrant young lady, her full lips parted as she smiled, revealing perfect white teeth. The King of England had already fallen in love with a secretly obtained portrait of her, but in the flesh, this visage was intoxicating. Her black hair had been braided into plaits and wound around her head, and her eyes glowed like a stoked fire, enormous and black. Marguerite d'Anjou was but fifteen years old.

Suffolk had come to France at the urging of his young master, the King of England, who had made him promise to obtain the lady for him. His patron, Cardinal Beaufort, had told him that the marriage would form the centerpiece of the peace negotiations labored on for the past two years. It was now Suffolk's duty to interview the lady herself and ascertain if she were truly fit to be England's queen. He offered his arm. "What do you know of England?"

"There has been a war between the English and the French for the past one hundred years," replied Marguerite. "So far, no one has won this fight. Though the English gained a great victory at Agincourt thirty years ago when King Henri's father was king, they have not been able to press their claims to the throne of France. If I were King of England, I would sue for peace."

"So, you would never make war?"

"I did not say that. If an enemy dared to attack me, I would mount my best horse and lead the charge."

"Marguerite!" exclaimed her mother Ysabeau, the Duchess of Lorraine, who walked a few paces behind. But Suffolk laughed, delighted.

"But you need men to fight for you," he observed, patting her arm. "How would you persuade them?"

"A queen must be many things," said Marguerite. "She must be a good wife to her lord and provide him with heirs. She must be a gracious hostess to everyone at court. She must find suitable husbands for the young women under her patronage. She must be charitable to those in need. She must encourage education and art. But, above all, she must inspire her people." She turned her dark gaze up to Suffolk's face. "I say to you, sir, that if such a queen requested her people to fight for her, do you not think they would follow?"

Suffolk chuckled as he kissed her hand with a flourish. This young lady had just given a perfect description. "Tell me," he murmured, "do you seek to emulate anyone in particular?"

"My lord father," replied Marguerite without pause.

Suffolk glanced around, but her father was standing some feet away, engaged in animated conversation with his steward. He narrowed his eyes. Did she really mean that? Réné of Anjou, King of Naples and Sicily, was described as a man of many crowns and no kingdoms. He had been struggling to take control of his vast inheritance without great success, even being taken prisoner by Philip III, Duke of Burgundy.

"And my lady mother," remarked Marguerite.

That was more like it, thought Suffolk, smiling at her eager face. Duchess Ysabeau had raised an army to rescue her husband from captivity.

"And my lady grandmother," said Marguerite.

"The Duchess of Aragon?"

Marguerite smiled, showing off her perfect teeth.

Suffolk whistled under his breath as he stroked his beard. Yolande of Aragon had dominated French politics until her death two years ago. Suffolk had heard rumors that it was Duchess Yolande who orchestrated the appearance of Joan of Arc to inspire the French troops. If Marguerite were anything like her grandmother, she would be a formidable lady indeed. But perhaps she was exactly what the young king needed, for it was plain that he was weak and easily led by his councilors. The king's council was barely able to govern these days on account of the continuing feud between Humphrey Plantagenet, Duke of Gloucester, and Cardinal Beaufort. Suffolk considered. Should he be concerned about promoting such a charismatic young lady to be Queen of England? What of his own position? He was entirely dependent on the king's favor. He glanced over at her as she moved into the Abbot's parlor.

"My daughter likes also to dance," murmured her father, standing at his elbow. He signaled to a servant to pour wine. "My daughter requests that she dance the Tarantella for you."

Suffolk inclined his head.

Marguerite began the dance by curtseying low, first to Suffolk, and then to each of her parents. She danced lightly, moving through the supple rhythms with ease and grace, her steps matching the stress patterns exactly, her bearing and gestures adding beauty to the music.

Suffolk watched for a few minutes. The young lady was beautiful, personable, articulate, and displayed impeccable carriage. She smiled at him as she danced, and he could not help smiling back. He did not fear her, for he and Marguerite were going to be the greatest of friends. He turned to René. "Your Grace, you have a lovely daughter. She has all the qualities one would hope for in a queen. I would now like to make a formal request for the hand of your daughter Marguerite."

"By all means," agreed Réné. "My daughter is a jewel, as you can see. Her mother and I are happy that you think her worthy to be Queen of England. But there is one matter I should warn you about. It shames me to say this, but I have no money, so I will be unable to provide my daughter with a dowry."

"No dowry?" exclaimed Suffolk.

Duchess Ysabeau raised her head, and Marguerite paused for a measure while she shot a sharp look in Suffolk's direction. Then she began to dance once more.

Réné lowered his voice. "I inherited the Duchy of Anjou ten years ago, but I get no revenues from it because it is owned by your king. I tried to claim the Kingdom of Naples but was forced to cede it to my cousin Alfonso of Aragon. My friend, I am poor and cannot provide for my daughter as I would wish."

"But surely you don't mean to send your daughter to England with nothing."

"I would be better able to provide for her, mon ami, if I had my lands back. I demand that King Henri give me the counties of Maine and Anjou as part of the marriage settlement."

Suffolk choked on his wine. "But the English people will never agree," he said between coughs. "If you insist on this, Your Grace, you will make your daughter unpopular. The English will resent her for the terms of this treaty. Is that how you wish her to begin as Queen of England?"

Réné made a dismissive gesture. "I don't see that the opinions of peasants should have any bearing on matters of state. The King of England will protect Marguerite from all that."

"England is not like France, my friend. People are in the habit of expressing their opinions much more freely. Being unpopular with the people could be costly. The King of England has to please the London merchants; otherwise, they will not give him loans."

Réné shrugged. "Those are my terms. Charles, Count of Nevers, wants my daughter also, so I suggest you hurry."

Suffolk glanced at Marguerite again. She was perfect, and the King of England was already in love with her; he would never forgive him if Marguerite didn't become his bride.

CHAPTER 13

Pontoise, English France
Saint Joseph's Eve
March 18, 1445

Cecylee shivered, the piercing air of March sending threads of freezing air through the thick fur mantle. She stood a little way back from the riverbank, careful not to get too close to the soft mud oozing up between the reeds and river grasses and threatening to soil her slippers. This Saint Joseph's Eve, she stood by the banks of the Seine, awaiting the queen's entry into Pontoise.

Cecylee measured time by how long it had been since Joan's passing. Before, everything seemed filled with sunlight. Now, the clouds had rolled in. How long would it be before she could join her daughter? It had already been three years.

Richard had agreed to name Blaybourne's son Edward and christened him in a small private ceremony in the chapel of Saint Romain where Joan was buried. One month after Edward's first birthday, Cecylee bore a son that Richard named Edmund, after his uncle Edmund Mortimer. Richard was ecstatic about this son's birth, and a magnificent ceremony for his christening was held in Rouen

Cathedral with a large number of dignitaries present. As a mark of special favor, the cathedral chapter allowed Richard to use Duke Rollo's font for Edmund's christening. Much was made of this honor, for this was the font at which Duke Rollo of Normandy, an ancestor of William the Conqueror, had been baptized into Christianity in the year 912. It had been kept covered and unused for over five hundred years.

Eleven months after Edmund's birth, Cecylee gave Richard a daughter named Beth.

Cecylee had mixed feelings about bearing so many children in such a short span of time: Joan, Nan, Henry, Edward, Edmund, Beth. She was in her prime, yet the fear of death was a continual presence. Now she stood with Richard, holding Nan's hand as she peered through the murky gloom for the barge that bore the new Queen of England from Paris. Sixteen-year-old Marguerite d'Anjou had been married by proxy to twenty-three-year-old King Henry of England a couple of weeks back and now began her journey to England.

Cecylee had heard much of the new queen. She'd heard that Marguerite d'Anjou had won golden opinions at the French court where she'd been living for the past year with her aunt Queen Marie d'Anjou of France. Charles of Valois, Duke of Orléans, was reported to have said that this woman "excelled all others, as well in beauty as in wit, and was of stomach and courage more like to a man than to a woman."

"Are they here, Mama?"

"Not yet, my sweet. Are you sure you're warm enough?"

"I am perfectly comfortable," replied five-year-old Nan gravely, her blue-grey eyes bearing Richard's expression. "Chatelaine keeps me warm."

Cecylee smiled, adjusting the child's soft fur hood. Nan was inseparable from her kitten. The tiny grey animal had hooked its claws into the thick sable so that it reclined on Nan's shoulder. "She's not too heavy for you?"

"Not yet," replied Nan.

"You shouldn't have allowed her to bring that cat," muttered Richard.

"She adores Chatelaine," whispered Cecylee. "Besides," she added, tilting her head as a sudden thought struck her, "it looks like a fur collar, don't you think?"

Richard's smile eased away from the lines of his face.

"Why don't you take her for a walk?" murmured Cecylee, thinking it would be well for Richard to spend time with his daughter.

She clasped her hands together for warmth beneath her furs as they left. Now that Marguerite d'Anjou was Queen of England, she was no longer the first lady of the land. She would have to yield precedence to a girl fourteen years younger and of an age to be her own child. If Marguerite bore the king's sons, Richard would cease to have any claim on the English throne. Perhaps it would be best if she and Richard went back to their estates in England, even to Richard's favorite residence at Fotheringhay, and lived out their lives in peace. As it was, Richard did not have many friends among the councilors who surrounded the king. They were divided into two camps. The Duke of Gloucester, supported by Richard, argued vociferously for the continuance of war in France; Cardinal Beaufort and his allies Suffolk and Somerset favored peace. The king was entirely dominated by Beaufort, Suffolk, and their cronies, who would stop at nothing to get their way, including accusing Gloucester's wife of witchcraft.

She crossed herself and shivered. At least they'd got rid of York by posting him abroad.

"Well met, my lady York," said a soft voice.

Cecylee turned to see Jacquetta de St. Pol, Duchess of Bedford, smiling. The Duchess was a lady of her age, elegantly dressed in grey furs that set off her grey eyes and pale complexion. She had caused a scandal some ten years before when, as a recent widow to the powerful Duke of Bedford and aunt-by-marriage to the king, she had married Sir Richard Woodville, a mere knight. Cecylee had admired Jacquetta for the courage she'd shown in braving the wrath of the King of England to marry this man who had been but a chamberlain to the Duke of Bedford.

"May I introduce my husband, Sir Richard Woodville?"

A man with a well-cut profile came forward and bowed low. Cecylee felt a twinge as she stared at this handsome face now emerging from a bow.

He looked down and smiled. "My lady York: The pleasure is all mine."

Cecylee's cheeks burned as she compared him with Blaybourne. Everyone sneered at Sir Richard's low birth, and yet his manners were courtly, his bearing elegant. The conundrum of Blaybourne reappeared: How could a mere peasant have the manners of an aristocrat? Didn't blood run true? How could this be possible unless he had some blue blood in his veins?

"Handsome, isn't he?" murmured Jacquetta.

Cecylee started and blushed as she realized she must have been staring at Sir Richard, almost as if she were trying to make out his shape from beneath the folds of the lavish cloak he'd wrapped himself in.

Jacquetta chuckled deep in her throat.

Cecylee stiffened.

"This is our eldest child," said Jacquetta nudging a diminutive form towards her. "Make your curtsey, chérie."

A tiny figure swathed in a green velvet cloak swept a deep curtsey. As she bent her head, a lock of hair spilled from her hood. The color was golden, vibrating with light.

"This is my Élisabeth."

Cecylee looked down into a pair of brown eyes. How strange. For wasn't brown a warm color? This child's eyes were cold, the color of stream-washed stones.

"How old is she?"

"Nigh on eight," replied Jacquetta.

Jacquetta was her age. She had a beautiful daughter Joan's age, and she had married for love. Cecylee might outrank Jacquetta among the ladies of court, but God was punishing her.

"Mama?" Cecylee turned and saw that Nan and Richard had returned. She made the introductions.

"I don't like Élisabeth," whispered Nan as Richard made conversation with the Woodvilles. "She stares at you in a mean way."

"Hush, my sweet," replied Cecylee, looking around to see if anyone had heard her. "Ladies do not pass remarks about people in public."

A slap of water made her turn. From the direction of Paris, a dark shape emerged silently through the mists. Several swathed figures sat in it, but the only color that emerged from the deep gloom was a faint gleam of gold shining dully from the head of one of the figures. Propelled by the rhythmical rising and falling of the oars, the barge drew closer, and fanfare shattered the quiet. Richard took her hand, and they moved across the thick carpets that had been placed at shore's edge as the crowned figure arose and stepped lightly to land.

"By the Grace of God, Marguerite, Queen of England and France, and Lady of Ireland!" the herald roared.

Suffolk disembarked next and knelt. "My dear lady," he said in his mellifluous voice, "May God bless you and keep you. This day is a blessing, for England gains a great queen."

A chill wind blew as Marguerite hastened forward to help him up. "Rise, *mon cher ami*." she said. "I am most grateful for all that you have done for me. You have my most especial favor."

Suffolk patted her hand and smiled as Richard thinned his lips.

CHAPTER 14

Pontoise, English France

When Marguerite d'Anjou first met the English Court at Pontoise on Saint Joseph's Eve in March 1445, the Duke of York was the first to kiss her hand. Marguerite was struck by the somber coloring of his raiment and the serious expression on his face. But as she motioned him to rise, a smile lit his face, warming those blue-grey eyes. Just behind Duke Richard was his wife, who sank into a deep and graceful curtsey with her head bent. Duchess Cecylee was very pretty in an English sort of way, with grey eyes, a lily-white complexion, and fair hair that had been braided up into an elaborate hairstyle. She wore a grey gown of fine wool, further setting off those eyes. For a woman who had already borne her lord six children, the Duchess was enviably slender. It was obvious her lord adored her, for he could scarce keep his eyes away.

As the duchess rose from her curtsey, she smiled, making her grey eyes sparkle. "Welcome to England, my dear," she said in that ugly, clattering Norman French with its rounded vowels, sharp consonants, and frequent heavy stresses.

Marguerite flinched. She would have to accustom herself to the elegant and beautiful French language being mangled in such a fashion.

"My lord Duke and I hope you will be happy in England," continued the duchess. "We will try to make it so."

As she spoke, Duchess Cecylee took in Queen Marguerite's appearance. But she lowered her lashes and said nothing.

Marguerite lifted her chin. How dare the duchess criticize her.

York cleared his throat. "We are blessed indeed with the arrival of this most beauteous princess from France." He murmured various other compliments, but Marguerite was distracted by Duchess Cecylee, who beckoned to a young boy to come forward. He held various packages done up in twine.

"I have this day been to the merchants of Pontoise," she remarked.

York raised an eyebrow as he turned to his wife.

She put a hand on his arm. "Dickon," she said, "you know we women must look our best for the state banquet we are to give our queen tonight." She turned to Marguerite. "May I present to you my maid Jenet?"

A slender brown maid curtseyed low.

"Jeanette is from Picardy," continued the Duchess in her heavy Norman-French accent, "but has lived many years in England and knows English fashions. If it pleases you, I would like to invite you to my apartments after Mass to see what I have bought."

Marguerite's cheeks warmed. Had they heard she'd been so short of money she'd been obliged to pawn her silver plate to the kind-hearted Countess of Somerset so that she could pay the wages of her sailors? Marguerite involuntarily glanced at her new friend Eleanor Beauchamp, Countess of Somerset, who stood by her side.

Marguerite turned back to Duchess Cecylee. "I thank you, madame, for your most kind attention, but I have brought with me five barons and baronesses, seventeen knights, sixty-five squires, and sundry others. King Henri has been kind enough to provide me with the services of the Countesses of Suffolk and Somerset. Therefore, I can manage, I assure you."

Duchess Cecylee compressed her lips, a perfect rose pink filling her lily-white complexion. An elegant lady in sky-blue satin took this opportunity to move forward. She dropped an exquisite curtsey. "My lady Queen, I am Jacquetta de Saint Pol, Duchess of Bedford, and sister to Isabelle of Luxembourg, Countess de Guise."

Marguerite smiled into the lovely face of this stranger who pronounced French so beautifully. Isabelle de Guise was married to her father's brother Charles, the Count of Maine.

"How is dearest Isabelle?" continued Jacquetta, as Marguerite motioned her to rise. "Has she had her child?"

"Tante Isabelle is very well and sends you her love," replied Marguerite, delighted to meet the countrywoman she'd heard much about. "She was brought to bed by a beautiful daughter called Louise." Marguerite motioned Jacquetta to a seat: "What can you tell me of England?"

"Many things, chérie, but all in good time. May I present to you my husband, Sir Richard Woodville?"

Sir Richard came forward, bowed low, knelt, and kissed the Queen's hand. "Enchanté," he murmured, smiling up at her.

"And here is little Élisabeth, my eldest," continued Jacquetta as a diminutive figure curtseyed low.

"Ma petite," exclaimed Marguerite, raising the child from her curtsey. She planted kisses on each soft cheek of the golden child.

"If it please you, my lady Queen," lisped Élisabeth. She looked at her mother, who nodded. "It is my greatest wish to be your damsel."

Marguerite smiled down at her. Élisabeth was tiny but so perfectly formed. She seemed like a creature out of a fairy tale. "But of course, chérie. I would be most happy to have my little kinswoman at my court." As she gently tilted the child's chin, she noticed the Duke and Duchess of York standing together.

"I had no idea the Woodville woman was related to the queen," York muttered to his wife.

"Only by marriage," replied Duchess Cecylee in her clear, bell-like tones. She glanced at Marguerite, then lowered her voice, but Marguerite's keen ears were still able to pick up her muffled tones.

"Did you see how patched and mended her gown was? It looks as if she has only one gown."

"She has no dowry," whispered York. "I received this morning a letter from Gloucester. He deplores her lack of dowry and has publicly accused parliament of having bought a queen not worth ten marks."

Marguerite stiffened as she gently took her fingers away from Élisabeth's face.

"Are you unwell, my lady Queen?" whispered Eleanor, Countess of Somerset.

"There's no point in standing here." Duchess Cecylee's clear voice carried over to where the Queen sat with her attendants. "Let us go, my lord. 'Tis clear we are not wanted." She swept off, leaving Marguerite staring after her.

York flushed, bowed to the Queen, and hurried after his wife.

"Do not mind her," murmured Alice de la Pole, Countess of Suffolk coming into the room with refreshments just as my lady York disappeared. "Many call her Proud Cis."

"I do not mind," replied Marguerite, lifting her chin. "She may be *Duchesse*, but I am Queen."

CHAPTER 15

Y ou must try harder to win her favor," murmured Richard as Queen Marguerite appeared at the top of the stairs leading into the great hall. "I'm depending upon you to become her friend. You can offer Nan to be her damsel if you wish."

Cecylee fingered an emerald necklace. She should not have swept from the room like that, and she couldn't understand why she had been overtaken by such ill-temper. She turned to Richard. "I thank you for your suggestion, but Nan is over young for that at present. Mayhap when she is older."

As Marguerite arrived at the bottom of the stairs, Cecylee sank into a low curtsey while Richard bowed, murmured various compliments, and offered Marguerite his arm. Cecylee walked behind on the arm of William de la Pole, Earl of Suffolk, the rest of the English court following. Cecylee frowned as she caught sight of Mistress Élisabeth Woodville dressed in a gold and green silk gown, her shimmering hair streaming down her back under a matching cap of gold and green.

Richard took Marguerite by the hand as he placed her in the seat of honor to his right. Cecylee sat on his left, next to the Earl of Suffolk, while Alice of Suffolk sat lower down. Richard had ensured that Marguerite was furnished with a fork, a new-fangled implement that the French court had adopted but was not yet common in England. He took care to cut up the choicest pieces of meat into small morsels so that she could pierce them with her fork and eat in one mouthful. As he did so, he murmured various compliments.

"Our last queen, Catrine de Valois, was fair but not as lovely as you," he remarked, kissing the tips of Marguerite's fingers with a flourish.

Cecylee had never seen Richard pay court to another woman.

Marguerite smiled and leaned towards Richard: "I have learned something of your history. Was not Catrine de Valois wife to King Henri, the one who fought us at Agincourt?"

"Indeed, yes." York picked up a flagon of wine, raised an eyebrow, and at Marguerite's nod, refilled her goblet. "His queen came to England to make peace, madam, like yourself."

"Tell me about England. Where do you live?"

York sipped his wine and smiled. "I have several residences, but my favorite one is at Fotheringhay."

"Foh-dring-hey." Marguerite turned the name slowly over on her tongue.

Suffolk laughed. "We will make an Englishwoman of you yet, my lady!" he bellowed, causing Cecylee to jump. He rose to his feet: "A toast to our queen." The other men rose also.

"May our queen live a long and happy life." Suffolk glanced at Richard. "And with no enemies to mar her reign."

"To our queen," roared the other men as they pounded the tables and drank.

Duke Richard sat down and took another sip of his wine. "That is my wish also, my Queen," he remarked softly. He put his goblet down. "Fotheringhay is dear to my heart. My castle sits on top of a tall hill around which the River Nene curls."

"It sounds lovely," murmured Marguerite as she ate a morsel of food.

"It would give me the greatest pleasure if you were to visit us there. I could show you the church tower I designed."

Marguerite stopped eating and stared. Cecylee watched the expression on her face. Did she think we English were uncouth and wild savages?

"Tell me about your *Tour*," said Marguerite.

"I had it built ten years ago, shortly after I came into my majority," replied Richard, cutting off a small portion of the roasted duck now placed before them. He laid it neatly on her trencher, put his knife down, and leaned back in his chair. "It is octagonal and commands a fine view of the surrounding countryside."

"Why did you make it octagonal?"

Richard laughed. "Perhaps because it is unusual. To my knowledge, the only other octagonal tower is the Lantern Tower of Ely Cathedral. I did not want it to be round or square because that would have made it look like a fortress." He rubbed his forked beard. "I wanted something that conveyed elegance and grace, qualities that I fear we are sorely lacking in England." He picked up Marguerite's hand and kissed it. "But you will remedy that, madam, of that I have no doubt."

Cecylee's stomach clenched at Marguerite's smile.

At length, the ladies rose to escort the queen upstairs to her bedchamber.

"I wish to learn English," remarked Marguerite as she entered the dark room with handsome carved furniture and heavy draperies, "but what should I read?"

"Have you heard of Master Geoffrey Chaucer?" asked Duchess Cecylee.

"Does he make shoes?" replied Marguerite, indicating that the ladies should sit around her.

My lady York laughed merrily. "No, no," she replied as soon as she could. "Though I see why you might think so. One of his forefathers must have been a chaucelier or shoemaker, for him to have the name Chaucer. But you should read him. He writes in English."

"What does he write about?"

Duchess Cecylee's grey eyes sparkled. "If you wish to understand the English, read the Canterbury Tales. There you will find people from every station in life. It will interest you greatly."

"I believe Master Chaucer was your mother's uncle, was he not?" murmured Jacquetta, stroking her daughter's hair.

Marguerite winced.

Duchess Cecylee turned pink. "An uncle-by-marriage." She lifted her chin. "I am not ashamed to be related to the greatest poet of the land. In any case, I am not the only one here to call Master Chaucer relative. My lady Suffolk is his granddaughter."

There was dead silence as Marguerite looked from Duchess Cecylee to Countess Alice and back again. How was it possible for these great ladies to have relatives who were not aristocratic? This mixing of classes wasn't right. Peasants should know their place and not get above their station.

"My lady Queen," lisped Élisabeth, "would you like for me to bring you some lavender water?"

"A goodly suggestion," remarked Countess Alice, rising and curtseying low before Marguerite. "I fear you are greatly fatigued, madam."

"Perhaps I should say my adieux," murmured Duchess Cecylee, "unless you wish me to stay, my lady Queen?"

"I will see you on the morrow," replied Marguerite, and so Duchess Cecylee curtseyed and made her way back to the great hall.

Alice clucked her tongue as she directed the servant girl to stoke up the fire. Élisabeth fetched a bowl of lavender water while Jacquetta unpinned Marguerite's headdress.

"Soon, you will be in England, and you will see things for yourself," said Alice. "Suffolk and I are blessed to have many good

friends at court, like Cardinal Beaufort and his family, the
Somersets." She nodded towards Eleanor Beauchamp, Countess of
Somerset, and smiled. "The king favors them greatly. So, you do not
need to worry about the Yorks and what they think. They are not in
favor at court. Indeed, the king has not seen his cousin York now for
four years. And Gloucester, the king's uncle, has been much
discredited due to the foolishness of his wife."

"What did she do?"

"The poor lady was very unwise—" began Countess Eleanor.

"Eleanor Cobham was indicted on charges of conspiring to kill
the king by means of witchcraft," said Jacquetta.

Marguerite turned in her seat to look both ladies in the face.
"Why does York support Gloucestre then? Surely his behavior is most
treasonous."

Alice sighed. "I do not understand York, save that he has a most
unwholesome ambition."

"York is completely untrustworthy," said Jacquetta. "He thinks
only of gaining power as if he is not the wealthiest peer in the
kingdom." She turned to Élisabeth. "Kneel, chérie, with the bowl just
so. Now hand the queen a napkin."

Marguerite smiled as she took the linen offered by the eight-year-
old and slowly dipped her fingers.

"And his wife is little better," said Alice. "She is not called Proud
Cis for nothing."

"The Duke of York was most charming to me tonight," remarked
Marguerite. "And I have heard it said he is talented at administration
and an excellent general."

"He can read Latin fluently," said Eleanor.

"He is well educated and intelligent. I grant him that," said
Jacquetta. "But everything he does is governed by ambition. Why do
you think he has taken such care to win golden opinions in France?"

"Do you think he should be recalled to England?" asked
Marguerite.

"Suffolk says there are others who could govern Normandy who
are more loyal," whispered Alice. "You might want to suggest to the
king, my lady, that it would be most wise to keep an eye on York—"

CHAPTER 16

Placentia Palace, Greenwich, London
October 1445

I had to pawn my collar. And now I'm back in England, what thanks do I get?" Richard, Duke of York, set his mouth into a grim line. It was seven months since he'd met Queen Marguerite in Pontoise and two months since King Henry had recalled him from Normandy.

Humphrey, Duke of Gloucester, shook his head and set his wine cup down. "I see nothing good in the fortunes of England. The king is so easily led. I know not why he's not more like his father, Great Harry. You would think a great warrior would breed a more warlike son." His voice trailed off as he stared gloomily out of the window at the thick fog that pressed inwards.

Richard had known Gloucester since he was a boy. When Richard had arrived at court after the death of Cecylee's father, Gloucester, also of the Plantagenet line, had befriended him and persuaded him to use his wealth and family connections to act as a counterpoise against the ambitions of Cardinal Beaufort. Richard studied the face of his great mentor: The years had not been kind. Age had thickened his small frame, and his dark hair was nearly white.

Small wonder, thought Richard, with all he has had to endure in recent years.

"I adored my brother, the king," said Duke Humphrey. "I'll never forget the day we fought together at Agincourt. He was my hero, and I always considered it my sacred duty to further his war policies in France. His aim was to defeat the French and annex the whole of France to the English Crown."

"And I support you in that aim. I hate to see my labor in Normandy go to waste."

"I know, my friend. You don't know how much I appreciate your support. Without it, I would be a lonely man indeed. Cardinal Beaufort, his great-nephew Somerset, and his protégé Suffolk are all against the war, and they are in with the king."

"And now the queen."

"And now the queen," repeated Gloucester. "It's been a little over six months since the king's marriage, and already you and I are left out in the cold."

York poured more mulled wine and took a sip.

"Have they given you a position on the king's council?"

"No."

Gloucester sighed. "Of course not. After what happened to me —"

"What happened exactly?"

Gloucester drained his wine cup and held it out for Richard to pour another measure. "I was doing what I've been doing for the past twenty-five years, campaigning for the continuance of the war in France. We were so near victory, and we could have done it if only the king had given us money. But Beaufort and his friends dominate him. I protested vociferously against their anti-war policies; I believe them to be a betrayal of everything Great Harry stood for. They didn't like what I said and set out to ruin my credibility."

He drained another wine cup and slumped in his seat. "Around the time you arrived in Rouen, my lady wife was attending a dinner in London when she was arrested on charges of witchcraft. She and several others were tried. Her clerk was hung, drawn, and quartered. Her woman was burned at stake. My wife was sentenced to do three public penances, and then they shut her up in prison for life. I had to sit silently by because they would have destroyed me as well. You have no idea what it was like seeing the lady you love being ruined before your very eyes."

Richard looked away. How would he have felt if Cecylee had been accused of witchcraft? He shuddered. Though Cecylee had wronged him greatly, he loved her still. One of the few pleasures in a life filled with duty was returning to the home she'd created for him. Richard always felt at peace when he saw her smile, inhaled her scent, and drank some concoction she'd prepared with her own hands. He didn't think he could bear it if Cecylee were shut up for life. It would be like quenching a candle flame. That was why he'd been unable to lock her up as she deserved. He couldn't quench her spirit. He looked up. Gloucester was blowing his nose on a handkerchief. "Was it true that Duchess Eleanor made a waxen image of the King?"

Gloucester sighed heavily as he wiped his eyes. "My wife liked to dabble in witchcraft. She had her horoscope cast, and it is true she made a waxen image of the king and melted it in a fire. But what harm could she do? The king is a young man in the best of health. Nothing my Eleanor did could alter that."

"But—"

"It was foolish, indeed, yes. And the poor lady is paying heavily for it now."

"But you continue to attend meetings of the king's council?"

"Not often. No one wants to listen to me because of this unfortunate business with my wife. They've discredited me, I tell you. This is all the doing of Cardinal Beaufort."

"Are you sure of that?"

"As sure as I can be. He's been trying to oust me from power for the past twenty years, and he's succeeded."

Duke Humphrey went to his bookshelf. He'd invited Richard into his private library where spines upon spines obscured the walls; he owned over two hundred books, more than any other magnate in England. "Now, where was I? I wanted to show you the latest work by Aretino." He put on a pair of spectacles and ran his fingers across the leather spines. "Ah, here it is. The History of the Florentine People, published about a year ago by the Republic of Florence." He gave Richard a twisted smile. "I wonder what you will make of this, my friend." He opened the book at a well-marked place and read:

If one considers the savagery of Tiberius, the fury of Caligula, the insanity of Claudius, and the crimes of Nero with his mad delight in fire and sword; if one adds Vitellius, Caracalla, Heliogabalus, Maximinus, and other monsters like them who horrified the whole world, one cannot deny that the Roman empire began to collapse once the disastrous name of Caesar had begun to brood over the city.

Richard threw back his head and laughed. "An apt comparison to the tyranny of our own times."

"My lord!" A messenger entered, wearing the badge of the falcon and the fetterlock, showing the Yorkist affinity. He was wet and muddy from a hard ride. Richard nodded, and the messenger came forward, knelt, and bowed his head. "I have ridden in from Westminster, my lord, from a meeting of Parliament to tell you—" He paused for breath. "To tell your lordship that Adam Moleyns, the Bishop of Chichester, has accused you of financial malpractice."

Richard's skin prickled as he blanched.

"No!" Gloucester whirled around, sending the book crashing to the floor. He jabbed a finger at the messenger. "This is a ploy to keep you off the king's council. Don't you see? Moleyns owes his bishopric to Suffolk. How dare they accuse you!"

Richard turned to the messenger. "What exactly did the bishop say?"

"He told Parliament that the campaigns in France were ruinously expensive. He said that so much money had been spent on Normandy, it didn't seem possible it could have cost that much. Either the Duke of York was foolishly overspending, he said, or he had pocketed the money."

A bead of ruby red liquid inched over the rim and dropped onto Richard's hand. He put his wine cup down. "How can he claim I pocketed the money when the King never paid me my annuity?"

Gloucester picked up his book and placed it on the table. "We must avenge this insult." He stormed downstairs, shouting for his horse. York hurried after him. Both lords mounted their horses and set off at a fast gallop towards Westminster.

York and Gloucester vaulted off their horses, tossed their reins to the groom, and strode into Westminster Hall, where parliament was meeting. As the door closed shut, the heat of the room sucked them in. A fire roared in the grate, and familiar faces crowded the chamber. Richard waited for the sergeant-at-arms to announce them and for the Duke of Norfolk to invite them to speak.

"This charge would be laughable were it not so grave." York looked around the chamber of Westminster Hall, meeting as many eyes as he could. "I've always dealt honestly with the Crown. When my uncle, the Earl of March, died, the custody of those lands should have been turned over to me because I was his nearest living male heir. However, the Crown saw fit to grant my lands to Cardinal Beaufort. As a lad of fourteen, there was not much I could do about that. Seven years later, when I reached my majority, I was informed I would get my lands back only if I paid the king the sum of one thousand six hundred and forty-six pounds and sixpence. I swallowed this insult and paid the king in full. The king has not treated me so courteously. When I was appointed lieutenant-general of France, I was promised an annuity of twenty thousand pounds, which I never received. I had to use my own personal funds to secure Normandy. I have summoned my officers from Normandy who will give you a full accounting of the money I have spent. You will see that far from pocketing money, I am so deeply in debt I have had to pawn my collar to pay my soldiers. The crown owes me the sum of thirty-eight thousand, six hundred and seventy-seven pounds." York sank down on the bench next to Gloucester and wiped the perspiration from his forehead.

The Earl of Suffolk rose. "Call Master Elbeuf." He looked around the room as a round gentleman appeared, bowed low, and declared himself to be the comptroller to the Duke of York.

"Let us begin," intoned Suffolk. "You say Duke Richard arrived in Rouen on Saint John's Day in the year 1441. Tell us how much he spent that day."

It took several days for Master Elbeuf to explain to Parliament the details of my lord of York's expenditure while he was in Rouen, for he had kept detailed records. Everything that was spent between June of 1441, when Richard of York took up his position as governor of Normandy, and October 1445, when he returned to England, was laid before Parliament. When York's comptroller finally sat down, Suffolk rose. "Is Richard, Duke of York, guilty of financial malpractice or not? It is for you, my lords, to decide."

Richard bowed his head and covered his face with his hands.

"Where is Duchess Cecylee?" whispered Gloucester. "Surely your lady wife should be with you at such a time."

York smiled briefly. "Cecylee is breeding. We expect to have our next child in May. She has not been well, and I did not want her to become upset."

"Indeed," sighed Gloucester. "You are wise to let her stay at Fotheringhay."

"I had to insist upon it," remarked York. "You know how my wife is. She loves being at court, especially now that our new queen has made it livelier. Cecylee hates being left behind at Fotheringhay. The country is too quiet for her."

Several hours passed. Finally, John de Mowbray, third Duke of Norfolk, rose. As premier duke of the realm, he was tasked with adjudicating this matter. "We have come to a decision." He bowed to

Suffolk. "We find Richard Duke of York to be not guilty of the charge of financial malpractice."

There was a roar from Richard's supporters. Gloucester thumped him on the back.

"Indeed," continued Norfolk, "we find that York has conducted his affairs with great probity and thoroughness. We recommend that the Crown repay him his loan of thirty-eight thousand pounds."

CHAPTER 17

Westminster Palace, London
December 1445

"My dear lord. You must fulfill the terms of the treaty. Can you not see that?"

"My dear wife, sit you down, and we will talk," replied King Henry.

He enclosed her delicate hand with his own as he drank her in. Sixteen-year-old Marguerite d'Anjou was the most ravishing beauty. She was small-boned and slender. Her russet-colored velvet gown clung to her well-turned waist and hips, outlining her lovely bosom. She had a well-cut profile, with high cheekbones and deep-set black eyes. They'd been wed for eight months, and he had yet to make love to her. His confessor had forbidden it, saying that lovemaking was a self-indulgent sport and that he should not come near her any more than was absolutely necessary for the begetting of an heir. Henry had not dared to; One glimpse of his wife's naked body would send him into paroxysms of lust, and then his soul would be damned to the second circle of hell for eternity. For had not Our Savior Jesus Christ called on us to live chaste lives dedicated to God? Had he not commanded his followers to forsake all family ties?

"You agreed to return Maine et Anjou to *mon oncle*, King Charles."

He started. "Yes, dearest, I did, but I have not informed Parliament of this matter."

Marguerite leapt to her feet. "You are King of England!"

King Henry moved his head from side to side, his forehead creasing into a frown. "They are not going to like it," he murmured.

"What do you mean? Who is not going to like it?"

She looked so lovely when she was angry, the color mounting those pretty cheeks. How he longed to cover those rosy lips with kisses. But his confessor had told him that he must sacrifice himself to a life devoid of earthly pleasure so that he could lead the English people to the gates of heaven.

The confessor continued the work of pious Richard de Beauchamp, Earl of Warwick, who'd been his guardian from the time he was nine months. De Beauchamp had made the arduous pilgrimage to Jerusalem. He had been heralded the "Father of Courtesy" by the Holy Roman Emperor. He had instilled in the young king the values of kindness and piety, as well as a love for education. Indeed, he had been so successful in training his young charge in kingly craft that Henry had taken a precocious interest in politics. As a lad of twelve, he had attempted to intervene in some matter, astonishing his councilors. They had roundly told him to avoid becoming entangled in court intrigue and swayed by those who would manipulate him for their own advancement.

"Who is not going to like it?" repeated Marguerite.

"Parliament."

"Does it matter? Are they not peasants?"

"There are two knights from every shire in the country," replied Henry, eyeing his wife. Deo Gracias, but she was lovely. However, it was becoming clear that she didn't understand English customs. The King of England could not ignore his parliament, unlike the King of France.

"They are peasants!" exclaimed Marguerite

"They represent my people," replied Henry as he fingered the s-shaped gold collar around his neck. That and the signet ring on his

right hand were the only marks of distinction he allowed himself.
Otherwise, he dressed in unfashionable round-toed shoes and robes
of indeterminate darkness.

Marguerite started to pace. "The people. Who cares what the
people think? You should return those territories now as you
promised, or you will dishonor your good name."

Marguerite had been at the court of Charles VII for only a year.
She would have been perfect as Queen of France, thought Henry.
Instead, she was Queen of England, and someone needed to explain
to her about English politics, as de Beauchamp had done for him. But
de Beauchamp had been dead these six years. Henry frowned with
concentration. It was all so complicated. Where was the best place to
start? Should he begin with the duties of the king? But she knew all
about that. Perhaps he should tell her about the humble folk. But she
seemed not to be interested—

"You promised to cede *Maine et Anjou*."

"Yes, dearest, I did. But I have not informed all of my magnates.
Gloucester and York don't know about this provision of the treaty."

Marguerite snorted. "You are king. What are Gloucestre and
York to you? They must obey their sovereign lord."

"Your lady wife speaks the truth, my lord King," remarked
Somerset bowing low as he entered. Edmund Beaufort, fourth Earl of
Somerset, was a gentleman nearing forty. Despite his graying hair, his
appearance was pleasing, his charming smile showing he'd kept most
of his teeth. "Gloucester and York are like yesterday's vegetables,
rotten to the core. You need not worry about them."

Henry chewed his lower lip. Someone was always squabbling
with someone else. "York is one of my most powerful magnates," he
said slowly, glancing at Marguerite. As such, perhaps he should begin
Marguerite's political education by talking about this cousin. "He
owns vast tracts of land in Wales, Ireland, and thirteen English
counties. He has inherited great wealth."

"You are his liege lord," said Marguerite.

"He could make difficulties," replied Henry.

"What difficulties? What could he do?"

"He could embarrass me," responded Henry, looking down and fiddling with his ring. "He and Gloucester together."

"What does *Gloucestre* have to do with this?"

Ah, the list of things Gloucester had to do with this. Gloucester was his uncle and was regent of England before Henry assumed his majority. He championed the war in France. But beyond that, how could he explain to his wife that the King of England had to consult with his magnates on matters of grave import? He heard de Beauchamp's voice: "Never forget, my lord King, to consult your magnates. Woe betide you if you do not. Your great-great-grandsire, King Edward III, was a master of consultative kingship, and he ruled this land peacefully for fifty years."

"Gloucester is York's mentor," said Somerset, his voice gradually making its way through the thicket of Henry's thoughts. "They are the best of friends. Gloucester has always championed the war in France. York backs him up."

"That may be so," said Marguerite. "But it doesn't mean you can go back on your word." She knelt before Henry, taking his large hand between her two small ones. "My dear lord, you must sign. Can you not see that?"

Henry patted her hand as he gazed into the middle distance. He really needed to explain these things to her, but the hour of nones was approaching, and he must go to chapel. Afterward, he expected a visitor from Cambridge University to talk about his new college. Four years ago, Henry had laid the foundation stone for a royal college dedicated to Our Lady and Saint Nicholas, and he was most anxious to choose the provost and the twelve impoverished students who would study there. Henry had been pleased with his idea of having twelve students because it was the number of Christ's apostles, but should he increase it? Education was so important, and there were so many impoverished young men who would benefit. Seventy would be a goodly number, for it was the number of early evangelists chosen by Our Lord Jesus himself—

Dimly, Henry became aware of a dull and fiery light. He sat up in his chair. Had he gone to hell? Surely not; he didn't remember dying. He looked up to see Cardinal Beaufort standing before him, his red robes vibrating against the gathering winter darkness. Now well into his seventies, Cardinal Beaufort supported himself by leaning on a stick. Henry motioned him to sit.

"In the matter of your marriage treaty," said the Cardinal, "I can only advise you to abide by its terms. If you do not sign, you will be breaking your oath, and you will ruin your reputation."

"And mine," said Marguerite from her seat on a low stool by the king.

The cardinal bowed. "And your reputation, of course, my dear lady."

Henry stared at the floor. Where was Somerset? Hadn't he been here? And when had Cardinal Beaufort arrived? How much time had passed since Marguerite had started talking to him about Maine and Anjou? Was it hours or days?

The cardinal beckoned, and one of his clerks came forward with the parchment. He dipped the pen in ink and held it out for the king.

Henry looked away. He wanted more time to think. The situation was complex.

"Sign it!" shrieked Marguerite.

Henry jumped. The cardinal raised his hand. "My daughter—"

"Sign it! Sign it!" she screamed at the top of her voice. She lunged toward Henry, snatched the quill from the clerk's fingers, wrapped Henry's fingers around it, and started to guide the movement of the pen to form a signature.

Henry sat passively, fascinated by her energy. It emanated from her in waves, like narrow golden haloes. Henry never felt energetic, except when he was consulting with scholars. Recently, he'd had the idea of establishing several grammar schools around the country, so that poor boys could be educated—

Cardinal Beaufort rose. "You cannot do that, my daughter. It is not legal by the laws of England. You must wait and possess your soul in patience."

Marguerite flung the pen down and jabbed her finger at King Henry. "You don't care what this does to me or my reputation. You sit there like a larded duck and do nothing. Meanwhile, my father and uncle are left wondering what kind of man is this Harry of England that can't even keep his word." She sank onto the floor, sobbing, burying her face in her hands.

I don't sit here, thought King Henry. I am filled with thoughts and ideas. Haven't I explained this to you, my dearest? He put out his hand to touch her pretty hair, but she had gone. He drifted into a sea of disconnected thoughts and images. When he came to, he saw the face of the French ambassador looming before him.

Marguerite lifted her well-defined chin and turned to Henry. "I have here a letter to the King of France in which you give a solemn undertaking to cede the territories of Maine and Anjou to my father King Réné, by the thirtieth of April of next year." She laid the parchment in front of him.

Henry looked away. Now, where was he? It took him such a long time to get through his thoughts—

"You are doing this to please Charles VII, the King of France, at the request of your wife," remarked Marguerite as she dipped the pen in ink and held it out to him.

Henry looked at her. She had a dimple on her cheek.

"Please, my lord," she said sweetly. "For the love you bear me."

Love. That was the word. How he loved his wife. And she wanted him to sign this document. Aye. It was the only way he could show her that he loved her until he plucked up enough courage to take her to his bed. He picked up the pen and slowly signed his name.

Marguerite clapped her hands.

Silence descended. The next thing he knew, his wife was kissing his cheek. "Thank you, my most redoubted lord," she murmured.

Henry sank back in his chair, pleased that she was happy. Now, who should explain English customs to her?

CHAPTER 18

Eltham Palace, Greenwich, London
April 1446

I t is beautiful in London, my lady, at the queen's gardens in Eltham with the flowers so fresh after a shower," began Jenet. "Were there any celebrations? It's now a year since King Henry married."

"There was a service of thanksgiving held in their private chapel. As soon as it ended, the queen asked my lord to walk with her in the gardens. My heart sank, for you know how the Queen is, she never keeps still—"

Cecylee had sent Jenet to spy on Richard. Well, perhaps that was rather a dramatic way of putting it, but just as she was about to give birth to her seventh child, a message came from the Queen asking Richard to visit her at Eltham on a matter of some importance. Richard did not know what the Queen wanted, and Cecylee could not go with him. She instructed Jenet to go.

Cecylee gave Jenet a long list of things needed from London for the new baby's christening to provide subterfuge. But privately, she instructed Jenet to wear nondescript clothing, not pretty hand-me-downs, to keep her head down, and to speak only English, hoping that Richard wouldn't recognize her when she followed him through the streets of London.

"After the queen asked my lord husband to walk in the gardens, were you able to keep up with them?" she asked.

"Fortunately, my lord wanted to sit. He looked tired."

Jenet paused, and Cecylee nodded.

So let me tell you what happens next, my lady. The place where my lord and the queen sat is not far from the stables, so I was able to go around a corner out of sight but near enough to listen.

"I am so glad you could come," says the queen in her high-pitched, bell-like voice.

Holy Mother be thanked, I thought, it will be easy enough to hear everything she has to say.

"I understand your wife is about to birth your child."

"Yes, Your Grace," says my lord. "If she is a girl, the duchess and I would like to name her 'Margaret' after you. Of course, with your permission."

The queen clapped her hands together. "Another Margot!" she exclaimed. Then she got up and started pacing. "I have another matter I would discuss with you. You know, my lord, that one of the provisions of the Treaty of Tours is that the truce holds until July 1446?"

"Indeed, my lady."

"The King of France and I wish to bind together the royal houses of France and England. So, we propose to you un marriage between his daughter Madeleine de Valois and your eldest son."

There was a long pause, and it seemed to go on forever. Finally, my lord said, "You would like the Princess Madeleine to marry Edmund?" I know he said 'Edmund,' my lady, because his voice rises as he gets to the end of the sentence.

Next thing I heard was peals of laughter, followed by gasps of breath. Finally, the queen managed to say, "Surely, *mon duc,* you cannot have forgotten your own son's name. I mean your eldest son, your four-year-old son called Édouard – is it not so?"

Cecylee raised her hand to stop Jenet's narrative flow. Six-year-old Nan was tapping her arm. "Mama, they are arguing again. I have told Edward not to tease Edmund, but he just laughs at me and tells me to go away." She frowned. "Why can't they play nicely together?"

Cecylee felt her unborn baby kick as she laughed and kissed her daughter's soft cheek. Nan was going to be a wonderful mother. At six, she was already playing peacemaker to her brothers, trying to curb Edward's natural exuberance so that his much quieter brother got his fair share of playthings and attention.

"Do you see what I mean?" inquired Nan, pointing.

Cecylee glanced over to see four-year-old Edward stick his tongue out as he made a large hoop roll around the room by beating it with a stick while three-year-old Edmund stood there, balling his hands into fists and crying. She beckoned to Annette de Caux. "Take the children outside, for it is fine enough to play. And make Lord Edward share with his brother." Edward rushed off, laughing in his boisterous way, followed more sedately by Annette, who held Edmund's hand.

"May I stay and listen to Jenet's tale?" asked Nan.

"No, my child," replied Cecylee stroking Nan's dark brown hair, which coiled down her back in soft waves. "Jenet and I have something private to discuss. But when we're done, I shall tell you a story."

"You won't be long, Mama?" she called as she skipped away.

Cecylee shook her head, smiled, and turned back to Jenet.

The queen continued, "I mean your eldest son, your four-year-old called Édouard – is not so? Your French son, *monsieur le duc*." She pealed with laughter. "Not the other one, the three-year-old, what is his name? Edder-mund, so English. Oh, I cannot say it."

There was dead silence from milord, but the queen seemed not to notice. She laughed again and then continued, "You know, Édouard is so *charmant*. Don't you remember how he sang to me those songs last year? Why, he had not quite three years. And he looked so well, so handsome. Oh, I think he would be the husband for the little princess. She has only three years but is extremely pretty. I think that Édouard would want a pretty woman to be his wife, is it not so?"

There was another pause, and then I heard a deep intake of breath. "This is a great honor, Your Grace," my lord said, spacing out each word slowly. "But I must give a little thought to it. Edward is only four years old." His voice trailed off.

The next thing I noticed, milord was walking right past me. He disappeared in the direction of the river. I peeped around the corner to see the queen raise her eyebrows.

"This marriage has the backing of Suffolk," she called after him.

But my lord seemed not to hear.

The queen lifted her elegant little shoulders in a shrug and turned to go indoors. However, she caught sight of me and frowned. I made a bob, as if I'm an ignorant wench who's never seen the queen before and mumbled in English, as your ladyship instructed. She relaxed and walked off. Obviously, I can't have understood a word she said since she and my lord have been speaking French.

As soon as she was gone, I ran after my lord, keeping a distance. He went to the river, where some women were spreading out their washing to dry. There's a pile of wet clothing that needs attending to. So, I set to and lay it out on the bushes. It is indeed a fine day.

Meanwhile, my lord stormed up and down on the strand, saying to himself, "Edmund, Edmund, I want you to be my heir."

He was very loud, my lady. The folk by the riverside, the women with their washing, the fishermen, the tavern keeper, the barmaids, they all gaped, but one look at his fine clothing and aristocratic bearing, and they left him alone. Fortunately, he was ranting and raving in French, so they couldn't have understood him.

I edged closer, for he was muttering to himself now. "What can I give my son? What can I give my son?" I heard him swearing under his breath; he even called the queen something I should not like to repeat. Then he struck his fists together and roared, "By Our Lady, how these women torment me." He drew his sword and started whacking at the trees, hedges, weeds, anything that happened to be near.

Everyone edged back.

"She told me who my eldest son was! I know who my eldest son is, but she had the temerity to tell me who my own son is!" He worked himself into quite a lather by now.

The groom appeared with my lord's palfrey, but he took one look at him and hesitated. I signal for him to wait.

"I have it!" my lord exclaimed, sheathing his sword and panting hard. "I will make Edmund Earl of Rutland. That title belonged to the first Duke of York's heir, and it carries prestige. It will be my way of letting everyone know that Edmund is my true heir. I will have to give that bastard something, however, to prevent gossip." He paced up and down, rubbing his forked beard. "If I give that bastard the title Earl of March, it will remind everyone of that troublemaker, the last Earl of March, who plotted against King Henry V and succeeded in having my father executed." He struck one hand against the other and gave a harsh bark of laughter. "My wife will have to agree; she'll have no choice." Suddenly, he noticed the groom standing there with his horse. He stopped dead, got onto his horse, and thundered off. We didn't see him for the rest of the day.

Jenet paused to help Cecylee ease a cushion behind her back. She was so large now she could scarcely move. She motioned for Jenet to continue.

"I am loath to tell you, my lady, in your condition."

"I want to know!" snapped Cecylee.

Jenet opened a jar of ointment and massaged Cecylee's feet.

I spent the next several days going to Cheapside, to visit the drapers, silversmiths, and haberdashers, so that I could get everything to furnish the new baby's christening. On the evening of the fifth day, I am just returning to our lodgings when the groom mentions that an unnamed visitor was ushered into the duke's private chamber.

I think quickly. It is nigh on vespers, the evening is drawing in, and my lord has not yet returned. I go to the kitchen and bribe one of the cooks to let me wear a cap and a sack apron so that I look like a humble kitchen maid.

I pick up a tray of beer and make my way up the stairs. Keeping my face bent, I try out the local London accent on a dark-haired lady dressed in a red riding habit, sitting in a carved chair by the fireplace.

She shoots me a sharp glance and then returns to her thoughts. What can Duke Richard be doing with her?

Next thing, I hear a thud of heavy steps and my lord shouting for his bath. I use the time to look quickly around the room for a suitable hiding place, mending the fire as I do so. Dipping a curtsey to the lady's back, I make my way to a small door leading to a spiral staircase that goes back down to the kitchens. I close the door without shutting it, wedging some material from my skirts into it so that it stays open a crack. Balancing the tray on my knees, I sit and wait.

Eventually, my lord enters. I hear him whistling to himself as he enters the room, and then the sound ceases abruptly. Perhaps he's been stopped dead in his tracks with astonishment.

A chair scrapes back. "My lord of York. I wanted a word with you about—a private matter."

My lord does not reply at first. He pours himself some beer and then sits. "Yes?" His tone is terse, like that of a military commander.

"I bring you important news, for the which you will have cause to thank me."

My lord snorts, taking a gulp of beer.

"Your wife, Lady Cecylee—"

"What about my wife?"

"She is unusually broad-minded for such a great lady in her choice of companions."

"My wife is my private matter," says my lord.

"You are a great military man, Duke Richard," replies the lady sweetly. "But you have one weakness: your lovely wife. She has you wrapped around her little finger, doesn't she?"

The silence is taut.

"I think you should know who Lady Cecylee's lover was. He was the son of a blacksmith."

"No!" roars my lord. "He was a nobleman of the House of Savoy!"

"He pretended to be the Duke of Savoy's son, but he was not. He was only a blacksmith's son."

"How do you know that?" shouts Duke Richard.

154

"He came from the village of Blay, near Bayeux in Normandy. There is a merchant from Bayeux, at this very moment, awaiting you in the Blue Swan in the village of Greenwich. He knows her lover's family. Go you there, my lord. You will find that I tell you true."

Jenet paused and looked down. Cecylee tapped her on the arm. Jenet sighed.

My lord thrust the door open and shouted for his horse. He banged downstairs, each footfall getting fainter with each descending step. Shortly afterward, the sound of galloping hooves floated up through the open window.

My lord didn't return until dawn.

A while after the duke left, the door to the back stairway opened, and the lady stood there, smiling down at me. It was Lady Lisette, your brother's wife.

The tray of beer glasses rattled on my knees.

"Blaybourne," she snorted. "What a stupid name. It's obvious it is made up." She signaled for me to stand and walked ahead of me back into the room.

I followed her, head held high, and put the tray down on a table.

"As your lady's sister," Lady Lisette said to me, "I made it my business to find out more about her lover. I made some inquiries and discovered that there was a village named Blay near Bayeux. I sent my personal servant there, and he found Blaybourne's brother. He had an interesting tale to tell."

"My lady," I said. "Forgive my boldness, but what you did was not well done. It was not kind."

She slapped me. "Hussy!" she snapped. "Why shouldn't Lady Cecylee pay for her sins? She knows she's a sinner! Why, she's desperate enough to send her maid to spy on her own husband!" She laughed shrilly.

I rubbed my cheek.

She stared at me for a moment and then smiled: "Perhaps you should warn your lady."

CHAPTER 19

Placentia Palace, Greenwich, London
April 28th, 1446

Richard did not get much sleep for the next several days. Bad enough to have taken a lover—every time Richard imagined her in someone else's arms, his stomach churned. But to have lied? To have slept with a peasant?

A wine cup banging on the table pulled him out of his thoughts. As he looked at it, the ruby wine sloshed out, the cup skidded, and it fell to the ground with a clatter.

A servant scurried out to clear the mess, but Gloucester waved him away, went to his fireplace, and pounded the hood with his fist. "I don't believe it!" he roared.

Richard, Duke of York, sank back in his chair and wiped his face with the back of his hand.

A servant materialized with a bowl of water and a napkin for washing his face and hands, while another poured a full goblet of Gloucester's best claret. Richard downed his goblet and signaled for another. He nodded for the messenger to leave. He'd forgotten about this latest piece of treachery; he'd been so preoccupied with Cecylee. Really, he sometimes felt he barely knew his own wife.

Gloucester turned. "I can scarcely believe the king would do this. The English people won't abide it. We must go to court at once and learn the truth of the matter."

"What is this I hear about Maine and Anjou?" roared Gloucester, striding into the king's presence chamber, followed by York. He made only the most perfunctory of bows.

King Henry shrank into the cushions of his elaborately carved chair.

Queen Marguerite, however, rose from her low stool and stood tall, arms folded. "They belong to my father. It is part of the marriage agreement, is that not so, my dearest?" She turned to Henry.

"Yes," murmured Henry, moistening his lips with his tongue.

"It can't be true," said York, gazing at the King, who steadfastly refused to look him in the eye.

"It is," said Marguerite, lifting her chin. "My lord the king has solemnly promised the King of France that he will return these territories to my father by the thirtieth day of April."

"The thirtieth day of April?" stormed Gloucester. "You mean in two days?"

Marguerite nodded.

Gloucester paled.

"Does the council know of this?" asked Richard.

King Henry stared at the floor.

"What about the governors of Maine and Anjou?"

King Henry twisted his ring.

"You mean to say that you arranged this—these provisions of the treaty and told no-one?" roared Gloucester. "Not the council, not the governors, not the magnates, and least of all me?"

158

There was silence. As Richard studied the king, he saw the jaw twitch. Of course. This idea was too stupid, even for King Henry. "Suffolk knew, didn't he?" said Richard.

"And Cardinal Beaufort!" spat Gloucester.

"The Cardinal is a man of the church," said Marguerite. "You should not abuse—"

"This is absolutely breathtaking," shouted Gloucester. "I can't believe you would be so stupid. What? Give back the territories that we won under your glorious father? It can't be true!"

"It is," said Marguerite, coming forward, her eyes flashing. "And you, my lord, should mind your manners around the king."

"I have never heard of such addle-pated goings-on in all my days," shouted Gloucester. "You must be out of your mind!" He stormed off, banging the door behind him.

"Sire," said Richard, bowing low. "This is a most ill-conceived piece of diplomacy. Mark my words, you will live to regret it." He hurried after Gloucester.

Richard urged his palfrey into a gallop so that he could catch up with Gloucester, riding east to the city. What is he going to do now, thought Richard, following Gloucester along the Strand towards Saint Paul's Cathedral. As soon as they got to the churchyard, Gloucester vaulted off his horse, threw his reins to a groom, and mounted the steps of Saint Paul's Cross.

Richard followed.

The Londoners were enjoying themselves in the spring sunshine, it being that time of day after the main meal when people come out to pay visits, shop, and enjoy a fine afternoon stroll. In one corner of Saint Paul's churchyard, a number of well-dressed citizens fingered the leather covers and the crisp pages of those new-fangled printed books.

There were goldsmiths and silversmiths. There was a woman selling
spring flowers. There was even a horse merchant, whose restless
charges stamped their feet, tossed their heads, and added a pungent
odor to the scene.

Just outside the door of the church stood a group of London
merchants. The soft leather of their boots and gloves displayed their
wealth, as did the exotic and colorful material of their robes, their
jewel-encrusted collars, and the many rings on their fingers. They
were outdone only by their wives, who crammed as many necklaces,
rings, and brooches as possible onto their costumes. Richard bowed
to one beldame passing by. She had so much cloth in her headdress,
her husband must belong to the clothier's guild.

As Gloucester arrived at Saint Paul's Cross, the people
immediately began to gather, separating Richard from his mentor.
"Good Duke Humphrey!" they shouted. "'Tis Good Duke
Humphrey!"

Gloucester bowed. A tapster from a nearby alehouse ran up to
hand him a mug of ale.

He looks years younger, thought Richard, glancing at his friend
basking in the approval of the crowd. How ironic that it is the people
of England who respect him, not his aristocratic peers.

The crowd gathered around Saint Paul's Cross, buzzing with
excited anticipation as the horses neighed.

"I wonder what he's got to say," said the bookseller.

"I've never seen anything like it," said the flower seller. "Most of
them fancy people never bother with the likes of us."

"Duke Humphrey, he's good," said the horse merchant. "He talks
to us. Tells us what's going on."

"He's become a champion of good governance," said a well-
dressed gentleman.

Duke Humphrey held up a hand, and the crowd fell silent.

"My friends, I have come here today to tell you about a piece of
treachery. Nay, I can scarce believe it myself, and if any of you had
told me this, I would think I had had a bad hangover from the night
before."

Some youngsters in the crowd erupted into laughter. Their elders grew watchful and silent.

Richard accepted a tankard of beer and stood by Gloucester. He looked at the faces tilted up before him. They don't seem overawed, he thought, sipping his beer. This country is not like France, where the common people grovel before the aristocrats. These people seem to know that their voices count for something.

Gloucester raised his hand again. "Would you believe it, but in return for Margaret of Anjou, the Earl of Suffolk negotiated a marriage settlement in which we give away Maine and Anjou to the French."

The crowd recoiled. "No!" they shouted.

Richard grew uneasy.

"Yes, good people. Yes: I am sorry to tell you so, but there it is."

"What does this mean for trade, sir?" asked a man, a fashionably dressed woman on his arm.

"You lose the revenues from the counties of Maine and Anjou," replied Duke Humphrey. "You lose revenues from wine."

"Is our wine trade going to dry up?" asked one merchant with a red nose.

"Not unless we lose Bordeaux. So far, we are just talking about Maine and Anjou."

The crowd responded with a harsh bark of laughter.

"But I can tell you," continued Gloucester, "that the loss of Maine and Anjou means the loss of goodly fruit."

"No more pears!" exclaimed a young girl with golden hair hanging out from an upstairs window. "But that's my favorite fruit." Her high voice sailed over the noise of the crowd.

"No more Anjou pears, madam," said Gloucester sweeping her a low bow.

"Jacinda, do not shout out of the window. It is not ladylike." A woman with an elaborate horned headdress appeared and gently pulled the child away. "Please accept my apologies, my lord Duke," she called down. "She is very free."

"Do not worry, madam," said Gloucester bowing again with a flourish. "You have a charming daughter."

Applause and cheers greeted this remark.

"What about the landowners of Maine and Anjou, my lord?" asked a merchant dressed in fine crimson silk, rubies winking from the collar around his neck. "What about their lands and holdings?"

"A good question." Gloucester held up his hand to still the whispers and murmurings of the crowd. "They will be obliged to give up their lands. They will be forced to come home with nothing and start afresh."

The crowd erupted into boos and murmurs, which grew louder. Richard looked at his friend.

"I see you look puzzled, good people," remarked Gloucester, as the restless crowd grew silent. "Let me spell out the terms of the Treaty of Tours by which our king gained a wife. By this treaty, we give up Maine and Anjou. In return, we get exactly—nothing. That's right. Nothing. The queen did not even bring a dowry with her. Can you believe it? Can you believe that Suffolk would be so stupid, so asinine, so treacherous, as to throw away something that we gained in a fair fight for nothing in return?"

"No!"

Their roar threw Richard backward. He moved closer to Gloucester. "They're getting upset," he hissed.

Gloucester ignored him. "And all for a queen worth not ten marks," he remarked, holding up his tankard of ale. "I feel personally betrayed."

"We are betrayed!" roared the crowd. "A queen worth not ten marks!" They turned and hurried down Ludgate Hill in the direction of Westminster, shouting as they went.

"What are they going to do?" asked Richard.

Gloucester chuckled. "They are going to Westminster Palace to shout insults at the queen."

CHAPTER 20

The Herber, The Strand, London
February 1447

Nine months later, Humphrey, Duke of Gloucester, was dead. His great friend Abbot Whethamstead averred that he had died of natural causes, but my lady queen had put him under house arrest and charged him with treason on the grounds that he had spread rumors that Suffolk was her lover.

Richard dropped into a seat by the fire. "This is such a shock," he murmured. "I feel as if my sword arm has been cut off."

"Indeed." Salisbury sighed heavily as he took the seat opposite.

Richard stroked his forked beard and narrowed his eyes. "I like not the sound of this. It seems a trivial reason to arrest someone for spreading gossip. And Gloucester was a royal duke. He must have thought he was untouchable."

"One good thing to come out of this sorry matter is that you become heir presumptive," remarked Salisbury, "until the queen bears a son."

"Or until the king makes Somerset his heir."

Salisbury shook his head. "You have a point there, my friend. Without Gloucester, you have no one close to you on the king's council. What will you do?"

Richard sagged in his seat, his eyes on the flames that flickered before him. Life seemed as dark as the shadows of this room. Salisbury was right. He was completely alone. How was he going to protect Cecylee and their children? Nan was now seven years old. Edmund was nearly four, Beth was nearly three, and Margaret was going to have her first birthday in May. Then there was Cecylee's bastard son, who was rising five. "I have been away in Normandy these four years. Others have the king's ear."

"You have three daughters," remarked Salisbury. "You will have to marry them off."

"They are so young," sighed Richard. "Cecylee would never agree to it."

"Of course, Cis is not going to agree to it. But you have to focus on the larger picture. Who's going to champion Gloucester's cause of good governance if not you? Who's going to speak out for the common folk, if not you? Who's going to inherit Gloucester's political mantle, if not you? But enemies lurk in the shadows."

"True enough," said Richard, fingering his beard. "I'll have to be more temperate than Gloucester."

"Indeed. He was known for his fiery temper. But you must also protect your family. Your sons are not old enough to fight."

"True," said Richard, thinning his lips. "And Fotheringhay is not well defended. Perhaps I should send them to Ludlow, which can withstand a siege."

Salisbury rose and clapped him on the back. "A good thought. It will keep them out of the way. Ludlow is a good hundred miles from London, so they'll not easily be taken hostage. If you put your best men on the garrison, they will be safe."

Richard nodded somberly.

"And you must think of forming alliances with those who have the king's ear. They would make suitable husbands for your daughters. There's Suffolk's heir, John."

"No, no. His grandsire was but a merchant from Hull."

"He's wealthy and powerful. And his wife is kin."

"True, but I'd have to be desperate to marry my daughter into that family."

"Stafford's heir and Northumberland's heir are already married. So is Shrewsbury's heir. That leaves only the Tudors. They are of a suitable age. Edmund Tudor is turning seventeen, and his brother Jasper is sixteen."

"But they are loyal to the king, their half-brother," said Richard. "It is not likely I can persuade them to my cause."

"What about Exeter's heir? He is the same age as Edmund Tudor."

Richard looked up. "Do you think Exeter would be willing to follow me?"

"Yes. Granted, he has strong ties to the throne. But his ties are those of blood, not of dependency. He's not like the Tudors, who owe everything to their half-brother, the King. Everyone in Exeter's family was born the right side of the sheets."

Richard touched his gold collar with the spear-pointed diamond, which he'd recovered once the king had paid the debt.

"If you take my advice, you'll see about it now," said Salisbury, "before someone else comes along."

Richard grimaced. "Your advice is sound, my friend. My fear is that it will grieve Cecylee greatly."

Salisbury smiled as he shook his head at Richard. "My sister is a woman. And women are not logical about such things. You should not worry overmuch about her reaction. She'll get used to it."

"Cecylee is breeding again. I am loath to upset her."

"But this is an opportunity for your advancement. Surely you see that? You shouldn't throw it away because of the whims of a foolish woman. Even though she is my sister, and I love her dearly."

CHAPTER 21

Fotheringhay Castle, Northamptonshire
March 1447

Richard held a special ceremony for Edmund to invest him with the title Earl of Rutland, while Cecylee's son Edward was allowed only to style himself the Earl of March, there being no formal ceremony for him. Naturally, nothing came of the match that Queen Marguerite proposed between Edward and the French princess.

Cecylee was warned by these actions that Richard was seriously displeased. But he had yet to do his worst. Not more than a month passed before he decreed that both children—then aged four and three—should be sent off to live at Ludlow Castle, deep in the Mortimer lands on the Welsh marches. They were to have their own household and learn the manly arts of war.

Then Richard wasted no time in arranging a marriage between the Duke of Exeter's heir and their eldest daughter Nan.

"Not Nan! She is a child! She has but six years."

"The match is a good one. The Hollands have royal blood flowing through their veins."

"But what kind of a person is Henry Holland?" Cecylee bunched up the rich ruby fabric of her new velvet gown. "Though he's only sixteen, I like not what I hear of him. He's already gaining a reputation for cruelty, for riding his horses too hard, for tormenting his dogs. His people seem terrified of him."

Richard tightened his jaw.

She paced up and down, her skirts swishing in the rushes. She stopped in front of Richard. "I cannot believe you would do this. It is the height of folly to put Nan in his mercy."

He took her by the shoulders. His fingers closed into a vise-like grip. "Cis: You are fond of gossip. Holland will become Duke of Exeter when his father dies. He is as close to the throne as I am. This is a splendid match."

"It is not a splendid match!" she said hotly, enunciating each word. "You are taking Nan away from me to folk she does not know. Holland's mother has been dead these fourteen years. His second wife has been dead for eight years. There will be no ladies to take care of her. And she will become a stranger to her brothers and sisters. You have encouraged those greedy Hollands, allowed them to talk you into this marriage. They will have the revenues from all the lands that Nan will bring as her dowry now."

A vein throbbed near his temple. He came closer and snapped, "How dare you lecture me on my duties as a father when you so forgot yourself as to lower yourself with an archer."

She backed away.

"You lied to me, Cis!" He thrust his face into hers. "You didn't tell me your son was a low-born bastard, now did you? I would have sent him away if I'd known to be brought up by humble folk."

She clenched her hands. It had never occurred to her that Richard might think she'd deliberately tricked him. She took a step forward. "He was extremely well educated. He studied at university. He had pleasing manners."

"He was a peasant!" roared Richard. He took her by the shoulders and shook her. "Take hold of yourself, Cis, and stop making excuses. You slept with a peasant."

"But Our Lord and Savior was not ashamed to go amongst peasants, so why should I—"

Richard let go, went to the door of the chamber, and turned. "I need Exeter's support," he spat. "I have plans for the House of York. Nan is to marry Holland now, and I'll have no more said against it."

Before Cecylee could open her mouth to reply, he stalked out.

For the marriage feast, she dressed Nan in a gown of green silk embroidered in silver thread, complete with matching cap, under which Nan's hair fell down in long brown waves. Cecylee embroidered Nan's gown herself, stitching Anne, Duchesse of Exeter around the hem as if the monotony of the embroidery could somehow soothe her feelings.

At length, the feasting came to an end, and it was time for Nan to leave. Cecylee held her hand as they took the stairs for the last time to the courtyard where grooms waited with the horses and a litter for Nan, for she was too young to ride so many miles on horseback.

"Goodbye, my sweetest child," she murmured, stooping to kiss Nan's upturned cheeks. She squeezed Nan's fingers gently. "May God bless and keep you."

Nan's eyes grew round. "Mama, where am I going?"

"You are going to Exeter, to be with your new husband."

"But you're coming with me, are you not, Mama?"

Cecylee slowly sank to her knees before the tiny form and took Nan into her arms. She clung tightly and wept. It was a foolish thing to do, but she could not help herself.

Nan started to wail. "Mama. Don't let them take me! I'll be good, I promise. I don't want to go."

Richard walked up, his face thunderous. "Cis!" he snapped. "What are you doing? Why are you upsetting the child?"

She rose shakily to her feet, fumbling for her handkerchief.

Exeter came up behind Richard and glared. "Come now, child," he said roughly. "Leave off your crying. Be a good girl and get into that litter."

Nan edged towards her mother.

Cecylee's hand instinctively curved around the tiny fingers.

"I won't," said Nan and stamped her foot.

Cecylee's lips curved in agreement.

Richard clenched his jaw and, without a word, grabbed Nan. He hoisted her up and deposited her in the litter. The curtains closed.

"Mamaaaa!" she wailed, her voice muffled by the curtains. "Mama! Mama!"

Exeter got onto his horse, followed by his son Henry Holland, Nan's new husband. He signaled, and the whole procession moved off, several knights riding alongside the closed litter.

"Mama! Mama! Mama!"

The wailing voice grew fainter and fainter as the entourage disappeared into the darkness of the oncoming night. Cecylee buried her face in her hands and sobbed. She did so right in front of the servants; it was beyond her power to do anything else.

At length, she felt herself being gently led away. She threw herself onto her bed and howled.

She came to with a throbbing headache and eyes that were sore from weeping.

"There now, my lady, that'll do you good." Jenet opened the bed curtains and handed her a potion of her own making. "It contains valerian root and chamomile flowers."

Cecylee rose from the bed. "I cannot go on. When will I see her again?"

"You are being sorely tried, my lady. But you must make your peace with it."

"Must?"

Jenet shrugged. "Well, you tell me, my lady. Do you have a choice?"

Cecylee sank onto the window seat. "I had little idea marriage would be like this."

"But you knew women lose their legal rights when they marry."

"It's so easy for you. You have more rights than I. You, at least, can choose your husband. I had no choice. Nan has no choice. I wish I were a peasant."

"Sip some of this, my lady, please. It will do you a power of good. You must keep up your strength for the baby that's coming."

At those words, Cecylee drank some of the valerian and chamomile concoction. "Do I look dreadful?"

"Of course, you do. Your husband has been cruel to you."

She drained the rest of the cup. "He's angry with me."

"I know, my lady. You've wounded his pride and his masculine vanity."

Cecylee grimaced as she leaned back against the window seat. Joan, Nan, Henry, Edward, Edmund, Beth, Margaret. She counted them like beads on a string. This baby was growing large, and her back was beginning to feel its weight. If he was a son, she hoped that Richard would allow her to call him William after her brother Lord Fauconberg. "My marriage is past mending."

"I wouldn't say that, my lady. Duke Richard has not banished you. He spends a great deal of time in your company."

"But he sends my children away." Her eyelids started to droop. "I know I'm foolish about my children," she murmured. "But I cannot help myself."

"That is one of the best things about you, my lady," said Jenet taking the cup away and unlacing her gown. "How you love your children. 'Tis a pleasure to see."

CHAPTER 22

Dublin, Ireland
Late Summer 1450

A messenger from London."

Duchess Cecylee and Duke Richard, in the middle of holding their daily audiences in the great hall of Dublin Castle, looked to the far side of the crowd. As the travel-stained figure wearily knelt before them, Cecylee straightened in her seat. It was nearly three years since Nan had been married off to Exeter, and during that time, Cecylee hadn't seen or heard of her daughter. Her numerous pregnancies made it impossible to travel the two hundred and fifty miles between Fotheringhay and Exeter. Cecylee counted out her beads on a string: Joan, Nan, Henry, Edward, Edmund, Beth, Margaret, William, John, George. And so, Cecylee wrote to Nan. Her letters had been returned unopened. When Cecylee begged Richard to allow Jenet to visit, he'd refused. He would never forgive her for having taken a lover. Ever since, Cecylee sought out anyone who could give her news of her daughter.

"How go affairs in France?" asked Richard, motioning the messenger to rise.

"Not well, my lord Duke," he replied, bowing. "My lord of Somerset has handed Caen over to the French."

Richard recoiled. "What did you say?"

The messenger repeated it.

Richard shot out of his chair. "This is madness!" he stormed. "This means the end of English rule in Normandy!" He called for a scribe and dictated a letter to the King of England.

While Richard was preoccupied, Cecylee turned to the messenger: "Have you news of my daughter the Duchess of Exeter?"

The messenger shook his head.

"Find out what you can," whispered Cecylee, slipping him a sovereign.

A month later, he reappeared. "His Grace the King bowed to your wishes and summoned parliament," he began. "But after hearing Somerset's explanation, he decided to make him Constable of England."

Richard stared at him, the color draining out of his face.

Cecylee put her hand over Richard's. Turning to the messenger, she inquired, "What do the people say about this?"

The messenger bowed. "They murmur that Somerset must be the queen's lover, madam."

Cecylee flinched, but Richard laughed. "Small wonder they think that," he said. "Why else make Somerset Constable of England? I've never heard of rewarding someone for bad judgment. The queen must have made a special request. I must go home."

"My lord?" Cecylee looked searchingly into his face.

"Aye, 'tis time. While I struggle here to end the squabbles in Ireland, I see England spiral downwards into chaos. The people need me."

"But don't you need permission of the king?" said Cecylee, feeling the baby kick. In a few months, she would present Richard with another child.

Richard gave a harsh bark of laughter. "I fear matters have gone beyond that point. I must leave, and leave now," he replied, kissing her on the cheek.

And so, in the space of a few hours, Richard saddled up and left, taking the messenger and many others with him. It was not until the messenger had left that Cecylee realized she'd not had a chance to ask him about Nan.

Several days later, the messenger returned and was ushered into the solar of Dublin Castle, where Cecylee was packing up her gowns and jewels, surrounded by her women and children, for Richard had instructed his wife to make all haste in leaving Ireland. Baby George was suckling his wet-nurse, four-year-old Margaret was playing with Jenet, while seven-year-old Beth kept close to her mother. Though Beth was now the same age as Nan had been at her marriage, thankfully, her father had said nothing about marrying her off. Cecylee hoped that the deteriorating situation in England would keep him occupied for many moons to come. She motioned for the messenger to rise. "How is my lord?"

"In good health and spirits, my lady," replied the messenger, bowing. "He successfully crossed to Wales and rode to Ludlow. There, he mustered a force of four thousand men and marched towards London. He is in London now, seeking an audience with the king."

Cecylee sighed and crossed herself, praying that common sense would prevail and that Richard would be safe. Nothing had gone right for him in recent years. The queen, fearing him, blocked all of his attempts to participate in government. Instead of making use of his considerable talents, she'd appointed York to be the king's lieutenant in Ireland. The position sounded like a great honor, but Richard and Cecylee were both painfully aware that the queen had banished him from London.

"Have you news of my daughter, the Duchess of Exeter?"

The messenger hesitated and looked at the floor.

"You heard something?"

He coughed. "Yes, my lady. But nothing good, I am afraid."

"Tell me," said Cecylee, motioning Annette to take Beth and the other children away.

"I happened to have business in that part of the country, and so I rode over to Exeter Castle. It is a fine fortress, tucked into one corner of the City of Exeter, and the Duke of Exeter lives in a fine mansion within, so I am told."

"You did not go into the castle yourself?"

"Alas, no, madam. I was turned away at the gate. But it was nighttime, and there was a full moon, so I let my horse linger nearby and—" He ran his tongue over his lips.

Cecylee felt her unborn baby kick as she sank into her seat. "And what?" she whispered.

"I swear I could hear a cry coming from the castle."

"A cry? What do you mean?"

The messenger was silent.

She rose. "I insist that you tell me."

"It sounded like someone screaming."

CHAPTER 23

London
November 1450

Richard pulled his palfrey to a halt and turned his head at the clarion call. There it came again and again. As the notes died away, Richard's ear caught the thunder of hooves, and around a bend in the road came a large group of riders bearing the badge of the lion. John de Mowbray, Duke of Norfolk, had arrived as promised on the outskirts of London.

"Well met, nephew Norfolk." York clasped hands with his powerful nephew-in-law, the son of Cecylee's sister Cath. As premier Duke of the Realm, Norfolk's opinion counted.

"How is your lady wife?"

"She is recovering from the birth of our son Thomas," replied Richard, nudging his horse into a trot beside Norfolk's. "The child is sickly, and Cecylee spends every waking hour nursing him."

The horses' breath rose up into steam in the chill November air. It was two months since Richard had hurried back from Ireland to confront his cousin over the mismanagement of affairs in France. Henry had bowed to York's wishes and summoned Parliament to meet in London on November sixth.

As the procession wound its way through the narrow streets of London, the people of London opened their upstairs windows to look down on them. These upper rooms jutted out over the lower ones and were so close in places that it was possible for two lovers on opposite sides of the street to hold hands. When the people saw York, they took up his cry: "A York! A York! A York!"

"I see you are popular with the people," murmured Norfolk. "How many men did you bring?"

"Three thousand."

"A goodly number. I brought a similar number myself." He motioned for one of his men to dismount and knock at the nearest house.

Presently, the casement window above was thrust open, and a dame with an elaborately starched white headdress, setting off her rosy cheeks, looked down on their company.

"I have no rooms, good sir," she said when Norfolk's man explained what he wanted. "This house and all of the surrounding ones are taken by men of my lord of Somerset's affinity."

"There's not a bed to be had between here and Whitechapel!" exclaimed another woman, opening the casement opposite. "London's an armed camp. Why every fellow who fancies he can wield a stick has come here."

A child scampered into the street. York pulled on the bit so savagely, his horse reared. He quickly brought it under control. The child ran away unharmed.

"Holy Mother, be blessed," said a dame, turning her head. "'Tis indeed my lord of York. Good e'en to you, sir." She dropped a low curtsey that made her head disappear below the sill of the open window. "May God prosper your cause."

York smiled and waved. "Did you hear what she said? I must find Somerset."

"Is that wise?"

"A York! A York!" chanted the people, thrusting open their casements and leaning over the procession.

"Garday loo!" shouted a maid as she prepared to heave a bucket of slops out of the window. "'Tis my lord of York," hissed her mistress. "Wait."

"Thank you, good madam," said Norfolk, inclining his head.

"Save your wastewater for Somerset!" shouted a voice across the way.

The crowd erupted into cheers and guffaws.

"We must do something about the money woes of this country," said Richard, pacing up and down.

"Certainly, my lord," replied Sir William Oldhall, picking up his pen. Richard had known Sir William for years, first as a councilor in Normandy, and latterly as his chamberlain. The House of Commons had demonstrated their support of York by recently electing Sir William to be their Speaker.

"The king's councilors are prepared to discuss fixing the income for the royal household," said Richard. "But we need to go further. I propose that we pass an Act of Resumption that returns the huge swaths of land the king has given away to his favorites for the past thirteen years."

Sir William stroked his beard.

Richard smiled. Sir William was a wealthy Norfolk landowner with powerful friends and relations. "Find out if public opinion would support this demand."

Sir William rose. "We should also get a promise from the king to restore law and order in the shires." He bowed and left.

"The seamstress has arrived with your gown," said Alainor, now Duchess of Somerset, curtseying low before the queen.

Marguerite motioned her friend to rise.

Alainor slowly straightened but would not meet the Queen's eye.

Marguerite sighed. Alainor had been so kind when she'd first come to England, lending her money so that she could pay her sailors. But as her relationship with the Duke of Somerset had grown closer, the friendship with his wife deteriorated.

Marguerite could not really blame her. Like most aristocratic ladies, Alainor had been married off as a child. But when her husband died, leaving her a widow at the age of twenty-three, she'd fallen in love with Somerset and married him secretly.

But recently, Queen Marguerite had turned to her dearest cousin Somerset. Her great friend, the Earl of Suffolk, had been murdered that spring, and the queen needed someone to take his place in her counsels and as leader of the Court Party. She and Somerset saw each other every day, and he was beginning to look at her—

Marguerite never allowed herself to criticize her husband. She placed him in a special category, for he was like no man she'd ever known. Every day, he devoted himself to his prayers and to his charities. He was the most kind-hearted and sweetest-tempered lord, denying her nothing. Except that he would not, could not, Marguerite corrected herself, give her a child after five years of marriage. And she so longed for a baby, not only for political reasons but for herself. If only she could have a son, York would be put in his place, for he would no longer be heir presumptive. And if not the king, then who? Marguerite smiled until her gaze landed on Alainor.

She bit her lip as her lady-in-waiting gently put the purple velvet gown embroidered in crimson thread over her head.

Alainor gave Marguerite her mirror and stood beside her to study the effect of the gown. It set off Marguerite's sculpted profile and made her look much older than her twenty-one years. Marguerite sighed as she studied her face in the mirror, noting a couple of lines around her mouth. "How old I look. Don't you think so, Alainor?"

Alainor, who was some twenty years older than the Queen, glanced at her mistress, then turned and gathered up the Queen's discarded gowns. Marguerite looked glorious, but she wasn't going to tell her that. She, too, had noticed the way her husband looked at the queen. "It is true you have not the freshness you had when first you came to this land five years ago," she said. "But you have been sorely tried, my lady. Especially this year."

Marguerite caught her friend's hand as she passed by. "You are so good to me, Alainor. I do not understand why."

Alainor reddened as she averted her face. She turned to the queen's dressing table and busied herself with clearing it, putting the stoppers back on the jars of rosewater, lavender water, and angelica water.

There was silence.

"How I miss Suffolk," sighed Marguerite.

"Have they apprehended the villains?"

"No, no. It is all York's doing. He is so powerful he can do as he pleases. All he wants is to create trouble for me and my most redoubted lord, the king."

"The government of this country should not ignore the people of England!" exclaimed York.

The cheering was so loud it nearly lifted off the hammer-beam roof of Westminster Hall. On that cold and chilly November morning, the temperature inside the hall rose as more and more people squeezed in to hear what York was saying. Assembled at one end of the hall were the great magnates of the land at the high table on the dais. Around the walls and packed several men deep stood the men-at-arms with their quarterstaffs, their badges clearly showing their affinities.

Richard of York stood before the lords in front of the dais, half-turned to face the people who were crowding into the hall below. There was a little space between the steps that led down from the dais and the body of the hall. In the front row stood all the important citizens of London, including the lord mayor and his wife and several prominent merchants with their wives. Behind them were the people of London, looking expectantly at the almost stout figure with a forked beard pointing his finger at the lords on the dais.

"I tell you, the people make reasonable demands," continued Richard. "It is folly to tax them so heavily while royal favorites are richly rewarded. And not only that, these men - already bloated with wealth beyond the wildest dreams of any poor plowman or widow - do not have to pay taxes. Where is the sense in that? The country needs money, and so it should tax its richest citizens."

York's voice was drowned out in cheers.

"I ask this parliament to pass the Act of Resumption that requires royal favorites to return the land they have been given these past thirteen years so that the value of this land may be used to get this country out of financial ruin."

Nan's husband rose. "My lord of York, you have given a most interesting speech. But I don't think you can expect these lands to be returned. It would be like asking your lady wife to return a present you'd given her."

Exeter laughed, and the other lords laughed with him.

"I think we can dismiss these complaints," he continued. "They are trivial. What does an unwashed peasant know of land husbandry? I tell you these lands are in good hands, and they should remain so."

"You should not dismiss the concerns of the people so lightly," said York, reddening. He glared at Exeter. But Exeter ignored him.

"You should not be questioning the king's judgment," he remarked, smiling. "What makes you think you know better than our king?"

The hall buzzed like a hive of angry bees.

"What of the traitors?" bellowed someone.

"What about the loss of Normandy?" shouted another.

"Impeach Somerset!" cried a third.

At this, the men-at-arms providing protection for the noble families brandished weapons and shouted: "Give us Justice! Punish the Traitors! Give us Justice! Punish the traitors!"

Their voices echoed around that huge room, soaring up to the hammer-beams built in the time of Richard II and dropping down to the old stone walls built in the time of William II.

Richard of York pointed his finger at the lords. "I demand that you impeach Somerset. Now."

Marguerite bit her lip. From her chamber in Westminster Palace, she heard the roar of the crowd. No doubt, York stirred more trouble. She wished she were back in France. Her youth seemed so golden and faraway, a lost time that tugged at her heart. How could people who smelled so bad she wanted to retch, who went around with lice-infested hair, open boils, and unseemly rags, make things so difficult? Marguerite could not understand why anyone would bother to listen to them. Yet her husband was afraid of them, and York manipulated their opinions to his own advantage.

She must have spoken aloud, for Alainor made sympathetic murmurs as she folded up the queen's gowns.

"It is so lonely being queen," said Marguerite, looking out of the mullioned windows at the grey, pillow-shaped clouds that were scattering flakes of snow as if they were goose-down feathers.

"You are not alone!" exclaimed Alainor, turning and glaring. "Your husband, the king, indulges your every whim. And you have my Somerset."

Marguerite stared. She had never heard Alainor speak so disrespectfully. She opened her mouth to say something when Alainor interrupted. "My Somerset," she said, pointing her finger at the queen, "is devoted to you. He would do anything you asked. Anything."

"My Queen."

Marguerite turned, and Somerset came swiftly forward. He knelt and brushed her hand with his lips. Marguerite's mouth curved into a smile regarding her friend. Though he was old enough to be her father, Edmund Beaufort, now Duke of Somerset, had the looks and manners of a much younger man. She was so absorbed in gazing into his eyes she barely noticed Alainor whisking out of the room with nary a curtsey.

Somerset arched an eyebrow as he rose. "You seem troubled, my love."

"York is giving a speech before the Commons today."

"Ah."

Marguerite moved closer and placed her hands within his. "I fear for you, dearest cousin. I fear that he will try to destroy you." A tear ran down her cheek.

Somerset brushed the tear away with his finger and stooped to kiss her cheek. "York cannot touch me: I have your favor and the favor of the king."

"But he will try," said Marguerite, lifting her face to his.

He bent down and kissed her slowly on the lips.

A sound of mailed feet made them turn. A detachment of guards rushed into the room, followed by the Constable of the Tower, who unrolled a parchment.

"My Lord of Somerset, I hereby arrest you on charges of treason. I am bidden to take you to the Tower forthwith."

Marguerite recoiled. "You cannot do this."

"I have Parliament's authority," replied the constable, as the guards seized Somerset.

"I am your queen!" shrieked Marguerite.

But the constable merely bowed and escorted Somerset out.

Marguerite sank down onto a window seat, sobbing. She could not understand it. How could Parliament have more power than the queen?

Sir William Oldhall rose to his feet. "To the Duke of York!" he exclaimed, holding his wine cup high. "Today, he has set England on the right course—with the Duke of Somerset shut up in the Tower."

Applause and cheers came from the assembled company of merchants and noblemen finishing the splendid feast provided by the wealthy merchant who'd rented out his house to the duke during his stay in London.

"Sir William Oldhall, My Lord Mayor of London, and Master Simon Eyre, who graciously provided his house to me and this feast for us today, I thank you for your hospitality and for your vote of confidence in me. We have much to do to root out corruption and waste in this land."

Richard told the assembled gathering about his plans: How he wanted to raise revenues by cutting waste rather than taxing the poor. How he wanted to bring justice back into the land so that murderers could not escape their crimes by bribing local juries. As he spoke, people nodded. They smiled. Their confidence stoked his excitement. "We have impeached Somerset," he said, "and now let us turn our attention to other members of the Court Party who have profited so unscrupulously at the expense of the country—"

"There was a duke who went to the Tower, Inducas," sang the crowd outside, making Richard stop.

"Who loved a queen full many a day, in temptationibus," the crowd sang on, their voices muffled by the glazing in the windows.

"This queen was lusty, proper and young, Inducas
"She offered the duke a way out of jail, in temptationibus."

Richard strode to the window. Chairs scraped as the assembled company rose hastily and followed, thrusting open the casements. The crowd bubbled with shy merriment as they recognized Richard of York:

Hey hey, fiddle-de-dee
What kind of queen have we?
Loyal, loyal to those she loves
And she loves this duke.
Hey hey, fiddle de dee
What'll happen tonight think we?
Jump jump, jump into bed
And cuddle and kiss—

"Good people, what is this?" called Richard down to the crowd.

"Your bird has flown, my lord Duke!" shouted someone.

"Queen's got her lover back!" shouted another.

A messenger rode up and reined in sharply. The horse quivered, its flanks still damp from exertion. It snorted through its nostrils, sending great puffs of steam into the air. "I've come from the Tower!" he shouted, gasping for breath. "My lady queen went to the king and prevailed upon him to set Somerset free."

CHAPTER 24

1452 to 1453

Richard passed a hand over his forehead. The water trickling down his face was not from the rain alone. His show of force would be interpreted as an act of treason against the king.

He groaned as he slid off his horse. The past fifteen months had not been good. He hadn't been able to prevail in his plans for reform, and things went from bad to worse. Somerset, who just presided over the ignominious loss of Normandy, had been appointed Captain of Calais, the largest garrison maintained by the Crown. In August 1451, the entire duchy of Aquitaine surrendered to the French King. The merchants of England were shocked and dismayed, for, in the space of two months, they'd lost their grip on the lucrative wine trade that flowed through Bordeaux.

By summer's end, it was plain to all that King Henry VI had no plans to implement government reform. France was all but lost, his government as rotten as a barrel of bad apples, justice was as scarce as hen's teeth, and disorder and anarchy prevailed. Yet the king was content to let things remain as they were.

York worked tirelessly for months, courting public opinion and sending his agents up and down the country to tell the good people of England that the king was fitter for a cloister than a throne. Then York left Ludlow and led his army towards London, intending to take the capital. The Londoner's response was to man the defenses, for they knew full well that supporting Richard of York would be construed as treason.

Finding London barred to him, York swung his army south, crossed Kingston Bridge, and led his army towards Dartford. There, he waited for the king's army.

"My lord, there is an embassy come to speak with you from Her Grace the Queen."

Richard set his jaw. But he jerked up in surprise when a well-known figure was ushered in. "Salisbury!" he exclaimed. The Nevilles had been keeping distant from him during these campaigns against Somerset, and Salisbury had large problems of his own with the Percies.

"May I present my eldest son, Warwick?" Salisbury motioned to a tall, young man with fair hair. "And the Bishops of Ely and Winchester."

Richard snapped his fingers, and squires came forward to place chairs for his guests and to tie down the tent flaps, protecting the party from the soaking, cold rain.

The bishops sat, but Salisbury and Warwick remained standing. "I am come from the queen," said Salisbury, a member of the king's council, "to command you in the king's name to return to your allegiance."

York thinned his lips. "I have one condition: Somerset must be punished for his crimes against the state."

188

There was dead silence as his guests looked at one another.

Richard rose. "I will have the Duke of Somerset or die, therefore."

The Bishop of Winchester coughed. "Perhaps matters could be arranged to your liking if you were to have a private interview with the king." He looked at the Bishop of Ely.

Ely turned towards Richard, "I could engage Her Grace the Queen in a game of chess."

Richard smiled.

Next day, as Richard adjusted to the gloom inside the king's tent, the first thing his eyes lighted upon was Somerset. He jerked back.

Somerset bowed low with a flourish.

Another figure emerged from the gloom. It was the queen. She scowled.

Richard felt an icy finger crawling up his spine. Somerset was like a weevil who wouldn't go away.

"Welcome, my cousin of York," came the dull tones of the king's voice.

Coming forward, Richard knelt and kissed the king's ring. Then he brought out a parchment. "As you requested, my lord King, I have drawn up the list of articles of indictment against my lord of Somerset."

The king nodded slightly.

Richard slowly unfurled the parchment.

"What's this?" shrieked Marguerite.

Henry slid his eyes towards his wife.

"Give that to me!" she screamed, making to reach for the document.

Henry sat stone still.

"How could you connive in this underhanded way with this—this viper?"

Richard took a deep breath and looked up. "My lady Queen, you do me an injustice. I am merely asking for the law of the land to be followed and Somerset to be tried for his crimes."

"I am merely asking for the law of the land to be followed," sneered Somerset. "Poppycock. You want power, my lord of York."

"My cousin has come in good faith to sue for peace," remarked Henry.

Richard turned to look at his cousin. Henry rarely stood up to anyone, least of all his wife. But Marguerite turned on him. "How could you go behind my back to your own worst enemy?" She jabbed a finger at Richard: "He's as cunning as a fox."

"He has the support of the Commons," replied Henry, but Marguerite was not listening.

"How could you listen to him? How could you arrest my dearest cousin to suit the whims—"

"He has the support of the people," said Henry. "That does count for something in this country."

"The people. Piffle," retorted Marguerite. "He goes on and on about the supposed crimes of our dear cousin. But what of his own ambition? I tell you, my lord King, York should be arrested. *Immédiatement.*"

"No," said Henry.

The scene blurred before Richard's eyes. He'd dismissed his army. He'd come alone with only a few trusted retainers, believing he would have a private meeting with the king. How could he have blundered into this trap? Facing him, not two feet away, were his worst enemies. If they chose to arrest him—if they decided to try him for treason and execute him—Richard clenched his jaw as sweat trickled down his back. How was he going to get word to Cecylee?

An image of Cecylee filled his head as he'd last seen her. She'd looked like a wounded bird. And they'd been arguing.

About Nan.

When Cecylee had returned from Ireland, she'd insisted, with a persistence and determination he did not know she had, that he allow

her to send Jenet to Exeter to inquire into the health of their
daughter. Richard had agreed; he would have no peace unless he did.
Cecylee had packed up several boxes of things, medicines, Nan's
favorite sweetmeats, even some things she'd left behind when she'd
married Exeter and sent Jenet off. It took her three months to return,
bruises still visible upon her cheeks.

"I begged and pleaded my lady, but he wouldn't let me in. Why,
one of my Lord of Exeter's men hit me in the face when I told him
that your ladyship insisted that I see the duchess."

She rubbed a mark the size of a man's fist.

After Jenet had curtseyed and left, Cecylee had sat there silently,
staring at the fire. It had unnerved him to have his lively and talkative
wife sitting there, unnaturally still. Finally, she lifted her head.

"You've killed her, Richard," she remarked before she stalked out
and shut the door behind her.

He'd not been allowed into her bed since.

And now, as he took in his perilous condition, the hairs rose on
the back of his neck.

"I'll send for the Constable of the Tour," declared Marguerite.
"He is hard by."

"No," said King Henry.

Marguerite turned to pull the tent flap aside.

Henry rose. "I tell you no," he said loudly, his usually pale face
flushed. "I agreed to arrest Somerset to be tried on charges of treason.
He should be taken to the Tower."

Marguerite froze, poised in the action of leaving the tent. Her
black eyes lost their sparkle as her face slackened. "You cannot mean
that, my dearest lord."

She moved swiftly, knelt before the king, and took his hand.
"What has he ever done to deserve this?" She covered her face with
her hands and sobbed.

And so, the king agreed to let Somerset go free.

"Your lord is in grave danger."

Cecylee stared at Sir William Oldhall. Richard? Danger? As she sagged into the cushions of her chair, she thought she saw Blaybourne standing before her: "Would you have me?" he asked. "I have always loved you, my love," she said, the words torn from her lips. "I will keep you safe," he replied, as his face dissolved into the face of her father. "I will lock you up," said Earl Ralph, "for you may be queen one day."

Someone touched her arm; Sir William's face swam into view.

"My lady," he said, touching her with a mud-splattered glove, "you look overwrought. Would you like me to come back when you have rested awhile?"

Cecylee came to with a jolt.

"What has happened?" she whispered.

"He has been taken prisoner."

Cecylee felt the color drain from her face. She'd been married to Richard now for fifteen years, and her lady friends envied her for the way he doted on her. She was never long out of his company. She traveled with him everywhere. She sat in on the various meetings he held. She held court with him in the great halls of various castles. She provided him with counsel in the privacy of their bedchamber—along with other pleasures, which caused her to breed nearly every year.

Her lady friends sighed as they talked about how lucky they were if their husbands merely ignored them. One lady considered herself fortunate that her husband was never around. Too often, husbands shouted at their ladies, or worse.

"You are so lucky, Cecylee, to have a husband that loves you," ladies exclaimed.

And Cecylee smiled, blushed, and turned the conversation into another current. For how could she explain that, though things had mellowed, there were still tears in the fabric of their marriage? Richard had never forgiven her for Blaybourne, and she had never forgiven him for Nan. Their marriage worked because they never discussed certain subjects, and also, thought Cecylee with a sigh of regret because Richard still loved her. And now, she could not imagine a life without him. She counted out her beads on a string: Joan, Nan, Henry, Edward, Edmund, Beth, Margaret, William, John, George, Thomas.

"How many men can we raise?"

"Not enough to free him. His army is scattered to the winds."

"How can you be sure? We must be able to muster many men from our estates."

"We do not have much time, my lady," replied Sir William.

Cecylee set her lips. "We must fight our enemies some other way. We shall have to spread reports abroad."

Sir William glanced at her with a frown.

She placed her hand on his arm. "I am quite recovered from my shock, thank you, good Sir William. Let me explain. Since we cannot fight with an army, we must fight in the court of public opinion. The people of England should hear that my lord of York has been taken prisoner."

Sir William stroked his beard. Cecylee snapped her fingers and dictated to a waiting scribe:

Good People of England,
My lord of York, the People's Champion, has been arrested.
My Lady Queen made him ride ahead of her in her train, as if he were a prisoner.
She and my lord of Somerset have provided him with lodgings in the Tower.
Good people, I need your help in persuading Our Sovereign Lord the King to set him free.

She signed her name and instructed a servant to ride to the
collegiate church in the village of Fotheringhay and request the
scribes there, in the name of their duchess, to make a hundred copies
of the document. "While they do that, get a team of riders together so
that this can be placed in the marketplace of every goodly sized
town."

The man bowed and left.

"Now, master scribe, there is another message I would have you
write. Make it in the form of a report that a king's councilor would
have. Put into this that Edward of York, Earl of March, has mustered
an army of eleven thousand men and is marching on London from
Ludlow. Say that he is gathering strength at every turn as the people
rise to set my lord of York free."

Sir William shook his head. "'Tis fortunate that folk is not aware
the Earl of March is a lad of only ten years."

One month later, the king issued a general pardon to all those
who had risen against him. He graciously included my lord of York in
this pardon. Four months after that, King Henry visited York at
Ludlow Castle during his annual royal progress.

Duchess Cecylee was not there to greet the king, for she was
lying some one hundred miles away at Fotheringhay, heavily pregnant
with her twelfth child. When he was born, in October 1452, she

named him Richard after his father, in thanksgiving for her husband's release. Joan, Nan, Henry, Edward, Edmund, Beth, Margaret, William, John, George, Thomas, Richard, thought Cecylee, as she lay in bed, recovering from Richard's birth.

Despite the king's visit, no progress was made in the furtherance of York's wish that his voice be heard on the king's council. Instead, early next year, Parliament authorized the king to be able to raise twenty thousand archers at a moment's notice, fearing that York would rise again. Alarmed, Cecylee decided to make a private visit to the queen around Whitsuntide, in the year 1453.

"What good would it do?" asked Richard. "She'll just laugh in your face."

Cecylee's grey eyes flashed as she thinned her lips. "Someone heard screams from Exeter Castle," she reminded him coldly.

"You listen to gossip."

"The last time you said that to me, you forced Nan away from my side. The information I have comes from one of your agents."

"Cis, I'm so sorry—"

"Do you want me to help you or not?"

"You're going to tell the queen I'm loyal and acting in good faith?"

"Exactly," replied Cecylee, lifting her chin. "She will be moved by my plea to show pity for the children."

He turned away. How could Cecylee be so naïve? The queen hated him. On the other hand, his lady wife was greatly upset about Nan; he wanted to comfort her. He tingled as she gently touched his arm. Since he'd returned from prison, she'd thawed and allowed him back into her bed. In return, Richard had made a private vow that he would not marry off their daughters before the age of consent at twelve years.

"Remember, Richard, she knows little of me," remarked Cecylee. "I believe I can persuade her."

"How can you persuade her when she would never believe me?"

"Because we have a common bond, being ladies of high station."

"I don't see how."

Cecylee put her small hand on top of his and lifted her face.

"You know the queen is expecting a baby. I shall take it upon myself to bring her such things as a lady in her condition might like. Then I can advise her—"

"I still don't see what this has to do with politics. How does your knowing about breeding make you persuasive?"

"I will catch her when her guard is down. She will be feeling vulnerable, anxious about the ordeal she is to undergo."

York stroked his beard, regarding her. Sir William Oldhall had brought a full report of Cecylee's cool handling of the crisis that had nearly cost him his life. He'd described her brilliant idea of fighting in the court of public opinion. "At first, I did not know what she was talking of. Truly, I thought her wits had gone. But she was merely many strides ahead of me. You know how quick the duchess is."

Cecylee tilted her head as if she could read his thoughts. "I succeeded in getting you out of the queen's clutches alive."

He smiled as he bent to kiss his wife on the cheek. "So, you did, my Cecylee. That was a deed well done. Well, if you believe you can shift her opinion—"

Cecylee smiled. "You agree that I should try?"

CHAPTER 25

Placentia Palace, Greenwich
Whitsuntide
May 1453

Marguerite regarded Duchess Cecylee with narrowed eyes. "It is most gracious of you to receive me, madam," murmured the duchess as she rose gracefully from her low curtsey.

Duchess Cecylee looked younger than her years. Wasn't she at least ten years older than Marguerite? How did she manage to look so slender after bearing so many children? How did she keep those roses in her cheeks when she was always breeding? Even her teeth were good, whereas she, Marguerite, was growing old. Every time she glanced at herself in her glass, she saw hard lines around her mouth and crow's feet around her eyes.

The truth was she'd done her work too well. Wedded to the King of England as part of the peace settlement between England and France, she'd been tireless in her efforts to further the interests of her countrymen. And she had succeeded brilliantly. First Maine and Anjou, then Normandy, then Aquitaine. All of these domains had fallen into the French king's lap because Marguerite wielded power over the English king and over his supporters Suffolk and Somerset. These men listened to her as she told them that the war with France would come to an end only if the French got back the land that was rightfully theirs.

The only person who stood in her way was York, and he'd stirred things up to such a fever pitch that even she, the redoubtable Marguerite, was disquieted by the hatred shown her by the people of England. Their stony silence, glares, and mutterings caused prickles of unease to run up her spine.

And now York's duchess had suddenly appeared. What could she possibly want? Was there some advantage to be gained here? She motioned the duchess to sit, signaling for wine to be poured.

The duchess sipped her wine delicately. "I am concerned about some things you might have heard about my lord of York."

Marguerite stared. She had expected the duchess to congratulate her about her pregnancy, dispense such advice she must surely have gained after bearing her lord twelve children. She raised an eyebrow. "I do not listen to gossip."

Duchess Cecylee flushed.

"I was not talking of gossip, madam," she replied. She lifted her lashes to stare directly at Marguerite. "There have been some serious accusations made against my lord."

Marguerite rose, and the duchess scrambled to her feet. Marguerite stared, but Duchess Cecylee met the gaze squarely. What would happen if Marguerite stirred the pot?

"I have heard it said that York is planning to attack the king. Is that so?"

"No, madam, it is not," replied the duchess immediately. She smiled. "Of course, my lord is not without his faults. He can be sometimes—difficult."

That is putting it mildly, thought Marguerite.

"You know how husbands can be," remarked the duchess, tilting her head on her slender neck. "But there is one thing York would never do, and that breaks his oath. He takes these things very seriously."

Marguerite sipped her wine. "What mean you?"

"He took an oath of allegiance to your lord when he was crowned king. It would go against everything he stands for were he to break it now."

Marguerite frowned as she tried to concentrate. Suddenly, the dark room with its handsome furniture and heavy draperies felt unbearably hot. The baby kicked repeatedly. She drew herself up. "Your lord is ambitious. He is close to the throne. He has powerful supporters. Why wouldn't he try to gain power for himself?"

Duchess Cecylee sighed as she put her wine cup down. "Perhaps you do not know my husband as well as I thought. Perhaps you do not know he is deeply religious."

Religious? York? She'd seen him at Mass, but he seemed no more religious than the next man. "I always thought my husband was the religious one," remarked Marguerite as the room began to swirl.

Duchess Cecylee laughed, a bright tinkling laugh echoing the bright points of candlelight that were making Marguerite's head ache.

"Well, of course, madam, no one can match your husband for piety. My lord is not like that, but it does not mean religion is not important to him. Why, he prays every day, both morning and evening. He hears Mass with me every day. He visits our priest regularly—"

"Why are you telling me this?" Marguerite said, more abruptly than she'd meant. But she was dying for the duchess to leave so that she could go to her bedchamber and lie down.

"I want you to understand that my lord does not break his vows. Your lord was anointed king before God. My lord gave his oath of allegiance then. He is not some hot-headed young blade who would take power into his own hands because it suits him to do so."

"I see." Marguerite turned away to collect her scattered thoughts. But she was not feeling sharp today. She was aware that the duchess wanted something; there were undercurrents to everything she said. But today, she could not fathom the depths. The duchess talked in riddles, and her head ached. But before she let her go, she must exact a promise from her.

"So, you are prepared, Madame, to give me your assurances that your lord, the Duc de York, will never break his oath of allegiance to my lord, the king?

"Yes, madam. Just so," replied the Duchess, never breaking gaze.

Marguerite nodded slowly as waves of relief washed over her. "I thank you for coming to tell me this, duchesse. It has eased my mind greatly, for I worry much about my lord—"

Marguerite's knees crumpled beneath her. She sank into her chair.

Duchess Cecylee smiled. "Let us think of more joyful tidings. You are going to bear your lord a child. I have brought some things to relieve the pain and discomfort of breeding."

She signaled, and a maidservant appeared, bearing a basket full of herbs. Duchess Cecylee took out each carefully wrapped package.

"I have here chamomile to soothe the spirits, tansy to ease the joints, willow bark to cleanse the skin, and various other things that I think you might like to have."

She drew out a scroll of parchment. "I wrote down some things here so that you don't have to remember. Breeding can be exhausting."

Marguerite motioned for the maid to come closer so that she could see the contents of the basket for herself.

"Why, *duchesse*, that is most kind."

Cecylee patted her hand. "I have long experience in such matters, my dear. If I might be permitted to give you some advice—"

Marguerite nodded.

"Perhaps it would be better if you worried less about weighty matters of state and thought instead of giving your lord a fine and healthy son."

Marguerite bit her tongue on an angry retort. "Is there anything I can give you in return, my lady York?"

Duchess Cecylee looked down. "I hardly like to mention it," she murmured.

"Come now. You have been most kind to me. You have eased my mind. Is there anything you would like for your children?"

"If it pleases you, my lady Queen, I would like to have a pension of a thousand marks for myself and my children."

Marguerite's smile was genuine. So that was it. A request to buy York's loyalty. She would see to it immediately.

CHAPTER 26

What was he to do? Her belly had ripened like an exotic fruit. She was heavily enceinte—

Enceinte. Enceinte. Enceinte.

The word clanged in his head like a bell. King Henry closed his eyes.

It had been a warm day, but now he could feel cooler breezes touching his cheeks. Where was he? At his hunting lodge of Clarendon, outside Salisbury. It had been a beautiful day, and now it was evening. His servants bustled around, preparing a feast of roasted venison from that day's hunt.

Henry inhaled. The sharp tang of wood smoke mixed with roasted flesh assailed his nostrils. He shuddered. Henry left the hunting to others, preferring quiet rides through the forests where he could pray and meditate.

But now, what was he to do?

John Talbot, Earl of Shrewsbury and so greatly feared by the French generals, needed money. He'd swept through the region around Bordeaux, recapturing town after town. These successes were important for the English wine trade. It was important to support Talbot, Henry knew that. But something had happened—

"My lord King?"

King Henry blinked. His chamberlain, Richard Tunstall, bowed. "I have some goodly ale for you, sir. 'Tis a hot evening. Supper will be ready soon."

Henry nodded his thanks, and Tunstall bowed himself out.

Tunstall. Tunstall. Tunstall—had told him something. Henry frowned, clutching at an evanescent web of thought—

"The first comfortable notice that our most dearly beloved wife, the queen, was enceinte to our most singular consolation, and to all true liege people's joy and comfort."

Henry sank back into his carved chair and smiled. He remembered the message that Tunstall had delivered several months ago.

Now, what did it mean?

Henry frowned as the roots of his mind writhed. Men were like trees. And trees bore fruit. And Marguerite's belly was—like ripe fruit. Aye. She was bearing his child. She was bearing a child. She was going to have a baby.

But whose?

His?

Henry froze. Aye, that was the nub of the problem. He'd been trying to think of it for days, and here it was.

The baby.

Here it was.

Talbot. France. Aye, Talbot was dead. Aye, dead. Parliament had not voted Talbot the money. The King of France had invaded Aquitaine. With three armies. To Bordeaux. The French laid siege to Castillon. The English inhabitants asked Talbot to help. Talbot went to their aid. The French left. Talbot chased the French. They turned, pushing the English back to the banks of the Dordogne.

Talbot was cut to pieces.

With a battle-axe.

Henry put his ale down and rested his head in his hand. He pictured the Earl of Shrewsbury's murder. Not hungry. No. He could not eat roasted meat after that.

Henry closed his eyes. It was his fault. Henry's. He'd not given Talbot the money he needed. Now he was dead, hacked to pieces.

Bile rose in his throat. Sweat bloomed on his forehead.

They'd lost. Lost everything. In France. Everything his father had conquered. Everything they'd held for three hundred and eighty-seven years.

All gone.

Save for Calais.

Henry looked up. The sun was setting. A sunset. Sunset. Somerset. Somerset was a dear friend of the queen.

What should he do?

It was Somerset's. Yea: That was it. And he could not recognize a bastard. It was against God. But they would ask him, ask him. They would insist.

Henry half-shut his eyes. His magnates stood in front of him. They had huge, staring eyes.

"You must," they said.

"No," replied Henry.

They stared.

Stared.

"Disappear," said a voice.

"Disappear."

"Inside."

"Go."

On the fifteenth of August, the feast day of the Assumption of Our Blessed Lady, and around one month after the loss of everything in France, Our Sovereign Lord the King was at dinner in his hunting lodge of Clarendon, near Salisbury, when he complained of feeling unnaturally sleepy.

The next day, he went mad.

This piece of news was kept from Richard of York, for the queen and her councilors feared that on receipt of it, he would seize power. They were most alarmed by this turn of events. The king seemed to have taken a sudden leave of his senses. His head lolling, he spent his days in a chair, looked after by attendants. He could neither walk, nor speak, nor understand, nor recognize anyone. It was as if he were in a kind of waking sleep. He was then thirty-two years.

The queen—determined to keep the condition secret—took the king to Westminster and summoned a horde of doctors. They tried everything, to no avail. The king was described by his physicians to be non compos mentis. Perhaps, they suggested, their sovereign lord was possessed by devils. Various priests were invited to exorcise any evil spirits, to no avail. The King was sent to Windsor to live out his days in seclusion.

And so it came to pass, at a time that could not possibly be worse, that England lost her head of state. This event put an end to any hopes of unity—however slight—between the opposing factions of government. It brought Queen Marguerite, who little understood English politics, to the forefront of power. And it removed the last check on feuding magnates and on the rapaciousness of the Court Party.

On the thirteenth day of October, some two months after this catastrophe, the queen went into labor and brought forth a son she named Édouard, after King Henry's favorite saint, Edward the Confessor, whose feast day it was. The birth of the queen's son meant that neither York nor Somerset would be named heir presumptive. But at Windsor, the king was still in a stupor and did not even know he had a son.

That same month, the baby prince was baptized in a grand ceremony in Westminster Abbey. The queen did not attend, for it was not customary for a lady to appear in public after the birth of her child until she had been churched. As sponsors for the prince, the queen chose the Duke of Somerset, the Archbishop of Canterbury, and York's sister-in-law Anne Stafford née Neville, Duchess of Buckingham. My lord of York was not best pleased by choice of Somerset to be a sponsor for the new prince.

It was around this time that rumors began to swirl like the dead leaves of November: Folk whispered that the new baby was not the son of the king at all, for who could imagine saintly, pious King Henry siring a son? Indeed, it seemed more likely that the baby prince was the son of Somerset, who was known to have a rather intense … friendship with the queen.

But now, the queen and her advisors realized they could not conceal the king's condition indefinitely, for he showed no sign of recovering. The queen—whose motto was *Humble and Loyal*—did consider the possibility of allowing the king to abdicate in favor of his son, thus granting herself fifteen years of untrammeled power as Queen Regent. Strangely, the lords of the council were unenthusiastic about this plan. But if not the queen, who was to be regent?

The birth of a son and heir necessitated the summoning of the magnates so that the baby prince could be formally acknowledged as heir-apparent to the throne. On the twenty-fourth day of October, therefore, Somerset, in the name of the queen, summoned such a council. York's name was omitted. This drew a storm of protest, especially from Norfolk, and so Somerset was obliged to invite York after all. When my lord of York finally arrived, he lost no time in gathering support against Somerset and the Court Party.

A little matter of the long-standing feud between the Nevilles and the Percies precipitated a change in the fortunes of my lord of York. Two things of note happened in the year 1453. In August, members of the Neville family were traveling to a family wedding at Sheriff Hutton when they were set upon by the Percies. This event drove the Nevilles—who had hitherto supported the House of Lancaster—to seek the powerful protection of York.

Another event confirmed this change of allegiance. Since the early part of 1453, Richard Neville, Earl of Warwick, had been involved in a bitter dispute with Somerset over the ownership of substantial lands in Wales that had formerly belonged to the House of

Beauchamp, in particular the lordship of Glamorgan. Warwick had held this lordship since 1450 and had administered it well. But early in 1453, Our Sovereign Lord the King, in his infinite wisdom, granted it to Somerset. Warwick fought for his rights and, in the process, realized what my lord of York had had to contend with all these years.

It so happened that York was Warwick's uncle-by-marriage, and Warwick himself was the most powerful Neville in his own right. This shabby treatment led Warwick to take sides, and whither Warwick led, so did the House of Neville follow. From the year 1453, therefore, Richard of York was to enjoy not only the influential support of my lord of Warwick—who was one of the richest and most powerful noblemen in England—but also of his father Richard Neville, Earl of Salisbury, Duchess Cecylee's eldest brother. Together, York, Salisbury, and Warwick made a formidable team that would influence the course of events for the next several years. As M. de Commines, the French Ambassador was later to write: It would have been better for the queen if she had acted more prudently in endeavoring to adjust the dispute between the Nevilles and Somerset than to have said, "I am of Somerset's party. I will maintain it."

Finally, my lord of York had acquired powerful allies among the magnates.

CHAPTER 27

October 1453

The queen could not keep the news of the king's condition hidden. Ancient custom demanded that the king recognize his heir, and so a deputation of twelve lords, spiritual and temporal, took the baby prince to visit his father. The cat came out of the bag as the sight of his heir failed to pull the king out of his strange state.

What to do? Parliament could not pass legislation confirming the child's right to the throne until the king acknowledged his son. The queen, who spared little thought for the people of England, found that her determination to conceal the king's condition cost her heavily, for folk interpreted the king's seeming hesitation as evidence that the baby prince was definitely a bastard!

Warwick wasted no time in making hay out of this predicament. He went before the people at Saint Paul's Cross one day in late October when it was fine but chill. London was bursting at the seams as all the magnates were in town to attend the christening of the baby prince, together with their servants. Folk scurried hither and thither, shopping for vegetables, for simples, for thread and bolts of cloth, at the grocers, the apothecaries, and the haberdashers, when my lord of

Warwick appeared before them, dressed in a purple velvet cloak flung over a crimson velvet tunic. He stood tall in his black leather riding boots at the top of the steps leading to the cross, his long gloves slicing the air.

"I have come, good people, to bring you tidings from court in the matter of the queen's child."

A ripple of laughter went around the crowd.

"I know you must marvel at the king's hesitation." Warwick paused; the crowd rustled and went silent. It would have been possible to hear a needle fall.

"Why?" asked Warwick, his word as clear as a bell. "Why does the king delay in acknowledging the child to be his son?"

The question dropped into the cold air. The crowd rustled and came to life as people turned to one another. Their murmurs grew louder and louder.

Warwick held up his hand. "One of two things is true about this child," he said. "Either he has appeared as a result of fraud, smuggled up the backstairs into the queen's chamber after her own child died. Or he has come into this world as the offspring of an adulterous relationship."

The crowd roared with catcalls and whistles.

Warwick smiled and accepted a cup of ale from the keeper of the tavern hard by Saint Paul's Cross. The tavern stood empty as its inhabitants spilled out onto the street, sipping ale, cider, and mulled wine, and dressed in everything from poor person's homespun to the magnificent furs and jewels of the London merchants and the aristocracy. The barman set up a line of boys to run into the tavern and get as many tankards of ale to the earl and his other customers as was needful.

"Thank you kindly," said Warwick to the barman as he quaffed the brimming tankard. "You brew the finest beer in London."

The barman flushed with pleasure at the laughs and cheers from the crowd. He signaled for more ale.

Warwick held up his hand and waited for silence.

"The king has not acknowledged the child as his son," he said slowly. "And furthermore, he never will."

There was a sudden intake of breath.

"It's true!" exclaimed a young woman, holding a twig basket that held a dried-up turnip, a withered carrot, and some wilted sprigs of rosemary. Her high voice sailed over the noises from the crowd. As people turned to stare, she went bright pink.

"Holy Mary, Mother of Christ!" she exclaimed, blushing again as she crossed herself.

"Indeed, madam," said Warwick, stepping down from the cross, bowing, and offering her one of his cups of ale. "You put it well." He turned to the crowd as he remounted the steps of the cross.

"It is very shocking, is it not, that a crowned Queen of England, a queen anointed by holy oil, would stop at nothing to gain power? That such a queen, invested in spiritual power by the Archbishop of Canterbury, would lie to us? That she would stoop so low as to foist her bastard on us? What does she think we are, good people? Stupid?"

The crowd roared with laughter.

Warwick laughed along with them, and then he held up his hand. "Good people, we must be serious now, for things are not good in this land of ours. We've lost our wine trade, our cloth trade, prices are going up, and it is getting harder and harder to feed our families."

People nodded and edged closer.

"Now, I am for the good of this country. I think this country should be prosperous and strong."

"Hear, hear!" shouted someone from the back of the crowd.

"But things must change," said Warwick. "Things must change for the better. And I want you all to know one thing. I want you to know that I will defend the interests of the people with all my power."

He looked around the crowd. "I will defend the interests of the people with all my power," he said again and then bent down and seized another brimming tankard, which he held high in the air. "To the people of England," shouted Warwick, then quaffed it in one gulp.

"To Warwick!" roared the people as they raised their tankards, wine cups, hats, hands, and daggers.

"A Warwick! A Warwick! A Warwick!" chanted some apprentices at the back of the crowd, who then took up the chant.

Warwick smiled warmly and held out his arms.

The crowd silenced immediately.

"Now, good people, I know many of you go to bed hungry and that you don't have enough to feed your children. I have a surprise for you."

He paused and scanned the crowd.

Everyone's face was turned towards him.

"I would like to invite you to my house on the Strand, where I roast six oxen every day. There, you may have as much meat as you like, and you may carry away as much meat as you can, provided that it fits onto the point of one dagger."

By these means, Warwick won the affection and esteem of the people of England, who put their greatest faith and trust into his hands.

Queen Marguerite swore never to forgive him.

CHAPTER 28

Feast of Saint Anselm
November 18, 1453

T he queen behaved as if the birth of a son consolidated her power and standing in the country.

On the eighteenth day of November 1453, around a month after the birth of the baby prince, all noble ladies were summoned to Westminster Abbey to participate in a magnificent ceremony for the churching of the queen. But Cecylee was too distracted to get caught up in the excitement, for she realized that after a span of more than six years, she would finally be able to see Nan.

Heart in mouth, Cecylee looked around the crowded room. Alice Chaucer, Duchess of Suffolk, was laying out the Queen's robe, which had been trimmed with over five hundred sables. She was helped by Eleanor Beauchamp, Duchess of Somerset, and Anne Beauchamp, Countess of Warwick. The rising temperature of the room mingled the odors of woodsmoke, wet leather, and the slightly rancid smell of fur pelts as more ladies crowded into the room.

Cecylee made her way to the only casement that was open.

And there she was.

Nan.

Only her blue-grey eyes were recognizable, but even these had changed. Gone was the wide-open innocence of the six-year-old child whom Cecylee had last seen. In their place was a hard, shut-in quality, as if a portcullis had gone down.

"Nan," called Cecylee softly as she came closer. "Nan. It is you, isn't it?"

She examined the pallid countenance of her elegantly thin daughter, trying to reconcile the sharply etched profile of this young lady with the soft curves of the six-year-old girl.

Nan didn't respond.

Cecylee scrutinized her daughter. Nan was magnificently arrayed in blue velvet embroidered all over with silver thread. Her brown hair was neatly coiled around her head. She wore a heart-shaped headdress with a translucent veil and the requisite number of jewels. Outwardly, Nan looked like a duke's wife. But her face was white, her eyes dull, and her clothes hung on her.

As Cecylee stared, Nan kept her eyes lowered, hands clasped in front of her, the very picture of a decorous noblewoman.

"What is wrong?" Cecylee whispered.

Nan favored her mother with one brief glance before lowering her lashes again.

Cecylee's hands trembled as she eased her daughter into a private corner of the room.

"He mistreats you, doesn't he?"

Nan stared at the floor.

Cecylee gently tilted her chin with one finger, but Nan closed her eyes.

"My dearest child, I will take you home if you wish."

Nan turned away.

Cecylee twisted her hands together. Where was her daughter? She remembered how Nan had looked after her brothers Edward and Edmund. She remembered how she'd adored Chatelaine and wept for several days when the little thing had been killed. She remembered her smile.

"Nan, come home with me. I beg of you."

214

Nan remained silent.

"Nan?"

Nan stared at the floor.

"Nan!"

Not a flicker passed across Nan's countenance.

"Nan, speak to me please, my sweet."

Cecylee's voice grew louder. She took a deep breath.

Nan edged away.

Cecylee looked around the room. Her eyes lighted on Jacquetta Woodville, Duchess of Bedford, who stood by the fireplace with her sixteen-year-old daughter, Élisabeth, now Baroness Grey, after marrying Sir John Grey of Groby. Both ladies were admiring one another's clothes, exchanging morsels of gossip and child-rearing advice. Tears pricked as Cecylee compared their easy relationship with the difficulties she now encountered with her abandoned child.

Nan spoke. "Go away."

Cecylee strained to hear those softly spoken words.

"But I'm your mother!"

Too late—others were becoming interested in their conversation. Jacquetta lifted her head and turned, scenting out a morsel of gossip. She turned back to Nan, who stared at her with thin lips. Her expression reminded Cecylee of how her aunt Isabel—Richard's sister —would look at her most disapproving.

"Please," Cecylee whispered as she touched the sleeve of Nan's gown. "Please let me take you home. I'll make it up to you, I promise."

Nan was silent. There was no expression on her face.

This was not Nan. This was what remained of her.

There was a rustle as Jacquetta appeared with Élisabeth in tow. With only the briefest of nods to Cecylee, she turned to Nan. "Chérie, you seem discomposed. It would never do to spoil our lady queen's triumph, now would it?"

Her words were like a dagger, shredding Cecylee's heart. "There is no need—"

But Jacquetta ignored her.

"Come with me, my sweet," continued Jacquetta smoothly to Nan, "and let my Élisabeth help you find your place."

Nan rose obediently and allowed the ladies to take each arm.

Cecylee rose also. "Nan—"

But Nan had gone.

Tears blinding her, Cecylee sank onto the window seat. Had Lisette's curse come true? She buried her face in her hands, tears trickling through her fingers. She took in great gulps of air as her chest heaved. Gradually, the room became silent. Cecylee blindly felt for her handkerchief and looked up.

They stared back.

The queen had arrived.

Cecylee rose, curtseyed, and took her place at the front of the procession. She was first lady of the land. She grabbed one corner of the queen's train and held her head high. But the magnificent service was a blur. Cecylee could see nothing.

CHAPTER 29

January 1454

The queen returned to the political scene with great determination. Motherhood transformed her, and not for the better. She became fiercely protective of her son's rights, and she aimed to crush the House of York. From that moment on, a bitter struggle ensued, not so much between the king and York or even between Somerset and York, but rather between my lord of York and my lady queen. York had won over the majority of the magnates and would seize power if nothing were done. It was imperative Édouard be declared heir to the throne of England.

"We must take the prince to Windsor," said Somerset, kissing Marguerite on the lips when she expressed her worries to him. He bundled her into her warmest furs, handed her the baby, and they set off to visit the king.

"My lord King!" said Somerset, speaking loudly and slowly as they entered the king's presence. "You have a fine son. All you need do is bless him." He took the prince in his arms and knelt.

King Henry sat in his chair, dressed in a faded blue robe trimmed with ermine. He stared vacantly.

Somerset brought the baby close so that the child was nearly sitting in the king's lap. The baby prince, restless, kicked out, one slipper hitting the side of the king's leg.

The king started. His head lolled.

"Place your hand on the prince's head and declare him to be your heir, I beseech you."

The king drooled, and a servant hastily wiped his mouth with a napkin.

Marguerite took the baby from Somerset.

"There are evil people who would deny him his rights," she said. "There has to be a formal announcement that he is your son otherwise York will seize power."

The baby turned pink and wailed.

The king stirred and turned in the direction of the sound. But his eyes were empty.

"Bless your son, my dearest lord," said Marguerite.

The king slid down in his seat as his head fell to one side.

"My dearest Queen, I fear he cannot do so," said Somerset, signaling for the servants to hoist the king up in his chair. He covered her hand with his own. "I grieve to tell you this, but we have to admit defeat."

Marguerite handed him the baby and rose. "I do not admit defeat." She snapped her fingers. "We'll ride for London at once."

She swept into her rooms at the Palace of Westminster, demanding that her scribe attend her immediately.

"My love," said Somerset, hurrying behind her. "What can you do? The king recognizes nobody."

"Many magnates are reluctant to support York's bid for the regency because it might look as if they were committing treason. So, I am drawing up a bill."

Somerset looked over her shoulder as the scribe wrote to her dictation:

Item the first:~
I, Marguerite, Queen of England,
desire to have the rule of the land of England in its entirety;

Item the second:~
I, Marguerite, Queen of England,
desire to have the power to appoint the Lord Chancellor, the Lord
Treasurer, the Lord Privy Seal and all such other officers of the land;

Item the third~
I, Marguerite, Queen of England,
desire to have the ability to give all bishoprics and all other such
benefices within the King's gift;

Item the fourth~
I, Marguerite, Queen of England,
desire to be granted by parliament an annuity consisting of monies
for upkeep of the king, the prince, and myself—

CHAPTER 30

January 1454

My lord of York and others of his affinity learned of the queen's plans for herself and England when a large crowd gathered outside Warwick's London residence, The Herber, now a focal point of opposition.

"We won't stomach foreigners," they shouted.

Inside, Warwick met with York, Salisbury, and Norfolk. On hearing the crowd, he went to the window and opened the casement.

"I pray you, good people, what is the meaning of this?"

"Queen's got the whip hand!" shouted one.

"She wants to rule!" shouted another.

"That one's a manly woman!" shouted a third. "Doesn't like taking orders."

"Ooh!" shouted the crowd.

"We don't want her!" shouted a fourth.

"We don't want her!" chanted the crowd.

"My lord of Warwick!" bellowed a beldame dressed in a purple velvet gown and a plum-colored horned headdress, "are you aware the queen has drawn up a bill giving herself supreme power over England?"

Warwick paled, clutching the casement. "God's teeth!" How was it possible? Warwick employed many spies in the queen's household and had yet to receive this news.

The crowd roared with laughter.

York, Salisbury, and Norfolk hurried to the window.

"A York! A York! A York!" shouted the crowd as York appeared.

"What mean you, madam?" bellowed Warwick, beckoning to the beldame. "How came you by this information?"

She sank into a low curtsey and beckoned to a young girl. "This is my maid Popelina, who has a sister who is washerwoman to the queen. Today, I allowed her to have the afternoon off to visit her sister."

Warwick leaned out of the window and beckoned. "Come closer. We'll not bite."

The crowd laughed and made way for a fresh-faced girl of around seventeen, who now appeared and bobbed a curtsey.

"Tell us your story," said Warwick.

"'T'was not more than an hour since, sir—I mean, my lord. I was just helping my sister make up the queen's bed with fresh linens. We were spreading them out on the bed and tucking the corners just so. The queen is very particular about the way her bed is made—"

The crowd guffawed with laughter.

"What did you hear?" asked Warwick. This information was fresh from the oven if it were less than an hour since she'd heard the queen speak.

"Well, sir. The queen was in the next room talking to someone —"

"Her scribe," put in the beldame.

"Her scribe. I heard her say that she desired to rule England."

The crowd booed loudly, then rustled with mutterings.

"What else did she say?"

"Something about making a chancellor and making bishops— and money. That's it. I was bending over a tuck and smoothing it down, and I was thinking, Holy Mother Above, the queen wants to be king. I ran off as soon as I could to tell my mistress, for she told me always to keep an ear out for anything the queen might say."

222

"And so, I brought the matter straight to your lordship," put in the beldame, "for I thought you ought to know."

Warwick thanked her and, with a nod, sent someone to ascertain if the story were true. If it were, he would employ Mistress Popelina to turn down beds for the queen in every corner of the country.

The Lords and Commons were offended by Queen Marguerite's highhandedness and took note of the people's determination not to be ruled by their haughty and arrogant French queen. And thus, many lords who might not otherwise have done so first began to support Richard of York.

In March of the year 1454, the sudden death of the Archbishop of Canterbury gave great urgency to the matter of a regency, for the archbishop's successor could only be chosen on the authority of the king. A regent was needed.

Before reaching their decision, the lords of the council made one last visit to the king to see if he showed any signs of recovery.

He did not.

And so, they sent for the Duke of York, closest of the lords to the throne of England by reason of his descent from the second and fourth sons of King Edward III.

On the twenty-seventh day of March in the year 1454, the Lords in Parliament nominated Richard of York to be regent of England. He was to enjoy the same title and powers and the same limitations on his authority that Humphrey, Duke of Gloucester, had enjoyed during the long minority of King Henry VI. The Lords decreed that York should neither have title of governor nor regent, but should be named Lord Protector and Defender because it conveyed a personal duty of protecting the realm both from enemies without as well as rebels within. They further stipulated that if the king did not recover, the office of protector should devolve upon Prince Edward when he achieved his majority. As this would not happen for at least fourteen years, great trust was put in York's hands.

CHAPTER 31

April 1454

Richard of York bowed low, unrolling a scroll and scanning it briefly. He lifted his head. "From now on, you will reside at Windsor with your lord husband, the king."

"You cannot order me to do that."

York smiled. The last time he'd met the queen, she'd held his life in her hands. Now, he held power.

"Have you not heard, my lady, that I am regent?"

Marguerite bit her lip.

"You will leave within the hour."

She was silent.

He turned to Somerset, who stood by, handling the baby prince. "And you, my lord, will go to the Tower to answer charges of treason."

"No!" shrieked Marguerite. She flung herself between Somerset and York. The baby prince wailed.

Her extreme action took Richard aback.

"My lord of Somerset will be well treated in the Tower. He will be tried by his peers in the House of Lords, as is his right. There is no need to be hysterical."

"He's not going," shouted Marguerite.

York nodded, and the Constable of the Tower entered the room with an armed escort.

Marguerite shrieked again, the baby echoing her shrieks.

York sighed. Why did she have to make things so difficult? He was saved by Somerset, who put his hand on her cheek.

"My dear lady and my love, be not so fretful. All will be well." He handed her the baby prince: "See how fine our prince is. No one can take that away from you."

"But they will try," said Marguerite, sweeping York a look. "Oh, how I know it. Already, York—"

Somerset took the queen's hand and kissed its palm.

York nodded, and the Constable of the Tower read out the indictment, charging Somerset with treasonable acts and summoning him to the Tower to await his trial for impeachment. Handing the baby back to Somerset, Marguerite leapt to her feet and seized the parchment.

"Of course!" she cried. "It is signed and sealed by the hand of York. Oh, he will stop at nothing to destroy you."

Somerset glared, handed the baby prince to the queen, and took the document. He scanned it and looked at York, who folded his arms and waited. By now, the room was filling with armed guards. He turned to the queen.

"Marguerite, don't take on so. You know I must go."

"There must be something I can do."

Somerset shook his head.

York signaled; the guards took each arm and led Somerset off.

Marguerite collapsed into a heap of tears. York waited. After she'd sobbed herself dry, he said, "You will leave within the hour. Your household will follow in a few days."

"The prince?" she whispered.

York paused and regarded her. Now she looked vulnerable and young. "The prince as well," he said slowly. "But once you reach Windsor, you will not leave."

"You can't do that," she replied, rising. "I am queen."

"It is not seemly for a woman to meddle in government as you have done, my lady. You should spend your days with your baby and your husband. That is your place."

Marguerite stamped her foot. The baby prince woke up from his brief slumber and wailed.

"How dare you insult me in this fashion!"

"No one wants you to be queen, my lady," replied York. "Saving, of course, yourself."

He paused again and looked at her. She was as willful as Cecylee, but unlike his wife, York found that he did not care for her at all. Strange, for she was a handsome woman. "You will do as I tell you. The country is in a grievous state, thanks to you. Now you will rest at Windsor and mind your family, as a good wife should."

He turned to go.

"I'll not consent to this!" screamed Marguerite. "You cannot treat your queen thus! I will not have it!"

York sighed and signaled to his marshal, who nodded. Several more guards entered Marguerite's chamber.

"I do not like to force a lady, but you give me no choice."

The guards surrounded the chamber, and one of them plucked the baby prince from Marguerite's arms and handed it to a nursemaid.

Marguerite screamed so loudly that Richard wanted to cover his ears. As his men hesitated, he nodded again. A couple of guards took her by the arms and dragged her away.

"I'll not forgive this!" she shrieked. "I'll never forgive this outrage!"

"We have not a moment to lose," said York as he took his seat as the head of the king's council.

"Indeed," replied Salisbury. "There are the Percies in the North still harrying our lands. Something needs to be done to curb their quarrelsome nature."

"There is the matter of the Crown's finances," said York. "We need to make adequate provision for the king's household without incurring further debts or draining the exchequer."

"The position of Archbishop of Canterbury lies vacant," put in Warwick.

York leaned back in his seat. "I've thought of that. It's vital we have someone reliable and loyal to our affinity."

"Whom do you propose?" asked Norfolk.

"Thomas Bourchier, the Bishop of Ely, would be a fine candidate. He's brother to my sister's husband, Viscount Henry Bourchier."

The lords deliberated on this matter for some time but finally agreed that my lord of York's choice was sound.

"What mean you to do about the Percies?" asked Warwick.

"I shall visit them next month," replied York. "While I am away, you, my lord of Salisbury, will manage affairs in London."

Salisbury smiled and nodded. One of Richard's first acts upon becoming regent was to install Salisbury as Chancellor of England.

"There is also Lancastrian disaffection in the north and the west, provoked by Exeter," remarked Warwick. "He must be curbed."

York winced. Nan's husband was proving to be difficult to handle. Moreover, Cecylee had returned from the Queen's churching ceremony brokenhearted, convinced Exeter was brutalizing their

daughter. She had taken to her bed. Nothing Richard could say
would comfort her. Only his successes of the past several months had
caused her to smile at him again. Richard regretted once again
arranging that marriage with Exeter. Exeter spelled trouble. He
should be watched.

Richard said aloud, "I think it would be prudent to hold my lord
of Exeter at Pontefract."

"But he's your son-in-law," exclaimed Salisbury.

"That may be. But he does not act as kin. His allegiance is to the
Court Party, and he has made that very clear to me on a number of
occasions. I do not have much choice. Exeter is dangerous."

Warwick nodded. "Holding Exeter at Pontefract does make him
a hostage for the good behavior of his affinity."

CHAPTER 32

November 1454

What is the news from France?"

Cecylee distracted herself by talking to the French Ambassador. The king's Lancastrian supporters surrounded her, eying her warily. These days, she spent all of her time at court, entertaining foreign diplomats. Fifteen months had passed since the king had fallen into his strange state, but he showed no sign of coming out of it. Joan, Nan, Henry, Edward, Edmund, Beth, Margaret, William, John, George, Thomas, Richard, murmured Cecylee to herself as she walked along the corridors. She found that living in Marguerite's magnificent palace of Placentia, wearing bejeweled dresses, and being treated as queen could not stem her sadness nor stop her sleepless nights. Every time she turned around, something happened to rub her wound raw. Jacquetta, Duchess of Bedford, had just left this very room after telling her that Nan would bear a child in the spring.

Cecylee had listened calmly, but as soon as she left, motioned to the French Ambassador to sit beside her.

"Ah, my lady York, the news is not so good."

Cecylee raised her eyebrows politely as she signaled for wine. If Nan were expecting a child in the spring, then she would be a grandmother before she turned forty.

"Do you mean that matters between King Charles of France and his son, the Dauphin Louis, have gone awry?"

The ambassador sighed. "You are too well informed, Madame. Indeed, it is a matter of grave disquiet that the king and his heir do not see matters in the same light."

How would Nan fare without her mother to help her? Cecylee leaned forward.

"Is it possible that matters might get worse?"

"I hope not, Madame."

She sighed. Perhaps families were difficult for everyone.

"I think I can speak for my husband as well as myself when I say that I hope matters will mend in France. But what is your opinion of the situation?"

The ambassador coughed. "I know that many are anxious to prevent war."

She studied him for a moment. War. That was a strong word for a family quarrel. "So, the king would send an army against his son?"

The ambassador recoiled. "I did not say that, Madame."

"No, you did not," replied Cecylee, signaling for a servant to refill the ambassador's wine cup. She would have to find a way of sending Jenet with a basket of herbs and things for her daughter's lying-in. "But it is a possibility?"

The ambassador sipped and coughed again, putting his cup down to speak. The arrival of her nephew Humphrey, Earl of Stafford, Anne's eldest son, interrupted them.

"My wife has given me a son," he exclaimed.

Cecylee started, jolted out of her thoughts. She signaled to the servants to refill the wine cups.

"Congratulations, my lord," she said, handing him a brimming cup. The Buckingham line would be secure. Cecylee kept her celebrations from seeming too joyful, however, as the Staffords were staunch Lancastrians. She silently wished she could be delighted by the birth of Nan's child. Perhaps it would not be a good idea to send

Jenet to her. She needed to send someone who did not obviously
come from herself, as such overtures would be unwelcome. She
repressed the now-familiar pricking of tears and looked up.

The lords eyed her.

"How have you named the child?" enquired someone.

"We have named him Henry, after the king," replied Stafford
with a smile.

"Let us drink to that," shouted another. And before she could
open her mouth, they raised their wine cups. "To the king!" they
roared.

Cecylee drank also, hoping the gesture would be appreciated by
Richard's rivals. As she took the wine cup away from her lips, she
became aware of someone in the doorway.

It was Richard. He entered the room slowly, followed by
Salisbury and Warwick. Many pairs of eyes watched in silence the
triumvirate that now governed England. Richard took a wine cup
offered to him by a servant, raised it, and said, "Congratulations,
Stafford, on the birth of your son. To Henry."

The others raised their goblets and drank again.

There was an awkward pause.

"My lords," said York setting his wine cup down. "I request that
you draw up ordinances for the reduction and reform of the king's
household."

"What ordinances?" snapped Buckingham, not moved by the
toast to his grandson.

"I have to reduce costs to avoid draining the exchequer."

"You have to—poppycock. This is aimed at our lady queen."

"Everyone will be affected," replied York. "There is no avoiding
that."

"You must see, my lord of Buckingham, that the Crown has no
money," put in Cecylee. "No one likes reducing costs. But it must be
done."

Buckingham snorted.

"Our households are to be cut," said Edmund Tudor, Earl of
Richmond, who stood there with his brother Jasper, Earl of
Pembroke.

"And we are half-brothers to the king," put in Pembroke. "Our
households will be only seven in number under my lord of York's
plan. An entourage only equal to that of the king's confessor."

"How can you allow that?" exclaimed Henry Percy, Earl of
Northumberland. "It's a disgrace!"

"We agree with my lord of York that such reforms are in our
sovereign brother's interests," said Richmond.

"Otherwise, he would be destitute," said Pembroke. "Surely
you've not forgotten the time when our sovereign king and his lady
queen sat down to a feast at Epiphany only to be told by their steward
there was no food to be had?"

Cecylee glanced at Richard, who was standing there silently. This
cannot be easy for him, she thought. He has to be so patient.

Richard cleared his throat.

"I want you all to know that I have removed Exeter to
Pontefract. He will stay there to cool his heels for a while."

Cecylee breathed deeply and smiled. Maybe I can be with Nan
after all. She drew herself up and looked around her. The lords were
standing there, stony-faced. "Let us pray," she said slowly, "that such
reforms as my lord has wisely proposed be acceptable to all, for they
are very necessary to the good governance of this realm."

CHAPTER 33

Feast of the Christ Child
Westminster Palace, London
December 25, 1454

Richard of York rose in his seat, lifted his wine cup high, and toasted the king's health.

Duchess Cecylee and everyone else followed, saluting the king at a formal banquet that was hosted by York as part of the festivities for the Feast of the Christ Child.

Cecylee had just put her wine cup down and turned to congratulate Richard on the efforts he was making when a messenger rushed in.

"The king awakens. He awakens!"

A roar erupted as everyone rose to their feet and eyed one another. Without further ado, the entire court abandoned the Christmas feast and rushed to the stables calling for their favorite horses. Meanwhile, servants appeared with mantles of sable, fur-lined hoods, gloves, and boots to protect everyone from the winter weather.

It took the rest of the day to ride the thirty or so miles from the Palace of Westminster, where Christmas Court was held, to Windsor

Castle, where the King was in residence. The entire court came in a rush upon the royal family.

The king sat in a high-backed chair, smiling vaguely.

The queen knelt before him, holding her fourteen-month-old son Édouard. "See what a fine son you have, my King," she said.

"This child is heaven-sent," replied King Henry in a low, clear voice. "His birth must have been a miracle of the Holy Spirit."

The queen's face was a picture. She searched her husband's face, her own puckered in bewilderment. The entire court exploded into laughter. Truly, King Henry had returned to the land of the living, for only he would make such a pronouncement.

There was an awkward silence, then Warwick strode up. "This so-called prince," said he, jabbing a finger at the infant on Marguerite's lap, "is no son of yours, Sire." He bowed low before King Henry, then turned to face the entire court. "He is Somerset's son."

A roar of noise broke. Marguerite rose, clutching the child to her, who bawled lustily. "How dare you!" she shrieked, spitting at Warwick, who took a step backward. "You slander me with your lies, with your defamation. But I fight!"

She looked around the room. "I will fight you all if I have to!" She stormed out.

Cecylee was stunned. She knew the queen and Somerset were lovers, for Richard had told her about his visit when, as the newly-made Lord Protector of England, he had shut Somerset in the Tower and banished Marguerite to Windsor. Somerset had been holding the baby as if he were his own, and Richard repeated their conversation, complete with lover's words.

Now Marguerite displayed no guilt at her actions. Cecylee's never-quite-dormant anger welled up. How dare Richard manipulates her to feel guilty for her one night of sin? How dare he make her feel like an animal in a cage? She would be taken out for petting once in a while, but if she bit, she would be thrust back in her cage, and the door slammed shut.

Cecylee took a breath and closed her eyes. What would happen now? Richard was no longer regent. She was no longer queen.

CHAPTER 34

Spring 1455

Though many wept for joy and declared the king to be well mended, nevertheless, he was not the same. His strange illness left him at the mercy of his domineering lady wife and quarrelsome nobles. From now on, royal authority would be in the hands of a weak king, debilitated by a long sleeping sickness that might recur at any time.

Events moved swiftly downhill after that Christmas Day. On the ninth day of February 1455, King Henry appeared in Parliament, whereupon he graciously gave thanks to all present and dismissed my lord of York from the office of protector. As soon as York relinquished his appointment, Salisbury was dismissed from his position as chancellor, and Exeter was set at liberty from his confinement at Pontefract. Naturally, the queen lost no time in setting her lover free from the Tower and restoring to him the offices of Constable and Captain of Calais.

Upon hearing the news of Somerset's release, Richard of York and others of his affinity rode out of London to Yorkshire. York went to Sandal Castle and Salisbury to Middleham. Somerset already filled the king's ear with talk of how my lord of York wished to depose the king and take the throne of England for himself.

Through his numerous connections in London, Warwick learned that Somerset was planning to hold a secret conference at Westminster. Warwick urged York and Salisbury not to wait to see what Somerset might do but instead to recruit an army. This they did without further ado, and levies were summoned to muster both at Middleham and Sandal while Warwick began to assemble a large army of his own at Warwick Castle.

CHAPTER 35

Sandal Castle, Yorkshire
May 1455

Exeter's return from Pontefract prevented Cecylee from attending her daughter's lying-in. She later heard that Nan gave birth to a healthy daughter, whom she named Anne after herself.

Perhaps it was just as well it was too dangerous to travel, mused Cecylee, sitting beside Richard on the dais of the great hall at Sandal Castle. Her belly swelled with her latest pregnancy. Joan, Nan, Henry, Edward, Edmund, Beth, Margaret, William, John, George, Thomas, Richard. This child would be her thirteenth.

It was May, and the door to the hall had been left open to allow in the fresh breezes of spring. Cecylee half-listened to the stream of petitioners filing into the hall to discuss their problems with the duke and duchess, instead idly wondering if she would survive this latest pregnancy. A royal messenger bearing the leopards of Anjou and the lilies of France finally grabbed her attention.

"I bring a summons from my lord the king!" he cried, kneeling before Richard.

Richard frowned and tore open the parchment. His face went white.

"My lord, what ails you?" whispered Cecylee. She got to her feet slowly, heavy with pregnancy.

Richard handed the parchment to her. The king had summoned York, Salisbury, and Warwick to meet him before a great council of England to be held on the twenty-first day of May in the year 1455.

Cecylee scanned the document and bit her lip. She glanced up and signaled to the royal messenger to leave, then turned to Richard.

"My lord, you cannot go."

He clasped her hands. "You think as I do."

She stared into his grey-blue eyes, thinking. What will become of the children if their father is murdered? I might not survive many moons longer. "I well remember what happened to my lord of Gloucester," she murmured under her breath.

Richard set his lips, clasping Cecylee's hands within his own. Then he strode briskly to the door and summoned the messenger back into the room.

"Tell our sovereign lord that I am loyal to him and that I will obey the summons."

The muscles of the young squire's face relaxed as he nodded and bowed.

Then he left.

Cecylee smiled up at Richard. "You will strike first?"

"Exactly so." Richard bent and gave her a peck on the cheek. "Take good care of yourself, my sweet," he murmured, laying a hand on her belly.

York led his army southwards to London with the intention of intercepting the king, the queen, and Somerset before they left for

Leicester. With him were Salisbury, Viscount Bourchier, and others, which numbered some six thousand men with their affinities. At the same time, Warwick led an army of one thousand across England from Warwick Castle to meet up with York and Salisbury on Ermine Street.

On the twentieth day of May, York's army, now numbering seven thousand men, arrived at the village of Royston in Hertfordshire. While there, York learned that the royal army was about to leave London without the queen, who had taken the baby prince to Greenwich. On the twenty-first day of May, the Yorkist army marched into the nearby village of Ware. By the early hours of May 22, York's scouts advised him that the king was making for Saint Albans, and so York swung his army around and, just outside that town, drew it up into three parts to be commanded by York, Salisbury, and Warwick.

The royal army, numbering some two or three thousand and commanded by Humphrey Stafford, Duke of Buckingham, arrived in Saint Albans early on the morning of May 22. For three hours, York delayed starting the battle, making every effort to induce the king to listen to his complaints about Somerset's misgovernment. To no avail. The king sent back an uncharacteristically harsh reply.

"He refuses to accede to any of your demands," exclaimed Warwick.

"Somerset is behind this," muttered Salisbury.

York rose. "Let the battle begin."

So saying, he mounted his charger, put on his helmet, and ordered the trumpeters to sound the alarms. He rode in front of his troops and spoke.

"Today, we stand at a turning point. Either we retreat to the misgovernment of the past, or we advance into the future, rid of all the traitors who would bleed the land white for their own gain."

"A York! A York! A York!" roared the troops.

"We have a hard fight ahead of us," shouted Richard. "I represent Job, and our Sovereign King is like King David, and together we will overcome Somerset."

The troops cheered, and the Battle of Saint Albans began.

York and Salisbury lead the charge from the East, along Saint Peter's Street, Sopwell Street, and other roads leading to the marketplace in an effort to storm the barricades the Lancastrian commanders put up to defend the town.

Many of the Lancastrian persuasion suffered that day. Henry Percy, Earl of Northumberland, husband to Cecylee's sister Alainor, perished in battle. Both Buckingham and his son and heir Humphrey Stafford were grievously wounded. But the big prizes were the death of Somerset and the capture of King Henry.

On May 23, 1455, York and Salisbury, preceded by Warwick bearing the king's sword, escorted our sovereign King Henry VI back to London, whereupon my lord of York assumed a new role as chief advisor to the king. He was immediately appointed to the position of Constable of England.

In the next week, the various members of the Court Party—Buckingham, Wiltshire, Shrewsbury, Richmond, Pembroke, and some others—made peace with Richard of York. Pembroke was especially anxious to devise a way of reconciling all parties, and during the long hot summer months of 1455—while Cecylee waited for her youngest child to be born—he spent many hours with York discussing how best to achieve such a reconciliation.

But though Somerset was dead, his faction remained, and there was considerable bitterness amongst those who had lost their loved ones at Saint Albans.

CHAPTER 36

July 1455 to January 1458

By the beginning of July 1455, Richard of York had
established himself as the effective ruler of England. As a
mark of his newfound power, he gave Salisbury the
influential office of Chancellor of the Duchy of Lancaster. Around
this time, Cecylee gave birth to a daughter. Though she survived the
birthing of her thirteenth child, the baby died soon after. Cecylee
named her Ursula in honor of Saint Ursula and her eleven thousand
virgins.

Richard could not spare the time to grieve with his wife, for the
king experienced another episode of his strange illness, and he
assumed complete control of the governance of the country on the
nineteenth day of November in the year 1455. Richard was once
again appointed Protector and Defender of the Realm.

For the rest of the year, York and his allies formulated a radical
program of reforms to bring order to the royal finances and the
patronage of Crown lands. These ideas did not make him popular
with the magnates. When King Henry regained his senses, these
magnates surrounded him with complaints. In February of the year
1456, King Henry appeared in Parliament and—in a manner very

similar to that of the year before—revoked my lord of York's appointment. He then ordered substantial changes to York's Act of Resumption. Despite this blow, York and his followers cooperated with the Court Party, and York himself remained a dominant voice on the king's council.

Queen Marguerite—who disliked Londoners—spent the spring of 1456 traveling around the country. While she was away, the king heeded York's advice and appointed Warwick to be Captain of Calais. This appointment was the most important military command within the king's gift. York was anxious that it should be given to Warwick to reward him for his crucial support at the Battle of Saint Albans. The queen had wanted to bestow this gift on Somerset's son and heir. By taking advantage of the queen's absence, York prevailed over the king.

With this coup, York allowed his guard to slip. He let the king go on royal progress around the country while he departed for Fotheringhay to spend time with his wife. The king went to Chester to reunite with the queen. With the king in her clutches, the queen prevailed upon him to dismiss persons of York's affinity from the government. Her plan was to throw York into the Tower and have him executed. But Buckingham persuaded her to banish him to Dublin instead.

Cecylee never forgot the way Richard looked when he came to her with news of this latest reprieve. Grey with fatigue, his expression made her bury any irritation. She sent him to Ireland with a kiss, promising that she would arrive soon. Then she went through the whole turmoil of packing up and organizing their trip across country from Fotheringhay, in Nottinghamshire, to Wales, where they took ship to Dublin. With her were fourteen-year-old Beth, twelve-year-old Margaret, eight-year-old George, and five-year-old Richard. At least the Irish had been right glad to see the Duke and Duchess of York return to Dublin, and so their sojourn provided some respite for poor Richard.

In January 1458, Richard of York was recalled to England by the king, who commanded all magnates to attend a peace conference at Westminster. Richard used the opportunity to forge new alliances.

"The time has come to marry Beth off."

"Couldn't she stay awhile longer? She is still young."

"Cis, we've had this conversation before. This is a splendid match. Beth will be Duchess of Suffolk."

"But first, she will be the Duchess of Suffolk's daughter-in-law. Alice Chaucer, the present Duchess, is of hardy stock. She might last a long time."

"Beth will be with her kinswoman then, for you are related to the Chaucers too, my sweet." He put his arm around her waist.

Cecylee let him hold her for a moment, then pulled away.

"But I may not see her again," she said, trying not to sound too shrill. "I never see nor hear from Nan. She sent me no word when her daughter was born." She knelt. "Please, Dickon, I ask only for a few more years. Surely you could grant me that?"

Richard gently pulled her to her feet. "I cannot grant your wish. The marriage documents have already been drawn up; everything has been signed and sealed."

"Without my knowledge?" she flashed out.

Richard stiffened, and his eyes went the color of steel.

"But why John de la Pole?" she asked, seeking to soften his gaze. "He is the son of your great enemy Suffolk."

"True," he replied, allowing the muscles of his face to relax. "But the son is made of different mettle than the father. Sir John has been loyal to the House of York." He clasped her hands within his own. "I nearly lost my life last year. I must use what time I have left to build affinities to protect our family. Surely you see that?"

Beth was married to John de la Pole within the month.

CHAPTER 37

1458 to 1459

The next move in this game of chess came from Queen Marguerite. Naturally, she wanted to oust Warwick from the Captaincy of Calais, so she summoned him to appear before the king's council to answer charges of piracy.

Her complaint stemmed from an incident in which Warwick sent a small flotilla of ships across the channel into the Thames estuary to capture three Italian ships loaded with English wool. The king himself had allowed the Italian merchants to load their ships with wool, but Warwick, ever attuned to the feelings of the Londoners, sent his ships to get the wool back. The king was unable to stop him, for he had but one ship.

This exploit earned Warwick tremendous popularity, for the London merchants, the source of so much of England's wealth, were ignored and slighted by the government. Warwick used his position as Captain of Calais to put together a fleet of ten ships, which he used to intercept Burgundian, Hanseatic and French ships and to further London's wealth. The Londoners regarded these deeds as nothing less than heroic, but the queen was not best pleased.

If the queen believed she could get rid of Warwick easily, she was to be disappointed. Warwick responded to her summons by arriving in London in July 1458 at the head of six hundred armed men. When the queen tried to press charges, Warwick protested he was being treated unfairly. His protests encouraged his supporters, of which there were many, to run riot in London.

In the mêlée, the Attorney General was murdered.

Over the next several months, various scuffles broke out between Warwick's supporters and those of the Court Party. When the queen persuaded the council to draw up a warrant for his arrest and committal to the Tower, he realized it was no longer safe to remain in England. Warwick—whose motto was Seulement En, or 'One Against Many'—returned to Calais, remaining a continuous thorn in the queen's side. Marguerite was now determined to take decisive action, and in the latter months of 1458, she left London to raise an army.

Richard responded to the deteriorating situation by deciding that Fotheringhay Castle was no longer safe. As soon as the winter frosts melted away, heralding in the spring of 1459, Cecylee packed up the household, and they left for Ludlow on the Welsh Marches because it had stronger fortifications. With them went the younger remaining children: Margaret, thirteen; George, nine; and Richard, six.

Cecylee had seen scarcely anything of Edward during his childhood and young manhood, for Richard had packed him off to Ludlow at the age of four to provide company for his three-year-old half-brother Rutland, groomed to be the Yorkist heir. With the storms of Richard's political life and thirteen pregnancies, Cecil could make only rare visits to Ludlow, for Fotheringhay Castle was a distance of one hundred and twenty-five miles away.

So when she entered the great hall at Ludlow Castle, and a young man came towards her, Cecylee's heart stilled. He wore a tight tunic of dark blue velvet trimmed with gold thread. His long legs were encased in stockings that were half blue, half gold, with the seam up the middle of each leg. He was tall. His hair was golden, and his dark blue eyes were sharp with intelligence. His tunic ended at the hip, showing off legs that were long and very shapely.

He knelt down and kissed her hand. She froze.

"Madam. Mother. You look unwell. May I get something for you?"

He signaled for a servant to bring a chair. As he poured a cup of wine, he peered at her anxiously.

"You look as if you've seen a ghost," continued the young man.

"I have," she murmured, slowly sipping the wine he'd given her. For there, standing before her, was the veritable image of Blaybourne.

Cecylee glanced at Richard, who quickly understood. His expression hardened.

Ignoring Edward, he turned to the other young man standing quietly by. It was then that Cecylee noticed her other son, Edmund, Earl of Rutland, aged sixteen years. Though he was tall like Edward, he greatly resembled Richard.

"Well met, my son," said Richard a little too loudly as he put his hand on Rutland's shoulder.

Rutland's pale face lit with a smile.

"Let us go to the stables to pick out a fine stallion for you, my son," said Richard, with just the slightest emphasis on the repetition. He steered Rutland away from Edward. They disappeared outside and did not return for the rest of the day.

Richard spent much time with Rutland as they settled in, personally supervising his training in the art of warfare while Cecylee was thrown into the company of her eldest son. She hadn't realized how much she longed for Blaybourne until then. Edward was very much like his father, not only in looks but also in wit. Although it was hard—even for his mother—not to notice he already boasted a notorious reputation for womanizing, Cecylee stopped her ears.

Edward was beguiling. He was charming. He made her feel that she was at the center of his life.

This gave her a confidence about him she should not have had.

One incident struck a discordant note. As she was eating a light supper with the younger children, Richard came in hot and flushed. He made a gesture with his thumb and forefinger to let her know that he wished to speak with her privately.

She nodded to Jenet and left.

When she entered Richard's private dressing room, Edward was there.

"Where is he?" Richard asked angrily.

"My lord, I am truly sorry. I cannot remember—"

"You cannot remember?" thundered Richard.

Cecylee put a hand on Richard's sleeve. "Edward. What has happened?"

He went down on one knee. "My lady mother, I crave your pardon and that of my lord father."

Richard bristled but said nothing.

"Rutland and I were out riding when my horse went lame. He agreed to let me ride his horse. I am not sure where I left him."

"Edward," exclaimed Cecylee, "how can this be? Gentlemen are trained to know always where they are. How can you successfully win battles otherwise?"

He hung his head.

Cecylee looked at Richard, staring at her with a grim countenance.

"He does not know because he was drunk at the time, is that not so, you oaf?"

He poked Edward with the toe of his boot.

Edward stared at the floor.

"He promised to ride straight back to me," said Richard. "And then to bring Rutland a new horse. Instead, he delayed, chasing wenches, is that not so?"

Cecylee's cheeks grew warm.

"I found him," continued Richard, "in a local stew, sodden with drink. When, finally, I roused him, he could not remember where he'd left Rutland."

There was silence for a moment. Then Richard prodded Edward again with the toe of his boot.

"You, sir," he shouted, "will mount up with me and a party of men-at-arms and set out to find Rutland. We'll search until we find him. If I find he's been taken hostage by the other side, you'll pay dearly for this, do you understand?"

Edward went white.

"Good God, man," thundered Richard, "there's a war on. Or were you so sunk in debauchery you forgot that too?"

A day later, they returned with Rutland and the lame horse. Edward was given a sound beating by the sergeant-at-arms to curb his tendency to be irresponsible. My lord believed the beating would teach him that lesson.

CHAPTER 38

Spring to Fall 1459

As the shadows grew shorter and the sun rose higher in the sky during the spring of 1459, York at Ludlow and Salisbury at Middleham summoned their vast following of tenants and retainers to counter the activities of the queen and her conscripted army. Late in June, the king held a great council at Coventry, attended by the Queen and five-year-old Prince Édouard. All lords were summoned to attend, including York and Salisbury. Instead, they sent an urgent message to Warwick at Calais, begging him to come to their aid.

Warwick raised two hundred men-at-arms and four hundred archers, all of whom wore red jackets sporting his badge of the bear and the ragged staff. Leaving Cecylee's brother and his uncle William Neville, Lord Fauconberg, in charge of the garrison at Calais, Warwick crossed to England and landed at Sandwich in Kent. Not pausing to draw breath, he pressed onto London.

On September 22, 1459, Warwick entered London unopposed. He left the next day at the head of a well-armed force, making for Warwick Castle where the Yorkist lords had planned to meet. However, the queen's army got to Warwick Castle before Warwick

did, and since Warwick did not have enough men to risk a
confrontation, he turned his army toward Ludlow, where York and his
army waited.

Meanwhile, Salisbury left Middleham for Ludlow with his army.
On September 23, Salisbury was approaching Market Drayton when
his scouts warned him the route was blocked by part of the queen's
army. He drew up his forces in battle order on nearby Blore Heath
and waited.

By dark, the Yorkists were victorious, and Salisbury anxiously
pressed on to the safety of Ludlow. Unfortunately, the queen was
waiting with the rest of her army at Eccleshall Castle, not ten miles
away. Salisbury's solution was subterfuge: He gave his cannon to an
Augustinian friar with instructions to fire it off intermittently during
the night.

When my lady queen arrived the next morning, she found a
frightened friar, a deserted campsite, and a field strewn with corpses.
Salisbury was nowhere to be seen, for he had already arrived at
Ludlow.

CHAPTER 39

October 1459

Queen Marguerite wasted no time. She mustered an army of thirty thousand and marched towards Ludlow. Richard responded by leading an army of twenty-five thousand out of Ludlow towards Worcester with the aim of getting to London. The queen's army blocked him, however, so he returned to Ludlow, encamping south of the town at Ludford Bridge.

On the evening of the tenth day of October, the queen arrived in Ludlow and pitched tents.

A murmuring of male voices came from the direction of the great hall. It was late, pitch black, and cold. Cecylee lit a lantern, slipped out of bed, put on a fur-lined robe and slippers, and went to investigate.

"Aren't you going to fight a battle?" she said as she entered.

Richard came and took her hands.

"Our men are deserting. They are going over to the other side as we speak."

She shivered. "What will you do?"

"We are going abroad, for we must escape capture," said Salisbury.

"My lord father and I are going to Calais to bide our time," said Warwick. "We will return to fight when the time is ripe."

"We'll go to Ireland," said Richard, putting a hand on Rutland's shoulder.

"I shall stay," said Edward, "and take my lady mother, my brothers, and my sister Margaret to the abbey at Wigmore."

"No," said Cecylee.

"Cis! It's for your own good!" exclaimed Richard.

"There is no time to get us to safety," she replied. "Besides, the country is crawling with Lancastrian spies."

"Mother," protested Edward. "You are not safe here."

"I shall stay and intercede for the people of Ludlow," she remarked, lifting her chin.

Five pairs of male eyes stared at her, widening in disbelief.

Richard interposed. "I'll not allow it," he said, his mouth tightening into a grim line.

"They'll not harm a woman with three children. We shall dress in our finest clothes and array ourselves in front of the market cross at Ludlow. We'll be on public view. They'll not dare to mistreat us."

The silence was broken by Salisbury's sudden bark of laughter. "How like Mama you look. Do you remember the night when she expected a Percy raid and had you spirited off to the South of England under armed escort?"

Cecylee smiled at the memory. Mama had acted like a tigress to save her.

"What of Margaret?" asked Rutland quietly.

As usual, he'd found the weak spot in the plan. Cecylee was not happy at the thought of her beautiful thirteen-year-old daughter being surrounded by rude soldiers.

"I'll not allow it," repeated Richard.

"We have no choice," she replied. "It is imperative that you all leave and leave now. There is not a moment to lose."

The silence held, and then York nodded somberly.

Salisbury, Edward, and Warwick said their farewells quickly and left. Richard wrapped his arms around her and gave her a peck on the cheek.

"I leave Ludlow in your care."

He signaled to Rutland, who knelt at Cecylee's feet for her blessing.

Then, they were gone.

Book IV: Two

Murders Reaped

*To all sicke men is given a lybertye to have all such things
as may be to their ease…
If any man fall impotente, he hath styll the same wages
that he had when he might doe his best service, during my
ladyes lyfe.*

*FROM ORDERS AND RULES OF
THE PRINCESS CECILL
QUOTED BY
JOHN WOLSTENHOLME COBB (1883)
HISTORY & ANTIQUITIES OF BERKHAMSTED*

CHAPTER 40

Ludlow, Welsh Marches
October 13, 1459

A low, rumbling sound could be heard faintly in the distance. It grew louder. It shimmered with the addition of the high jingling sounds of harness and bridle. A trumpet sounded a blast, and the folk of Ludlow came to their doors, braced for the worst. A chill wind lifted my veil, fluttering from the point of my tall henin. To greet the queen, I arrayed myself in a dress of pale green damask woven with gold thread, worn over a violet chemise. I had not thought to put on my mantle, believing we would be back in the castle soon. But the neckline of my gown was edged in miniver, and that helped to ward off the cold.

My three children stood with me; Margaret, running a rosary through her fingers as she recited the prayers I'd taught her; George, shifting impatiently from one foot to the other as he fingered the exquisitely bejeweled dagger his father had given him; and Richard, who had turned seven only ten days before. Richard was dressed in his favorite shade of grey, which set off his grey-blue eyes. In contrast to his brother, he was quiet, far too quiet. The only emotion he showed was when he clutched at my hand when, with a roar, the queen's army flooded into the marketplace of Ludlow. The sound was deafening as the children and I were suddenly surrounded by the grinning, leering faces of unwashed, unshaven men, brandishing weapons.

"Well, well, and what have we here?" said one of these churls, sidling up to Margaret, eyeing her in a thoroughly disgusting fashion.

Margaret had dressed in her best sky-blue damask, setting off her creamy skin and rich dark-brown hair. She edged closer to me, shivering. How I wished that I had made her put on her thick fur mantle, for she needed it now, more for protection from leering eyes than for warmth.

I stepped forward. "I am Cecylee, Duchess of York. I wish to speak to the Duke of Somerset." Henry Beaufort, now Duke of Somerset, had been given command of the Lancastrian army at the age of three-and-twenty years. I knew little of this young man, but surely he could not be as bad as his father, who'd been one of Richard's greatest enemies.

"You do, do you?" answered the fellow. "I'm sure he'd like to speak to you too." This remark was followed by loud guffaws from the other men.

A film of sweat blossomed on my forehead, dampening my wimple. I flushed and clasped my hands together to still their shaking. I hadn't thought that the men might refuse my request.

But a stir started quickly, and the Duke of Somerset rode into view, followed by Humphrey Stafford, Duke of Buckingham, and Henry Percy, Earl of Northumberland, the commanders of the queen's army. With one motion of Somerset's hand, the churls fell back. He dismounted.

"Duchess," he called as I curtseyed low. "Where is your lord? Your brother? Your older sons?"

"They are not here," I replied.

I put my hands on my boys' shoulders to remind them of their manners. They bowed under the gentle pressure of my fingers.

"I am here, as you see, with my younger children. I beg you to be merciful."

"Beg?" His eyebrows shot up. He put his hand to his chin, considering. "I don't think I have ever seen you beg, Duchess Cecylee."

My cheeks warmed. I had not expected to be forced to answer the accusation of Proud Cis now. I looked at the ground. It was filthy. If I knelt down, I would ruin the gown Jenet had finished only the other day.

I bit my lip, shot Somerset a look. He stood there, hand to chin, one eyebrow raised, regarding me with ill-concealed amusement. In the distance, the folk of Ludlow edged away from their doorways, forming a large silent crowd. They craned their necks, and I recognized the pleasant young woman I employed to clean my chamber. What about those poor people? One ruined dress was nothing. They were my people; I was their liege lady. It was my duty to protect them.

Without a second thought, I knelt in the filth. It squelched noisily as I lowered myself to my knees, and an unpleasant smell assailed my nostrils. I looked up and raised both hands in supplication.

"My lord of Somerset, I beg you. Be merciful to the good folk of Ludlow. They have done nothing wrong."

"Where is York?" snapped Northumberland, coming up by Somerset's side.

Somerset regarded Northumberland, then turned back to me. "We are prepared to be merciful to you and yours," he said, "if you tell us the whereabouts of York, March, Rutland, Salisbury, and Warwick."

I froze.

"You're upsetting Mama," put in George suddenly. He stepped forward, his hand on his dagger.

George had turned ten yesterday, and it had taken hours to get him ready, for he was fond of clothes. He had already discarded twelve suits before settling on a bright green tunic decorated with gold thread.

"It matches your gown, Mama," he said, smiling his charming smile so that I wouldn't be angry with him for being made to wait.

Before I could prevent him, George continued, "You shouldn't make Mama kneel in this filth. She has ruined her best gown."

My sides ached as I held in my breath. The last thing I wanted was for my boy to speak out.

Fortunately, Somerset laughed. "And who are you, my little lordling?"

I put my hand on George's arm and gently withdrew his hand from his dagger. "This is my son George."

Somerset pointedly turned his back on the boy and leaned in closer. "Out with it, my lady. I think you know where the Yorkist lords are."

I lowered my lashes and stared at the ground. What could I say? I knew that once these Lancastrian lords got their hands on them, they'd never come back alive.

"Torch their houses!" someone bellowed.

I scrambled to my feet and tugged at Somerset's sleeve. "My lord, I beg you. Be merciful. What have these people done?"

He disengaged my arm roughly and spat out a response. "You can stop all this, my fine lady." He eyed my spattered skirts. "Just tell us where they are."

"Never!" I cried.

A high neighing made me turn. Marguerite d'Anjou, Queen of England, dressed in cloth of gold, sat on a black horse. As the queen eyed me grimly, I journeyed back in time to when I'd last seen her and asked for a pension of one thousand marks in return for Richard's loyalty. My cheeks warmed, ice crawled up my spine. What was I doing here with three children? I shouldn't be putting their lives in danger. I should have gone to the priory at Wigmore as Edward had suggested. After all, the queen could kidnap the boys. Why wouldn't she? She had already taken two of Salisbury's sons.

The queen's hard voice cut through my wandering thoughts. "My lady York well met. I see you have mislaid your husband."

George opened his mouth, and I put a hand on his shoulder to forestall him. Perhaps I could persuade her to be reasonable, one woman to another. Wrinkling my nose, I again lowered myself to my knees as the men guffawed, making cracks about the state of my garments.

"Madame!" I said, "I beg you for the love of Christ, be merciful to the folk of Ludlow. Prevent your soldiers from torching their homes, from looting, from rampaging."

I paused and bit my lip.

"You lied!" exclaimed the Queen, pointing her whip at me. "You came to me all those years ago, begging me not to notice your lord's treacherie. Why should I listen to anything you say now? You are two-faced Madame. You are duplicitous."

I trembled as I bowed my head. I learned then that Marguerite never forgot the wrongs done to her.

"So, you imagine we are animals," continued Marguerite. She raised her hand. "Let us show my lady York."

She let her hand fall, and the Lancastrian beasts set to work. By the time they'd finished, Ludlow was nothing more than an ash-heap. When they'd finished with the town, they went into the castle, and all of our costly furnishings, clothing, and books were thrown about, looted, and burned.

I was forced to watch with my three children. The worst part of this harrowing and humiliating experience was the sound. The sound of horses panicking, people screaming, fire roaring, people begging for their lives, women pleading to be spared from rape.

By the time they'd finished, dusk was falling. It was the worst day of my life. Most of all, my children had to go through it. Margaret wept silently, her face smudged from the smoke blackening everything. George clutched his dagger so hard it made his fingers bleed. But the worst was the effect it had on seven-year-old Richard. He disappeared. I could not rouse him. He just stared at me. Silent.

At length, they arrested and escorted us to Stafford Castle, the residence of the Duke of Buckingham, and my sister Anne. I hadn't seen much of Anne since we were children, and I wondered how she would be now. After all, her husband and mine were mortal enemies.

"Cecylee."

I turned, and there she was. My sister, only looking older.

She came forward, lines of concern etched on her face, and kissed me on the cheek.

I don't know why it was, perhaps because she suddenly reminded me of Mama. But suddenly, I broke down.

Anne took in the sight of my three children, filthy and exhausted, and immediately ordered hot baths and refreshments. She took me by the hand and led me into her chamber, where I was given a much-needed bath and some fresh garments. Anne's servants arrived, bearing hot possets, and we sent the children to bed.

"Where is your husband?" she whispered as we sat by the fire.

"You know I cannot tell you that."

She sighed. "Wherever he may be, he has left you to bear all this by yourself. Why, leaving a lady and three children to face down a whole army—"

"That was my idea," I interrupted, my cheeks burning. "My lord was against it, but he had no choice."

"You mean he was not able to anticipate the situation?"

"No," I replied, looking away. "Things moved so fast."

"I worry greatly for your safety, Cecylee," said Anne, leaning forward and patting my hand. "If a lord cannot protect his wife and children, who will?"

I hung my head as I knotted my fingers together. My feelings simmered just out of reach.

CHAPTER 41

Stafford Castle, Staffordshire
Autumn 1459 to Summer 1460

Richard and his allies determined to launch one final, decisive attack against the Court Party, and this naturally meant invading England from Ireland and Calais.

I knew little of these matters, for I was under house arrest, and scarcely any news got through. Anne was kind but loyal to her husband, the Duke of Buckingham, and she never discussed matters of political import. For the first time since that fateful summer when I'd met Blaybourne, I was separated from Richard. I couldn't even send or receive letters.

As the months passed with no word, my feelings gradually unraveled. I was furious with him for blundering yet again, leaving the children and me in such a perilous situation. I'd never seen an army before and had no idea the situation could be so dire. I imagined that I would kneel before the Lancastrian commanders, and they would honor my requests. They would lead me back to Ludlow Castle and then march on somewhere else. It never occurred to me that they might sack and burn the village of Ludlow, loot and destroy my possessions, and force me to watch the horror of it all with three children. Of course, Richard must have known how bad things could've been. But he'd fled anyway.

As I saw the damage that had been done to the children, I grew angrier and angrier. Margaret seemed unable to stop weeping. George talked about killing people with a disquieting light in his eyes. But Richard was the child who worried me most, for he did not seem like a normal seven-year-old. During the day, he was silent. At night, he couldn't sleep from the nightmares that haunted him.

I tried to make life as normal as I could for the children. I had Richard sleep with me at night while George and Margaret slept together. But what was I to do about Margaret's constant weeping? It grated on everyone's nerves. One day, we sat with the ladies of Anne's household, embroidering, when I noticed how accomplished Margaret had become.

"My sweet," I said as an idea struck me. "How would you like to embroider some shirts for your father?"

"Father?" whispered Margaret, after looking around to be sure no one was listening.

I smiled sadly. Margaret was already acting far older than her thirteen years.

"It would mean a great deal to him."

Margaret smiled for the first time in many weeks.

I kissed her. Then my thoughts turned to the other Richard, my youngest son.

"It worries me that Richard is so silent," I murmured as Margaret dried her tears, opened her needlework box, and started hunting for skeins of silk. "Does he talk at all when I'm not around?"

"Not really," replied Margaret, threading her needle. "He seems to enjoy reading books."

Wasn't that an unusual occupation for a seven-year-old? "I would like you to spend more time with him. He needs to be with people."

"I could ask him to walk with me when I go outside with the others." Anne had four daughters living at home who were around the same age as my children.

"A good thought, my love," I said rising and smiling at her. "And now, I must see to George."

With his father gone, George saw himself as the head of the family and strutted about self-importantly, earning him laughs and sneers from those of Buckingham's affinity. I sighed as I made my way to his chamber. The boy was charming and intelligent, but—

"My lady," called Jenet softly. She came forward and put her mouth close to my ear. "The London merchants have given my lord of Warwick eighteen thousand pounds."

I stared at her. That was an enormous sum of money. It could only mean that the merchants were full weary of the bad government of the king and had actually paid Warwick to invade England. I opened my mouth when Jenet indicated with her eyes that someone was watching.

I turned slowly around. It was Anne.

"Cecylee!" she exclaimed, kissing my cheek. "What are you doing here?"

"Looking for George," I replied. "I am worried about him. He has so much energy and not enough to do."

"That's very true," said Anne, laughing, taking my arm.

Had she noticed Jenet? I guided Anne downstairs in the opposite direction. "George isn't a scholar," I continued. "He needs something to channel his considerable energies." And dull those bloodthirsty thoughts.

"'Tis time he became a page," remarked Anne. "Perhaps he could serve his uncle Buckingham."

I thanked her as I smiled my misgivings away. I hoped George would behave himself, not speak out of turn, nor divulge matters best to be silent about. Most of all, I hoped that George's position in Buckingham's household did not mean that he was being held hostage against the good behavior of his lord father.

In June of 1460, my nephew Warwick arrived in Kent. My lady queen was unable to prevent this from happening —or prevent the arrival of my brother Salisbury or that of my son Edward, Earl of March. Her sailors mutinied, and thus the Yorkist ships passed them by, unmolested.

I bit my nails to the quick on hearing this news, whispered to me by Jenet. Warwick was taking a great risk by occupying a town in Kent, for his lands and sphere of influence lay in the distant north and west. This meant that he had to take London before he could reach his lands.

He was held in such esteem and affection by the people of Kent and the Londoners; however, I need not have worried. When he sent messages asking for support, the mayors of the little Kentish towns readily complied. Soon, men flocked to Warwick's standard in large numbers. Then, though my lady queen tried to prevent the Yorkist lords from entering the city of Canterbury, their sympathizers gave them the keys. The gates were flung open, and the people gave Warwick, Salisbury, and March a warm welcome. During their short stay, Warwick secured the good offices of the papal legate, which had the effect of encouraging the bishops to join the Yorkist cause.

News of the invasion had by now reached London. The mayor of that city, anxious that he not been seen as treasonous, sent a cautiously worded message to Warwick, advising him that he would not be permitted to enter.

It did not matter.

Warwick had so many friends among the merchants and the people that the mayor was persuaded to reconsider.

On the second day of July, the gates of London were
thrown open, and the Yorkists lords entered the city,
followed by around forty thousand armed men.

"Their plan now must be to gain control over the king,"
I murmured to Jenet as we sat outside with our sewing.
Stafford Castle was quiet, all the menfolk gone to the
queen's army, commanded by Buckingham.

"Your son Edward and my lord of Warwick are to leave
London for Coventry where the king resides," she
whispered.

However, the king left Coventry and marched to
Northampton to take refuge in the almost impenetrable
Fen country surrounding the Isle of Ely. The queen's army
arrived in Northampton to protect the king, drawing itself
up in battle order.

On the tenth of July, Warwick's army arrived. He tried
to avoid battle by sending the papal legate and other
bishops to the king to beg an airing of the grievances of the
Yorkist lords. My lord of Buckingham accused the bishops
of hypocrisy and advised the king to pay them no heed.

At two o'clock in the afternoon, with the rain teeming
down, watched by the papal legate and the Archbishop of
Canterbury, Warwick ordered his trumpeters to sound the
call to battle. Edward commanded the vanguard. His
advance across the Nene marshes was met with a deadly
series of volleys from the Lancastrian archers.

CHAPTER 42

Stafford Castle, Staffordshire
July 1460

As I stepped onto the castle battlements, a cooling breeze lifted my veil. I looked for George, but he was nowhere to be seen. Thank goodness that George had been considered too young to fight; for Buckingham would certainly have taken him when he left the castle a fortnight ago. I could only marvel at my good fortune. Buckingham had been courteous and, more importantly, had refrained from making hostages out of my two boys. I thanked God every day for their safe deliverance while I awaited tidings of the latest conflict.

Though it was hot, the commander of the garrison at Stafford Castle did not allow his men to relax. All were stationed at their posts and had to remain there while Anne directed her servants to pour watered-down ale. Leaving Anne behind me, I wandered along the parapet encircling the castle wall. I came upon George engaged in assisting a squire with the commander's heavy armor. While the two boys tightened buckles and tied laces, the commander scanned the horizon.

I watched for a moment. This son reminded me most forcibly of my father. Like him, George was an amusing and lively companion. Even his gestures were similar as he told jokes. His bright eyes took everything in, and I sighed once more with sorrow as I thought of the horrors he'd seen that day at Ludlow. At that moment, he glanced up.

"Mama!" he called, looking like the young lad he was.

I smiled into his blue-green eyes. "Well met, my son."

"And how does my nephew?" remarked Anne, coming up silently behind me.

"Well, madam," responded George gravely. "I've been learning all about how to clean armor and which order the pieces go on."

"Lord George has a quick wit," remarked the commander, bowing. "He'll make a fine squire someday."

There was an awkward pause. How I wished this war would end. I turned to look at the horizon, which shimmered in the heat.

"Someone's coming," remarked George in a whisper.

I shot my son a look, then scanned the horizon again.

"To your posts!" roared the commander. "Ladies, I must ask you to wait below."

"George!" I exclaimed as fear gripped me.

"Mama!" he exclaimed, mimicking my tone.

I watched helpless as George scampered away.

"Leave him be," said Anne quietly. "He'll only fret if he's mewed up with us."

I sighed as I followed Anne downstairs. I went to my bedchamber to see Richard, who was feeling poorly. I wondered if he would survive this latest bout of illness. I'd lost so many children, two daughters and four sons who'd never grown up, locked in my memory as the small children they'd been when taken up to heaven. I recited the litany now as I looked down at Richard's wan face: Joan, Henry, William, John, Thomas, Ursula.

Sitting down, I took Richard's small hand in mine. What kind of man would he be? He was tenacious. He'd shown that by the way, he clung on through the worst of his illnesses. He was already showing the promise of a fine mind, preferring to play chess and read books. And he was preternaturally serious, just like his father.

I smiled, thinking of Richard. We'd met in December 1423 at Castle Raby. I'd been a lively eight-year-old sent out one bright December day to tend to my roses when I saw a strange boy watching me.

When asked who he was, he drew himself up stiffly. "Richard, Duke of York."

I tossed him some pert reply and turned my back on him while humming a favorite air. When I turned around, he was still there. "You're so serious!" I exclaimed. "Don't you ever smile?"

At that, he had smiled. Tentatively.

And now, I hadn't seen him in nine months. I'd grown accustomed to life without Richard and found that it suited me. Most of all, I reveled in the freedom of making my own decisions without the need to consult him. I felt a twinge of guilt. How was he faring in Ireland? I'd heard nothing—

A door banged, and then there was the sound of heavy feet. I bent over my son to hide my fear. The child was stirring.

"Mama?" he said sleepily. Then suddenly, his pale face lit with a smile.

I swung around.

"Edward!" I exclaimed.

Any misgivings I had about Edward vanished as I took him in, standing in front of me, tall and gleaming in his suit of armor. I thought he'd never looked so handsome, and my heart caught in my throat.

"Mother," he said, bowing. Then he kissed me on the cheek before turning to the bed. "And how goes brother Richard?"

To my amazement, Richard pushed himself up in bed and leaned forward eagerly. Under his older brother's smile, Richard shed years, looking like a little boy rather than an old man.

"I bought you a gift," remarked Edward.

How had Edward found the time to get his little brother a gift?

Edward reached into the folds of his tunic and drew out a horseshoe. "'Tis from White York, my stallion that helped me win the battle."

"Battle? What battle?" I asked.

"All in good time, Mother," replied Edward. He turned to Richard. "Tuck it under your pillow for good luck."

"I wish I could fight like you," remarked Richard, gazing at Edward with shining eyes.

"You do fight," said Edward, patting his shoulder. At that moment, the door blew open, and George entered, followed by Margaret. "Tell us the news!"

Edward gave an account of the Battle of Northampton, and I could hardly believe he was alive. "You were under fire from the Lancastrian archers, and the weather was atrocious?"

"Aye," agreed Edward. "The mud was thick and viscous. That's how White York lost his shoe. But the Lancastrians could not fire their cannon because the rain was teeming down. When we reached their defenses, Lord Grey de Ruthun gave the signal, and his men helped us over the barricades."

I clasped a hand over my mouth. Edmund Grey, a faithful supporter of the Lancastrian cause, threw his allegiance in with the House of York? "He should be rewarded," I breathed, drying my hands on my handkerchief. "I am most grateful that Lady Fortune was with you that day."

Suddenly, my mind jolted awake. What was Edward doing at Stafford Castle?

I turned to him. "Buckingham?"

Edward looked grim. "I bear bad tidings. He's dead."

CHAPTER 43

July to October 1460

The Battle of Northampton lasted the space of one half of an hour, and at the end of it, Warwick, March, and Salisbury took possession of the king and conducted him to Delapré Abbey. My lady queen fled with her son to Scotland.

Though I was free from house arrest, my heart bled as I said my farewells to my sister Anne. But she seemed to take the news of Buckingham's passing with a kind of stoic resignation. Her family flocked to her side. Their silences and stares convinced me to be quick in my leave.

Now I was free. As free as a lark to soar up into the air and sing merrily. I traveled to Baynard's Castle, my London residence, taking the children with me.

On the eighth day of September, Richard, together with Edmund, returned from Ireland. He sent a message asking me to meet with him in Hereford. I sighed, for it was not going to be easy to be Richard's wife again after the freedom of the past few months.

Leaving the children behind in London, I took a horse litter, choosing this somewhat queenly mode of transportation because I did not feel like riding the hundred or so miles. Taking a litter hung with blue velvet curtains and drawn between two pairs of fine horses was not only a stylish way of greeting my long-absent husband. It also had the effect of prolonging my journey.

While I journeyed, I had the leisure to ponder. How unfortunate that Richard was not a person to whom folk warmed easily, for he had many good qualities. He cared deeply about the people and had been loyal to King Henry until the King's misrule had driven him to take up arms. But Richard also had his flaws. He was arrogant, he was proud, and as always, he was too serious for his own good. While I journeyed to Hereford, I wondered how he would be now.

When finally, I saw him, it was as if a stranger were standing there. Richard had grown stout during his sojourn in Ireland. His hair and beard had gone grey, and there were harsh lines around his mouth. But when he caught sight of me, his smile made him look like the young man who'd courted me.

He eagerly helped me down from the litter, so caught up in greeting me that he didn't notice the expensive mode of transportation. "Cis! You look as fair as ever. Christ! How I've missed you."

I smiled as I submitted to his embraces. Then I looked around. "Why are your men in such livery? They are bearing the Royal Arms." I turned to stare at him. "That's treasonous, Richard."

Richard's mouth set in a grim line, following the creases of the new lines around his mouth. "I wish to make my pretensions to the throne clear. I will not be gainsaid by anyone, not even you, Cis."

And with that, he strode off.

Richard was not in the most communicative of moods as he and I traveled to London at the head of a large retinue. I tried to persuade him to discuss his plans with me. To no avail. Had Richard even consulted with his allies? The night before our arrival in London, growing anxious, I forced the issue.

I ordered the cook to prepare Richard's favorite dishes. I had my women dress me in a gown of lilac brocade, for it was one of Richard's favorite colors. Then I sent a message inviting him to my tent.

By the time he arrived, I'd given instructions to put thick carpets on the floors, light candles, and arrange flowers. A group of musicians sat in one corner, playing some of his favorite airs. He smiled as I took him by the hand and bade him sit beside me.

First, I presented him with gifts from the children, including Margaret's beautifully embroidered shirts. Then I signaled for the servants to bring out the meal. Only when he'd finished eating and was well watered with wine did I broach the topic. Signaling for the servants to leave, I stroked his hand.

"My lord," I began in a low tone, leaning forward, "What mean you to do once we arrive in London?"

"I mean to claim the throne for myself."

"That is your right, but do others know of your plans?"

Richard's eyes went from being the gentle grey-blue of waves rippling by the shoreline to the flinty grey of a winter sky. "Why should I tell anyone? Think you I should ask permission?"

I stroked his hand again, for he was so irritable these days. "Of course not," I said soothingly. "But don't you think it might be better to make sure they agree with you?"

"Of course, they agree with me. That's why we're fighting, isn't it?"

I sighed and pressed ahead. Richard could be heavy weather, but it was imperative to nudge him in the right direction. If he were going to succeed in his ambitions, he had to get the backing of the magnates, as well as the citizens of London. "Does Salisbury know that you're marching to London to take the throne of England?"

The silence stretched on. "No," said Richard reluctantly, crumbling his bread.

"I think," I whispered, "I think you should dictate a letter to him and to the other magnates explaining what you intend to do."

Richard frowned and stopped crumbling bread. Finally, he nodded. "I give you my word."

I sagged with relief and gave him my most dazzling smile.

On the tenth day of October, Richard and I arrived in London. Much to the marvel of the folk of the City of London, our trumpeters bore the sovereign arms of England. We proceeded to Westminster Hall, where Parliament was to meet. Dismounting at the door, Richard caused the sword of state to be borne before him. He strode through the throng of magnates and made his way to the throne, whereon he placed his hand. Placing his hand on the throne was the clearest signal Richard could give that he thought he should be king.

There was dead silence.

I looked for my relatives, for Salisbury and Warwick, confident that they knew and approved of this gesture. I expected them to come forward and acclaim Richard as their sovereign.

The silence continued dismay on even friendly faces.

They were completely ignorant of his plans.

Mortified, I would have vanished in a puff of smoke at that instant if I could. Richard had lied to me. I looked at his shadowed face as he stared at the throne. He'd never done that before. What did it mean?

Richard lifted his head and flushed purple. "I am the heir general of King Richard II, and I tell you, I have waited too long. I shall be crowned King Richard III on All Hallows Day."

There was silence. All Hallows Day was less than three weeks away.

Archbishop Bourchier of Canterbury, the kinsman by marriage Richard had placed in that position so many years ago, came forward: "My lord. Perhaps you should obtain an audience with King Henry to discuss your claim."

Richard bristled. "I should obtain an audience with Henry of Lancaster?" he spat. "Say, rather, he should seek an audience with me. He is the usurper, descended from a line of usurpers, who illegally wrested the throne from King Richard II." Richard's voice grew louder and louder during this speech until he was bellowing at the magnates in that echoing hall.

He swept them one final look of disgust, then stormed out.

Conversation buzzed as soon as he disappeared. With flaming cheeks, I took the opportunity to slip away to Baynard's Castle. I ordered the main meal to be served and pushed my food around my plate while waiting for Richard to return. Had the many years of frustration not only soured his temper but also turned him into a liar?

Eventually, Richard stormed in again, surrounded by men-at-arms. Without greeting me, he went to the sideboard to pour himself some wine.

Suddenly Warwick appeared. "Why didn't you consult us?" he roared, too angry to bother with a greeting. "This is madness. Why should our lord king be deposed now? He's ruled us for thirty-eight years. There's no precedent for your arrogance."

"How can you stand by a king who has promulgated decades of misrule upon this land?" Richard shot back.

Warwick came closer. "We took oaths of allegiance. Including you. He is our anointed king before God. Surely you're not thinking of arrogating the power of God to yourself."

Richard clenched his fingers around his wine-cup. "Kings have been deposed before. Henry's grandfather usurped the throne from King Richard II."

"Does your cursed ambition know no bounds?" bellowed Warwick. "King Richard was a tyrant, King Henry is a good man. He's saintly and pious. He's been good to the magnates, and you took an oath of allegiance to him."

This noisy row drew the whole household. Seventeen-year-old Rutland now appeared. When he saw Warwick castigating his father, he approached his cousin. "Fair sir, be not angry, for you know that we have the true right to the crown and that my lord and father here must have it."

Warwick flushed and bit his lip, for Rutland was correct. Richard had the better claim to the throne.

Eighteen-year-old Edward had been lounging at the table cracking nuts, seemingly uninterested in the row. But now he looked up and remarked, "Brother, 'tis not wise to vex Warwick."

Warwick smiled. Turning away from Richard and Rutland, he made a great show of speaking only to Edward.

CHAPTER 44

Palace of Westminster, London
October 16, 1460

Norfolk, premier duke and earl of the realm eyed Richard grimly. "We have taken our oaths, and we stand by that."

Richard signaled to his scribe, who unrolled the parchment and set it on the table. "This shows that I am the rightful claimant to the throne," he said loudly. "This is my genealogy, showing my descent from King Edward III. I am descended from his second son, Lionel of Antwerp, through my mother, Lady Anne de Mortimer. My cousin, Henry of Lancaster, is descended from his third son, John of Gaunt."

Richard no longer referred to Henry VI as king; he was always Henry of Lancaster. I looked at Richard, trying to follow his mood. We stood in the great hall of Westminster

Palace as Richard formally presented his claim to the great magnates of the land. At least he was calmer than he'd been a week ago. This time, he'd asked Salisbury and Warwick for their opinion. They advised him to go to the lords without them to see more clearly what kind of support he would get.

What would Richard be like as king? I didn't like to think about it. He had many enemies and lacked the ability to deal with them. His temper was short, and being an unpopular king would shorten it further. He was stubborn and too arrogant to take advice. I'd seen these traits grow worse as he gained power. Worst of all, his actions might harm the children. Nevertheless, it remained my duty to act as Richard's loyal wife.

"Why didn't you put forth your claim before?" said John de Vere, Earl of Oxford. "It would have saved us a passel of trouble had you spoken up."

Richard flushed. "Though truth for a time may rest and be put to silence," he replied, "yet it never dies."

"Humph," snorted Oxford.

"My lords," said Viscount Henry Bourchier and Richard's brother-in-law. "Should we not discuss this now? Duke Richard has presented his case and furnished his genealogy. I suggest we take some time to study it."

Voices murmured, and robes swished as the lords peered at Richard's parchment.

"This claim is a nothing," sneered Nan's husband, Exeter. "It derives through a woman. And we know women are good for only one thing." He laughed.

My lips thinned as I glared. Being so close to him and having his vulgar remarks shoved into my face made me physically sick. How was Nan? I knew only she'd given her lord one daughter some five years before. My anger welled up and veered rapidly from Exeter to Richard and back again. Like a weathervane in a storm.

"My lord of York's claim is derived from his lady mother, Anne de Mortimer," said Bourchier.

"But the whole claim is dominated by females," objected Somerset, fingering the parchment. As the son of Richard's greatest enemy, Henry Somerset was the last person who wanted to see Richard's claim prevail. "Look at this." He pointed with one finger. "Not only is the claim though his mother Anne de Mortimer, but also though his great-grandmother Philippa, daughter of Lionel of Antwerp."

"His claim would be far stronger if it were through the male line," said Northumberland.

"Like that of our lord king," chimed in Somerset.

Richard glared but was prevented from speaking by Bourchier. "Women may inherit, my lords."

He looked at Norfolk in appeal. Norfolk's opinion carried weight.

"When there is no male heir, then yes, a woman may inherit," said Norfolk. He'd been studying the parchment intently, and now he took off his eyeglasses and shook his head slowly. "I am sorry to say this, my lords, but indeed I think my lord of York has the better claim."

Richard beamed.

There was a roar of disapproval.

Richard went white.

My heart sank. Just as I feared, Richard did not have the support he needed. The better claim to the throne didn't matter—his enemies would fight him tooth and claw.

"We cannot change horses in midstream," said Northumberland.

"It's unthinkable to renege on our oaths of allegiance," said Oxford.

"York cannot be King," shouted Somerset.

"My lords, my lords," interrupted Bourchier. "Some compromise must be possible." He looked at Norfolk.

"We could disinherit Prince Édouard," said Norfolk slowly, "and make York heir-apparent."

"That way, York could succeed on the king's death," remarked Exeter with a sneer.

That was not what Richard wanted; ten years older than the king, he was likely to die sooner.

CHAPTER 45

November 1460 to January 1461

On the eighth day of November, in the year 1460, Richard was proclaimed heir-apparent to the throne and Protector of England by the Act of Accord. All the lords, spiritual and temporal, swore allegiance to him as the king's heir, and he, in turn, swore allegiance to Henry of Lancaster and the lords, saying he would abide by all conventions and compacts. Richard of York now ruled England in the name of the king.

I sat by his side at the Palace of Westminster and endured the uneasy atmosphere of a court torn by factions. Richard seemed to believe his position invincible. But I couldn't sleep at nights. From the north, news was not good.

Marguerite reached a settlement with the Queen of Scotland and was resting at Falkirk when news of the Act of

Accord broke. Furious her son had been disinherited, she amassed an army of some twenty thousand men. She acted so swiftly Richard realized what happened only too late. That November, at York, Queen Marguerite challenged Richard to settle the issue of succession by a contest of arms, then marched her army south.

Richard sent my son Edward to Ludlow to repair the damage done by the raid of 1459. Then with Rutland and Salisbury, he marched out of London on the ninth day of December at the head of an army of around six thousand men to meet the queen, leaving Warwick in charge of London.

I settled down to celebrate Christmas with my three youngest children, making many visits to Warwick's residence on the Strand. There we enjoyed the hospitality of his wife Anne and two daughters, Bella and Nanette. I allowed myself a much-needed respite, relaxing at Warwick's well-appointed house, surrounded by the good wishes of the London merchants and the people of London. I was grateful that Bella and Nanette were good companions for my boys. Even eight-year-old Richard managed a shy smile when his four-year-old cousin Nanette greeted him. He sat down and began to teach her chess.

"She's too young for that," exclaimed George, who was now eleven. His mouth crammed full of fruit, George held out a sticky hand.

"Come, Bella," he said to his nine-year-old cousin. "Let me show you the steps to the latest dance."

I smiled at the handsome pair they made. My children were happy. I should try to be so, for their sake.

"I miss Father," whispered fourteen-year-old Margaret, sitting down beside me.

I covered her cold fingers with my own. "So do I," I replied, looking at the thick snow falling outside. I shivered at the thought of Richard having to endure that cold. "Let us pray that he finds some peace and joy this Christmastide."

"Your lord is gone, madam," said the messenger, crossing himself.

"You say he was cut down?" I took a shaky breath.

"He was pulled off his horse."

My hands flew to my mouth to prevent shrieks, for I didn't want the children to hear.

Everything went black.

When I came to, I was bewildered to find myself in my bedchamber in the middle of the day.

Jenet wiped my face with a lavender-scented handkerchief. "You've had a nasty shock, my lady."

I gazed up into her brown eyes. "Is it true?"

Jenet nodded.

I looked away. Only forty-nine. If only I'd loved him as he deserved. He'd never had an easy life. Orphaned by the time he was four. Then he married me—

By the time Richard reached Sandal Castle in Yorkshire, the poor weather left few supplies. He spent Christmas there and, shortly afterward, sent a party of men to forage. They were ambushed by Lancastrian scouts. On hearing of this, my lord of York rode out of Sandal Castle with Salisbury and Rutland in a heroic effort to protect his men. The whole Lancastrian army surrounded him. They pulled him off his horse and murdered him. Salisbury was killed during the ensuing battle. Rutland was murdered in cold blood after the battle ended. He was only seventeen years old.

As the truth of what had happened dribbled into my mind, I became ill. I sobbed for days as my heart squeezed out drops of guilt and pity. Only after my tears dried did my anger surface. Why had he impulsively rushed out of the castle? Didn't he have scouts who could tell him that a whole army was waiting to cut him to pieces? His stupidity cost not only his life but those of our son Rutland and my beloved brother Salisbury.

But he'd done his duty; I wept one night as his face floated before me. He couldn't let his men be cut down without trying to save them. And people respected him for that, extolling his knightly virtues whenever they came to console me.

"I'll make it up to you, my love," I murmured into a pillow.

Over the years, at the Augustinian priory at Clare in Suffolk, I erected a shrine to my lord of York in the form of a repository of documents and other memorabilia commemorating his life. I built an image of the lost heroic father, the worthy statesman, the pious man chosen by God to be king, and the courageous warrior beleaguered by his enemies. It was imperative that the House of York pull together to fight its enemies. And folk needed a hero to inspire.

And so, my marriage came to an end. But I did not have the luxury of grieving forever, for there was a war on.

After a month, I sat up in bed and took a deep breath. I was free. As a fabulously wealthy woman, I could live in comfort for the rest of my days. There would be no more pregnancies. I could indulge my slightest whim. And best of all, I need never marry again, for I was far too powerful to be cozened by an ambitious aristocrat seeking to feather his nest. I closed my eyes and silently thanked Our Blessed Lady.

CHAPTER 46

February to March 1461

After the massacre at Sandal Castle, Edward gathered the Yorkist forces together and fought a battle at Mortimer's Cross, which he won on the Feast of Candlemas, the second day of February in 1461, just a month after Richard was murdered.

The main part of the Lancastrian army moved south, marching toward London via Grantham, Stamford, Peterborough, Huntingdon, Royston, and Saint Albans. My lady queen was unable to pay her soldiers, so she gave them license to loot. They robbed, burned, raped, and pillaged their way through the countryside. They sacked priories and abbeys. They burned whole villages, barns, and manor houses. Many people fled south from the wrath of the northerners, carrying with them dreadful tales of atrocities.

These reports caused many towns to switch sides, furthering the Yorkist cause.

On the twelfth day of February, Warwick rode out of London at the head of a large army, making his way north. He met the queen's army at Saint Albans on the seventeenth. Thus the Second Battle of Saint Albans commenced. Warwick would have won this engagement but for the treachery of one commander who held back, then raced to join the Lancastrian side. Under the cover of darkness, Warwick gathered up the remnants of his army and marched west to meet Edward of York.

As news of Warwick's defeat reached London, panic spread. Streets emptied as merchants shut and locked their shops. Folk barricaded themselves inside their houses. Some wealthy merchants even went abroad. The queen sent a deputation to London's mayor to negotiate the terms of the capital's surrender. She ordered the Londoners to proclaim Edward of York a traitor and assured them of amnesty.

The Londoners did not trust her.

My lady queen countered by sending four hundred of her elite troops to march on Aldgate, where they demanded admittance to the city.

The people of Aldgate barred their entry.

Another group of the queen's men made it to Westminster but were driven away by the indignant Londoners. And so the queen retreated to Dunstable in Bedfordshire, some forty miles to the northwest.

I was staying at my London residence of Baynard's Castle, increasingly concerned that George and Richard might be taken hostage for Edward's good behavior. Early one morning, I put them on a ship bound for Burgundy, where they would remain under the protection of Duke Philip until it was safe for them to return. Margaret remained in London with me, and every day we went from house to house, accepting hospitality from the good folk of London while persuading them to stay with the Yorkist cause despite the terrifying tales they were hearing about the queen's army.

On February 27, Edward rode into London at the head of twenty thousand knights and thirty thousand foot soldiers. I was reading in my solar at Baynard's Castle when the roar of the crowd reached my ears. I rose and went to my prie-dieu to pray. When I rose, the shouts of the crowd had become more distinct.

"Hail to the Rose of Rouen," they roared. One imaginative young man sang:

> *Let us walk in a new vineyard,*
> *and let us make a gay garden into the month of March,*
> *with this fair white rose and herb,*
> *the Earl of March.*

Smiling, I walked outside with Margaret. Edward was here, the Londoners behind him.

"Mother!" he exclaimed, vaulting off his gelding. "My fair sister!"

"Well met, my son," I said loudly and clearly so that the crowd could understand. I had not seen Edward since the death of Richard. Now, he was the head of the House of York. Nearly nineteen, he cut a striking figure, and he held the Londoners in the palm of his hand. With him was his cousin Warwick, already beloved of the people.

"Greetings, dear nephew," I said, kissing Warwick's cheek. Warwick was an ambitious, proud aristocrat who wanted to serve as the king's chief minister, but he had no thoughts of being king himself. As the grandson of Joan de Beaufort, born of an adulterous relationship between John of Gaunt and Catrine de Roet, Warwick did not have a tenable claim to the throne. And so, he supported his cousin Edward.

We waved to the crowd. Then I took them inside for mulled wine and counsel, which I invited Margaret to attend, believing she should understand matters of state.

The discussion was not congratulatory. Edward's position was not strong. Technically, he was an attainted traitor. He lacked funds, as well as the support of the majority of the magnates.

"It is imperative that you have the support of the London merchants," I remarked.

"Don't worry, Mother. We'll test the waters first," said Edward, kissing my cheek.

CHAPTER 47

Saint John's Fields, London
Sunday, March 1, 1461

For the first time in a long time, it was safe enough to go out, and the Londoners wanted to see the army defending them from the marauding Lancastrians. After morning Mass, they poured out of the northern edge of the city toward Saint John's Fields, where the Yorkist army camped.

It was a cool, blustery day with the wind whipping the ladies' veils around their faces. Fine ladies huddled in their mounds of sables, while their less well-off neighbors donned thick, woolen mantles. Warwick vaulted off his horse and strode among them, basking in their affection and warmth, the Bishop of London at his side. Someone even found a couple of wooden boxes for him to stand on so that he could be seen by all.

"Good people of London!" he exclaimed. "You may want to know why I say that King Henry is a usurper."

The crowd laughed and inched closer.

"It's simple," remarked Warwick. "My cousin Edward is descended from Edward III's second son, while Henry of Lancaster is descended from Edward III's third son."

"What happened to Edward III's first son?" someone asked.

"A goodly question," replied Warwick. "Edward III's first son had an only child, who became King Richard II. But King Richard had no children, and so his line died out."

"So, you are saying that the Earl of March is the legitimate heir to the throne?" asked a well-dressed young man, wearing a thick mantle of beaver fur.

"Exactly, my friend," replied Warwick. He turned to the Bishop of London.

"Good people," intoned the bishop, "we want to know your opinion. Think you that Edward, Earl of March, should be King of England?"

"Yea! Yea! King Edward!" shouted the crowd, clapping their hands.

The soldiers of the Yorkist army accompanied this acclamation by drubbing on their armor.

"We must call a council here at Baynard's Castle," I said when Warwick returned bringing news of what happened in Saint John's Fields. Certainly, events proceeded apace, and it was best to strike while the iron was hot.

"We must invite the Archbishop of Canterbury, all the bishops, and all of the peers. Parliament is in session, so it will be an easy matter to manage. I will have the invitations sent out now."

I snapped my fingers, sending people in all directions.

On the third day of March, the magnates present at the meeting that I convened at Baynard's Castle agreed that Edward should be offered the throne.

Still, I couldn't sleep that night. How was it that everything Richard had striven for so mightily was dropping into Edward's lap? The people of London scarcely knew him, yet they'd taken him to their hearts. Was it out of respect for the late duke?

I felt a twinge of guilt, then quickly suppressed it. Since Marguerite did not feel guilty about her illegitimate son, why should I? Richard was in heaven, and nothing could hurt him now. Clearly, no one knew that Edward was not the duke's son, not even Edward himself. I vowed to keep it that way.

Next morning, Warwick was ushered in just as I was breaking my fast.

"I come with a petition, dear Aunt!" he cried in ringing tones.

I rose, thanking Our Blessed Lady that my sleeplessness of the night before had caused me to rise early and put on my finest attire. Behind Warwick was a crowd of familiar faces. This could only be a deputation from the Lords and the Commons. I beckoned to my steward. "Ask Lord Edward to come at once."

When Edward walked in around an hour later, he looked every inch a king. I regarded him with astonishment, feeling again that now-familiar quandary that Blaybourne used to put me in—that a peasant could look like an aristocrat.

"God Save King Edward," raised a faint voice.

I turned around.

"'Tis the crowd outside," remarked Warwick. "They followed me all the way from the Herber and have been waiting."

I smiled. "Let us open the door, therefore, that we may hear them."

"King Edward! God Save King Edward!" chanted the crowd outside as my steward slowly opened the heavy oak door.

My chest swelled as tears pricked.

Warwick went down on one knee. "We humbly beg you, Edward, Earl of March, to accept the crown and royal dignity of England."

Wasn't it fortunate that I named him Edward? His name reminded everyone of his descent from King Edward III.

"Aye!" exclaimed the Lords and the Commons. "We beg you to accept the crown."

"Avenge us on King Henry and his wife!" chanted the crowd outside.

Edward bestowed his dazzling smile on everyone and made a pretty speech, in which he accepted their petition.

Warwick summoned London's leading citizens to Saint Paul's Cathedral, where they enthusiastically acclaimed their new sovereign. Truly, Edward behaved like a king that day. He made a thanksgiving offering to God, then processed to Westminster Hall, where he took the oath of the new monarch.

I found it all I could do to keep from weeping, my son attired in royal robes and the cap of estate, enthroned on the king's bench to the cheers of the greatest magnates of the realm.

Afterward, everyone formed up in procession and went past delirious Londoners who threw snowdrops and wintergreens at their new sovereign. They went to Westminster Abbey, where the abbot and monks presented Edward with the crown and scepter of Saint Edward the

Confessor. Edward made offerings at the high altar and the Confessors Shrine before seating himself in the coronation chair. He addressed the congregation, explaining to them why he was their rightful king. When the lords asked the people if they would have Edward as their king, their roars were loud enough to lift the roof. The magnates then knelt, one by one, to do homage to Edward while the monks sang the Te Deum.

On the thirteenth day of March, Edward left for the north.

CHAPTER 48

Baynard's Castle, London
April 3rd, 1461

On the third day of April, I received a letter from Edward. I called my household together and read it to them from the steps of the dais of Baynard Castle's great hall.

Well-beloved Mother, we greet you well.
It has pleased God to grant us a great victory at Towton this twenty-ninth day of March, in the first year of our reign.
We now advance on London, where I shall soon greet you in person.

"Edward the King!" Cups and tankards clanked, and everyone toasted my son. The noise they made carried

outside, and an excited crowd gathered. I ordered my
steward to proclaim the news of Edward's victory and
provide a cup of ale for anyone who wanted to toast him.
Then I mounted the stairs to my bedchamber to read the
rest of the letter.

*On the twenty-eighth day of March, I sent Cousin
Warwick to secure the bridge over the River Aire, but we
were ambushed, and many of our number were killed.
Cousin Warwick was wounded in the leg, but it was just a
graze. When the news spread, the soldiers were full
dismayed.*
*But Cousin Warwick saved the day by killing his own
horse, in full view of the army.*
*He told them that he would fight on foot and die with his
men rather than yield another inch.*

I lay back against my pillows. How proud my father
would have been to see how indispensable the Nevilles had
become to the House of York. Just as Salisbury had
supported my lord, so now his son Warwick supported my
son.

*Though the Lancastrians destroyed the bridge,
we managed to cross the Aire and set up camp that night
on the other bank.*
*Did I forget to mention that the weather was atrocious?
My men had to endure driving snow and hail.*
*Baron John de Clifford, whom you well know was
responsible for brother Rutland's murder, died.*

310

I shivered and crossed myself, trying not to think of another bitter winter day when my son, husband, and brother had been cut down by those Lancastrian beasts.

That night, I stayed in Pontefract castle.
The next day, I drew my men up in battle formation near unto the village of Towton.
We fought all day long, from around eleven in the morning to well past compline, in the midst of a thick blizzard.
As dusk came on, Norfolk sent in a strong force, and the Lancastrians fled in a rout.
Maybe forty thousand souls perished that day, the bloodiest day on English soil.
I have given the gravediggers extra wages, for their labor will be long and hard.

I crossed myself and murmured a prayer. How like Edward to remember the common folk. My heart swelled; he had endured a hard and bitter fight, and he had won. Now, I would be able to summon George and Richard home from their exile in Burgundy.

Written at Towton, the thirtieth day of March, by your most loving son,
Edwardus Rex.

A month before his nineteenth birthday, Edward became King of England, styling himself Edward IV. Henry of Lancaster and Marguerite d'Anjou were in York when they heard the news of their defeat. They fled north. Exeter was on their train.

Edward had won an important victory, yet it was incomplete. Henry of Lancaster, his wife, and her son was still at large, Marguerite vowing she would be revenged on the House of York.

CHAPTER 49

April to November 1461

Throughout April and May of 1461, I received numerous letters from Edward telling me of his affairs.

Well-Beloved Mother,
I write to you from the fair city of York, where I shall rest to celebrate Easter.
My first act on arriving was to order the decent burial of my beloved father, uncle and brother.
I hope, dearest Mother, this will give you some peace…

I felt the now-familiar rise of bile at the hideous way my menfolk had been treated. I retreated to the privy. After murdering them, the Lancastrian beasts struck their heads off their bodies and put them atop pikes above Micklegate

Bar, the main gateway into the city of York. These beasts even put a paper crown on my lord's severed head before moving off.

Later, propped up in bed with a cup of Jenet's soothing mint potion, I read the rest of the letter.

We are to set off north tomorrow in pursuit of the Bitch of Anjou.
My scouts tell me she is working her way towards Scotland with her family…

In early May, Edward left the north and returned to London, where he received a hero's welcome for saving the city from the savagery of the northerners. Unfortunately, he was unsuccessful in preventing the Bitch of Anjou, Henry of Lancaster, and others from reaching refuge in Scotland.

On the twenty-eighth day of June, in the year 1461, Edward was crowned in Westminster Abbey. On that day, he made his younger brother George the Duke of Clarence. Richard was allowed to remain under my care.

I was determined to do something for my eldest daughter Nan. When Marguerite d'Anjou and Henry of Lancaster fled north into Scotland, Exeter had followed, leaving his wife and daughter behind. Edward declared him to be a traitor and in the normal course of affairs, would have confiscated his lands. Yet he offered to restore Exeter's lands to Nan that she might live comfortably for the rest of her life and provide for her daughter, who would now be a wealthy heiress.Nan was at first unwilling to agree, certain that her husband would eventually return. She gave in only after seeing Edward's coronation. I wanted her to stay awhile in Baynard's Castle, but Nan refused.

"I must manage my lands, madam," she told me. "There are many out there who would take Anne's inheritance away. I must ensure that does not happen."

I could not fault her reasoning. Nan was like a whipped horse. Only time and the greatest patience would enable her to trust anyone again.

On the thirty-first day of July, Edward appointed Warwick to be Warden of the East and West marches on the northern border, thus combining the Percy's share of the defense with that of the Nevilles, for the Percy Earls of Northumberland were Lancastrian still. This was a rich and well-deserved reward for the cousin who'd proved himself a loyal friend. Edward also made him chief advisor, giving him the responsibility of defending the kingdom and of foreign policy.

Not more than a month passed after Edward's coronation before King Charles VII of France died. He was succeeded by his son Louis, who had been friendly towards the Yorkists. But matters between the new kings of England and France did not proceed smoothly. One September day, Edward was closeted in his study with his cousin Warwick, tackling the numerous problems facing England, when a young man flew in and bent at the knee, sweat pouring down his face.

"My lord King: I have here a letter to the queen." He paused and flushed red. "Pardon me, I mean Marguerite of Lancaster."

Warwick swung around. He cut a magnificent figure in a tunic of red velvet, a cloak of purple draped elegantly over one shoulder. "A letter?" he snapped.

"Yes, Your Grace. I mean, your lordship. I'm sorry, good sirs, my wits are that addled—" He gasped for breath.

Edward came forward. At six feet four inches, he was about six inches taller than his cousin. He also dressed magnificently. Today he was wearing a blue satin tunic, slashed to reveal a silver silk undershirt. He placed a large hand on the messenger's shoulder.

"Take a breath, my good man. You look as if you've run all the way from Scotland." He called to his squire. "Bring a cup of ale for this good fellow."

"That's very kind of you, sir, I mean, my lord, Your Grace—"

"What is your message?" snapped Warwick, his grey eyes hardening. Now in his early thirties, his fair hair was beginning to grey, and he had lines of experience around his mouth and eyes.

Edward smiled gently and patted the messenger again.

"Have some ale and tell us how you came by this letter."

"One of your spies intercepted it," replied the messenger, quaffing his ale.

Edward held his hand out and scanned the letter.

Madam, fear not, but be of good comfort, for we have been summoned to see King Louis. Therefore, beware ye venture not your person by sea till ye have other word from us—

Edward glanced up as Warwick came forward. His young unlined face showed little emotion, save for a clenching of the jaw. Silently, he handed over the letter.

"Christ's bones!" exclaimed Warwick. "I thought we had the favor of the new King of France. It is said he hates the House of Anjou. But that doesn't stop her from seeking his aid."

Edward moved to the table in the middle of the room and unrolled a large map that showed England, Scotland, Wales, and France. "We could be invaded at any time," he remarked. "Where do you think she's likely to strike?"

Warwick motioned for the messenger to leave and pointed to the Cotetin peninsula of Normandy. "Her plan might be to try and capture the Channel Isles to make a bridgehead to England from France."

"At the moment, she's in Scotland," replied Edward. "She can only attack the Channel Isles if she's in France. And that depends on King Louis giving her money."

"I have it on good authority that she's already exhausted her own funds. That letter can mean only one thing."

Edward looked up.

"She's worn out her welcome at the Scottish court," remarked Warwick.

Edward frowned. "She might strike from the north."

"Aye, she might," agreed Warwick, rubbing his chin. "All we need is more unrest there."

"Therefore, I think that you, cousin, should march to Alnwick," said Edward, pointing to the far north of England, "and capture it."

"Right," said Warwick, nodding. "I'll go there forthwith. We cannot have the Bitch of Anjou take a major Northumbrian stronghold."

He bowed and disappeared, followed by his large train of retainers, all bearing his badge of the staff and ragged bear on scarlet tunics.

Warwick captured not only Alnwick but also Bamburgh Castle, thus ensuring that the new king had the most important Northumbrian strongholds to serve as a bulwark against any invasion from Scotland.

On November 1st, 1461, Edward opened his first parliament. On that day, he made his youngest brother Richard, Duke of Gloucester, and sent him to live at Middleham, with my blessing, to train as a knight under Warwick's supervision.

CHAPTER 50

Summer 1463

The crowning of my son Edward seemed to be a vindication for all the sacrifices made. I was given my lands back and admitted to the highest councils of the land. Folk said that Duchess Cecylee ruled the king as she pleased. Never before had a lady had such influence unless you counted the activities of Queen Alainor of Aquitaine of three centuries before. No more would England have to endure a warrior queen who struck terror into the hearts of men with a rampaging army of animals she was unable to control. Instead, I modeled myself on Queen Alainor, known for her fair dealing whenever she dispensed justice at the various assizes held around the country.

In all of this, I was ably assisted by my nephew Warwick. And yet this was a time of peril for the new king, for the Bitch of Anjou was creating havoc, both by negotiating with the French and Burgundian princes and by repeatedly taking the Northumbrian fortresses. Finally, Warwick arranged a peace conference between Edward, King Louis XI of France, and Duke Philip of Burgundy, in the summer of 1463. The objective was to close France and Burgundy to Marguerite d'Anjou and Henry of Lancaster.

After that, Warwick set about finding a suitable bride for Edward, for in the two years he had been king he'd not had time to think about this matter.

"The Duke of Burgundy has offered his two nieces," I remarked, "Lady Marguerite de Bourbon and her sister Jeanne."

"How old are these ladies?" asked Warwick.

"Lady Marguerite has twenty-four years. Lady Jeanne, her sister, is a little younger. She has twenty-one years."

Warwick steepled his fingers as he leaned back in his elaborately carved chair. How he reveled in his power and influence. Indeed, in those days, Warwick appeared to have so much power that folk called him The Kingmaker. Or as one wit at the French court put it: "They have but two rulers in England, Monsieur de Warwick and another whose name I have forgotten." At that moment, he was securing the northern border, negotiating with the French and Burgundians, and helping Edward sort out the country's finances and judicial system. He strode about, followed by his huge army of retainers, always busy, always preoccupied.

"Edward has now twenty-one years," he remarked. "He might be happier with someone younger."

I nodded. "Perhaps you are right. There is a younger lady with whom I have been in correspondence. Lady Isabella of Castile has now turned twelve. She is very suitable, for she is the half-sister of King Henry of Castile and possible heiress to the throne of Castile."

"What of Lady Bona of Savoy?"

My ears pricked up as an image of Blaybourne dressed in his finery materialized. I was now so confused about the swirl of events surrounding my lover that I knew not whether he was a humble archer, a scholar, or a nobleman called Philippe of Savoy.

"Tell me about her."

"She is sister to the Queen of France. Her father is Duke Louis of Savoy, the eldest son of Duke Amadeus of Savoy."

Since Richard's death, I'd made discreet inquiries and learned that Philippe of Savoy was the youngest son of Duke Amadeus. Strangely, he remained unmarried. Lady Bona would be his niece and thus a possible cousin to Edward.

"She is a little older than Princess Isabella," continued Warwick, "and would now be turning fourteen."

"She would be able to bear Edward sons sooner. But what are the political implications?"

"This match would close France to the Lancastrian exiles," replied Warwick. "As we speak, the Lancastrian usurper Henry is at large in Scotland, while the Bitch of

Anjou and her son Édouard are in Burgundy, pleading for the duke to give them succor."

"We should do something about that."

Warwick smiled. "We need do nothing, dear Aunt, providing that France is on our side. It is King Louis's ambition to crush Burgundy. And he will succeed. He's crafty and wily, and France is a much greater power than Burgundy."

"That may be so," I replied. "But is Louis trustworthy? King Henry of Castile is weak and, therefore, malleable. I have it on good authority that he would be pleased to marry off his half-sister Isabella to a foreign power, for he has a newborn daughter to think of, and the Lady Isabella is her rival for the throne. I believe he would agree to very acceptable terms."

The door opened, and Edward suddenly appeared. "Mother," he said. "What are you discussing?"

"Your marriage," I replied, smiling up at him. He was my golden boy with his unusual height, thick head of golden hair, and bright blue eyes.

"We were just talking of two promising young ladies," said Warwick. "Isabella of Castile and Bona of Savoy."

"And what do these ladies look like?"

"Lady Isabella is highly intelligent and pleasing to look at," I replied, making a mental note to obtain a portrait of her. Of course, Edward would want an attractive wife.

"Does she have violet eyes?" asked Edward. "Or hair the color of silver?"

There was only one person who met that description, and that was Lady Eleanor Talbot, the youngest daughter of my dearest friend Margaret and now Lady Butler. She'd been married years ago.

Warwick looked at Edward intently. "Do you have someone in mind?"

Edward shrugged and smiled.

I waited for him to speak, a strange sensation of unease crawling up my spine.

"Do not look so serious, Mother," said Edward finally. "I wish only for a beauty."

"And that you shall have," declared Warwick, rising and slapping him on the back. "I have already turned down two ladies your mother suggested on the grounds they were too old."

Edward grimaced.

"I understand your tastes," said Warwick. He glanced at me and forbore to say more.

I thinned my lips. It was greatly disquieting that every young woman in the land was flinging herself at Edward.

"Find me a bride who is young, lively, and very beautiful," said Edward, clasping Warwick's hand. And with a quick kiss on my cheek, he disappeared.

CHAPTER 51

The Abbey of Our Lady and Saint John the Evangelist
Reading, Berkshire
September 14, 1464

Knowing that my son had chosen for his motto *Confort et Liesse* or "Comfort and Joy" should have prepared me. For Edward had one fatal flaw, he could be dangerously impulsive.

One fine September day in the Year of Our Lord 1464, I was waiting to talk with him about his forthcoming marriage to the Lady Bona of Savoy when the door to the chapter house burst open, and everyone poured out. Edward hurried over.

"What's happened?" I asked, noticing the hubbub and the long faces of his councilors.

"Mother, I am married. I have just told my councilors —"

"Married!" The color drained from my face. "Who is she?"

"You do not know her, Mother. She is Dame Élisabeth Grey."

"Dame Grey. You mean she was married before?"

"Yes," he replied.

My stomach lurched, and I staggered.

Edward signaled to hovering servants to bring me a chair and some wine. At another signal, everyone left. I sat and sipped my wine slowly while marshaling my swirling thoughts. Eventually, I looked up at Edward. "Who are her parents?"

"Her mother is Jacquetta of Luxembourg, the daughter of the Count of St. Pol."

I knew that name—it could not be. "Her father?"

"Earl Rivers."

"You mean that jumped-up squire Sir Richard Woodville," I snapped, "Sir Nobody."

Edward winced.

I knew who Dame Élisabeth Grey was. Her mother Jacquetta had created a scandal nearly thirty years before when, as the widowed Duchess of Bedford and aunt-by-marriage to the king, she had married Sir Richard Woodville shortly after her husband's death. Sir Richard was far below her in rank and only had his good looks to commend him.

As for Dame Grey, that doll-like child now had gilt-gold hair, pointed features, and a sly smile. She was a year older than my beloved daughter Joan would have been had she lived, which meant that at twenty-seven, she was five years older than Edward. She was the widow of a Lancastrian knight who'd fought against us in the recent wars—Sir John Grey of Groby. She had two boys. She was poor. She had a large number of relatives. In short, she had nothing to recommend her. Moreover, she and her mother had interfered the day of Marguerite's churching, the day I struggled to have Nan come home to me. I turned on Edward.

"How could you be such a fool?"

He flinched.

"How long have you been married?"

He flushed, and the silence held. Finally, he lifted his chin and looked at me squarely. "Since May."

"Since May? Edward that cannot be so."

There was silence again.

"Are you saying that you have been married for the past four months?"

"Yes, Mother."

"Why didn't you tell me?"

He hung his head. A flush crept up his neck.

I sagged in my seat. If only I'd been allowed to spend time with Edward when he was growing up. If only Richard hadn't taken him away.

"Edward," I said, "I am devoted to you, you know that. I have worked tirelessly for you all my life. Why could you not confide in me, your own mother?"

"I knew you would talk me out of it."

I looked at him steadily for a moment. He was a coward, as well as completely irresponsible. "Do you truly think she is suitable?"

"Yes."

I picked up my wine-cup. "The fact that you have been married for four months and have told no one will indicate to everyone you do not think her to be suitable."

"She is the most beautiful woman in England."

"I am glad you think so." I put my wine-cup down. "Did the wedding occur in a church?"

He shook his head.

"Who were the witnesses?"

"Élisabeth came with her mother. There was the priest."

I gazed at him. It was like his christening that underhanded affair in a private chapel away from prying eyes.

"That was a very private ceremony," I murmured eventually. "I was planning a magnificent celebration for you, my son, something that would befit a King of England. I was hoping to meet your bride beforehand to welcome her into the family."

Edward took my hand in his. "And you will know Élisabeth," he said. "Mother, I would like you to befriend her."

I stared at him and withdrew my hand.

"How well do you know her?"

"I have been courting her for several months."

I tapped the arm of my chair to control my surging feelings. My golden boy had just crushed all my hopes and

dreams. "There are many reasons to marry," I said. "If you
had to marry for love, could you not have chosen someone
who you had serious reason to believe would make you
happy?"

"She does make me happy."

"How?"

He flushed.

I drained my cup of wine. "Remember, Edward, you
have a soul to keep. Your wife will have a great deal of
power over you."

"She is sweet and charming."

"She wants to be Queen of England."

Edward fiddled with his ring.

"She will not make you happy. Apart from that, there
are political reasons for not marrying her."

I rose and stood stiff and tall.

"When you succeeded my lord of York as head of the
family, you assumed certain duties and responsibilities. You
are now king, and it is the king's duty—for the sake of his
family and his country—to marry into a noble or royal
house from the continent to enhance his status and increase
his possessions. Your cousin has traveled to France on your
behalf, and negotiations for your marriage to Bona of Savoy
are now far advanced."

"Cousin Warwick will accept my marriage."

I raised an eyebrow: "You didn't confide in your
cousin?"

Edward was silent.

I folded my arms. "It is the height of folly to antagonize the Earl of Warwick so unnecessarily. Why, he was expected to conclude these marriage negotiations within the month."

Edward twisted his signet ring again.

"As you know, I have also been in correspondence with Isabella of Castile in case the French marriage negotiations broke down. Either of these princesses would have been fit to be your queen."

"But I don't know them," protested Edward. "What makes you think they would have made me happy?"

"They are young," I ticked my fingers. "Bona has fifteen years, and Isabella has thirteen. They are schooled to be queens, having lived their lives in the finest courts of Europe, and it was my hope, as your mother, to train them myself. I wanted to tell them about you; I wanted to mold them to English life and to the ways of your life. I wanted to supervise their religious instruction and to educate them in literature and the arts, the way my mother did."

"Mother!"

I glared. "I would have ensured they had your best interests at heart."

There was silence.

I had said everything I could. Was there any way of annulling this ridiculous marriage?

But Edward said nothing.

"It is wholly inappropriate," I remarked, staring at his downcast eyes and shut-in face, "for a monarch to marry his own subject where no honor or lands can be gained by it. A rich man marries his maid only for a little easy pleasure. In such marriages, folk admire the maid's good fortune but think her master lacks judgment. And in this matter, there is no difference so great between any master and maid in this land as between you and this widow."

I paused.

Edward did not react.

"And the fact that she is a widow makes everything much worse."

Edward lifted his chin and stared at me.

I gazed back. There was a long silence. Finally, I snapped, "This marriage is a blemish and a disparagement to the majesty of a prince!"

I swept out.

CHAPTER 52

Westminster Palace, London
Feast of Saint Lucy
December 13, 1464

It was as if I'd never spoken.

Later that September, at Michaelmas, Dame Élisabeth Grey was escorted into Reading Abbey by Warwick and George. The Serpent was presented to the magnates and the people as their Sovereign Lady, and the whole assembly of people knelt to do her honor.

Except for myself.

I could not submit.

I made my displeasure clear by being absent.

My absence was noted by everyone.

Edward had disgraced himself with this awful marriage. In turn, I styled myself Queen by Right.

From then on, there were two queens at Edward's court. I remained in the queen's apartments, and Edward was forced to build a special wing onto one of his palaces to accommodate the Serpent and her entourage. Shortly after her elevation, she got her revenge in the most predictable way. The horde of poverty-stricken relatives descended on the court and proceeded to elbow their way into the aristocracy. I enumerate as follows.

> *Item: Margaret Woodville, sister to the Serpent, married October 1464 to Thomas Fitzalan, Baron Maltravers, the Earl of Arundel's heir.*

> *Item: Catherine Woodville, sister to the Serpent, married April 1465 to Henry Stafford, Duke of Buckingham, my sister Anne's grandson.*

> *Item: Martha Woodville, sister, married in June 1465 to Sir John Bromley.*

> *Item: Jacqueline Woodville, sister, married February 1466 to John le Strange, Baron Strange of Knockin.*

> *Item: Thomas Grey, the Serpent's eldest son, married in October 1466 to Nan's daughter, Anne Holland.*

> *Item: Mary Woodville, sister, married January 1467 to William Herbert, Lord Dunster, the Earl of Pembroke's heir.*

Item: Eleanor Woodville, sister, married July 1467 to Sir Anthony Grey.

Item: Anne Woodville, sister, married in July 1467 to William, Viscount Bourchier the eldest son of Richard's sister Isabel.

What more need I say?

"Cecylee, Queen by Right, Duchess of York," roared the herald.

There was a stir as I lifted my chin high and sailed into the room. I dressed in my usual dark colors worn since my lord of York's death. This time my gown was midnight-blue velvet, the neck and bodice covered in a white silken scarf, over which I wore a simple white headdress surmounted by a coronet.

Everyone sank like a wave as I approached, the gentlemen bowing, the ladies curtseying. All except for one figure, dressed in cloth of gold brocade with a plunging neckline to set off the emeralds around her neck. The dress formed pools of gold as it flowed around her feet. This figure stood motionless with her back erect as I approached. At the end of that long hall, I found myself finally face-to-face with the Serpent, my daughter-in-law, Edward's wife, and soon-to-be crowned Queen of England.

We stared at each other for several minutes. In that huge hall, thronging with hundreds of people, the silence was deafening. Finally, the Serpent's mouth curved into a smile.

"Well met, Mother!" she cried out, louder than I would have liked, as the room rustled to life. "You are welcome, indeed, to our Christmas Court."

I stiffened as she took my arm, but the Serpent held me in a vice-like grip. I looked around for Edward, but he was nowhere to be seen.

"Edward has been detained," said the Serpent, as she led me along the corridor, followed by her ladies. "In the meantime, I wanted to invite you to my private chambers so that we could have a quiet talk."

As we arrived, the door shut behind us, and the Serpent signaled to her women to pour wine and bring out refreshments. She indicated a seat for me to sit in, but I shook my head.

"As you wish," she remarked, shrugging. And smiling, she sat down.

Her ladies followed suit, some of them smiling behind their hands.

How dare she sit in my presence?

The Serpent leaned back in her chair and sipped delicately from a crystal goblet that sparkled with gold lights reflecting the gold of her dress. She watched me for a moment. Finally, she spoke.

"Queen by Right," she murmured, twisting the goblet between her fingers so that the reflected colors moved hither and thither. "An interesting title, madam. Did you inherit it from someone in your family?"

I glared at her. The sound of smothered giggles struck my ear. It was followed by shushing sounds.

The Serpent fastened her eyes on her goblet and kept them there until the room was completely quiet. Then she looked at me.

"Has a Queen of England ever ruled through her son?" she asked.

"Yes," said I, raising my chin. "Queen Alainor of Aquitaine, of blessed memory—"

There was a splutter behind my back. I turned to glare in that general direction. When I turned back to the Serpent, she was leaning forward in her chair, her brow furrowing in concentration.

"She was the mother of Richard, Coeur de Lion," I explained.

"I see." The Serpent turned the crystal goblet in her fingers. These goblets had recently come into fashion. Edward had imported them from Venice, at great expense, for the Serpent was determined to emulate the luxury of the court of Burgundy. Even if it meant plunging the Crown into debt.

"Was Richard, Coeur de Lion, actually married?" asked the Serpent.

"His mother found him a suitable bride in the Princess Berengaria of Navarre," I replied.

The Serpent remained in her chair, leaning forward, looking up at me with one eyebrow raised. She held the exquisite goblet poised delicately between the fingers of two hands.

"I see," she said evenly.

Again, there was a splutter behind me.

The Serpent sighed, put her goblet down, rose, and beckoned to someone behind me. Everyone in the room rose also.

A rosy-cheeked giggling child of around six or so jumped out and after a vain attempt to stifle her giggles, sketched me a very shaky curtsey.

The Serpent smiled. "May I present to you my sweet sister Catherine?" She turned to her sister: "Be off with you, child, for we have serious matters to discuss."

The child giggled and ran off, followed by her governess.

The Serpent turned back to me. "Are you sure you wouldn't rather sit?"

I cleared my throat. "No, I thank you."

The Serpent resumed her seat, and everyone in the room sat also, leaving me standing.

The Serpent signaled, and a servant rushed forward to refill her crystal goblet. She took a sip turned to me.

"Now, where were we?" she remarked as the room fluttered with sounds of whispers and giggles. "Ah, yes. You were telling me of King Richard's marriage."

I glared at her. "You should not be sitting there, madam. Your family is Lancastrian. You fought against us in the recent war. I lost my husband, son, and brother to Lancastrian beasts who—"

I gulped for air, unable to bear the images that rose up. "You were damsel to the Bitch of Anjou. You are two-faced, madam. You are duplicitous."

"But the time has come to put that behind us."

"I never forget," I replied. "And you should not. Your husband died too."

The Serpent glanced at me, biting her lip. She lowered her eyes and played with her crystal goblet. "Families are so interesting—"

"Indeed," I exclaimed. "Your family, for instance, madam. Your father is a jumped-up nobody, and I understand that you are descended, on your mother's side, from the fay Melusine, the sorceress who vanished in a puff of smoke when forced to attend Mass."

I paused and jabbed my finger at her. "Your wiles, and that of your mother, have entrapped my son, bewitched him, so that he lost his reason and married you."

A hush fell as the Serpent stared at me, her face white. Witchcraft was a serious accusation, and she knew it.

My head high, I turned on my heel and left.

I swept into my chamber and took breath.

Good.

I had made my feelings clear.

My shoulders relaxed, the bottled-up frustration of the past several months leaking out.

I had just crushed my mortal enemy.

I lost no time in going to see Edward to discuss the evils of his marriage. I pointed out that since there were hardly any witnesses, it would be an easy matter to get it annulled.

He heard me out, then turned to me and smiled. "Madam, I am well content with my lovely wife, and I pray you be content also. Both Élisabeth and I already have children. England will have heirs."

I stared at him, speechless with indignation. It was only then that I realized I did not know my son at all.

CHAPTER 53

Queen's Apartments, Westminster Palace, London
Feast of The Epiphany
January 6, 1465

*To the Steward of Fotheringhay Castle, Northamptonshire,
Greetings.*
May it please you to know that
Cecylee, Duchess of York, Queen By Right,
*has come to the end of her stay in London and will be
arriving in Fotheringhay in ten days.*
*See to it that all necessary provisions are made against her
return.*
*Given, this sixth day of January, in the Year of Our Lord
1465.*

I took this document from my scribe, read it through, and smiled. I intended to use my new title until I could persuade Edward to find another wife. As I congratulated myself on putting the Serpent in her place, the door to my chamber burst open. It was Cath.

"Cis, dearest: I wanted you to be the first to know. I am to marry Sir John Woodville."

Cath was no longer young, for she was sixty-seven years old. Still, she was a handsome woman who would have looked younger had she not lost most of her teeth. Every time she smiled, she drooled.

I handed her my handkerchief and signaled for the scribe to leave. "You mean to tell me, sister, the Serpent has commanded you to marry her brother John?"

Cath threw back her head and laughed: "Fancy calling Edward's queen The Serpent. What has she done to you to deserve that name?"

"She has wormed her way into the House of York like a canker eating at an apple. Now she is commanding you to marry her brother."

"He's a lovely young man."

"How old is he?"

"He's—nineteen, I believe she said."

"Cath!"

Cath flushed.

"You know how this is going to look."

"But I'm lonely."

"A lady of your years matched to a callow youth of nineteen!"

"But you know how much I like male company—"

"How could you agree to it?"

"—and I've had three husbands taken from me."

"You know folk will not be kind."

"I don't see why I shouldn't marry this charming young man."

"She's trying to humiliate you. The Serpent wants your money. After burying three husbands, she knows you to be wealthy."

"But he's sweet!"

"I'm going to see her now."

"But Cis—" Cath plucked at my sleeve.

I brushed her off. "This isn't about you, Cath. She's trying to humiliate the Nevilles, the House of York, and me. I must put a stop to it."

I came upon the Serpent seated on a gilded chair with her ladies around her. She was embroidering a magnificent altar cloth made of cloth of gold and purple velvet. She wore a silver dress that reflected the blood-red rubies at her throat and on her fingers. She looked up as I entered but did not rise.

"Good Morrow, Mother." She signaled to her ladies to put the altar cloth away and bring out refreshments in the form of oranges, figs, nuts, and warm spiced wine.

"I wish to talk to you."

"About your sister's forthcoming nuptials?" The Serpent leaned back in her chair as she peeled an orange with a bejeweled dagger. While she talked, the blade flashed as it went in and out, separating the peel from the sweet, luscious fruit within.

"I cannot allow it to happen."

"And what does your sister say?"

I hesitated. The room rustled with the sounds of the ladies' heavy skirts dragging across the Turkish carpets as they went about their duties. Finally, they took up position around their mistress. A sea of staring eyes met mine.

The Serpent paused, holding the dagger balanced between thumb and finger, and studied me for a moment. "Your sister is older than you, is she not? Surely old enough to decide her own fate."

A murmur of laughter ran around the room.

"When I told her of my plans, she seemed delighted. As I remember, she called my brother John a sweet boy. So, I made the old dame happy. What's wrong with that?"

"You know what's wrong."

The Serpent put her dagger down and stared: "My sweet brother is delighted to make your sister happy. Your sister is happy with my choice of bridegroom, so what could your objection be?" She paused for a moment, put her hand to her head, and frowned in concentration as her ladies tittered behind their hands.

"It couldn't be my brother's—bloodlines, now could it?"

I glared.

"I believe that the last time I had the pleasure of your company, you described my father as 'jumped up.'"

"I did. I also said—"

"Perhaps it would help, good mother, if I told you more about Maman, my mother."

"Your mother? She was the cause of a great scandal. She was the king's aunt, and she married well beneath her."

"I would like to tell you about Maman's family," said the Serpent, handing her cup to one of her ladies and rising. She took my arm.

"My mother has many interesting people she can claim relation with. Surely you know that my mother's father, the Count of St. Pol, was related to the Holy Roman Emperor. Or that my mother's mother was an Italian princess, descended from the Orsinis?"

She turned to look at me. "You look surprised, good mother," she cooed. "I see you did not know that."

The candles flickered as my vision narrowed. I knew her mother, Jacquetta, Duchess of Bedford, was of a higher social station than her father, for I remembered well how she would constantly talk of her family in France. But I'd never really believed her connections were so illustrious. Perhaps because it seemed obvious, she would exaggerate in an effort to cover up her husband's humble origins.

"Are you not descended from Queen Alainor of Aquitaine?" said the Serpent.

"Indeed I am."

"And would you have been happy if your son, the king, had married one of Queen Alainor's descendants?"

I gripped the back of a chair. If he'd done that, wouldn't everything have been different?

The Serpent turned slightly, the silver dress fanning out across the floor in a curling wave. She smiled.

"You see, Mother, your son was dutiful after all. I also am descended from Queen Alainor."

I glared at her. How like her mother, to exaggerate her claims.

"That's not true."

"Indeed, it is. I am descended, by my mother, from Simon de Montfort and his wife, the Lady Eleanor, one of Queen Alainor's granddaughters."

I shook my head but could not rid myself of a pounding headache.

"So, you need have no further worry about allying yourself with the Woodvilles." The Serpent drew her arm through mine and ushered me out of the room. "We are truly blue-blooded. Your sister will be safe with us."

The door closed shut, and I was left in a dark corridor. I shivered with cold. The Serpent's family had fought against the House of York in the war. She was responsible for the murder of Richard, of Salisbury, and of Rutland. Her people were the ones who'd put their heads on top of pikes at Micklegate Bar. She should not be Queen of England.

Within the month, Cath was married to the Serpent's brother John. Much sport was had at poor Cath's expense. One wit described her as *a slip of a girl*. Another referred to this sham arrangement as the *Diabolical Marriage*. I was forced to attend the wedding ceremony, which I found humiliating in the extreme. Just as the Serpent had intended.

CHAPTER 54

Greenwich Palace, London
Feast of Saints Philip & James
May 3, 1465

At nineteen, Margaret was the most beautiful lady at Edward's court. She greatly resembled her dead sister Joan, with her flawless lily-and-rose complexion and chestnut brown tresses. On this birthday, Edward held a feast followed by dancing to celebrate. Margaret stood in a circle with other young folk, following the beat of the drum first left, then right, that accompanied the recorder and dulcimer, while the dancing-master instructed them on the latest dance steps.

I stood in the garden, enjoying the music while I gave directions to Edward's head steward, having taken in hand the lavish preparations for Margaret's feast.

An unpleasantly shrill voice made me turn.

"Nineteen, is she not? 'Tis full time she was married."

As soon as my eyes met the Serpent's, she took my arm. She chose her moment well, for she was in front of hangers-on and had a vice-like grip that was not easy to dislodge.

"My brother Ned would be the perfect match for Margaret," she remarked. "Why, the king, your son, thinks highly of him."

My cheeks warmed as my stomach turned over. Ned Woodville was one of those gentlemen who seem always to be underfoot, dicing, singing, and not doing anything in particular. Why the king had made him Admiral of the Fleet, heaven only knew. Doubtless, it had something to do with the Serpent, for he had no qualifications that I could see, having never fought a sea battle in his life. His bleary eyes and late risings rather told me that he led a life given over to debauchery and drink. Unfortunately, Edward seemed to attract many such followers to his court.

"No need to gape, good mother: You have been remiss. Why haven't you married her off before?"

Why indeed? Margaret was my youngest daughter. I could not bear to part with her. Of course, I must one day. But only to someone who was worthy.

The Serpent continued, "'Tis four years since Edward became king. You've had plenty of time to choose a suitor."

"No."

"'Tis true, I tell you. Why, he was crowned king in June of 1461, near unto the Feast Day of Saints Peter and Paul. You cannot tell me your wits are so addled—"

"Out of the question."

"Why?" The Serpent opened her gold-brown eyes wide. "You don't mean to say my brother is not good enough? That is absurd. Your son, the king, has heaped honors on him. I'm sure he would agree to the match."

The ground heaved, and the Serpent's voice receded into the distance as she said, "Think on it, good mother, I beseech you. 'Tis time for her to be married. 'Tis full time."

Her mouth widened into a smile as I sank onto the nearest seat.

She left, followed by ladies who did not trouble to hide their smiles.

I must protect Margaret at all costs. Where was Edward?

When I arrived at the king's apartments, Edward was closeted with Warwick.

"We need an alliance with France," said Warwick as I entered.

"But an alliance with Burgundy would bring in more trade," replied Edward.

"It is imperative we seal a compact with King Louis," said Warwick. "Otherwise, he'll give shelter to the Lancastrians."

"Louis is too slippery to be trusted," remarked Edward, "so he might do anything. But the London merchants need the trade with Burgundy."

He caught sight of me and instantly came forward. "Mother?"

I sank wordlessly onto a seat while Edward waved away Warwick and sent for wine.

"Mother, what's wrong?"

I sipped my wine, playing for time. Now that I was with Edward, I had no clear idea of what to say.

"I've never seen you look so upset, Mother. Whatever has happened?"

My intuition told me not to mention the Serpent by name. On the other hand, discussing Margaret's marriage with Edward when I had not prepared him for this topic of conversation was going to make me look ridiculous. But I had no choice, so I plunged ahead.

"It's about Margaret."

"Margaret?" Edward's brows furrowed. "You do not mean to say she has gone off and married without my permission?"

"Nothing like that. But I am anxious that she marry well and marry soon."

Edward's blue eyes bore into mine. "Is that all? Why, Mother, you do surprise me. I thought something truly awful had happened."

"Edward, I need your help. Margaret must be married and married soon."

"All in good time, Mother. Why the rush now?"

I avoided looking at him. "Is there no prince or duke abroad who needs a wife? I would have my Margaret make a splendid international match."

Edward picked up a scroll of paper and began tapping it with his ring finger. "I have received news that the Duke of Burgundy's heir needs a wife. Charles of Charolais was married to Isabelle of Bourbon. The news from Burgundy is that Countess Isabelle has recently died. Now that would be a good match."

"Oh, yes, Edward. That would be just the thing for her."

"But what of your nephew Warwick? He wouldn't be pleased if you supported a Burgundian alliance."

It was true. Warwick and Edward did not go in the same direction regarding England's foreign policy. They were like an ill-yoked pair of mules, with Warwick pulling towards France and Edward pulling towards Burgundy. I had hitherto supported Warwick's efforts in gaining an alliance with France. I felt that I should stand by him after Edward betrayed him by secretly marrying the Serpent. Now, matters were different: I would do anything to save Margaret from a Woodville alliance.

I rose and assured Edward I would deal with Warwick provided Edward gave his solemn oath that he would lose no time in seeing about a marriage between Margaret and Burgundy's heir.

Edward threw back his head and roared with laughter.

"Really, Mother. There's no need to be so anxious. You know I'm very keen on the Burgundian alliance. I assure you I will do all in my power to see to this match." His eyes bored into mine. "Mother," he remarked. "You have been acting oddly, you know. Am I missing something?"

I smiled as warmly as I could and assured him that standing in the sun had not agreed with me.

Then I hurried back to the garden and spoke to the steward once more about the arrangements for Margaret's birthday feast.

CHAPTER 55

Greenwich Palace, London
June 1465

The Serpent was crowned Queen of England on Whitsunday, just at the end of May. I did not attend. While I lay in bed, I braced myself for what might follow.

She didn't keep me waiting long.

"Ah, good mother, there you are."

Edward was nowhere to be seen. As usual, I was surrounded by her people. As always, the Serpent took my arm in her insultingly overly familiar manner.

"I've been meaning to talk to you about Richard," she said as she took me through a tunnel overhung with lilac. It's sweet, almost sickly scent was overpowering.

"Richard? You mean, my son Richard?"

"How old is he now?"

I paused and glared at her. Her ladies stared at me, so I was forced to answer. "He has about twelve years."

"He's growing up," she exclaimed. "We do not have much time."

"What does this have to do with you?"

She smiled. "Ah. Now we come to the point." She took my arm again. "You see, good mother, I have Richard's best interests at heart. Now, Warwick—"

"What about Warwick?" I demanded, drawing my arm away.

"Now, now. There, there." She patted my arm. "There's no need to be so suspicious." She pouted, but there was a glint of amusement in her eyes. "I have a plan for Richard." She took my arm again.

I withdrew it and glared.

She smiled and folded her arms. "I think Richard should be moved from Warwick's care to that of my brother. Do you not agree?"

It was the custom for young noblemen, like Richard, to be taken away from their families at the age of seven or eight and sent to train in the arts of war in another household. I had sent my youngest son to be trained in the household of my nephew. However, the Serpent and Warwick loathed each other.

I glared. "Richard is in my keeping."

"He's in Warwick's keeping," she pointed out, "and I do not think Warwick is—satisfactory. Richard would do much better if he were under the care of my brother, Sir Antony Woodville."

I froze. Of all her siblings – and the Serpent had many
– Sir Antony was the most widely respected. He was
learned, cultured, and had a great reputation in the jousting
field.

"What say you, good mother?"

"I have to think of Richard's wishes," I replied. " He has
not had an easy childhood, and he is happy at Middleham
—"

"How strange that the wealthiest peer in the realm,
your husband, the Duke of York, should have so many
sickly children," she remarked. "Let me see, you had five
daughters did you not? But two died." She ticked them off
on her fingers. "Joan, the eldest, and Ursula, the youngest.
And you had eight sons, did you not, Madame? And of
those sons, five died. Henri, Edmund, William, John,
Thomas. So many sons, so many good fighting men for the
House of York. But they died."

"What exactly is your meaning?" I snapped.

The Serpent edged away, making fluttering motions
with her hands. "You do frighten me so, Mother dear when
you get angry." She paused and flashed a sidelong smile.
"And you do get angry, do you not?"

I compressed my lips. Since the day my father had
given me that beating, I had always been angry.

"Maman," she remarked, speaking now of her own
mother, "had fifteen children, six sons, and nine daughters,
and they all survived. And she had considerably less money
than you. Now, why would that be? Was it all the riding
around you did when you should have been confined to

357

one of your husband's castles, awaiting the birth of his children?"

I made a wall of silence between us.

"They do say," continued the Serpent, putting her hand on the gnarled bole of a tree, "that Richard greatly resembles his father, the old duke. Was the duke as puny as your son Richard? Was he as short, as pasty-faced, and—deformed?"

"Richard is not deformed!" I exclaimed. "He injured his shoulder at the quintain when he was practicing his jousting. Such injuries are common, as you well know."

The Serpent was silent for a few moments. "So, the duke, your husband, was not strong. Perhaps he could not sire healthy sons. Or perhaps it was your fault."

I clenched my hands so tightly together my nails drew blood.

"Yours was a perfect marriage, except for all those dead children." She paused to pick a red rose. "We Woodvilles take good care of our own. My brother is a good man. Think on it, good mother, I beseech you. For truly I have Richard's best interests at heart!"

She swung around, her green silken skirts making whorls, and left, trailing brittle laughter.

CHAPTER 56

Westminster Palace, London
December 1468

Three years and more passed. In July of 1465, Henry of Lancaster was captured and brought to the Tower. In October of 1466, Edward agreed to a treaty of friendship with Philip of Burgundy. From France, the Bitch of Anjou stirred things up by sending Warwick a message. She extended the hand of friendship, deducing correctly the frustration he must now feel.

Matters were not helped, when in July of 1468, Margaret finally married Charles of Burgundy. I did not attend the wedding myself, for it was not the custom to do so for foreign matches. But I listened avidly to the reports of the magnificent ceremony in which the streets of Bruges were hung with priceless tapestries. The parades, feasting,

masques, and allegorical entertainments so impressed
everyone that folk called it "The Wedding of the Century."

Now it was December of 1468, and I arrived to
celebrate Christmas Court with Edward and his Serpent-
Queen. I stood by the window, wrapped in a thick fur
mantle, my hair in its night plait, gazing at the wintry scene
before me. It was so cold the frost had swirled patterns onto
the icy windows, and the scant vegetation had hardened
into ice. What would befall the House of York this season?

I didn't have long to wait, for the door to my chamber
burst open, and my nephew Warwick strode in.

"This is insupportable!" he roared.

I bade him sit and signaled to Jenet to bring hot mulled
wine and wafers.

But Warwick paced around my chamber, his face
flushed darkly, a vein throbbing in his temple.

I waited.

"Cousin," he said finally. "What shall I do about my
daughters? There are no eligible heirs to the peerage left for
them to marry."

Warwick had no sons, so Bella and Nanette were his
heirs, standing to inherit substantial holdings from their
Neville, Montacute, and Beauchamp forbears. They were

both of an age to marry—Bella, seventeen, and Nanette, twelve.

"You have just come from the Serpent," I stated.

Warwick's mouth crinkled in amusement as I handed him a cup of wine. "You have a gift for nicknames, Aunt."

"What did she say?"

"She had the insolence to suggest that Bella marry her brother, Dick, while Nanette should be betrothed to Ned Woodville."

I nodded. "She must be getting desperate to marry off Ned. She once had the temerity to suggest that my Margaret marry him."

He narrowed his eyes. "But Margaret married Burgundy."

My cheeks warmed. I put my hand on his arm. "I know you spent many years working for the alliance with France. But Edward wanted an alliance with Burgundy, and he can be obstinate."

"He was not always that way," said Warwick, his voice rising. "Before he acquired a wife—"

"Before the Serpent came, he was easy to manage. You and I both know that. But now he is different. The Serpent is ensconced in his life, whether we like it or not. Edward will not be ruled by either you or me, so we must devise some other plan."

Warwick glowered. "Those sisters of hers have swept the aristocratic marriage market clean. There is no one suitable left in England. I will not have her loathsome Woodville brothers get their hands on my wealth."

I understood, already alarmed about the marriage prospects for my son George. George was such a handsome boy, tall and blond, the very image of my father. Yet I was having trouble procuring a bride for him. Two years before, Duke Philip of Burgundy had offered his granddaughter's hand in marriage, but Edward would not hear of it. I'd been stunned when George told me the news. In having made a bad marriage, did Edward begrudge a good one for his brother?

At nineteen, George was now the age Edward had been in the first year of his reign. He needed something to do, but the king seemed disinclined to use his brother's talents. George was well educated; I had seen to that. And he showed signs of being a talented administrator, like his father. Yet, if Edward were not going to give George a position in his government, surely he should allow his brother to marry a foreign princess and use his talents abroad?

As if reading my thoughts, Warwick said softly, "It seems the king doesn't want George to marry Mary of Burgundy. So, what would you think if George married my Bella?"

I leaned forward, smiling. It was a brilliant idea. "But what of Richard?"

"He can have Nanette."

I mulled this over. I liked it. Warwick's plan did mean giving up any hope of brilliant international marriages for my boys. But with Edward in his present mood, it wasn't likely he would allow Richard to marry a foreign princess any more than he had allowed George to marry Margaret's stepdaughter. The Neville heiresses were the most suitable young ladies in the whole of England.

"I like it. But we should move cautiously so that Edward doesn't know our full intentions. Richard and Nanette are full young and can wait a while. I propose that we focus now on getting George wed to Bella. Let me speak with George first."

And so, I summoned Jenet to attire me for my appearance at Edward's court and sent a page with a message for George.

"Mother," said George, coming forward to kiss my cheek. "Do you not like my new suit of clothes?" He smiled down at me as I examined him closely. Today he was resplendent in a tunic of purple decorated with intricate gold embroidery. His stockings were of purple and gold, with the seam up the middle of each leg. His sleeves were slashed to show the gold shirt he wore under his tunic. His blue-green eyes glowed with excitement. How he loved being at court.

I smiled back at him. "You have such a good eye for color, George," I remarked. "That purple brings out the color of your eyes." I turned around on my stool so that

Jenet could pin on my headdress, a pointed henin with a veil of translucent silk.

"Hurry, Mother," he said. "It would not do to be late."

"George." I smiled. "Your mother is an old woman. She is not as fast as she was when she was a girl."

"Nonsense, Mama!" he exclaimed, offering me his arm. "Old? You'll never be old."

I laughed out loud. George always had that effect on me. Though I was fifty-three, George made me feel younger. "I have three grown daughters," I reminded him. "It would not be seemly for their mother to look like a maid."

George threw back his head and roared with laughter. "Now, Mother," he said. "You know you are looking very well."

It was true. Prodded by George, I'd finally decided to abandon my widow's weeds and put on something more cheerful. Today I wore a gown of sky-blue velvet edged in ermine, with silver embroidery running down the sleeves and over my skirts.

Jenet put the last pins into my headdress, and I rose and signaled for her to leave. "I have something important to ask you, my son," I said, leading George to a window seat. "As you know, I think it high time you were married. But I want your opinion on this matter." I paused and looked at him closely. "How would you feel about marrying your cousin Bella?"

At once, his face lit up.

"It would make you happy?"

"Yes, Mother. I am very fond of my cousin. She makes me laugh and—" He flushed. "I've always found her beautiful."

I smiled as I kissed his cheek. "Let's ask Cousin Warwick to join us."

Warwick was delighted, and as my nephew and my son conversed, a scene played itself out in my mind, something I had been vaguely thinking of but had not articulated. When folk grows old, it is the custom for the widowed mother to live with her eldest son in a quiet retirement. But I had been too deeply wounded by Edward's marriage for that to be possible. Suppose I lived with George instead? I adored George; he always made me feel cheerful and energetic. And Bella would be a fine wife for him. Perhaps I could live out my life in the company of George and his family.

George offered me his arm, and we left for the formal banquet that Edward was giving as part of the Christmas celebrations at court. These celebrations were very elaborate, both in terms of the number of courses served, as well as the strict protocol the Serpent insisted on. I was very glad to have my handsome son beside me, radiating energy and good cheer, for I found these occasions wearisome in the extreme.

"Now remember," I said in a low voice, "today is the feast of Christ's birth, of peace and joy upon the land. We must put on a good appearance of one happy family. You understand, my son?"

George's expression darkened.

"You will be polite to the queen." I was careful not to call her by her nickname in front of George because he was acquiring a disturbing tendency to blurt out secrets. But now I was going to take George firmly in hand. First, it was imperative that he learn some skills to arm himself against the Serpent's poison.

"What would you have me do?" said George, his lower lip jutting out sulkily.

"The only way to deal with her is to be polite and ignore everything she says. She will attempt to bait you, to goad you into saying things you should not say. Remember, it gives her the greatest pleasure to upset us. You must, however, remain silent or turn the conversation. Try not to listen to her, and whatever you do, you must not rise to her bait. She is adept at spotting her opponent's weaknesses."

George nodded, and I took his arm again. I resolved to stay as close to him as I could without being too obvious about it.

The Serpent was ensconced by the fire, clad in a magnificent dress of silver and blood-red brocade. In four and a half years of marriage, she'd given Edward two children, both daughters, and now she was heavily pregnant with their third child. Edward sat next to her, and of course, her numerous Woodville relatives surrounded them:

her father and mother, her six brothers, and her nine sisters with their stolen husbands.

I was forced to sit by the windows, facing them, with Warwick and his family on one side and George on the other. Icy fingers of air made their way through the casements, chilling my fingers. I placed them in the folds of my new velvet gown.

A flurry of movement caught my eye. One of the Serpent's sisters, Jacqueline, had wandered over a few feet away and started nibbling at some nuts. She looked like a rabbit with her fine, strong teeth, and as she talked, she continued to nibble.

"How fare you, sweet Johnny?" she said to her brother. Sir John Woodville was a well-made young man of three-and-twenty years.

"I fare well," he replied evenly.

"How does marriage suit you?" Nibble, nibble.

"She is very kind."

"She does not excite your passion then?" Nibble, nibble.

John sighed but made no reply.

"Is she not too old for you?" Nibble.

John occupied himself in taking his new kid gloves off. They were dyed black to match his hose and fit perfectly to his shapely hands.

"How have you the patience to bear it? Why, she has no teeth, her breath is foul, and she—"

John shushed his sister with a wave of his hand.

I turned. Cath stood in the doorway. Her eyes moved slowly around the room, and as they lighted on her husband John, she smiled. She went over to kiss him full on the lips.

"I found the tincture I told you about, the one for sore throats and colds. Come with me, my darling."

During this speech, John made various gestures intended to slow the volume and rapidity of Cath's speech. At seventy-one, she was deaf and difficult to understand, having lost most of her teeth. She stood there, looking at her husband lovingly, drooling; when suddenly noticing this, she fumbled for a kerchief, flushed, and excused herself.

Poor Cath; my heart ached. I glanced at my son Edward. He was talking to my Richard, clapping him on the back and laughing merrily. And Richard's face showed an unusual amount of animation.

I made myself sit ramrod straight in my seat, gritting my teeth to forestall the impending headache always produced by the Serpent's presence. But

Jacqueline had not the good manners to hide the look of disgust on her face. "Couldn't you get this marriage annulled?"

Her bell-like voice rang out as silence suddenly filled the room. My gorge rose. I stood.

"Don't you think you should keep your wicked thoughts to yourself?" I snapped. The nibbling stopped.

The Serpent, her face impassive, rose and faced me. Casually stifling a yawn, she lumbered slowly towards

George and held out her hand. "Come, brother. Come, keep me company. You know how to play piquet, no?"

George flushed as he rose and bowed to her. They went to sit near the fireplace with her family.

I went slowly back towards my place near the window, taking care to take a seat that was in earshot of the proceedings.

"You're a good-looking boy; you should be married," the Serpent said.

Nineteen-year-old George smiled but refrained from saying anything.

The Serpent deftly cut the cards and shuffled. "I have a little sister."

"Another sister?" blurted out George. "I thought your sisters to be all married."

"All except for one. My sister Agnes would do very well for you."

I should have been prepared for this, but I was not. Was there no end to the Serpent's coils? I drew my handkerchief from my sleeve and dried my moist palms.

"How old is the lady?"

"She turned twelve last month. She's a sweet child and well suited to you." The Serpent stared at George as she dealt the cards. "She pouts, and sulks, and is easily led." She paused and smiled. "She would be the perfect playmate for your little games."

George sat stone still, a flush spreading slowly up his neck, staring at the card-strewn table before him. Suddenly, he leaped up, knocking over his chair. "How dare you insult me like this!" George jutted out his lower lip, making him look exactly like a sulky child.

The Serpent smiled sweetly.

I put my finger to my lips, but George ignored me.

"I already have a bride," he said.

The Serpent's cat's eyes went wide.

"Sweeting!" she called across the room to Edward. "Were you aware that your dear brother planned to marry?"

Edward rose, his blue eyes blazing. "Who is she?"

George faced him, scowling. "You don't have any right —"

"Who is she?"

George flicked a look over at me.

I nodded.

"Cousin Bella."

"What?" roared Edward.

"Why not?"

Edward shushed him with a wave of his hand. "I expressly forbid you," he said loudly into the dead silence that followed, "to marry your cousin Bella."

"It's not right!" exclaimed George. "You block me at every turn. You prevented my marriage to Mary of Burgundy. Now you won't let me marry Bella. Just because you've married a whore yourself doesn't mean you can prevent me from making a good match."

Edward went white. "You will apologize," he said in a voice that cut like a knife.

George glared at him as Warwick went to stand by his side.

Edward put his hand on the Serpent's shoulder. "You are talking of my wife, your liege lady, and my Queen."

The Serpent covered his hand with her own and turned to smile up at him. They were a fortress together against the rest of the world. How had I failed in my attempts to pry Edward away from the Serpent?

My belly filling with ice, slowly, I stood.

Gradually, everyone in the room turned to stare at me.

"I am displeased with you, my son," I said. My voice rang like a bell in the thick silence. "You have grievously offended your family, your cousin Warwick, your brothers George and Richard, and your mother. I am deeply hurt by what you have done. All my life, I have supported and cherished you, yet how do you repay me?" I paused and jabbed my finger at the Serpent: "By marrying someone who is not worthy."

Edward flushed and took a step towards me. He said loudly, "She is worthy, Mother."

I lifted my chin and stared him down. "She is a canker in the House of York. She is destroying it even as we speak."

Edward narrowed his eyes and went pale. The silence was deafening.

"I am disappointed. I thought you once worthy to be my lord husband's heir. Instead, I see you betray your father's low origins."

There was a swelling murmur as folk turned to each other and whispered.

"My father was the Duke of York."

"Your father," said I, my voice tinkling like ice, "was an archer on the Rouen garrison. His name was Blaybourne. His father, your grandsire, was not even a knight, but a humble blacksmith—"

"You lie!" roared Edward, coming towards me.

"I do not," I replied. I turned to face everyone in the room. "I am willing to go before a public enquiry to answer any questions, even to swear an oath on Holy Writ or saint's bones or a vial of the most precious blood of Our Lord and Savior Jesus Christ, that what I say is most true. This man," I indicated Edward, "Is a bastard. He is a fraud and an impostor, and I have made him so, for I loved and dedicated my life to him."

My voice broke. How I had loved Blaybourne. How I had allowed Edward's likeness to my lover to blind me to his faults.

"I see now how wrong I was. For you cannot make a noble out of dross. He is my child, yes, but no blood relation to the Duke of York, my late husband."

My voice rose at the end of this speech. I felt someone beside me. It was Richard.

"Mother!" he exclaimed, his blue-grey eyes cloudy with distress.

Was he worried about his own paternity? I would set the record straight.

"The true heir to the throne of England is my son George, followed in succession by his younger brother Richard. They are my lord husband's legitimate heirs."

My voice rang eerily through that packed chamber. I paused for a moment, then allowed Richard to lead me to my rooms.

The last thing I remember just before the door shut was a tableau of Edward, white and shaking on one side of the room, and George, standing proud and tall on the other side of the room, his blue-green eyes blazing with excitement.

CHAPTER 57

December 1468 to March 1469

Within the hour, I left for Fotheringhay. It was time for me to retire and lead a life of quiet contemplation.

They came for me in March.

I was standing in the collegiate church of Fotheringhay, talking to the glazier who had just finished beautifying the windows in my direction.

"We come from the king!" someone shouted.

I ignored this individual, for I was not accustomed to being greeted in such a rough manner.

My steward appeared, breathless from running. "They say they are from the king, madam." He bowed.

I turned and fixed the churls with an icy stare. There were ten of them, dressed simply, in leather jerkins and nondescript woolen clothing. They carried quarter-staves and sported daggers in their belts. They looked like the sort of rude men-of-arms one would use to garrison a castle, not deal with a great lady. The person with the loud voice took a scroll out of his leather bag, unrolled it, and declaimed as follows:

> *From Edward, King of England, to Cecylee, Duchess of York,*
> *Greetings.*
> *I, Edward, King of England,*
> *do arrest you, Cecylee, Duchess of York,*
> *on the charge of treason for bruiting abroad scurrilous rumors about my person.*
> *I command you, therefore, to follow these men to Berkhamsted, where I shall confine you under armed guard for the rest of your life.*

I frowned. Before I could make sense of this, one of the churls grabbed my arm. "It is time to go, my fine lady."

I shook him off.

"We have orders to escort you to Berkhamsted."

"Impossible. I cannot go now. And be so good as to take your filthy paw off my arm."

The men guffawed. "I see you are not called Proud Cis for nothing," one of them remarked.

"Proud Cis! Proud Cis! Proud Cis!" chanted the others.

A cold wind blew, and my flesh hardened into ice. If these men truly were from Edward, it meant there was nothing he might not do to insult and humiliate me.

"I demand to see the warrant," I said, my voice high.

The men laughed again. "Quite a mouse we have here," remarked one wit.

My steward stood in front of them. "You are insulting the king's mother."

The loud-mouthed man curled his lip. "If she tears it up and burns it, let her know that I have other copies, signed and sealed by the king's hand."

I took the warrant from my steward and scanned it. It was signed by Edward, I recognized his writing and his seal.

I crumpled onto a stone seat. "What about my household?"

"The king, your son, declares that you will do without a household. You are to leave forthwith. He will brook no delay."

I left Fotheringhay, the home that Richard and I had made together for over twenty years, to the sounds of my household weeping. They did at least allow me to ride my best palfrey and to wrap myself up in furs to keep out the cold. But the weather was bitter with icy winds by day and frosts by night. As I rode the eighty miles to Berkhamsted in Hertfordshire, I wondered if I would die from cold, damp, sorrow, and humiliation. Bitterly did I regret my words. Far from abandoning Edward, the Serpent had drawn even closer and connived to send me to Berkhamsted in disgrace.

At length, we arrived. My head reverberated with the sound of the Serpent's brittle laughter as I looked around. The towers leaned, and the roof over the great hall had fallen in. My rough escorts left me in the muddy courtyard, sitting bedraggled on my coffer. It was sleeting hard. They took my horse away and drew straws to determine who would guard me while the others foraged.

The dull afternoon was darkening slowly when, through lines of sleet, a black shape came into view. I stiffened. Was this figure Death? Had my Lord Richard come for me? Or was it one of the men, determined to humiliate me further?

"My lady," said the figure in a high voice, "my name is Ghislaine." She curtseyed low, muddying her skirts as she did so.

I beckoned, and the figure let down her hood. She was a finely made girl of around twelve or so with delicate pale features and grey eyes.

"Child, what are you doing here?"

"My parents are gone, so I must find my own keep," she replied. "The sisters at the convent of Ashridge took me on as a maid. They asked me to walk over here to see if you needed anything."

I took breath. Ghislaine's pale face surrounded by wisps of hair beaded with moisture and her patched clothes stirred a memory. Hadn't Blaybourne said that he was turned out of his home at the age of seven, no one willing to look after him?

I sat upright on my seat and patted the girl's head. "We must get out of this sleet, child, or we shall both catch our death." I looked over at the guard who had been left to watch me: "You, sir. What is your name?"

To my astonishment, he bowed. "Gerard, my lady, at your service." After the rough treatment this past week, I had not thought anyone would be polite to me again. Gerard was a short, compact gentleman, of around five and twenty, with a spade-shaped beard and square hands.

"Master Gerard," said I, rising. "If you would be so good as to follow me with the cart, I will show you where to put everything." I turned to Ghislaine. "Do you know how to make a fire?"

"Yes, my lady," she replied, curtseying again. "And I can cook and sew."

"That is well enough, for now, child. Let us get out of this evil weather."

There was but one room fit for habitation, and that was solar. It was a large room, big enough for my furniture. But to get to it, one was obliged to walk up a rickety staircase open to the elements, then heave open a door that was hanging off its hinges. Somehow, Master Gerard hoisted all of my possessions up those stairs without dropping anything and arranged the furniture in my direction.

I had my bed put against the inner wall and the carved chairs set on each side of the fireplace. I directed Gerard to put the hangings up to ward off the damp chill that pervaded the place.

Clearly, the Serpent hoped I would make a quick end of it here.

I resolved to disappoint her.

I told Ghislaine to make the fire, put the water on to boil, and arrange my down bedspreads, cushions, pillows, and gleaming gold cups while I unpacked my dresses from the coffer.

The door banged to and fro on its weakened hinge, letting in flurries of snow, as well as drafts of cold air.

"Good day to you, madam," said a voice.

I turned. A young woman in a Benedictine habit was curtseying.

"Though it be so dark, you can scarce tell it be day," she remarked. "I am Sister Avisa, of the Benedictine Order of Nuns at the convent of Ashridge, beyond the hamlet of Friesden, not four miles hence. We have come to make you welcome."

She waved in a young man, who bore the royal arms of the leopards of Anjou and the lilies of France.

He knelt and handed up a letter from Edward, which announced the birth of his third daughter. The child was to be named Cecily in my honor.

I looked up to scrutinize the countenance of the messenger before me. But his expression revealed nothing.

I walked to the window to collect my thoughts. It was sleeting hard again, and everything dissolved into grey shadows as afternoon waned into evening. What was the meaning of this? The last time I'd seen Edward was just after I told everyone he was illegitimate. He'd been furious, and when he was furious, he could be terrifying. Since that day, he'd sent no message to me. The only communication had been that arrest warrant.

I read the letter again slowly. In Edward's fine Italic hand, it told me I would be allowed to return to court, provided I made a public apology to the King and the Serpent and retracted my words.

Tears filled my eyes. I brushed them away and turned to Sister Avisa.

"I am greatly fatigued," I told her. "Would you see to it that a suitable gift is sent for the child, and please tell my son I am retiring from the world?"

"Do you wish me to add anything else?"

"Tell him that I am retiring to my new home in the country that he was gracious enough to give me."

Sister Avisa curtseyed silently and left.

I sank into my chair and covered my face with my hands.

I would not know Edward's children well. I saw the two so-called Little Princes in the Tower—Edward of Westminster and his brother, Richard of Shrewsbury, the Duke of York—fewer times than I could count with the fingers of one hand.

A week later, my steward from Fotheringhay, my maid Jenet, and others of my household arrived with more of my things.

"But what will the King say?" I asked as my people from Fotheringhay bowed and curtseyed before me. "He'll not allow you to stay."

"He'll not cause me to go," declared Jenet. "I was worried sick about you. You know how susceptible you are to the cold, and the weather has been evil. Look at the way you're coughing, even now. 'My place is with my lady,' I said to myself. "For no one else can make the cold tinctures that she needs."

"And I am right glad to see you," I replied, kissing her on the cheek. "And all of you are welcome," I added, "if you wish to stay in this grim place."

They assured me that they wished to stay with such a kind mistress and set about making needful repairs.

Slowly, life returned to normal.

Unfortunately, the same could not be said for my nearest kin. Things had curdled to sourness betwixt my son and my nephew. Warwick had given up much of his life, as well as a portion of his considerable fortune, to support the House of York. And what had Edward done for him in return? Promoted the Serpent's family at the expense of everyone else.

Now he made difficulties with the marriage between George and Bella. Edward's opposition did not prevent Warwick from working behind the scenes to obtain a papal dispensation so that the marriage could proceed.

I gazed out at the gloomy skies that seemed to hover over this ruined castle. What would Edward do when George defied him and married Bella?

CHAPTER 58

June 1469 to September 1470

In June of 1469, three months after I was taken from my home in Fotheringhay, news came that George plotted to overthrow Edward.

I motioned the messenger to leave and went to my prie-dieu for prayer and reflection. Wasn't this what I wanted? But what about George? Would he have the backing of the magnates and the citizens of London? Or was this a ploy by Warwick to seize power?

I let the polished jet beads of my rosary slip through my fingers. George was in great danger, I was sure of it. As his mother, I must do everything in my power to protect him.

And so, I hurried to Canterbury, where he was then staying, awaiting a favorable tide that would take him to Calais.

"My son," I said. "Do not do this. It will ruin your life."

"Edward is a bastard. You said so, yourself. Mother, I am the legitimate heir to the throne."

"I know, my son. But I know also that Edward has been anointed king, and that he is popular with the people."

"Warwick is more popular."

George had a point there. The people were growing weary of the taxes Edward imposed on them, and there was unrest in the north.

I took a deep breath then played my last card. "Warwick does not want you on the throne."

George's eyes narrowed. For a moment, he looked exactly like Edward. "How do you know that?"

"I feel it in my bones."

"Then why is he supporting me?"

"He is using you."

George turned away. "Go home, Mother, and leave me in peace. I have pledged my word to Warwick's cause, and I'll not go back on it."

I argued with him for an hour or more, but there was nothing I could do to sway his judgment.

And so, I returned to Berkhamsted.

At the beginning of July, George set sail for Calais with Warwick and his family. Shortly afterward, the unrest in the north boiled over. Edward did nothing. Instead, he took a boat to Fotheringhay and spent a week in my newly refurbished apartments. With the Serpent.

On the eleventh day of July 1469, in defiance of Edward's wishes, George wed Warwick's daughter Bella in the Church of Our Lady in Calais. Then, Warwick issued a proclamation calling on the king to remove the Woodvilles from their high offices. Warwick sailed for Kent, marched on the city of London, where he was welcomed with great acclaim, then went north.

On the twenty-sixth day of July 1469, Warwick scored a resounding victory at the Battle of Edgecote Moor.

Edward, who had been woolgathering in the middle of the country, now sought shelter in a little village called Olney. When news of Warwick's victory broke, all the lords left him, saving only his distant cousin William Hastings, whose father had long served the House of York, and my youngest son, Richard, Duke of Gloucester.

On the second day of August 1469, Edward was captured and brought before Warwick and George.

On hearing this news, I fainted.

When I came to, I went to my prie-dieu and spent the rest of the day on my knees in prayer. For if Edward were now to be executed, I would be responsible. Little did I think that my bitter words would be used against him so quickly and to such lethal effect.

The next morning, I sent a messenger to invite the nuns from the house of Ashridge to join me at Berkhamsted Castle. Thus, I gradually fell into the habit of rising early to pray at matins, of having religious works read aloud while I dined, and of relaxing in the evening with my women over a glass or two of wine. The daily rhythm of prayer, as well as the company of the good sisters, helped me to keep my sanity.

For the news sent me spinning, like a top.

The Serpent got exactly what she deserved, forced to lodge in the Tower in scant state. Now she would know how it felt to come down in the world. Her mother's arrest on a charge of witchcraft was only to be expected since it was well known she practiced the black arts. That is exactly how she trapped my son into that awful marriage. The capture and beheading of the Serpent's father and one of her brothers were regrettable. But how else was one to get rid of the Woodvilles? They were everywhere, a blight on the White Rose of York.

Then I received a tear-stained letter from Cath in which she bewailed the passing of her fourth husband, Sir John Woodville:

My Johnny was so sweet, wrote Cath, *and such a good husband to me. I cannot imagine what he did to deserve such a death. I hope, dear sister, your dislike of the Queen did not cause you to say things you might regret. You always were headstrong, you know.*

I crumpled up the letter and tossed it in the fire. Then I took to my bed, Jenet fussing over me with her tonics and tinctures.

Yes, the Serpent had gone. But what about my sons? What was going to happen to Edward, George, Richard?

Despite his popularity, Warwick did not have the authority to rule. Without the support of the magnates, ruling England would prove impossible, and the majority of the magnates thought that this time Warwick had gone too far. By summer's end, Warwick was losing his grip, and the country was descending into anarchy. In London, angry mobs demanded the release of the king.

Edward was released from captivity and taken to York, where his supporters and the magnates acclaimed him.

Early in October of 1469, Edward left York with his supporters and returned to London to the great joy of its citizens. One of his first acts was to give Richard, then only seventeen years old, full powers to secure the Welsh strongholds from rebel hands.

I smiled when I read a letter from my youngest son, in which he earnestly told me how he had successfully carried out the king's instructions. I locked the letter away in a box I kept by my bed to read when my spirits became low.

Although Edward behaved courteously towards George and Warwick, it was plain to all that things were not going their way. By February of 1470, Warwick's desperation with the situation had reached such a pitch he incited a rising in Yorkshire and Lincolnshire. His plan was to distract Edward in this manner, then enlist the help of the French king in deposing him.

This time, Edward acted quickly and marched north. The king's army confronted the rebels at Empingham in Rutland on the twelfth day of March 1470, and it struck so swiftly that Warwick and George had no time to bring in reinforcements. The rebels fled with such speed they left their jackets behind. And so, this battle became known as the *Battle of Lose-Coat Field*.

On the twenty-fourth of March 1470, Edward issued a proclamation calling Warwick and George traitors and rebels. They fled to Calais, taking Warwick's wife, George's wife, and Bella's younger sister, Nanette.

Then tragedy struck.

On the sixteenth day of April 1470, Bella, heavily pregnant, went into labor.

Our first child could not be saved, wrote George in a letter to me, *for we were all on a ship at anchor in Calais Harbor, and Edward's henchmen would not let us land in Calais.*

When Cousin Warwick pleaded with them, saying that his daughter was like to die, they replied they had received direct orders from King Edward himself.

Can you believe it?

I had not thought him to be cruel.

Bella lost a lot of blood. She owes her life to her mother, cousin Anne, who is skilled in midwifery.

I shook my head. The continuation of the war was making men bitter. Even Edward, usually so genial and tolerant, forgot his knightly code. Taking George's letter, I went to my prie-dieu and placed it between my hands. I spent an hour or so praying to God that George and Bella would have healthy children.

Things continued to go badly for George. Warwick gained an audience with the King of France and was persuaded to make reconciliation with Marguerite of Anjou, then staying at the French court with her son, Édouard. As I had foreseen, George was set aside. For King Louis XI thought it better to try and reinstate Henry of Lancaster rather than put George on the throne, telling Warwick that George was unreliable.

It did not take George long to realize what was afoot, and the letter he wrote me was an angry one. I resisted telling him off. Instead, I wrote a soothing note in which I expressed the hope that he might reconcile himself to Edward, for he is your sovereign lord, I wrote, and greatly beloved by the people.

I wondered how Louis XI had persuaded Marguerite d'Anjou to make peace with Warwick. I had an opportunity to find out when the French ambassador traveled up from London to pay his respects.

"It was not easy, Madame," he replied, smiling faintly in reply to my question. "Queen Marguerite cried out that Warwick had pierced her heart with wounds that would bleed until Judgment Day when she would appeal to the justice of God for vengeance against him."

"Not an auspicious beginning," I remarked, signaling for more wine to be poured.

Now that I had been at Berkhamsted for over a year, the place was beginning to look like a royal palace again, where I might entertain visitors without embarrassment. Edward had graciously forgotten to take my revenues away from me, so I was able to pay for the upkeep and refurbishment of this place, which had been home to so many English queens.

"It was not an auspicious beginning," agreed the ambassador, wiping his lips with a napkin. "But King Louis is very patient. He heard her out and, when she finished, told her bluntly that while her arguments might be valid, she should put her personal feelings aside if she wished to win the throne back for her husband."

"And she agreed to this?"

"Only after a discussion that lasted many, many days."

On the fifteenth of July 1470, Warwick's wife, Anne, and his daughter Nanette were formally presented to Marguerite d'Anjou. Ten days later, on July 25, Nanette was betrothed to Marguerite's son Édouard in Angers Cathedral. Five days later, on July 30, Warwick swore to keep faith with the Lancastrians on a fragment of the true cross.

In August, Edward, who had ignored the warnings from his diplomats and went hunting, was drawn north to Yorkshire by news of a rebellion.

On the thirteenth of September, Warwick's fleet of ships arrived in the West Country harbors of Dartmouth and Plymouth. So many men flocked to Warwick's banner, by the time he reached Coventry, he had an army numbering some fifty thousand men.

Edward marched south to deal with Warwick's rebellion only to find his soldiers deserting in large numbers. And so, he fled to Burgundy, taking with him his boon companion

William Hastings, his brother-in-law Rivers, and my
youngest son Richard.

CHAPTER 59

October 1470 to October 1471

My three sons now fought over the throne of England. It was impossible for me to take sides; however much I disagreed with Edward over his choice of wife, he had been a good king. Moreover, Richard, of whom I was so proud, adored his brother, the king. He had followed him into exile, even though it meant fighting against his former mentor and friend, Warwick. As for George, I could never now think of him without the greatest anxiety. What was to become of him? His life seemed rudderless and dark.

We rode into London at the head of a triumphal procession, wrote George, *and made homage to King Henry.*

*Cousin Warwick ordered the king to be newly arrayed in a
robe of blue velvet, and we rode from the Tower along
Cheapside to the Bishop of London's palace.*

*Warwick had him sit on the throne and placed the crown
on his head.*

He paid him great reverence.

*But I could not help noticing that King Henry sat on the
throne as if he were but a sack of wool.*

Was he always like that, Mother?

For you knew him well in his younger days.

I smiled grimly as I tucked that letter away. The fact the
King Henry seemed so inert caused a small spark of hope to
light in my heart. But where were Edward and Richard?

Soon after, I received a letter from Richard.

Madam,

I recommend me to you as heartily as is to me possible.

*Edward and I and others of our party have arrived in The
Hague, so you need fret no more, Mother.*

We are safe.

We are going to seek out Charles of Burgundy,

*and in my next, I hope to bring you tidings of our sister
Margaret.*

On the second day of November 1470, the Serpent
gave birth to a son named Edward. It should have been a
day of great rejoicing, for, after three daughters, she had
given Edward his heir. But the Serpent was perching in

Westminster Abbey, where she had taken sanctuary. And Warwick reigned supreme.

However, the birth of the Yorkist heir disquieted Warwick. On the thirtieth of December 1470, his fourteen-year-old daughter Nanette was married to seventeen-year-old Édouard of Lancaster, now styled Prince of Wales, in the Château d'Amboise. Marguerite of Anjou was in attendance.

Then, Warwick blundered.

I received this news one cold, wet morning in February of 1471 when a messenger ran into the great hall of Berkhamsted Castle.

"He's ordered the Calais garrison to attack Burgundy!"

I straightened in my seat on the dais and frowned. "What mean you, my good fellow?"

The messenger gasped out something that I could not clearly hear.

I signaled to my steward. "Bring a pitcher of ale and some pies from the kitchens."

As he hurried off to do my bidding, I recognized the messenger as being one of my late husband's agents. I beckoned him closer.

"Tell me your message more slowly, my good friend. Of whom are you speaking?"

"Warwick, my lady. Warwick has ordered the Calais garrison to attack Burgundy."

"Are you sure?" I said, watching his face closely.

The messenger gazed squarely into my eyes, his expression never changing.

I frowned as I settled more comfortably against the cushions in my carved chair: "That seems extremely foolhardy. If he did that, there would be no better way of throwing Charles of Burgundy into Edward's arms."

"Indeed, madam. Which is why I am here. To bring you good comfort."

I smiled. Edward and Richard would have an opportunity to invade England after all. But their path would be fraught with danger.

"Tell me about the London merchants," I said, motioning him to rise. "Do they know of this matter?"

"Indeed, they do, and they are furious. They do not want England dragged into a war with Burgundy without Parliament's consent. They know this could ruin their trade. And so, they are refusing to lend Warwick any more money."

The tide is turning, I thought, giving the messenger a sovereign.

On the fourteenth of March 1471, Edward landed in Ravenspur, Yorkshire, with an army funded by the Duke of Burgundy. Four days later, on March the eighteenth, he was welcomed into the city of York. On the twenty-ninth of March, Edward appeared before Coventry, one of the most heavily fortified towns in England, for his spies had told him that Warwick was there with seven thousand men.

Edward spent three days sending formal challenges to Warwick to come out and fight, to no avail. Edward then marched his army to Warwick and captured the castle. There, he was formally proclaimed king.

I took this opportunity to write to George:

My beloved son,
You can see how little you stand with Warwick, for I am
told that he recently forced you to hand over some of your
property to Marguerite d'Anjou.
I pray you, therefore, to put aside your differences and give
Edward your assistance in regaining his throne.
Edward is generous with his rewards, and your elderly
mother will rejoice to see her sons reunited.

On the third of April, George, Duke of Clarence, led
his army of twelve thousand men into King Edward's camp
at Banbury and knelt in submission. On the eleventh of
April, another messenger ran into Berkhamsted Castle.

"The king has arrived in London!" he exclaimed.

I rose from my seat, flooded with energy. "Heavens be
praised. How was he greeted?"

"With great joy, madam," replied the messenger
bowing. He handed me a letter with a flourish. "He had
with him his brothers of Clarence and Gloucester."

"Thanks be to God," I exclaimed, crossing myself.

Edward's letter invited me to meet him in London. And
so, it came to pass that Edward, George, and Richard
attended a solemn service in my private chapel on April 12,
1471, Good Friday.

As I walked down the stairs into the great hall of
Baynard's Castle to greet my three sons, I finally felt some
measure of peace. How wonderful that they were together

at last. For this was the way, it was supposed to be, brother
supporting brother.

To celebrate the occasion, I invited several leading
citizens of London and their wives. It was heart-warming to
hear so many kind folk inquire after my health and express
their delight that I was back in London. I was in the middle
of talking with Sir Simon Eyre, former sheriff and mayor of
London, who was telling me his memories of my lord
Richard, when twenty-eight-year-old Edward strode
boisterously into the hall, looking fit and lean after his
exertions in the field. As was his wont, he had no trouble
filling that huge room with his presence.

"Mother!" he bellowed, kissing me on both cheeks.
"How good it is to see you again."

I had no time to register any emotion, for he
immediately turned away and began shaking hands,
clapping people on the back, and patting arms, laughing
boisterously all the while as the Londoners crowded around
him.

He was followed by Richard, now eighteen years old
but looking ten years older. As usual, Richard seemed
content to remain in Edward's shadow, looking watchful
and grave, while Edward charmed everyone.

I took Richard's hands in greeting as he kissed me on
both cheeks. He would never be indolent like Edward, but
would he be as well-liked? He was too difficult to read.

Last to arrive was George, making an awkward third
spoke of a wheel. He pecked me on the cheek, then circled

the room, studying his brothers, running his tongue over his lips.

What was going to happen to George? Would he ever keep his word again? Or had he been corrupted beyond redemption by Warwick?

Edward held a great counsel at Baynard's Castle, then marched north to deal with Warwick. On Easter Sunday, at dawn, near the village of Barnet, Edward fell upon Warwick's army and soundly defeated him. Warwick was cut down fleeing from the scene. When Marguerite d'Anjou, newly arrived in England, heard the news, she collapsed into a faint. Her commanders persuaded her to stay and fight.

This time, Edward wasted no time in marching out of London to the West Country to intercept Marguerite and Édouard to prevent them from crossing the Severn into Wales.

On the fourth of May 1471, they met at Tewkesbury, near Gloucester. With the help of my youngest son, Richard, Duke of Gloucester, Edward won the day. And Marguerite's son Édouard was cut down.

I closed my ears to tales that Édouard survived the fighting and was murdered after the battle in cold blood by my three sons. I tried not to hear the whispers that Henry of Lancaster, the former King Henry VI, was struck down while at prayer. Some said that Richard of Gloucester was responsible for his murder. That he had come up silently behind King Henry before cracking his head open with a mace.

I turned a deaf ear to these rumors because I was grateful that the Cousin's War was over. Nearly ten years after my lord's murder, the House of York had prevailed.

On the twenty-first of May 1471, Edward was formally welcomed into London by the populace. In his train was Marguerite of Anjou, enduring the taunts of the crowd as they threw rubbish at her. Meanwhile, on the twenty-second of May 1471, Henry of Lancaster's corpse was taken to Saint Paul's so that all might pay their respects. The people of London were saddened by Henry of Lancaster's passing but thankful to be rid of their weak king. Marguerite was imprisoned in the Tower of London. But Edward, in a merciful gesture, sent her to live in Wallingford Castle so she could be near her great friend Alice Chaucer, the Dowager Duchess of Suffolk.

Dearest Mother, wrote Beth,
you may have heard that the former queen has come to live nearby, owing to her friendship with my mother-by-marriage, Duchess Alice.

Edward wrote to me, asking me to accompany the Dowager Duchess as much as possible on her visits to the former queen.

I assured him I would do my best, for you know I am good at keeping quiet.

I laughed. George's nickname for Beth had been "Mouse." She had been such a quiet child in contrast to her noisy siblings. I picked up the letter.

*I take my basket of sewing things and sit in a corner
making clothes for my children, doing the fine needlework
you taught us, Mother, while the ladies talk.
So far, I have nothing interesting to report to the king, for
while Marguerite bewails her state, the duchess comforts
her with gifts and wise sayings.
She has made sure that the former queen is comfortably
appointed at Wallingford Castle, with three women to
serve her.
I will write more when I have news.
I pray for you every night, dear Mother.
Your loving, Beth,
Duchess of Suffolk.*

I sighed, tucking the letter away. At least one of my
daughters was nearby and dutiful. Margaret wrote
wonderful letters, but I never saw her now that she was
Duchess of Burgundy. I scarcely saw Nan, and when I did,
it was like speaking to a stranger. And though things were
somewhat mended between Edward and myself, they were
not the same. I was ashamed that George must stomach a
bastard half-brother on the throne of England. If only I had
said 'no' that far-off evening thirty years ago.

But one cannot undo the past.

CHAPTER 60

October 1471

I was most proud of my youngest son, Richard, Duke of Gloucester, whose motto was *Loyauté Me Lié* (Loyalty Binds Me). Richard was the hero of the Battle of Barnet, holding the line against overwhelming odds so that Edward did not need to send in his reserves until the last moment. The king could be very generous, and Richard had been heaped with honors for his role in the Yorkist victory. After the Battle of Tewkesbury, I orchestrated a campaign whereby my daughters pleaded for clemency on George's behalf, which Edward eventually granted. But he refused to give George anything. This led to an outbreak of feuding between my two younger sons, and it erupted at around the time when my quiet, hard-to-read Richard decided to marry.

Richard and I had been the best of friends ever since the Serpent tried to take him from Warwick and send him to her brother Sir Anthony Woodville. On that evening long ago, I invited Richard to dine with me to ascertain his wishes. Not surprisingly, he preferred to stay with Warwick. As he left, I made a casual remark: "My son, I wish for you to find happiness in this life."

He looked at me, puzzled, his grave expression making him look much older than twelve years.

I touched his cheek with my finger. "When I was a girl, I danced and sang and played music all day long. I think of my childhood as a golden time. I was always misbehaving, but you, my son, have not had that. The war took your childhood from you. I wish I could lighten your cares. You are too young to be so serious. But then, you are just like your father."

Richard's face came alive. "Am I really?"

I nodded. "You look exactly like him. You have his nut-brown hair, his blue-grey eyes, his small build. And you have his serious personality."

"Is this true, Mother?"

"Richard! You didn't think—"

"No, Mother," he replied, flushing. He fiddled with a ring Edward had given him. "I don't look like Edward or George—"

That was true. Both Edward and George were blond giants.

"That is because Edward and George both take after my father, especially George," I told him. That was not quite true. Edward looked exactly like Blaybourne, but I didn't tell Richard that. "Meanwhile, you look like your father. How odd you both share the same name."

"Tell me about my father," he said eagerly.

And so, over the months and years that passed, I gradually told Richard about my lord of York, and from that day forward, we became the best of friends.

I suppose my guilty feelings caused me to overdo the image I gave Richard of his father. In his eyes, Richard of York became a hero, a shining warrior, an upholder of knightly virtues, the perfect gentleman. What harm could there be in it? It gave my romantic youngest son something to reach for, something to measure his conduct by. Such a different standard from the frivolity and debauchery of Edward's court.

And now, nineteen-year-old Richard had come to visit me at Berkhamsted. As always, I was delighted to see him. As was our custom, we went into my private chapel to pray for a while before sitting down to talk. This time, Richard was not as quiet as usual. He kept pacing back and forth, fiddling with the signet ring.

I ordered refreshments, then waved my people away.

"What is it?" I poured the mulled wine, for the October days were chill, and Richard had ridden at break-neck speed from London by the look of his boots.

"I wish to marry, Mother," said Richard, tossing his gloves onto a nearby coffer. "I wish to marry Nanette."

My head jerked up. Richard had just been preoccupied with fighting for the Yorkist cause. Where had he found the time to think of taking a wife?

"But Nanette is recently widowed," I said. Not long after her father Warwick had married her off to Édouard of Lancaster, he'd been killed at the Battle of Tewkesbury. "What about a foreign princess? There is Mary of Burgundy, who has now fourteen years."

"I want Nanette." Richard's tone was quiet but firm, his grey-blue eyes dark with intensity.

I recognized that look. It was the exact same expression my lord had had when he'd asked me to marry him all those years ago.

Sighing, I motioned him to sit beside me. "Nanette is lovely and perfectly suitable. Yet—"

"What, Mother?"

"She is—delicate. I am not sure she will be able to give you children. Even trying to have one child may be too much for her."

Richard paled, and his face went still. He was silent.

At last, I gently touched his arm. "Richard, my son, I am deeply sorry if I have wounded you. I did not know how much you cared about her."

"I have loved her from the moment I set eyes on her."

"But you were only eight! She was four."

"She was an angel," murmured Richard.

"Why did you not say so before? My son, you carry too many burdens. I had no idea. How you must have suffered when you heard—"

"She'd been married to that brute Lancaster?" Richard smiled wryly. "Part of me died, but it inspired me to fight."

"And you fought brilliantly, my son. I'm so proud of you."

Richard smiled. "So, you will help me, Mother?"

I laughed. "Why do you need my help?"

"She's disappeared."

"Disappeared? What do you mean?"

Richard sagged in his seat.

I frowned. "She was staying with George and Bella, wasn't she?" I fumbled in his silence. "She's at his London residence, the Herber."

"When I went there yesterday to visit her, George refused to let me see her. This morning I returned with some men-at-arms, determined to see her. We searched the house but could find her nowhere."

I stared. No. It could not be—

For the first time in many moons, my spine prickled with unease. Nanette was co-heiress with Bella of Warwick's vast estates. Was George preventing Richard from marrying Nanette so he could receive the revenue exclusively for his own use?

Richard lifted his eyes to mine. "Exactly so, Mother. Nanette could not have disappeared of her own accord. George must have hidden her somewhere."

"What do you want me to do?"

"I would like you to talk to George and Edward if necessary."

"Will the king agree to your marriage?"

"When we won at Tewkesbury, Edward said I could have anything I wanted. I told him I wanted Nanette."

"And?"

Richard met my eyes and smiled in a way that made his face glow. "He roared with laughter and slapped me on the back."

"Where is she?"

George remained silent, his hand clenched around a cup of wine. As usual, he looked magnificent in a ruby-colored tunic, his long sleeves brushing the floor, cut to show off the white velvet undershirt he wore beneath. But he was already on his third cup of wine, and it was only mid-morning. At twenty-two, my son was still handsome, but his reddening nose and slackening paunch told of a life that lacked purpose. Edward had pardoned his brother for plotting to take the throne of England. But he kept him on a tight leash and gave him little to do.

I sighed. "My son, this is serious. If anything happened to Nanette, you would be in grave trouble. Edward is testing you."

"Nothing will happen to her!" George interrupted flushing.

"How do you know that? Do you know where she is?"

I was interrupted by the sound of hooves, of metal clanging, and of male voices shouting. There was a jingle of spurs as someone ran up the stairs.

It was Richard.

I'd never seen him look so angry. He looked exactly as his father had the day he discovered my affair with Blaybourne.

"I cannot believe it!" he shouted. "You took her to a common cook shop where I found her working in the kitchens!"

Flushing crimson, George rose from his seat and fumbled for his dagger.

"George!" I said.

It made him stop in his tracks. George had hidden Nanette in a cook shop? She had been forced to work in the kitchens? George's sense of humor seemed to have become oddly twisted.

"George," I said, "Is this true?"

George flicked his eyes away and pursed his lips.

As he did so, I thanked God silently that I had chosen to live out my declining years as abbess of a Benedictine Order rather than with George and his family. For something had gone horribly wrong. George was charming. He was intelligent. He was well educated. As a boy, he'd always been my stalwart, defending the family during his father's absence like a bulldog.

What had happened? I'd never known him to behave like this. Had the death of his first child warped him somehow?

"It is true, Mother, I tell you," said Richard. "I went there myself. I saw Nanette with my own eyes. She was disheveled, dirty, and very, very scared. She had given up hope of anyone finding her."

He turned back to George. "What were you trying to do?" he roared. "Murder her? You know Nanette is not strong. Yet she was doing back-breaking work in a fiery kitchen by day and sleeping in a freezing attic by night!"

"George," I said. "How long did you plan to keep her like this?"

"Until Richard left her alone," replied George. He strutted over to his brother, jutting his chin out. "Where is she?"

"I have her in safekeeping."

"I demand that you return her to my house," said George, putting his hands behind his back, which made him look even more like a strutting cock.

Richard clenched his jaw, and his lips thinned.

I hurried over to stand between my sons, putting my hand on Richard's sleeve. "Where is she, my son? Is she safe?"

Richard stopped glaring at his brother. "Have no fear, Mother," he said, patting my arm. "She is safe in Saint Martin-le-Grand in Newgate Street. I have put her into the care of her uncle the Archbishop of York."

Archbishop George Neville was a nephew of mine, the younger brother of Warwick. I had known him all his life. Indeed, he had been one of the children I had been minding in the garden at Bisham when I met my lord Richard as an adult.

"You have done well, my son. How long do you plan to keep her there?"

"Until our marriage takes place," replied Richard.

"No!" roared George.

"You cannot prevent my marriage to Nanette. She is not your ward. Nor can you take her away from our kinsman, the archbishop."

"Edward will agree with me," said George, turning to go.

"He'll agree with me," responded Richard, more quietly, following his brother.

Edward, at length, was able to persuade Richard and George to bury their differences. George agreed to the carving-up of Warwick's estates after receiving the greater share of them and was created Earl of Warwick and Salisbury in right of his wife.

On his marriage to Nanette, Richard received Warwick's estates in Yorkshire, Northumberland, and Cumberland, which included Sheriff Hutton and Middleham. Richard and Nanette married in the spring of 1472. They had but one child, a son whom they named Edward after the king.

CHAPTER 61

1473 to 1478

During this time, my prayers were answered, and George and Bella had more children. Their second child, named Margaret after my daughter, the Duchess of Burgundy, was born August 14, 1473. Their third child, named Edward after the king, was born February 25, 1475.

However, tensions rumbled on between my sons. George and Edward barely tolerated each other, and even Richard grew more critical of the king. In 1475, Richard had gone over to France with the army, ready to give the French another Agincourt. But Edward allowed himself to be bought off by the King of France like a wealthy merchant who would prostitute his services to the highest bidder.

"This is insupportable," Richard told me later. "Edward does not behave as a prince of blood. He cheats us of an honorable peace at Picquigny."

I could only sigh. Every year, Edward did something that seemed to demonstrate his low origins.

In the summer of 1476, Richard finally prevailed upon Edward to re-inter my lord of York in a proper resting place at Fotheringhay. Richard acted as chief mourner and led the seven-day procession from Pontefract – where my lord had been hastily interred after his foul murder – to Fotheringhay.

I wished to be present, of course. But in the end, I begged off, saying it was too painful. The reason was that the Serpent insisted on being there, and Edward was unable or unwilling to say no to her. Richard blamed the delay of the re-internment on Edward's irresponsibility.

I had other things to think of. One day earlier in that year of 1476, I was at my prayers when the steward announced the Duchess of Suffolk. I was surprised; January was a bad time for traveling. I rose at once.

"Mother, dearest!" Beth kissed my cheek as she entered my bedchamber. Her black woolen cloak was covered in snow from the storm outside.

"My dearest child, what has happened?"

"My lord John and our children send you their affectionate greetings. They are well."

"But?"

Beth drew up a chair and bade me sit.

"Margaret?" I whispered.

"Nan." She sat down beside me and took my hands. "Nan is dead."

"No."

"Yes, Mother."

Rising swiftly, I nearly knocked over my chair. "No. It can't be true." I folded my arms over my chest and gazed at the white flakes tumbling down outside. "After all these years, I've been trying to reach her…"

Beth was silent.

"How did she die?"

"In childbirth, Mother."

"Childbirth? I didn't know she was expecting."

"Her daughter Anne died last year, at the age of twenty."

I sank into a chair, my arms wrapped around me, and rocked to and fro. Nan's daughter, Anne Holland, had been married to the Serpent's son Thomas Grey. He'd made her die in childbirth.

"Nan decided to have another child. The child lives and is called Anne St. Leger."

"I didn't know," I whispered. "Was she happy, with her —her lover?"

"They were married, Mother dear," said Beth, chafing my cold hands. "Anne got her divorce three years ago and has been married for two years."

"It's all my fault," I burst out, rising. "I should never have let her go. I'll never forget the day she was torn away from me. If only—"

The rest of the sentence disappeared as I flung myself onto my bed. "If only I'd never met Blaybourne," I sobbed into a pillow, "then Richard would not have punished me with Nan's marriage."

Beth sat by me and held my hand.

"We can't have run out of time." I wept. "I had plans to see her again."

Beth summoned Jenet, who mixed up a potion to help me sleep.

I slept that day. But it was many moons before I slept well again. The sands of time had run through my fingers, and Nan was gone, dead at the age of thirty-six. I paced around my chamber during the dead of night. Why hadn't I done more to reach her? Dark waves of guilt washed over me as I gazed at the stars.

In October 1476, Bella presented George with their fourth child, a son they named Richard. But she never recovered. By mid-November, she was so ill she was taken home to Warwick Castle to die. She passed on just before Christmas 1476, at the age of twenty-five. Their child died ten days later.

George was heartbroken, and I was consumed with worry. Naturally, George wished to marry again, for he had

two children under the age of five. His first choice was
Mary of Burgundy, now nearly twenty years old. On her
father's death in January 1477, she had become the heiress
to his vast duchy. But Edward thwarted George at every
turn, and the Serpent added fuel to the fire by proposing
her own brother Anthony Woodville, Earl Rivers, as
bridegroom. In the end, Mary married Maximilian of
Austria with Edward's blessing.

George's second choice of bride was Princess Margaret
of Scotland. But Edward again forbade the match.
Surmising that the Serpent was responsible for these
decisions, George decided to strike at her through one of
her women, Ankarette Twynho, who'd served Bella before
her death. Taking the king's justice into his own hands,
George arrested, tried, and executed Dame Twynho on the
grounds that she had poisoned Bella, being the means by
which the Serpent had put a curse on Bella to make her die.

Edward was furious but did nothing.

"The king is showing a great deal of forbearance," I
remarked, listening to Robert Stillington, the Bishop of
Bath and Wells, explain the situation. "You have seen
George much of late. How is he?"

Bishop Stillington cleared his throat. "I have some news
that I fear will greatly distress you, and that is the reason for
my visit."

I gripped the chair handles.

"The Duke of Clarence is publicly declaring the king to
be a bastard."

"Not that," I murmured. But of course, he would say such a thing. I had taught him to say it, and it was becoming clear that in the wake of Bella's death, George was becoming unhinged.

The bishop signaled to my women. "I fear I have greatly distressed you."

I waved them away and sipped my wine. I must do penance for my sins, and the one way I could do that was to hear the worst.

"What else does George say?"

The bishop sighed and lowered his voice: "He declares the king to be a necromancer and says that his marriage to the queen is null and void because tradition forbids the King of England to marry widows."

I shook my head. "George is not well. The death of his wife has been a great shock."

"You might be right, my lady. His actions seemed designed to cause the most offense. Why, yesterday, he publicly accused the queen of murdering his duchess by poison and sorcery. And he refuses to eat or drink anything at court."

My hands trembled as I put my wine-cup down. "What of the king?" I whispered.

"He is very patient with his brother."

But that could not last much longer. As I paced my chamber that night, gazing at the moon, I could imagine the Serpent's reaction:

"I tell you, he's gone quite mad," she would say. "He thinks he can do anything he likes, such as storming into your council chamber and demanding that the king's justice be overturned."

Edward would sigh. It was true that George was becoming a problem, but he was loath to act. His brother was amusing. And they were both so alike, much more so than their youngest brother Richard. "George has no real power. He is greatly upset by his wife's death."

"Edward! He's dangerous. Don't you remember how he plotted against you with Warwick? But worst of all is what he's said against me. He says I'm not your legitimate wife!"

"No one takes him seriously."

"Sweeting, think about this. If Clarence believes I'm not your legitimate wife, then what is he going to think about our children? He's going to say they are bastards. And so he'll not allow our Edward to inherit the throne. What say you to that?"

"You have a point there."

"And so, you will see to it that Clarence is removed, won't you, my sweeting?"

And so it came to pass that George was incarcerated in the Tower of London. Months passed, and Edward did nothing. Then, he summoned Parliament to meet in January 1478 to try George publicly for his offenses.

"I have a copy of the attainder with me."

The Archbishop of Canterbury, Thomas Bourchier, handed me his scroll and bowed. Thomas Bourchier, a kinsman-by-marriage of my lord husband Richard, had been chosen by Richard to be Archbishop of Canterbury when he was regent of England. Over the years, we had developed a close friendship.

"Pray be seated," I said, "and read it to me. My eyes are tired today." I sat opposite him in front of the fireplace, my face concealed by shadows.

The Archbishop cleared his throat. "The king read the indictment himself. He accused his brother, George, Duke of Clarence, of new treasons to exalt himself and his heir to the regality of the crown of England. He said that he had ever loved and cherished his brother, giving him so large a portion of possessions that seldom had been seen. The duke's love, for all this, did not increase but grew daily more and more in malice. He falsely and traitorously intended the destruction and disinheriting of the king and his issue."

I put my hand in front of my face as the Archbishop stopped. I could not deny the charges. And, yet, Edward had never handled George well. What would have happened if George had been allowed to have a position in

Edward's cabinet? Would he have used it to try and take the throne that way?

"What will happen now?"

"The Lords and the Commons demand that the sentence be carried out."

I gripped the chair so hard, my knuckles went white. If that were true, George would suffer the full horrors of a traitor's death, the hanging, the drawing, and the quartering. Couldn't Edward lock him up for the duration of his lifetime? But Edward had done that for Henry of Lancaster, only to find he became the focus of opposition. Henry of Lancaster had been removed, a threat to Edward's throne.

I pinched my lips together and rose, then wobbled. The Archbishop rushed to put a hand under my elbow. I sank into my seat.

"I must write to the king."

Dear Edward, I wrote,

Archbishop Bourchier has told me that George has been indicted on charges of treason.

I beg you not to let him die a traitor's death.

I humbly request that you commute the sentence to a beheading, or some other way preferred by George, and that you allow it to be done privately to spare our family further scandal.

In sorrow,

Cecylee,

Duchess of York.

I gazed out of the window. It was bitter cold, and I struggled to keep my heavy fur wrapped around me as I stood there, sleepless. Dawn came, black changing to grey and white. It was February 19, 1478, a cold day under the clouds, snow falling. Wisps of chill damp infected my bones as I knelt to pray for the soul of my son George.

Had he been executed the night before?

What had become of him?

I was near unto sixty-three years, yet hours went by as I continued to fast and pray, moving my lips over the prayers composed by Saint Bridget of Sweden:

O Jesu,
endless sweetness of all that love thee,
a joy passing and exceeding all gladness and desire,
the savior and lover of all repentant sinners ...

A voice softly said, "Mother?"

Slowly, I opened my eyes, and through my cloudy vision, a face gradually came into focus. The face seemed to be George's. But it dissolved and became Richard's. I'd never noticed Richard to be like George before.

I tried to move but could not.

Someone lifted me up and gently set me into my favorite chair. The room came to life as folk stoked up the fire and bustled around with cups of mulled wine and refreshments.

"I cannot eat," I murmured.

Richard sat down beside me. "I'll not have you go as well."

An image of George the day I'd faced down the Lancastrian army at Ludlow filled my head. How bright and handsome he'd looked in his suit of green and gold, chosen especially to match my outfit. He showed little fear, even when the army burst into town, staring at everything with his unusual blue-green eyes. And now I would never see him again.

"Mother," came a voice. "Mother, where are you?"

"George?" I murmured. Someone's warm hands picked mine up, and Richard's face wavered into view. "You must eat, Mother. You'll make yourself ill if you do not."

I took my handkerchief out of my sleeve and dabbed my eyes. A procession of people filled my mind's eye: my beloved Joan, my lost daughter Nan, my murdered child Edmund, my lord husband Richard, and my dearest friend and confidante, Mama. I sagged in my seat, bone weary. Truly, I was living a long and unhappy life. Lisette's curse had come true. Maybe if I continued to fast, I could see Mama again.

But Richard was by my side once more. He cut a small morsel of my favorite honey wafer put it on a plate. Then he stared me down until I took a nibble. He handed me my wine cup and used the power of his blue-grey eyes to encourage me to take a sip.

"You're so quiet, Mother."

I lifted my eyes. "George?"

Richard slumped in his seat and took my hands. "He's gone."

"How?"

"I'm not going to tell you."

I stared at my hands as tears slipped past my lids and down my cheeks. I was responsible for George's death. By announcing the king's illegitimacy in front of everyone, I provided the motive to turn against his brother. George had always been intensely jealous of Edward, but I refused to see that. I believed I could manage George, but he was unstable and easily led.

What a sin I had committed by being unfaithful to my lord. Edward was not legitimate, but he'd executed the legitimate heir. What had I done? What monster had I brought into our family?

I stared into Richard's blue-grey eyes. Was I with my lord? No. Richard was the only son left to me, and I must protect him. I sat up in my chair.

"What will you do?"

"I have been loyal to Edward," replied Richard. "And will continue so while he lives. But I owe no loyalty to his wife nor to her numerous relations."

"The queen is dangerous," I remarked, rising. "Remember what happened when she stole the king's signet ring and had the Earl of Desmond and his two young children executed? And all because he made some unfortunate—and very true—remarks about the king's choice of a wife."

Richard glanced at me. "I'd forgotten that."

"You are next," I said, going to him. "Mark my words, if she has any excuse to rid herself of you, she will."

"I'm determined to fight for what is rightfully ours," he said. "And you must be determined, Mother, not to let George's … death get you down."

"You've given me hope," I replied as I blessed him.

I do not know what happened to darling George. He died in mysterious circumstances in the Tower on the night of February 18, 1478. Some say he drowned in a barrel of Malmsey wine. But I preferred to think that he died the more dignified death of beheading by an expert swordsman.

Poor George was buried in Tewkesbury Abbey, next to his wife, Bella.

Five years passed. The country seemed to be at peace.

Until one day, in early April 1483.

CHAPTER 62

March to April 1483

I knew nothing of these events until much later, for the Serpent neglected to tell me.

Edward loved fishing and had insisted on going out on a boat in the cold, blustery, wet weather of March 1483. It was not surprising that he caught a chill and had to take to his bed. But everyone expected him to recover, for he was only forty years old.

However, Edward was as intemperate in his eating habits as he was with his mistresses. Gone was the lean, muscular, and handsome youth crowned king at the age of eighteen. In his place was a man with an enormous stomach, who frequently purged himself for the pleasure of gorging on food and drink.

The Serpent summoned a horde of doctors, to no avail. Edward died on the ninth day of April.

If she did not act quickly, the Serpent's hold on power would disappear. Her first aim was to get her eldest son, twelve-year-old Edward, Prince of Wales, to London, where he would be under her care. For when his father died, the prince was some two hundred miles away at Ludlow. Fortunately, she'd used her charms to convince Edward to give the guardianship of his heir to her brother, Anthony Woodville, Earl Rivers, whose loyalty to her was unquestioned.

Her second aim was to deal with the king's younger brother, Richard of Gloucester, immensely powerful in the north of England partly because he owned an enormous amount of land and partly because he had the power to dispense the king's justice. It was imperative to keep the king's condition secret from Gloucester because Edward had named him Protector of the Realm until Prince Edward reached his majority.

But if Prince Edward were brought to his mother in London, he could be crowned immediately, and there would be no need for Gloucester to act as Protector.

The Serpent loathed and feared Gloucester, for he was close to me and, like me, had disapproved of Edward's marriage. Unlike George, Richard was crafty enough to keep his feelings to himself. But he'd made his displeasure with the Woodvilles plain by rarely coming to court.

The Serpent lost no time, apprising Rivers of Edward's death and urging him to bring the young prince to London.

To the late king's mother and younger brother, she wrote not a word, hoping we would not learn of Edward's death until it was too late.

CHAPTER 63

April 11 to 17, 1483

To Cecylee, Duchess of York, Greetings.
Madam,
It has come to my attention that you may not have been
apprised of the sad news of the late king's passing, here in
London, on the ninth day of April.
You should also know it was the late king's wish that his
brother, Richard, Duke of Gloucester, be Protector of the
Realm until such time as Prince Edward reaches his
majority.
Written this eleventh day of April, in the year 1483,
Thomas Bourchier,
Archbishop of Canterbury.

I sagged and dropped the letter. Edward dead? How could that be? He was only forty years old, and he was a vital, larger-than-life person whose ringing laugh made even the sourest person merry. Whatever had happened?

I sat in my chair for many moments, hearing the vast silence of his absence. I no longer went to court and had not seen him in years. My sons and daughters communicate with letters and visits. All except Edward, who never visited and rarely wrote. Over the years, I'd only been able to glean news of him from others.

But he was my son and had been a daily presence in my thoughts for the past forty years. Despite his irresponsibility and lack of taste, he'd been a strong king. He held everything together, keeping the factions of his government at bay by giving Richard power in the north while the Serpent's family had their power base in the south.

Now, what would happen?

The Serpent was well placed to seize power, for she was in London, and her relatives had been rewarded with positions in Edward's government. I gripped the arms of my chair.

What was going to become of Richard?

If the Serpent prevailed, she would strip him of his offices. She would take away his land and his home. She would leave him with nothing.

But she would not end there. No. She would find some way to incarcerate him in the Tower.

I picked up the Archbishop's letter. It was written two days after Edward's death. Had anyone told my remaining son? It reminded me of the time when Henry of Lancaster had gone mad, and the Bitch of Anjou had kept the news from Richard of York.

I sat up suddenly, berating myself for the sluggishness of my mind. Of course, the Serpent would not want Richard of Gloucester to know about his brother's death! I must write to him at once!

To Richard, Duke of Gloucester, Greetings.
Dearest Richard,
I write in haste to tell you that Edward the King passed away suddenly this ninth day of April.
I have a subtle suspicion that the Serpent may not have apprised you of this news, and so I urge you to move swiftly to protect your interests.
Perhaps you should have Prince Edward transferred to your care.
Written this thirteenth day of April 1483,
Your loving mother,
Cecylee,
Duchess of York.

While I anxiously waited for a reply from Richard, the Serpent held her first council meeting. First, she asked for a new bidding prayer to be said in the churches. This was customary on the death of a sovereign, but the Serpent had purposely worded it so that the name of Richard of Gloucester was left out.

The king's council should have voted this down, but it was packed with her friends and relations. There was the Archbishop of York and the Bishop of Ely, who had been friends of the king and queen. There was her eldest son, Thomas Grey, first Marquess of Dorset, who had control of the king's treasure and the royal ordinance. And then there were the aristocrats her sisters had married.

They agreed with the Serpent.

They agreed too when the Serpent requested they proclaim Edward Prince of Wales, King of England.

But when the Serpent requested that the coronation take place as soon as possible, William Hastings, the Lord Chamberlain, and Edward's closest friend objected.

"Why so hasty?" he demanded. "King Edward has a protector-designate."

It turned out that Edward had altered his will at the last minute to say that his brother of Gloucester should be protector-designate until Prince Edward reached his majority. The Serpent was not happy.

She turned to the Archbishop of Canterbury because he would officiate at the coronation. "What say you, my lord?"

Thomas Bourchier smiled slightly. "Perhaps it would be more prudent to wait."

"We've just declared war on France," remarked Dorset. "I think it would be wise to have a smooth transition. Crowning Prince Edward now would show the French that matters have not changed."

Smiling, the Serpent consulted her scroll. "What say you, my lords, to Sunday, the fourth day of May?"

They agreed.

The Serpent then requested that twelve-year-old Edward be escorted the two hundred miles from Ludlow to London by an army of soldiers.

"An army!" exclaimed Hastings. "Whom in this realm do you fear so much?"

"The king should have a suitable escort," remarked Dorset, allowing the Serpent to evade the question.

"But not an army!" shouted Hastings. "It will only sow trouble and bloodshed."

"I want no harm to befall my son," replied the Serpent.

"If you insist on this foolhardy whim, madam," replied Hastings, "then I'll retire to Calais."

This was no empty threat, for Hastings was the Governor of Calais, and it was from Calais that Warwick had plotted his coup against Edward.

"I suggest, madam," continued Hastings, "that you limit the prince's escort to two thousand men."

The Serpent looked around the table, but the king's councilors would not meet her gaze. She was forced to abandon her plan.

She summoned her scribe and wrote to her brother
Rivers for a second time, urging him to bring the prince
quickly to London.

A few days passed, then I received Richard's reply:

Dearest Mother,
I thank you most heartily for your message.
Indeed, no one had thought to apprise me of this situation,
saving yourself and Hastings.
I agree with your suggestion concerning Prince Edward's
person. If we do not win, we will be in grave jeopardy for
the reasons that you well know.
Written this seventeenth day of April 1483
Your loving son,
R. Gloucester

I smiled; Richard's plans were already well in hand. I
fingered my rosary beads. The next few days would
determine who would win, and it would be hard to wait. I
rang my bell. I would summon my women and design a
new altar cloth, which we would sew. And I would ask
Master Gerard to ensure that we had a goodly supply of
wine, for I found it most comforting in the evenings when
the shadows drew in.

I was going to need all the comfort I could find.

CHAPTER 64

April 20th to May 7th, 1483

By the greatest good fortune, the Serpent's brother Rivers planned to celebrate Saint George's Day in Ludlow and saw no reason to alter his plans. He ignored his sister's urgent pleas and did not leave Ludlow until the morning of April 24. This gave Richard a week to muster his forces before marching south.

Richard arrived in York on April 20 and sent out messengers to ascertain where the young king was. His plan was to intercept Rivers before he arrived in London. Fortunately, Rivers took his time. He did not arrive in Northampton with his charge until April 29.

I had a prior undertaking to meet with Rivers in Northampton, wrote Richard to me,
but he tried to slip through my fingers.

I put the letter down and frowned. Henry Stafford,
second Duke of Buckingham? What was Richard doing
with him?

Buckingham was my great-nephew but had not been
popular at Edward's court, being jealous, proud, and
ruthlessly ambitious. He'd never bothered to conceal his
hatred of the queen, who had forced him to marry one of
her sisters. He harbored a grudge against the King because
of a dispute over some estates. He was, I realized with
dismay, not unlike George. If Buckingham had now
switched his allegiance to Richard's cause, it could only be
because he hoped that Richard would reward him for his
loyalty by returning the disputed Bohun estates. Did
Richard know this?

I picked up Richard's letter:

*When Rivers arrived in Northampton with the queen
dowager's second son, Sir Richard Grey,
I received them graciously and asked them to sup with me.
I considered it wise not to betray my anger at River's gross
presumption at lodging the king so far away without
consulting me first.
Over dinner, I gently pumped Rivers for information, and
he acquainted me with the dealings of the council in
London.*

Suffice it to say, there appeared to be no place for me in the new king's government.

You may realize, dear Mother, how alarmed I was. But I concealed my feelings behind smiles and gestures of goodwill.

That night, Rivers and Grey slept in the accommodation I had arranged for them in Northampton, while Buckingham and I posted guards around that inn and along the road leading to Stony Stratford.

The next day, at dawn, Buckingham and I rode to Stony Stratford at full speed with Sir Richard Grey.

The king was full pleased to see us, so we dismissed his escort and his attendants and set off for Northampton.

"Madam."

I looked up as my steward bowed.

"A messenger has arrived from London."

I put Richard's letter down. "What is the news?"

"The queen dowager has taken sanctuary in Westminster Abbey with her five daughters, two of her four sons, and her brother, the Bishop of Salisbury," replied the messenger, kneeling before me.

Had Richard already succeeded in crushing the Woodvilles? But he was not yet in London. Or was this a clever ruse by the Serpent to make her look powerless and thus to gain sympathy? For she was not powerless at all. She was like a spider spinning a web.

I motioned for the messenger to continue.

"Your son, Richard, Duke of Gloucester, has imprisoned Rivers in Sheriff Hutton, Sir Richard Grey in Middleham, and others of their affinity in Pontefract."

By Our Lady, Richard had moved with lightning speed.

"When my lord duke was informed that the Archbishop of York had given the Great Seal of England to the queen, he removed him from office."

I smiled grimly and let out a breath. Archbishop Thomas Rotherham was known to be a staunch friend of the queen. Richard had performed magnificently. I picked up his letter again.

"What do the people say?"

The messenger coughed and looked at the ground. "Unfortunately, madam, they murmur that these actions are those of a tyrant."

I stared at him. Motioning for the messenger to leave, I ignored the prickle of unease that crept up my spine and the painful memories of my lord Richard's bid for power.

I am proceeding onto London with my nephew.
And, madam, I beseech you to throw off your present cares
and go to Baynard's Castle, your residence in London, so
that I may take counsel with you to my comfort.
Written at Northampton, the second day of May,
with the hand of your most humble son,
R. Gloucester

On the third of May, Richard of Gloucester set off for London in the company of his cousin Henry of Buckingham and the young King Edward V.

On the fourth of May, they entered London, and Gloucester lodged the prince in the palace of the bishops of London.

On the seventh of May, the Archbishop of Canterbury, on Gloucester's orders, recovered the Great Seal of England from the queen dowager.

CHAPTER 65

Baynard's Castle, London
May 7, 1483

What would happen to Richard when King Edward V gained his majority? My grandson already had twelve years. We didn't have long to act, for a precedent had been set by Henry of Lancaster, who'd declared his majority at sixteen.

If we did nothing, Edward would reward his numerous Woodville relatives once he came of age.

Thus, it was imperative we invalidated the will of the late king immediately. And so I summoned my dear friend Thomas Bourchier, Archbishop of Canterbury, to a private meeting at Baynard's Castle.

"My lord," he said when Richard explained what we intended to do, "everything is in order. The late king's will has been properly signed and sealed. What objections do you have?"

I took a deep breath. "There are things you know not, my lord Archbishop. Things that cause me great sorrow."

Richard signaled, and a servant brought me wine.

I sipped it slowly before continuing. "Long ago, when I was young, I sinned grievously against my lord husband. I bore a child that was not his."

There was a long silence as I thought of all that had gone wrong.

The archbishop leaned forward. "Are you speaking, my lady, of the late king?"

I nodded.

"You are quite certain, Lady Cecylee, that this is so?"

"I am willing to swear on holy relics," I replied.

The archbishop put his hands inside his long, wide sleeves and considered.

"If it be true that Lord Edward was indeed illegitimate, then he should have been debarred from ascending the throne of England. Thus, we have grounds for declaring his will to be illegal."

He turned to me. "Because you alone, Lady Cecylee, can answer that question, I believe it more politic if you would sign the statement declaring Lord Edward's will to be invalid."

Richard summoned a scribe, who drew up the document.

"What do you intend to do about Lord Edward's sons?" asked the archbishop in a low tone.

"I have not made a decision as yet," replied Richard. "Their mother is a dangerous schemer. I intend to deal with her, and with them, at a time and place of my own choosing."

On the tenth of May, Richard was made Lord Protector of England.

CHAPTER 66

Baynard's Castle, London
May 26, 1483

Richard sat tense in my big throne-like chair, taut as a harp string, turning his signet ring round and round. Any more of this, and he would snap.

"My conscience has tormented me for years," said our guest, Robert Stillington, Bishop of Bath and Wells. "But I made a promise to my king and liege lord, to your son, madam, that I would breathe no word of this to any living person."

I pressed a cup of mulled wine into Richard's hand and indicated a seat for the good bishop. The man was haggard with exhaustion, having traveled all the way from his seat at Wells, a distance of some one hundred miles.

"What has tormented you?" I asked, signaling to the servants to bring more wine.

"Madam. I ought to warn you. What I am about to say may horrify you and your son." He bowed to Richard.

I sat wearily in my chair, indicating to the servants to leave the flagon of wine and close the door.

"I know the late king's marriage to Dame Élisabeth Grey caused your family great pain," continued Bishop Stillington as soon as the door shut. "Perhaps it might have caused even greater pain had you known he was already married."

Richard recoiled in his chair. My hands shook, so I spilled some drops of wine.

I busied myself with my handkerchief, cleaning the spill away. Finally, I said, "Edward committed bigamy?"

"Yes, madam."

"Who was the lady?" asked Richard.

"Lady Eleanor Butler."

I put my wine-cup down. "Not Lady Eleanor Talbot, the Earl of Shrewsbury's daughter?"

"Yes, madam. She was married to Sir Thomas Butler, Lord Sudeley's heir, some thirty years ago. I do not know exactly when her husband died, save that he'd passed on by March of 1461 when first I met the lady."

I sat back in my seat, turning the cup in my hands. My head filled with an image of Eleanor, a child of such striking beauty back in Rouen. The youngest daughter of my dearest friend Margaret, she had hair the color of silver and deep violet eyes. She had been a quiet child with surprising flashes of naughtiness. Most of all, she'd been the playmate of my beloved Joan.

I blinked away tears as the image changed, and six-year-old Eleanor ran through the gardens of Rouen Castle hand in hand with three-year-old Joan.

Someone bent over me. It was Richard.

He chafed my hands. "You look pale, Mother," he murmured. He turned to the bishop. "My lady mother is distressed. Perhaps you should return."

At once, Bishop Stillington was on his feet, his face creased with concern. "Madam, I am more sorry than I can say to bring you such news."

I waved him back to his seat. "What you have told me is very shocking. Edward told me nothing of this—"

I broke off as I remembered something Edward had said. What was it? I grasped at a thread of memory. It had been around the time Warwick and I had been negotiating his marriage with Bona of Savoy. Yes, he'd asked if his bride-to-be had silver hair and violet eyes.

Richard returned to his seat. "Tell us how this happened, when it took place, and how you know about it."

"After the death of her husband, Lady Eleanor went to the King to ask him to return her manors. Her father-in-law, Lord Sudeley, had settled two manors on her at the time of her marriage, but after his son's death, he wanted one of them back. However, his lordship did not complete the required documents to transfer the title. At that point, King Edward seized her lands because the Butlers were

Lancastrians who had fought against him. Lady Eleanor was forced to move in with her father-in-law.

"Shortly afterward, she made her way to the Palace of Windsor to plead her case before the king. He was enchanted by her beauty. Lady Eleanor, however, rebuffed his advances, saying that she would not lie with him unless he married her."

"When did the marriage take place?" asked Richard.

"April of 1462."

I looked at the bishop. When did Easter Sunday fall that year? For it was customary for the Church to ban marriages during the Lenten season.

"How do you know this?" asked Richard.

"I was the officiating priest."

I grasped the handles of my chair and rose. "How could this have happened without my knowledge?"

The bishop went off into a coughing fit.

Richard filled his wine cup and motioned for him to continue.

"I married them in a private ceremony at a Carmelite house in Oxford. There were no witnesses."

I sank into my seat. "Are you saying that her lady mother did not know of this?"

The bishop nodded.

Richard leaned forward in his chair. "Why was the marriage kept so secret?"

The bishop bowed his head. "Lady Eleanor was deeply spiritual. She was beautiful both inside and out. She felt she'd sinned by agreeing to a clandestine marriage with

Lord Edward. She was greatly distressed to find herself expecting a child shortly after the marriage took place. She went into seclusion at the Augustinian priory of Wigmore, where she gave birth to a son."

"A son!" exclaimed Richard.

"Yes, my lord. A son named Edward after his father. The child was known as Edward of Wigmore."

"Why did no one say anything?" demanded Richard.

"Lady Eleanor made Lord Edward take a vow of silence. She felt she had wronged her family, wronged her mother, wronged you, my lady," he turned towards me. "She had great respect and love for both her mother and you," he bowed to me. "She did not want power for herself, and she disliked court life. She doubted her ability to be Lord Edward's queen. She wanted only safety and security for herself and her son."

"But if she had come to court as Edward's acknowledged lady and queen, the whole tone of the court would have been different," I said. What would have happened? Would Edward have been as greedy and debauched, lazy, and irresponsible? Maybe not. For I always thought that the Serpent's greed and selfishness brought out the worst in him.

Richard glanced at me, motioning for the bishop to continue.

"Lord Edward tried to change Lady Eleanor's mind, but he could not wait forever."

"And then another Lancastrian widow came along," I put in.

"Indeed," said the bishop. "When Lady Eleanor heard of Lord Edward's marriage to Dame Grey, she was heartsick. But after her hesitations, she did not feel it right to put forward her own claim. She entered the Carmelite priory at Ludlow."

"Is she alive?" I asked.

"No. She was buried on the thirtieth of June 1468. Truly, I believe, she died of a broken heart."

"What of her son?" asked Richard.

"The child did not survive her."

I rose and walked to the window to hide tears. How different everything could have been.

The bishop coughed. "Of course," he added, "this does have implications."

I turned.

"Since Lord Edward was previously married, his marriage to Dame Grey was unlawful," said Bishop Stillington. "And so, the children of that union are not legitimate, thus have no claim to the throne of England."

I glared. Had Edward let me ruin my reputation rather than admit he was a bigamist? Had he been laughing behind his hand while I struggled with the Serpent? What about all those freezing winters spent in a residence that did not have glazed windows? Or my years of remorse following my outburst?

I had gone through all that humiliation so that Edward could keep his secret. He must have kept it well, for the Serpent could not have known.

The bishop rose and made a deep bow to Richard. "You, my lord," he said, "are the rightful King of England."

Richard's face went quiet.

I looked up. Richard was the most sensitive of my children, the one with the finest mind. He could read Latin fluently and was exceedingly familiar with the laws of the land, having acted as Edward's Justiciar for the past twelve years. He would be a superb king, for he was just and would use his knowledge of the law to protect his people. But he was so modest, so unlike Edward and George.

"I did not look for this," said Richard eventually.

"No, you did not," I replied. "But it is yours by right. You know you can do it, for what is kingship if not administering justice to all the people?"

CHAPTER 67

Early June 1483

Richard immediately went about securing his claim to the throne. He didn't have much time, for the coronation of Edward's bastard son had been set for Saint John's Day, less than one month away.

On the fifth day of June, my son moved from Baynard's Castle to his own town house at Crosby Place in Bishopsgate, allowing him secret meetings with those of the king's council who supported him while continuing to hold open meetings either at my residence or at Westminster. During the open meetings, my son took control of daily matters of the government, permitting my grandson's coronation to go ahead.

But things did not proceed smoothly. For some unaccountable reason, Hastings saw fit to go over to the

Woodvilles. I suppose I shouldn't have been surprised, for Hastings was an unsavory character who'd led Edward into the depths of debauchery. Naturally, it was Hastings who'd suggested the boating outing that resulted in Edward's death. Folk said that they even shared mistresses.

On the ninth of June, Richard discovered Hastings plotting with the Serpent to remove him as Lord Protector. Up until that point, Richard hadn't disturbed the Serpent's sanctuary. But it was now imperative that Richard gain custody of Prince Edward's younger brother, the Duke of York before the Serpent could do further damage. To do this, Richard hit upon the clever idea of bringing forward the date of the coronation by two days to June 22, giving reason to place the young Duke of York in the Tower with his brother, the new king. If the king's brother were not allowed to appear at his coronation, even the Serpent would be embarrassed.

On the tenth of June, Richard wrote to the great northern magnates and the civil council in York, telling them of the Woodville plots and asking for arms and men.

On the eleventh of June, he ordered the executions of Rivers, Grey, and others of their affinity, ensuring that the Woodvilles did not regain power.

On the thirteenth of June, he divided his council. The open meeting met in Westminster and was ordered to finalize plans for the coronation. Richard's secret meeting took place in the Tower. During that, he publicly accused Hastings of treason and had him executed on the spot without a trial.

Folk will wonder why he did this. After all, Hastings was a nobleman, and the law said he had to be tried by his peers. But Hastings was a dangerous enemy, the Serpent's henchman, and spy.

On the sixteenth of June, Archbishop Bourchier went with many others to the sanctuary to confront the Serpent. They conveyed my son's request that nine-year-old Richard, Duke of York, be removed to the Tower. The Serpent expressed some reservations about her sons' safety. However, our kinsman Bourchier was able to calm her fears, and she handed over her youngest son.

I breathed a sigh of relief upon hearing the news. The Woodvilles were being stripped of their power, and all seemed much easier than I'd dared hope.

On that day, my son took up residence in the royal lodgings at the Tower. Shortly afterward, the two boys were moved to the inner apartments. They were never seen again.

CHAPTER 68

June 1483

It was now time for Richard to explain things to the good people of London.

"My son," I said, "You must tell them of my sin. How else can you claim the throne? If you don't explain that Edward was illegitimate, they will think you are usurping it."

"But, Mother, it would ruin your reputation, and for a lady of your years—"

"It is imperative that you get the Serpent out of the way," I said, interrupting. "And the only way to do that is to claim the throne of England for yourself. But you must get the backing of the Londoners. You cannot expect them to give you the throne, for they think it belongs to your nephew, whom they call Edward V."

There was a long pause. Richard got up and went to the window so that I couldn't see his face. But I could tell he was struggling mightily, for he twisted his ring and fiddled with his dagger.

Finally, he turned around. "If you're sure, Mother?"

I glanced down. This was not going to be easy. Women who erred were not treated kindly, and I was not looking forward to the effect these revelations would have. But I had to crush the Serpent. I lifted my chin. "I am sure."

But Richard procrastinated and allowed the coronation arrangements for my grandson to continue. He did not show his hand until Sunday, June 22, the day of the presumed coronation. Naturally, the Londoners were buzzing with anticipation.

Doctor Ralph Shaw of Cambridge University preached a sermon at Saint Paul's Cross in which he told everyone that Edward IV was illegitimate. Naturally, I was not present, and so I had to hear about it from members of my household. I thought that telling the truth about my sins would help my son Richard become king. But my informants told me something surprising. When Doctor Shaw made these allegations, the crowd became silent. When their murmurs eventually started up, it became apparent they didn't believe him.

464

Now it was my turn to be surprised. Why wouldn't folk believe it, especially as it happened to be true? I was not prepared for this. According to my informants—and I had many—people didn't believe that someone as pious as I could have sinned so greatly.

It was true that I heard Mass several times a day and that I was a Benedictine abbess. But I never thought of myself as more saintly than others. If only they knew! I was pious because I had sinned so greatly.

I was dismayed: Everyone knew the Londoners had to be on your side if you were to govern England effectively. What was going to happen to Richard?

"They didn't believe you." I exclaimed. "Why not?"

Richard sighed. In the pearly light of an early summer evening, he looked grey and drawn. "I don't know," he replied, sinking into one of my chairs. "What should I do now?"

I folded my arms. "Edward was always popular with the Londoners. It was the source of his power.

"Where does that put me, Mother?"

"They will know you in good time, my son. Meanwhile, you must develop a new strategy. It seems you are going to have to drop the story of Edward's illegitimacy; it is doing you more harm than good."

"What can I say?"

"Tell them the story of Lady Eleanor," I replied. "If they have difficulty in believing a pious old woman could produce an illegitimate son, they will have a much easier time believing that Edward was a bigamist. After all, they knew what he was like with women."

"That's true." Richard rose stiffly from his chair. "Why did I not think of that before?"

I put my hand on his shoulder, which felt fragile and bony to my touch.

"Because you're exhausted," I said. "And you have not been nourishing yourself for these past several weeks."

Richard took my advice and that very same day sent his cousin Henry Stafford, Duke of Buckingham, to the Guildhall to address the mayor, aldermen, and citizens of London.

Buckingham spoke eloquently on my son's behalf, glossing over my foolishness and instead of telling the good people about Edward's bigamous marriage with Lady Eleanor. He ended by appealing to them to offer the crown to my son Richard.

Again, they were met by that silence. Apparently, people were not happy about the way Hastings had been executed without trial. They were not happy that Richard

466

had not crowned his nephew as promised. They were very unhappy that he had a large army in the north that he could bring down on them at any moment. For they hadn't forgotten how they'd suffered under the Bitch of Anjou.

I sighed with impatience but trusted Richard's sterling qualities would sway them.

Buckingham remedied the situation by having his men throw their caps into the air and shout, "King Richard!"

The next day, there was a meeting of the Lords and Commons in Westminster. Again, Buckingham addressed them, dwelling on Edward's bigamy with Lady Eleanor. And so, they declared Edward's marriage to the Serpent to be invalid, their children illegitimate.

Richard's reign had begun, and I could finally retire in peace.

For my work was done.

CHAPTER 69

July 1483

My youngest son, King Richard III, dated his reign from June 26, 1483, the day he was installed on the King's Bench in Westminster Hall. He now had the title Richard, Duke of York, had striven for, the title that had been torn from him by his enemies in 1460. It was my son's task to ensure that he kept that title.

Richard was crowned in Westminster Abbey on July 6, 1483, in the presence of his beloved wife Nanette, who was crowned queen, and their only son and heir, Edward of Middleham. I was not present, not because I disapproved of Richard as certain folk claim, but because I was indisposed, the strain of the previous weeks finally coming home to roost.

However, I rose from my bed to give the new king my solemn blessing before he set out for his coronation.

Richard was anxious that his subjects should know their new king, so only two weeks after his coronation, he set off on a royal progress to travel around the country. He'd been traveling only three days when he decided to pay me a sudden visit early one morning.

"My son," I said, coming forward and searching his face. "What troubles you?"

Richard had acquired a healthy summer tan, but dark circles around his eyes betokened many restless nights.

"Come with me," I added, "and let us pray for guidance."

We went to my private chapel. It was a spare, white-washed room with a portrait of Saint Bridget and a statue of Our Lady carrying the Lord Jesus. The king and I spent the next several minutes in prayer.

Afterward, I led Richard back to the solar, now warmed by a roaring fire. Richard had been kind enough to restore all of my lands, and so I was able to entertain in rather better style than previously. I signaled to the steward to open my best Bordeaux, which I poured for him myself. Then I settled in a large carved chair with cushions and rug.

Richard put his wine cup down untouched, covering his face with one hand. I signaled for Mother Avisa to get me a tonic for headaches.

Then:

"Those accursed Woodvilles," he finally spat. "Am I never to be free of their plotting?"

I frowned at the rawness of his outburst. His life had not been easy of late, and he needed rest. Otherwise, he would damage his health.

He looked up. "Two plots have I uncovered: One is to spirit Edward's daughters out of their sanctuary in Westminster Abbey and send them abroad. The other is to rescue Edward's sons from the Tower."

"No." I put my wine cup down.

"Indeed yes, Mother," he replied.

I rose stiffly to my feet and went to put a hand on his shoulder. My son ached for comfort, I could feel it. "We must act decisively to stop this nonsense once and for all," I said. "We cannot lose heart now. You are the legitimate ruler of England. No one can take that away from you."

I sat next to him and chafed his hands. "As for Edward's daughters, all you need do is tighten your cordon around Westminster Abbey. You have enough men for the task. You must insist no one goes in or out of the abbey without your permission."

"What should I do about Edward's sons?"

I paused, for that was a knotty problem.

"We should plan for the future," I replied. "Of all my children, only Edward, Beth, George, and you have male heirs. George's son, Edward, Earl of Warwick, also has a claim to the throne, but he is only eight years old. He is too young and not strong enough in his wits to be a real threat to you as long as you keep him with a trusted member of the family. Perhaps you should have him stay with Nanette, as she is his nearest female relation. The poor child needs some kindness in his life, and your wife will be kind.

Richard's smile wiped away his lines.

"Beth has many sons, all strong and healthy," I continued. "And more to the point, they are loyal to you. If anything happened to your boy, perhaps you should consider making her eldest, John de la Pole, Earl of Lincoln, your heir."

The color drained from Richard's face.

I took his hands. "Richard, I know you find this painful, but we live in dangerous times. Your Edward is only seven years old and not strong. Beth's eldest son has twenty-one years old enough to assume the responsibility of being your heir. He can fight for you."

Richard made a face as I pressed a wine glass into his hands. He took a sip and put it down. "What about Edward's sons?"

"Folk do not want to believe they're bastards," I replied. "The Serpent and her horde of Woodville relatives will never stop plotting. Edward's sons are Woodvilles at heart, their mother saw to that. Edward was too weak-willed to stop her. As Woodvilles, they pose a danger to your throne. You've already discovered one plot. There will be others."

Richard nodded, and we gazed at the fire together.

"How I blame myself," I said, "for my own lack of responsibility. If Edward had not been born, none of this would have happened."

"Edward seemed like a hero to me when I was a boy," murmured Richard.

I winced. "The plain truth is that he and I were too much alike. I was irresponsible in the getting of him, and he was irresponsible in his marriages, particularly in bringing that awful Woodville woman into the family. His fault compounded my own. The worm in the apple was his wife, his second wife."

Richard was silent.

I leaned forward. "For the good of our family and for the good of England, we must set right these wrongs." I took both his hands in mine and gazed into his eyes. "We must destroy the Woodvilles once and for all."

Richard stared at me. "Do you really believe that?" he whispered. "Rid ourselves of those two boys in the Tower?"

I paused for a long moment. I could hardly believe what I was suggesting, but what could I do? The Serpent was dangerous.

"It grieves me much that you have to bear the weight of my sins and of Edward's folly," I murmured. "That you are the person burdened with putting everything right."

Richard sat for many moments. Finally, he rose and kissed me on the cheek.

"I thank you," he whispered softly. "You have given me the strength I need. It shall be done."

CHAPTER 70

Berkhamsted Castle, Hertfordshire
September 1483

Madam,
I beseech you most humbly for your daily blessing and
prayers for matters have been accomplished which you
know of.
I make a solemn oath that I will found a chantry at York,
where one hundred priests will say masses for my soul.
Written at York, the eighth day of September,
in the first year of our reign,
by the hand of your most humble son,
Ricardus Rex

I wobbled and sank into my seat, motioning Gerard to rise. He was now in his early forties, remaining at my side since the day I'd arrived at Berkhamsted some fourteen years before.

"How did it happen?"

Gerard hesitated.

"I must pray for my sins, of which there are many. But I cannot take responsibility for something if you keep me in the dark."

"Tyrell saw to it." Sir James Tyrell worked as a secretary in Richard's household.

"And?"

"Smothered," he said hoarsely.

My stomach churned. I sat up in my seat.

"They were smothered in their beds in the dead of night," continued Gerard.

"When?"

"The night of September third to fourth. Tyrell had to leave London at first light on the fourth to make it back to York on September the eighth for the investiture of Lord Richard's son, Edward. He left York on the night of August thirtieth to London to collect robes and wall-hangings for the investiture."

Richard's son and only child, seven-year-old Edward of Middleham, had been made Prince of Wales in a special ceremony held in York on September 8, 1483. It took about four days of fast riding to travel between London and York, a distance of some two hundred miles.

"Did they suffer?"

"I don't know." He avoided my eyes.

I rose. "Where are they buried?"

"Under the stairs in the White Tower. In a chest."

I rubbed my hands together to warm them. "Master Gerard, this has been most painful—"

"I'll not work for you no more," he growled.

"Gerard!"

"That was evil," he spat. "Pure evil."

"Gerard," I said, putting my hand on his arm, "You don't understand."

"I understand full well!" he exclaimed, glaring. "You murdered those two boys, innocent lambs they be. Why couldn't you let them live?"

"Because," said I, sinking wearily into my chair, "if they'd lived, we would have been killed."

"They wouldn't have killed you. They had the souls of angels."

"Maybe not, but their mother would have. She had to be crushed."

Gerard was silent for a moment, considering. "And would that have been so bad?" he asked eventually. "I mean, folk, they die all the time. What's so bad about being murdered? I mean, the way you done it, madam, you've put your immortal soul in harm's way. You will burn in hell forever. And I want no truck with that. I'm done. I'm going."

And he strode out, leaving me sitting in my chair, with the ghost-like forms of two boys filling my head. As I tried to reach for them, I felt myself turning to ice.

CHAPTER 71

September 1483 to August 1485

Richard didn't have an easy time of it as King of England. By late September 1483, rumors stirred abroad that the sons of the late king had met a violent end. In short order, this rumor became the talk of all the courts of Europe. Many switched allegiance to one Henry Tudor.

Henry Tudor, Earl of Richmond, was a totally unknown Lancastrian exile who would have remained obscure but for a chance meeting between his mother Lady Margaret Beaufort, and Richard's cousin Henry of Buckingham, himself a male heir to the Plantagenet line and possibly angling for the crown. Shortly after my son's coronation, Lady Margaret—a formidable, highly intelligent woman—managed to persuade Buckingham to abandon Richard's cause and join her son's. I am not sure how she did it, but she probably played on Buckingham's fears. For the southerners were not happy that Richard's loyal northerners were taking all the royal offices or that the so-called Little Princes in the Tower—Edward of Westminster and Richard of Shrewsbury—had disappeared.

Lady Margaret was a kinswoman of mine, by my mother. Like me, she descended from John of Gaunt and his third wife Catrine de Roet. It was ridiculous for Tudor to put forward a claim to the throne, for there were many descendants of the House of Lancaster abroad who had a much better claim that he. For instance, the King of Portugal and the Queen of Castile were descended from John of Gaunt's first and second wives.

It would be as ridiculous as if I'd claimed the throne of England on my own behalf.

In any case, it was unlawful, for the Beauforts had been debarred from succession by Richard II during the legitimization ceremony in the House of Lords that my mother attended in 1396. However, Lady Margaret Beaufort put ideas into her son's head, and thus Richard soon found his rightful claim to the throne challenged by this obscure upstart, aided and abetted by the treachery of his cousin Buckingham.

In early October 1483, Henry Tudor's fleet set sail from Brittany, intending to invade England, but a storm drove the ships back to port. In mid-October, Henry Tudor tried again, but on All Saints Day, Buckingham was arrested.

He was executed on All Souls Day.

On that day, Henry Tudor arrived in Plymouth, but on hearing of the collapse of the rebellion, sailed back to France and established a court in exile. His mother was detained but only kept under house arrest in the care of her husband.

Richard returned in triumph to London. But on Christmas Day 1483, Henry Tudor made a solemn vow in Rennes cathedral that when he became King, he would marry the Serpent's eldest daughter, Lady Bessy. To counter this, in January 1484, Parliament met and passed the Act of Titulus Regius, formally confirming King Richard III's title to the Crown. It also provided legal aid to poor people for the first time in history.

In March 1484, Richard finally persuaded the Serpent to let her daughters leave sanctuary, for their presence, there was a source of great embarrassment to him. She embarrassed him further by insisting that he swear an oath in public that he would protect them.

On April 9, 1484, one year after Edward's death, Prince Edward of Middleham died at the age of eight. The people attributed the loss of Richard's heir to divine punishment.

Worse was to follow. On March 16, 1485, Richard's wife Nanette died at the age of twenty-eight after a lingering illness that caused her to cough up blood. Rumors about his wife's death reached such a pitch that two weeks later, Richard was obliged to deny publicly that he'd planned to marry his niece, nineteen-year-old Lady Bessy— or indeed, that he'd had an unsavory liaison with her. I promised to see about finding a suitable bride, for Richard was young, nigh unto thirty-three years, the same age my father had been when he'd taken my mother as his second wife. The best way to put an end to such ugly gossip, as well as the Serpent's plots, was for him to marry abroad.

But reports from abroad were alarming, for Henry Tudor planned another invasion of England. Richard put aside thoughts of marriage, meticulously planning to fight for his throne. He chose Nottingham as his residence for the summer of 1485 for its central location. If Tudor landed in Wales, as seemed probable—for he was Welsh on his father's side—it would be easy for Richard to gather his forces to meet him.

On his way to Nottingham, Richard came to celebrate my birthday at Berkhamsted. For on May 3, the Feast of Saint Philip, I turned three-score and ten years, the biblical end of life. During his visit, he asked my opinion about the special ceremony he would hold before the coming battle commenced. Richard wanted to start afresh with his people, who continued to be wary of him after two years of rule.

"You must send for holy oil," I said. "Ask the priests to anoint you before battle. The anointing should take place in public, during a solemn Mass."

I paused to let Richard write down what I was saying.

"And you should also send for the coronation crown of Saint Edward."

"But, Mother, that's unheard of. The coronation crown is sacred. I could not take that with me into battle."

"The crown is holy," I replied. "It will give you additional authority and protection. You must wear it in procession at dawn on the day of battle."

Richard bent over his parchment again.

"The priests should go before you wearing their vestments and holding up their crosses. Then you should ride out in full armor, with Saint Edward's crown on your head. God will give you his blessing, and then you can overcome the tragedies of the past two years."

I paused, smiling at the magnificent image this created. Would this ceremony work? Would Richard truly be able to start anew with his people? Only if his people wanted it. So, who would be against it?

I turned to Richard. "Be wary of my Lord Stanley."

Lord Thomas Stanley's motto was Sans Changer or Without Change. And it is true he'd been loyal to Richard during Tudor's abortive plot to take the throne some two years before. But he was married to Tudor's mother, Lady Margaret, and his ability to avoid all the major battles of the recent war was second to none.

"If I may say so, my son," I said, chafing my hands because they had suddenly gone cold, "you have been far too lenient towards Stanley, especially towards his wife, Lady Margaret. She is the real threat, for she is Tudor's mother."

"But a woman cannot do much," began Richard when he saw my raised eyebrows.

"You know better than that!" I exclaimed. "A woman may do much as any man, given the opportunity." I drew myself up. "Lady Margaret is dangerous. Believe me, Tudor would be nowhere without his mother. She is the brains behind this campaign. She has the means, she knows everyone, she is here. That manor of hers at Collyweston is a beehive of activity. Heaven knows what she's up to."

"She is under house arrest in the custody of Lord Stanley. She can do no harm."

"I wouldn't be so sanguine. Clever women have ways of getting around their menfolk. Believe me, I grew up in a household of clever and resourceful women."

Richard laughed.

I could not help smiling, even though I regretted the somewhat colorful tales I'd told him of my girlhood. Was there no way of penetrating through that thick carapace of male vanity?

I drew myself up again. "Be wary. Your father made the mistake of underestimating a woman. When his commanders pleaded with him to stay inside Sandal Castle, he said he wasn't going to be so cowardly as to shut his gates to a scolding woman whose only weapons were her tongue and her nails. That mistake cost him his life."

"Do not worry, Mother. I am going to crush Tudor. Never believe otherwise!"

How I wanted to believe him. So, I put my sighs away and smiled as he knelt for my blessing.

My son Richard was a superb king, fair-minded and just. During his reign, he reformed the justice system by allowing the accused to have bail, protecting them from imprisonment before trial, and protecting their goods from seizure until they'd been convicted. Unfortunately, he made many enemies, for folk did not know him and treated him with great suspicion.

Many folk, not knowing my story, regarded the Little Princes in the Tower the rightful heirs to the throne. The disappearance of those two boys ruined Richard's credibility and clawed at him for the rest of his short reign.

On August 1, 1485, Henry Tudor sailed from Harfleur, Normandy. On August 7, he landed at Milford Haven, Wales. On August 22, 1485, he confronted King Richard.

King Richard had the upper hand; his forces ranged on top of a hill while Tudor's had to slog through the low-lying marshes. But Richard, a true gentle knight, plunged away from safety to take on his opponent, just as his father did at Sandal Castle in 1460.

And like his father, he was viciously cut down and murdered at the Battle of Redmore Plain, commonly known as Bosworth Field, by that upstart Tudor and his followers.

Tudor did not have a good claim to the throne and knew it. He also knew there were plenty of others who had a better claim. The rightful King of England was Edward, Earl of Warwick, poor George's only son, ten years old. Next in succession was his sister Margaret, who had twelve years. Tudor immediately clapped Edward, Earl of

Warwick, in the Tower, where he still languishes after ten years. Then he married poor Margaret to a knight well below her. A Sir Richard Pole.

My son Richard had no surviving children. Richard's designated heir, John de la Pole, Earl of Lincoln, was cut down by Tudor at the Battle of Stoke in June 1487. Other contenders were my bastard son's five daughters: Bessy, Cecily, Anne, Catherine, and Bridget. They were luckier than the others.

Tudor sought to heal old wounds by marrying the eldest daughter, Lady Bessy. If only he knew how little that helped his cause, for he would have been better off with George's daughter Margaret. But by that time, no one wanted to believe the tale of my affair of the heart. They assumed that Edward must have been legitimate because my lord of York never said anything to make them think otherwise.

What a hard world we live in. I little thought how my one night of transgression would cause so much grief. The dynasty now on the throne—the House of Tudor—is not legitimate. But what can I do? England has suffered much from my folly. Tudor seems keen not to speak of old mistakes; he governs on the principle of "least said, soonest mended." He and Bessy, my granddaughter, now have children of their own.

Richard's sudden death in battle made me rethink everything. Should I have glorified his father in the way I did? Perhaps if I hadn't, he wouldn't have been tempted to make that suicidal charge against Tudor. Should I have done more to come out of retirement to keep Richard's enemies at bay? He was so vulnerable, for people did not know him. He was forced to commit a terrible crime before he could establish himself on the throne. Should I, then, have discouraged Richard from being king at all when it was obvious the folk of London did not see him that way, preferring the Serpent's sons instead? Richard and his family could have lived in exile abroad. But would we have made it into exile safely?

Perhaps the biggest mistake I made was in letting my feelings for the Serpent get carried away. She was so easy to hate.

The hatred I fostered left poor Richard with some very bad choices when his half-brother Edward suddenly died. This is why I pray and do penance every day. I pray for the souls of the dead, for my sons and daughters, for my mother and sisters, and yes, even for the Serpent, for that poor lady passed away some three years ago, in poverty, at Bermondsey Abbey. She was so poor that her remaining son Dorset had to pay out of his own pocket for her modest funeral. Shockingly so for a former queen.

Tudor took her lands from her, claiming he was short of land. He forced her to enter a religious order, for she had nowhere else to go. Her only wish was to be placed at Bermondsey, where she could see the Tower, the place where her sons had disappeared.

An eye for an eye, a tooth for a tooth, two sons for a son.

How sad it all is.

EPILOGUE

She contynueth in prayer until the first peale of evensonge;
then she drinketh wyne or ale at her pleasure…
In the tyme of supper she recyteth the lecture that was had
at dynner to those that be in her presence.
After supper she disposeth herself to be famyliare with her
gentlewomen, to the secac'on of honest myrthe;
and one howre before her goeing to bed, she taketh a cuppe
of wyne, and after that, goeth to her pryvie closette, and
taketh her leave of God for all nighte, making ende of her
prayers for that daye; and by eight of the clocke is in bedde.
I truste to our lordes mercy that this noble Princesse
thus devideth the howers to his highe pleasure.

FROM ORDERS AND RULES OF THE PRINCESS
CECILL
QUOTED BY JOHN WOLSTENHOLME COBB
(1883)
HISTORY & ANTIQUITIES OF BERKHAMSTED

I t is the Feast of Saint Joseph in March 1495, and I
will have eighty years in two months. My mind
drifts back fifty years to another Saint Joseph's Eve,
when Richard and I waited by the banks of the Seine for
Marguerite d'Anjou to take her place as our new queen.
Nan was with us then, young, trusting, and happy.

I am full weary of this world, glad to be leaving it. But
before I go, I have an important task I must perform. I have
written to my daughter Margaret, Duchess of Burgundy, to
request a new Book of Hours. Tudor's spies will intercept
that document. Let them smile at the fancies of an old
woman. Let them think I need another magnificent prayer
book. Let them admit a party of nuns led by an abbess so
that my memoirs can be taken back to Burgundy before
that so-called King of England can pounce and destroy the
truth about who is the rightful heir to the throne.

I shiver with fear. The fire had gone down in my room,
so I rang my bell. A nun appeared I did not know. This was

not unusual; the sisters often take in new women as candidates to the religious life. I indicated the nearly dead fire, and she fed the flames. But I was struck by how clumsy and slow her movements were as if she were not used to lighting a fire.

"Is that all, madam?"

"Yes, I thank you. You may go now." I went back to my writing.

After several minutes, I raised my head. She was standing beside me, reading what I had just written:

This is for my great-grandchild Henry Pole, grandson to my darling son George, and the rightful heir to the throne of England. This is the story of why you and your future sons and heirs should be sitting on the throne of England, and not that upstart Tudor, who styles himself "Henry VII, King of England."

As soon as our eyes met, the nun made a perfunctory curtsey and disappeared, letting the door bang behind her.

Who was she?

I hid my memoirs in my fur wrap.

Half an hour later, the door to my chamber banged open, letting in a burst of cold air. I jerked my head up, and my eyes met those of the new nun.

"What are you doing here?" I demanded.

"I brought these for you, madam," she replied, putting a goblet of red wine, one of my magnificent gold cups, and a platter of cheese wafers on the table.

I eyed these refreshments warily while she poked at the fire.

After banging around with tongs and poker, she sat down, drew out a ball of yarn and some needles, and started to knit.

I glared at her. "I don't remember asking you to stay or even inviting you in."

"But your ladyship requires my company."

"I do?"

"Of course, you do," she said smoothly. "A lady of your position and years needs someone to sit with her."

"I manage very well by myself. And now I wish you to take that tray of food with you and go."

She continued to knit.

I glared at her.

She ignored me.

I rang my silver hand bell.

She got up, rolled up her yarn and knitting needles into her bag, picked up the tray of food. As she passed my chair, she put my silver bell on the tray, then paused in the doorway. "I don't think you'll need that," she remarked before leaving.

I felt the leather cover of my memoirs and smiled.

I fell into a light slumber. A blast of cold air made me sit up with a start. The door opened to Sister Ghislaine, cautiously poking her head around the door. "My lady?"

I moved slowly, for I was chilled to the bone, and my muscles were cramping.

"I am cold and famished," I said. "This fire needs to be attended to, and I have not had anything or seen anyone for hours."

Sister Ghislaine's eyes widened in shock. "My lady. How dreadful."

As she poked the fire, bringing it to life again, I fumbled with my fur wrap. Thank heavens, my book was still there. "Where is everyone?" I asked.

"Everyone is here. Nothing out of the ordinary has happened. We didn't disturb you because Sister Dangereuse—"

"Dangereuse." I interrupted. "You mean the new nun?"

"Yes, my lady."

"What a strange name," I murmured. "Did you know Queen Alainor of Aquitaine had a grandmother named

494

Dangereuse?" I snapped back into the present. "And what did Sister Dangereuse tell you?"

"She told us you were busy with your writing and had expressly commanded no one to disturb you."

Half an hour passed. I'd slumbered again when Sister Ghislaine knocked on my door.

"My lady, I have a tray of food for you, a light repast, and another poultice for your aching wrist."

She wound a tansy poultice around my wrist to ease the aching from all the writing I have done this day, then poured some hot spiced wine into one of my gold cups. She arranged dishes of pigeon pastries, lentils, and wafers on a small table. She stoked up the fire, for the room had become cold again. Finally, she put the silver bell back on my table.

"I thank you," I said, smiling at her.

Sister Ghislaine and I had become dear friends over the years, ever since my arrival here in the midst of a sleet storm in March 1469, twenty-six years ago. Ghislaine was a child of twelve, left at the house of Ashridge when both her parents died. Now she had taken her vows and was known for her skill in illuminating manuscripts.

There was a knock at the door. It was Mother Avisa, the Mother Superior, who managed our Benedictine cell. Now a plump woman in her fifties with square, capable hands, she sank into a deep curtsey, then sat in the chair I indicated.

"Where is the new nun?"

Mother Avisa sighed and looked at Sister Ghislaine.

"I have searched for her but can find her nowhere."

I picked up the leather book made to look like a prayer book and secreted it in my fur wrapper.

"Very wise, my lady Abbess," remarked Mother Avisa. She cleared her throat and coughed. "I do not know who Dangereuse is, but I can tell you that I accepted her because she came with very good references. As you know, since Sister Matilda's death, we have needed someone who is a skilled herbalist."

"Who recommended her?"

"Her letter of introduction was signed by Archbishop Morton himself."

I gazed into her face. Archbishop John Morton was the new Archbishop of Canterbury and extremely popular with Tudor the Usurper. His popularity was due to a diabolically clever idea of collecting fines, known as Morton's Fork. Under this scheme, you either paid the original fine whether it was fair or not, or if you did not pay, then you paid another fine for not paying the original fine. Needless to say, Tudor loved this idea, for he was the most grasping, the most avaricious, the most penny-pinching monarch ever to sit on the Throne of England.

"Archbishop Morton is Tudor's henchman." I said slowly. "That plot against Tudor in which Lambert Simnel impersonated my grandson, the Earl of Warwick, was supported by my daughter Margaret. And we know that Tudor's policy is to destroy anyone who might have a legitimate claim to the throne."

"Whereas my lady of Burgundy's is to annoy Tudor as much as possible," murmured Ghislaine.

I smiled. "She now has at her court another promising young man, this time someone known as Perkin Warbeck. It is possible that he could be one of Edward's bastards, dating from that time he had to take refuge in Burgundy more than twenty years ago."

"My lady of Burgundy also says he's another of your grandsons, the Duke of York," said Ghislaine.

I was silent. If that were true, it would mean that the Serpent had smuggled her younger son out before Richard disturbed her sanctuary. Could she really have done that? She was cunning enough and desperate. I put that thought away, for a headache threatened. "Perhaps he is," I murmured.

"My lady, they've arrived." Someone was shaking me.

I sat up slowly in my chair and blinked to adjust my eyes to the light of the candle.

Ghislaine was bending over me. "I'm sorry to disturb you, my lady, but they thought it best to arrive under cover of night."

"Whom do you mean?" I asked, my thoughts blurry from sleep.

"The party of nuns from Burgundy, my lady."

I sat bolt upright. "What hour is it?"

"Nigh unto matins."

Avisa bustled into the room. "It's quite a large party," she announced, rising from her curtsey. "Twenty men-at-arms, ten archers, a priest, three nuns, and the abbess herself. I have found places for everyone. There is someone who would like to meet privately with you now."

I looked up as a figure swept me a low bow.

"Olivier de Blay at your service."

I looked at the figure before me but couldn't see his face, hidden by shadow. I motioned him forward.

He bowed again.

Something familiar echoed. It was almost as if I were seeing Edward again. But how could that be true, for Edward had been dead these twelve years? Had my daughter of Burgundy sent me her latest protégé? What was his name? Oh yes, Lambert something.

"What did you say your name was?"

"Olivier de Blay."

"You seem familiar."

"I'm told I look exactly like my grandfather. Though I never met him."

He was dressed in a tunic of wine-colored velvet embroidered in silver. His stockings were a russet color. Of course. He had Blaybourne's build, nut-colored hair, long, expressive face, and shapely legs. But whereas Blaybourne's eyes had been hazel, this young man's were grey. I looked at his hand and saw a blue glint.

"Let me see your ring."

He drew from his finger a sapphire ring set in silver.

I took my sapphire ring from my finger and put both rings together. My ring nestled into the cutout shape of his sapphire, just as I had once nestled into Blaybourne's arms. My vision blurred, and I fumbled for my handkerchief.

The young man hovered nearby and handed me a glass of wine.

"After all these years, I have so many questions." I indicated a seat, and the young man sat in the carved chair opposite mine, stretching his long legs out towards the fire.

"My grandfather was humbly born. His father was a blacksmith."

"He told me that," I said, "but where?"

"In the village of Blay, near Bayeux in Normandy.

I frowned. "His name was not Blaybourne?"

"Being so humble, my grandfather did not have a last name. But when he arrived at the monastery in Caen, the monks asked him where he was from, and so-called him Pierre de Blay."

I smiled. What would Tudor say if he knew his wife had such peasant blood? I cleared my throat. "When last I saw him, he was dressed as a nobleman, and he had an entourage of pages, knights, and men-at-arms. That day, he gave his name as Philippe de Savoy, Count of Geneva."

"There was a gentleman of that name," replied Olivier de Blay. "He was the youngest son of Duke Amadeus of Savoie."

"But wasn't it dangerous for your grandfather to impersonate a nobleman?"

"He chose minor members of the nobility and was careful in his choices. After all, the Count of Geneva never came to Rouen."

"I've always wanted to know more about him. I had so little time."

"Did you know he was a spy?"

I stared at my guest as everything slid into place. The fact that Blaybourne knew so many languages. The humble background, the courtly behavior, the education at an Italian university. Even his advanced degree.

"I had no idea," I said, gripping the arms of my chair as I stared into the fire. The flames flickered, giving me an image of Blaybourne saying farewell to me all over again.

"He must have been in some danger while he was visiting me, for he had no protector."

The grandson smiled. "My grandfather was extremely well educated and valuable for that reason."

"Whom did he spy for?"

"The Medici bank of Florence."

Yes, he had used that name when giving me his last instructions.

"Banks need information about which way the wind is blowing before they lend money," continued the young man. "My grandfather was trying to find out whether the English were likely to win their war against the French so that the Medici bank could determine if it would be wise to give the English king a loan."

"Is that why he came from Pontoise?"

"Yes. After getting information about the campaign against the French, he planned to go to the court at Rouen to gather more information before returning to Italy. He was detained by a fair lady."

My cheeks warmed.

"The lady was enchanting, so I've heard," observed the young man smiling. "My grandfather delayed until he could do so no more."

"Until he had to leave," said I, conjuring up the image of the moment when Richard had announced his return outside Rouen Castle.

There was silence for a moment.

"He wasn't a nobleman," I sighed.

"No, but he could assume the guise of a nobleman. He said it made it easier to conduct negotiations."

"I always wondered how he managed to do that."

"The monks taught him his manners," replied Olivier de Blay. "As you know, some of them come from aristocratic families."

I nodded, too weary to pursue the matter further. "What happened to your grandfather?"

"He gave up the roving life of a spy, returned to Florence, and worked for the Medici bank in other ways. Several years later, he settled down, married a young lady whose father was a wealthy *marchant*, and produced a son. My father Cecilio."

"Cecilio?" I clasped my hands and smiled. "He remembered me!"

"He couldn't forget you."

"He was not happy?"

"He was well enough."

I looked down. Even when I was nine years old, marrying Richard hadn't felt right. Granted, I reveled in my power and influence. But had it been good for my soul? I examined my hands, now knobbled with arthritis. What would I have done had I known what that choice would entail? Would I have had the courage to leave three children and cause a scandal for a husband who loved me in exchange for a life of study and companionship with Blaybourne?

No. For the cost would have been too high. True, I would have been spared the drama and tragedy of a life encrusted with power. But could I have lived with myself?

I felt inside my fur wrap and brought out the leather-bound book, handing it to the young man.

"My life is in my memoirs," I said. "Take this book to my daughter Margaret for safekeeping. For Tudor would destroy if he knew of it."

The young man bowed.

"Tell me more about your grandfather. Is he alive?"

"*Non*, my lady, I regret to say not. He died some thirty-five years ago."

"The very same year as my lord husband," I murmured.

I leaned back in my seat, feeling Lady Fortune completing her circle. If I shut my eyes, I could see their faces: Mama's, Cath's, Anne's, Audrey's, and Jenet's. They were laughing at something I said.

We were sitting in Bulmer's Tower at Castle Raby, discussing Chaucer. The day was warm and fresh. Mama smiled at me and patted my hand.

NOTE

Cecylee, Duchess of York, died on May 31, 1495, at the great age of eighty.

She is buried in the Collegiate Church of Fotheringhay, opposite her husband, Richard, Duke of York.

This manuscript was taken to Margaret, Duchess of Burgundy, who placed it in safekeeping at the convent of Roosendael just before her death in November 1503.

Unfortunately, this convent was destroyed in 1576, during the religious upheavals of the sixteenth century.

The manuscript has only recently been unearthed.

WEBSITES

Instagram
https://www.instagram.com/
cynthia_at_cynthia_sally/

Pinterest
https://ru.pinterest.com/cynthiasallyhaggard/
thwarted-queen/

LinkedIn
https://www.linkedin.com/in/
cynthiasallyhaggard/

Website
https://www.cynthiasallyhaggard.com/about/

About the Author

Cynthia Sally Haggard was born and reared in Surrey, England.

About 40 years ago, she surfaced in the United States, inhabiting the Mid-Atlantic region as she wound her way through four careers: violinist, cognitive scientist, medical writer, and novelist.

Her first novel, *Thwarted Queen*, a saga about the Yorks, Lancasters & Nevilles, whose family feud inspired "Game of Thrones," won the 2021 Gold Medal IPPY Award for Audiobook, with the fab Diana Croft narrating..

Cynthia graduated with an MFA in Creative Writing from Lesley University, Cambridge MA, in June 2015.

When she's not annoying everyone by insisting her fictional characters are more real than they are, Cynthia likes to go for long walks, knit something glamorous, cook in her wonderful kitchen, and play the piano.

You can visit her at cynthiasallyhaggard.com

Would You Like To Be An Advanced Reader?

You'll receive a FREE book and other bonuses!
MEMBERSHIP includes:

a free book
advance review copies
newsletter.

Subscribe here: https://cynthiasallyhaggard.com/contact/ (and tap WIP Updates)

Your Opinion Is Important to Me...

Thank you for reading *Thwarted Queen*.

Reviews are so important because they allow people like me (an unknown Indie author) to find people like you (readers who enjoy historical fiction.)

An unreviewed book is like a rose gasping for water.

So if you enjoyed *Thwarted Queen*, you would make one author very happy by posting a short review at your favorite online retailer.

It only takes 5 minutes...

Thank you so much for your support!
Warmly, Cynthia

www.ingramcontent.com/pod-product-compliance
Lightning Source LLC
Chambersburg PA
CBHW020239120726
47904CB00001B/27